Reflection

MARY SHELDON

Reflection

KENSINGTON BOOKS
http://www.kensingtonbooks.com

KENSINGTON BOOKS are published by

Kensington Publishing Corp.
850 Third Avenue
New York, NY 10022

All Kensington titles, imprints and distributed lines are available at special quantity discounts for bulk purchases for sales promotion, premiums, fund-raising, educational or institutional use.

Special book excerpts or customized printings can also be created to fit specific needs. For details, write or phone the office of the Kensington Special Sales Manager: Kensington Publishing Corp., 850 Third Avenue, New York, NY 10022. Attn. Special Sales Department. Phone: 1-800-221-2647.

Library of Congress Card Catalogue Number: 2002112642
ISBN 0-7582-0308-X

First Printing: April 2003
10 9 8 7 6 5 4 3 2 1

Printed in the United States of America

For Aunt Rodie—
with lifetimes of love

ACKNOWLEDGMENTS

The grateful author wishes to thank the following people for sharing their expertise with me: Tiela Garnett, Marc Mantell, Christopher Stone, and Kate Supnik.

Also, my blessed family: long-suffering Bob, golden Lizy, and angel-sprite Rebecca.

My friend and agent, Dorris Halsey.

And the people at Kensington, especially Walter Zacharius, Laurie Parkin, Amanda Rouse, Janice Rossi Schaus, and Doug Mendini. Not to mention the one and only Ann LaFarge.

Thank you all.

PROLOGUE
ONE

June 1956

It was seven o'clock in the morning, and the Los Angeles sunshine was already heavily dosed with smog. The Princess telephone on Zoë's bedside table rang.

"Damn!" said Zoë sleepily. She groped through a tangle of pink satin sheets and finally found the receiver.

"Hello?"

When she heard the voice on the other end, she was no longer sleepy.

"Yes, Max?"

She edged out from under the sheets, sat down on the pink satin comforter and listened in eager silence for a few moments. Then she frowned, picked up a cigarette, and lit it. The tip smoldered and glared.

Well," she said abruptly at last. "I see. No, don't be silly—not your fault at all. It obviously wasn't meant to be. Anyway, thank you for putting in a good word for me."

Slowly, she put down the receiver. Then she sat back on the bed and finished the cigarette.

From the next room, there came a high, whimpering cry. Zoë sighed and crushed out the cigarette stub.

"I'm coming, baby," she called. "I'm coming."

Zoë arrived at Nate 'n Al's a few minutes before noon. As she sat in the booth, she caught sight of Hans Lasky coming into the restaurant. He looked thinner, grayer, but Zoë was touched to see how elegantly he had dressed himself for their lunch.

She settled her face into a pleasant smile as he approached.

"Dear Hans," she murmured, and kissed his cheek.

"Something's wrong," he said instantly. His accented voice was anxious. "What has happened?"

"I didn't get the job," she told him flatly. "Max called this morning. They decided to go with someone with more experience."

Hans frowned. "I'm sorry. I know how much you wanted it. But I think maybe this isn't a bad thing."

Zoë shook her head. "It would have meant Europe. Not to mention the prestige. It would have set me up for life—a few years over there, then I could have started my own agency."

"And why can't you start your agency now?"

Zoë's laugh was bitter. "Do you have any idea what that would take? You have to have a hell of a track record to get anything like that off the ground. And I've got nothing."

The older man shook his head and smiled. "Ah, but I have a track record, my dear."

Zoë started to say something, but he held up a hand. "I'll tell you what you do. You see a client you want, you tell these prospective mamas that if they sign with you, Hans Lasky will photograph their little darlings free of charge."

"Hans!"

He beamed at her. "And I'll put out the good word about you. 'Zoë Andrews—she's young, but believe me, she's the best children's agent in town.' You'll see—before you can turn around, you'll have all the big business you want." He patted her hand affectionately. "This call you got this morning, trust me, it's a blessing."

He picked up a pickle with a delicate hand and started to eat it.

"Think of Caroline," he added. "If you had gotten the job, what would have happened to her? She couldn't have gone with you."

"No," Zoë admitted. "I guess Barton would have taken her. He's planning on moving back to New York, as soon as the divorce is final." Seeing Hans's look, Zoë added rather acidly, "I wasn't planning on giving up my child, Hans. It would have been just for a year or two."

"But it never would have worked like that," he told her. "Barton would have wanted her to stay with him. No, it's far better like this. Babies belong with their mothers. So you will have Caroline and your agency as well. You wait and see."

Zoë put her hand on top of his and squeezed it.

When she got home, Daphne, the teenaged baby-sitter was sitting on the flowered sofa, watching television.

"Everything okay?" Zoë asked. "Caroline behave herself? She didn't throw any wild parties?"

The girl laughed. "She was perfect. I put her down for her nap a few minutes ago."

When Daphne left, Zoë went into the nursery. She walked over to the crib and touched the sleeping child.

"Well, baby doll," she whispered, "it looks like you're stuck with me. So let's make it into something grand."

Caroline opened dark blue eyes, and looked at Zoë.

PROLOGUE
TWO

June 1956

It was seven o'clock in the morning, and the Los Angeles sunshine was already heavily dosed with smog. The Princess telephone on Zoë's bedside table rang abruptly.

"Damn," said Zoë sleepily. She groped through a tangle of pink satin sheets and finally found the receiver.

"Hello?"

When she heard the voice on the other end, she was no longer sleepy.

"Yes, Max."

She edged out from under the sheets, and sat down on the pink satin comforter and listened in eager silence for a few moments. Then she smiled, picked up a cigarette, and lit it.

"Well, hurray," she said lightly, at last. "That's wonderful news. Tell them I accept. And thank you so much, Max, for putting in the word for me. I just need to get some things settled, and I'm all yours."

She said good-bye, and hung up the phone. She sat back down on the bed and slowly smoked.

From the other room came a small, high cry. Zoë stubbed out her cigarette.

"I'm coming," she called.

Caroline was lying in her crib, her face puckered and wet. Zoë picked her up and held her against her shoulder.

"It's all right," she told the baby. "Completely wasted tears. Zoë's here."

* * *

Zoë was the first to arrive at Nate 'n Al's. She waved at Barton when she saw him enter the restaurant. She could see he had dressed with special care.

He kissed her cautiously on the cheek and sat down.

"You're looking well."

"Thank you." She smiled at him graciously.

They talked idly for a few minutes, ordered coffee.

"So," Barton said at last, "why did you need to see me?"

Zoë took a breath.

"Are you still planning on going back to New York when all this is over?"

He seemed surprised by the question. "I don't think there's much point in my staying out here."

Zoë nodded. "Well," she said lightly, "You might not be going alone."

He drew in a breath, tensed. She realized that he thought she was referring to herself.

"What are you talking about?"

"Caroline," she said quickly. She strained to keep the light tone. "It looks like you'll be taking care of her for a while."

Barton blinked. "What?"

"I got a call this morning from New York. The Dawson Agency is starting an overseas branch—they want me to head it. It'll mean the next few years in Europe."

Barton started to say something—Zoë cut him off.

"It's a great opportunity, but it means that I can't take care of Caroline for a while."

There was a silence. "Why can't she go with you?"

"I'm starting up an agency, Barton. It's going to mean working round-the-clock, constant travel. I can't do that to her. And I want this job."

She smiled at him.

"It'll be great," she said lightly. "You won't even know she's there. You'll get one of those penthouses on Park Avenue, and you'll find a wonderful housekeeper." Her smile became a little sour. "Who knows—you might even get married again."

"I don't think that's going to happen," Barton said. "Listen, Zoë—are you serious about this? You really want me to take Caroline?"

"Well, I don't want you to," she said sharply, "but I don't see that I have a choice at the moment."

"And what happens after Europe?"

"I'll take her back, of course."

Barton shook his head. "No. That's not fair. I can't have her for a year or two, and then just give her up."

"Well, we'll worry about that later," Zoë told him hastily. "We don't have to work out every detail this second. I'm sure we can come up with a compromise."

"Maybe so. But we need to talk to the lawyers. Everything must be made absolutely clear."

She sighed. "All right, all right."

The waitress brought the bill. Zoë reached for her purse, but Barton stopped her.

"Let me," he said. He brought out his wallet, flipped it open.

"Congratulations on landing the job, by the way," he told her.

Zoë looked at him thoughtfully. "You know something? You're really quite a handsome man. I can see why I fell for you."

When Zoë got back to her apartment, Daphne was sitting on the flowered sofa, watching television.

"Everything okay?" Zoë asked her. "Caroline behave herself?"

The girl laughed. "She was perfect. I put her down for her nap a few minutes ago."

When the baby-sitter left, Zoë went into the baby's room. She reached through the slats of the crib and touched the tiny pink hand.

"Zoë's little star," she whispered. "Zoë's little star." She blinked back tears. "I've worked so hard for this, baby—and you'll have a great time in New York. But it won't be forever. I promise you."

Zoë picked the baby up out of the crib and held her. In the mirror she saw the two of them, the woman and the baby, reflected together. Her mouth tightened and began to tremble. She hugged Caroline so hard that the baby woke and began to wail.

PART ONE

ANGEL ON A CLOUD

CAROLINE

Caroline's first memory is of stealing the television set.

She is four years old. It happens on a day when her father is away on a business trip. He is away a lot—this will be the third time in six weeks. He is an architect: Caroline has seen his name—Barton Andrews—written on plaques in the lobby of many buildings. She cannot read the words, but she traces the letters with her fingers.

Caroline is proud every time she sees her father's name—he must be almost as famous as President Eisenhower. She goes up to passersby, and points and tells them, "That's my daddy." But she doesn't understand why he has to be away so often. New York has everything: the zoo, the park, the smiling doorman at the front of their building. And their apartment has everything, too: a toy closet in her room, a big television set in the den, and a balcony that lets you see a tiny, precious Central Park far below. But her father still leaves New York to go on his business trips.

Caroline is always sad to see him go. She likes having her father near her. He is neat and handsome, and his smell is safe and lemony. She likes going into his den and playing with his brass paperweights and his ivory chessmen. She likes it when he laughs, and when he tickles her before bed. She even rather likes it when he plays spelling games with her at dinner, though not as much as he does. But when he goes away, that's all right, too. In a way, it's even more fun. Because when her father is gone, she can spend more time with Laura.

Laura has been with Caroline always. She is old and very dark and smells like things kept secret. Laura is the most important person in the house. It is Laura's face that shines over Caroline every morning. It is Laura's hand that decides how much brown sugar Caroline will get on her oatmeal. It is the state of Laura's bones that determines whether or not there will be a trip to the park that afternoon. And it is Laura's mouth, comforting, which gives the last kiss before bedtime.

When Barton is away, dinner is not served in the dining room; Caroline and Laura sit on stools in the kitchen, eating lovely easy meals like creamed corn and canned peaches—not the fancy foods that Barton always wants Caroline to try.

"What if you grow up to be the ambassador to China or Mexico someday?" he asks her. "You'll have to eat everything you're given, or you'll let down the whole government."

Caroline doesn't want to be the ambassador to China or Mexico. She just wants to sit at the kitchen table, eating creamed corn forever.

After dinner, she and Laura play cards—they play Old Maid for so long sometimes that when Caroline closes her eyes afterward, she can still see the cards shimmering against the backs of her eyelids. She always wins the game.

"Not again! Boo hoo!" Laura pretends to cry. And Caroline rushes over and hugs her and comforts her and loves her, loves her.

Then, at bedtime, Laura tucks Caroline in bed and tells her scary stories about the Virgin Islands, where she came from. She tells Caroline about men who wear wooden masks and dance in the firelight. Caroline is frightened to death of these masks—she imagines the eyes, huge and dripping—but she doesn't tell Laura she is scared because she doesn't want the stories to stop.

Often, Barton is away on weekends, and these are the best times of all.

"Can we go to your house tomorrow?" Caroline asks Laura every time he leaves on a Friday night. "Please, please!"

Laura doesn't always say yes; she isn't sure that Caroline's father really likes their going. But every so often, she agrees.

It's an adventure to get up extra early and walk down the street to the subway. Then there is the thick warmth of the train to be enjoyed, and all the noises, which might be scary if Caroline weren't holding Laura's hand. And finally there is stepping off into a whole new place—a street very different from the one Caroline lives on.

There are no doormen in front of these buildings, and no flowers, but there are a lot of stray dogs and people sitting on the steps of their houses. Laura and Caroline walk down one street, then turn the corner, and there is Laura's house, blue and faded, and there is Laura's daughter Dale, small and big-haired, and there, best and worst of all, is Yvette.

Yvette is Laura's granddaughter, and she is six. Before Caroline met Yvette, back in the days when she had only heard her name, she thought Yvette would look like a special car she had seen on a television commercial. But Yvette turned out not to be curvy and red. She was as dark as Laura, with hair in tiny braids, tied with ribbons.

"Can I have hair like Yvette's?" Caroline had asked Laura.

Laura had laughed. "I don't think it would suit you."

"I don't care."

So that night, Laura put Caroline's hair in tiny blond braids all over her head. Caroline pretended she thought it was pretty, but she secretly knew it didn't look right. She asked Laura to take the braids out.

Everything about Yvette was interesting. She had a gerbil in a little cage. She had been to the Automat. She knew someone whose father had gone to prison. And she could hula hoop.

But the most exciting thing about Yvette's life was Playland. She got to go there twice a year, once in the winter and once in the summer. Playland sounded like the most wonderful place on Earth, bright as the cards from Old Maid, with licorice as long as your arm and pink spun candy like an old woman's hairdo.

Caroline could never hear enough about it.

"I went on the roller coaster last time I was there," Yvette tells her.

Caroline is awed. "The big one?"

"Yeah, that one."

"Did you go on the Tilt-A-Whirl?"

"Sure."

"And the elephants?"

"Oh, yeah. Though they're getting kinda babyish for me now."

But the greatest thing about Playland is the throwing game.

"You go up to this booth, and a man gives you these three rings, and you've got to throw them over the tops of milk bottles. And if you do it, you get a big prize!"

Caroline tenses. She knows what's coming next.

"Wanna see what I won?"

Caroline nods.

They go into Yvette's room. And there in the corner is the huge pink plush teddy bear, bigger than Caroline, bigger than Yvette, with a red ribbon around its neck, and a satin heart stitched onto its chest.

Caroline sighs with envy.

Yvette sees her face and chuckles.

"Well, maybe you'll win one too, someday."

Caroline nods, a little hopelessly. She has mentioned Playland over and over again to her father, but so far he has shown no signs of wanting to take her there.

"Anyway, we can practice," Yvette says brightly.

They do this every visit—they make their own "throwing game." They take all Dale's empty milk bottles and put them in the hall and try to toss cardboard rings around them.

As Caroline throws the rings, she dreams of the bear she will someday win at Playland. She won't choose a pink teddy bear, like Yvette's—no, hers will be turquoise, and she'll name it Rajah. She won't let go of Rajah for a moment. She'll take him with her on the Ferris wheel. He will be her partner on the giant slide. Rajah will feel fear along with her on the Tilt-A-Whirl.

She rings her third milk bottle, and smiles.

It is the end of December. Barton is away in Philadelphia for the weekend, and on Saturday morning, Caroline and Laura get on the subway and go to visit Dale and Yvette.

The clouds are low and cold. The streets up in Harlem are filled with trash and thrown-out Christmas trees.

Caroline is walking very quickly. She can't wait to see Yvette and show her what Santa Claus gave her—the big Chatty Cathy doll that really talked. Caroline knows that Yvette doesn't have a Chatty Cathy of her own, and she is sorry about that, but she still needs to show Yvette her doll.

When Laura knocks, the door opens right away.

"Hey," says Yvette. She looks at Chatty Cathy.

"I got her for Christmas."

Yvette nods politely.

"Look what I got," she says.

Caroline follows Yvette into the bedroom, and Yvette points to a table beside the bed. There, on the table, is a little wooden dollhouse, yellow with white trim. Caroline stares at it. Her mouth goes slack. Chatty Cathy is nothing. Even the huge pink bear is no longer wonderful. The dollhouse is something out of a fairy tale, the most adorable thing Caroline has ever seen.

She kneels and goes over every room. The tiny carpets, the flowered curtains, the beds dressed for sleep, the lamps, the pots and pans. It hurts her to look at it, it is so precious. It is a perfect world, something that the big world can't possibly touch or spoil.

"There's even a television," Yvette points out.

The television is the best thing of all. It's green with a tiny antenna, and the screen is only as big as a walnut. On that screen, Mrs. Do-Bee from *Romper Room* would be the size of a fingernail; Mighty Mouse would be no bigger than an ant.

Tears of longing come to Caroline's eyes. She rushes from the room and runs outside.

Laura follows her.

"What's wrong, baby?"

"I want Yvette's dollhouse!"

Yvette has come out. She sits on the stoop and listens.

Laura gives Caroline a hug.

"I'll tell you what. When we get home this afternoon, we'll make you your own dollhouse. I got these shoe boxes—we'll fix it up out of those. We'll make little curtains for it, and beds, and I'll knit you some rugs."

Caroline stops crying.

Yvette is outraged.

"You never knitted me rugs! Why can't I have shoe boxes for my dollhouse? Hers will be better!"

Caroline is happy. She imagines herself making bedspreads out of Kleenex and cardboard tables and chairs. But there is one thing she cannot make. She cannot make a television.

The idea comes to her while she and Yvette are having cookies. It is wrong, of course, but it must be done.

Yvette does not suspect at all.

"Do you want to play the throwing game?" she asks when the cookies are eaten.

"No," Caroline says.

Yvette is surprised and disappointed.

"Why not?"

Caroline shrugs.

"We should be getting back anyway," Laura tells her.

They get up from the table and say good-bye to Dale and Yvette. Caroline steps outside the front door.

"Wait! I forgot something," she says suddenly, and she runs back into Yvette's room.

Stealing the television set from the dollhouse doesn't take but a moment.

Throughout the long subway ride home, Caroline's eyes burn. There's a blind man staring in her direction; she wonders if he can somehow see what she has in her pocket. She does not say a word. Laura is busy knitting and doesn't notice. When they get home, the doorman smiles at her the same way as always; the elevator man gives his usual cheerful bow. Caroline cannot look at them.

She wonders if Yvette has found out yet that her television is gone.

Caroline knows she should give the television back, but she also knows that she won't. But she will make it up to Yvette somehow; the next time she visits, she will bring Yvette her toy koala. And her marbles as well; and maybe even her turquoise crayon.

* * *

Dinner is over.

"Ready for Old Maid?" Laura asks.

But Caroline tells her, "I just want to go to bed."

Laura frowns. "Are you feeling all right?"

"Oh, yes," Caroline says.

Laura takes Caroline into her bedroom, and helps her get undressed. The bedtime story and good night kiss seem to take forever. But at last Laura closes the door behind her, and Caroline is alone.

She sits up in bed. Carefully, she feels her way to the closet and turns on the light. She pulls out the tiny television set from the shelf where she has hidden it. Then she holds her breath, pushes the on/off knob, and waits for the picture to come on. It is time for *Sky King;*—any moment he will be taking off in a plane the size of a ladybug. But nothing happens. The tiny television screen remains gray.

Caroline pushes the knob again. Still nothing happens. Why isn't it working? Could it have broken in her pocket?

Then she smiles with relief. Of course. It needs light. Her father had explained it to her once. Light comes through a television set and makes the pictures. It's much too dark in the closet. That's why the set won't work.

Caroline goes back to her bed. Carefully, she places the television on her bedside lamp, under the shade and next to the bulb. It is very hot, and she has to be careful. She stares until there are bright spots before her eyes. It's starting to work—a little glow is beginning to light the television screen. *Sky King* will come on any second now. She gets under the bedcovers, still watching. Her eyes feel sore. She will close them for a moment, just a moment, to rest them.

There is a terrible smell. Caroline wakes up, choking and coughing. She opens her eyes. There, inches from her face, is something horrible, something shapeless on the lamp. She shrinks away. She cannot take her eyes off it. It looks like the masks Laura has told her about, the voodoo masks, with dripping eyes. And her television is gone. She looks wildly around for it and then she knows—the horrible thing is the television. The lamp has melted it. She knocks out at the television and it rolls under the bed. She screams and screams.

Laura rushes in. Her hair is in little rollers.

"Baby! What's the matter? What's that smell?"

But Caroline cannot tell her anything. She cannot tell of the theft, or of the murder of the television, or of the tiny corpse under the bed. She screams and screams with horror and with guilt and Laura holds her and rocks her.

She never asks to go back to Yvette's house again.

One night at dinner, Barton seems pleased about something.

"You've got a big day coming up," he says.

Caroline's eyes widen. Were they going to Playland at last?

"What is it?"

He smiles at her. "You're starting nursery school."

Caroline says nothing. She returns to her lamb chops, hoping that if she keeps quiet, the subject will go away.

But the subject doesn't go away.

"I'm excited—aren't you?" her father asks.

Caroline shakes her head. She isn't sure what nursery school is, but it doesn't sound good.

"You'll love it," he tells her. "You'll learn so much. It'll be just like the games we play."

Caroline doesn't especially care for the games she and her father play, but she can't tell him that. Her eyes fill with tears.

"I won't go."

Barton talks very gently. He tells her over and over how much fun nursery school will be. By dessert, though, his voice has gotten thinner, and then finally it snaps.

"Caroline, this is quite enough. Monday morning, you are going to nursery school."

Monday morning? Nursery school didn't start until Monday morning? Caroline is swept by a tidal wave of relief—Monday morning was forever away.

But Monday morning comes.

"Wake up, baby!" Laura is saying. "Today's the big day!"

She puts Caroline in her red-and-blue plaid dress, she brings out her new blue shoes. And when Caroline comes into the dining room, her father is there. She pretends she doesn't notice.

Finally the oatmeal is finished, her sweater is put on, and then she and Barton and Laura are going down in the elevator. They pass the lobby and the doorman hails a taxi.

Caroline clings to Laura, but finally her hands are untangled and she has to get in the taxi. Caroline rolls down the window and holds out her arms to the tiny, sobbing Laura who is getting smaller by the second, shrinking into a dollhouse doll.

Nursery school is bad. There isn't anything Caroline likes about it—not the other children, not Mrs. McElroy, the teacher, not the graham crackers.

Every morning she begs Laura not to make her go. Some mornings, when her father is away, Laura gives in and lets Caroline stay home. She does not get out of bed on these days; she just lies under the covers, safe.

But in October, everything changes. A new boy comes to nursery school. Davie is skinny and blond, and he eats his lunchtime apple in little curving swoops. At recess, he stands by the jungle gym and gives a Tarzan yell.

Caroline has always wondered about falling in love, and she knows that she has finally done it.

Everything is different now—she can't wait to get to nursery school every morning. She spends the whole time watching Davie, and making up stories about the two of them.

She imagines getting trapped high up on the jungle gym.

Help! Help! she'll cry, and Davie will rush right out of class and rescue her.

Thank you, she'll say. *You saved my life.*

And he'll take her hand and they'll play together all recess, building sand castles and going on the seesaw, just the two of them.

Usually Caroline takes the school bus home, but one day she has a doctor's appointment, and Laura says she will pick her up from school in a taxi.

Caroline can't wait to have Laura come to school, and for Davie to meet her.

After school is over, the children wait by the front railings. At last the taxi pulls up.

"Laura!" Caroline cries.

Davie turns at the sound, and Caroline knows he is watching her. She rushes to Laura and hugs and kisses her even harder than usual. She wants to be sure that Davie sees.

But when she looks over, there is a strange expression on Davie's face.

"Why are you kissing her?" he asks Caroline with distaste. "She's only your maid."

Caroline stares at Davie. Then she stares at Laura.

Caroline no longer hugs and kisses Laura whenever she picks her up from school. And even when Davie is not around, she starts acting differently. She treats Laura more cautiously, more coolly now. She makes herself remember that Laura is not her real family. She is only the maid. The Old Maid.

In January, Caroline's father gets a big assignment—he has been asked to design a new office building in Washington, D.C. He tells Caroline all about it, and she feels grown up and important, listening to him talk.

One afternoon, a few weeks later, he calls her into his den.

"Come here, Caroline; I want to show you something."

There, on the big glass table, sitting on a board, is a tiny high-rise building. It is wonderful. There are miniature walkways and trees, and even tiny people. Tears prick Caroline's eyes.

"Is it for me?"

Barton laughs. "I'm afraid not. This is what we call an architectural model—it's a miniature version of that project we're doing in Washington. Tomorrow I'm showing it to the people in charge."

"Can I have it when you're done?"

He looks more closely at her and his eyes grow watchful.

"Caroline, this is only for looking at—understand? I don't want you going anywhere near it. It's very delicate—touch it the wrong way, and weeks of work will be down the drain." He tweaks her ear. "You wouldn't want that to happen, would you?"

"No," Caroline says.

Barton leaves the apartment soon afterward for a squash game. Within seconds, Caroline is back in the den.

Of course she won't hurt the model. Of course she doesn't want weeks of work to be down the drain. But she must see if the model has an inside, if it's full of furniture, tiny desks so that the people can sit down.

She leans in and tugs gently on the top of the building. It doesn't move. She pulls a little harder, just a little, and suddenly the board slips. The building tilts, flips, and crashes down to the floor. Caroline staggers back, the roof of the model in her arms.

She stares in terror at what she has done. There is only one word in the universe to pray, and she prays it.

"Laura!"

Laura rushes in at the scream. At first, she does not say a word. She surveys the roofless building, the skewed velvet lawn, the tiny fallen people. "Well," she says, "looks like they had themselves an earthquake."

She puts the board back on the table, hurries into the kitchen for some glue, and starts to work. Caroline stands beside her, barely able to breathe. It isn't going well. The model can't be fixed. Her father will kill her. Laura keeps trying. She sings in a soft little voice about the big earthquake at the office building. Then suddenly, incredibly, everything is looking better—much better. The lawns are smoothed, the people are righted. The loosened windows are glued into place—now the roof is back on. Everything looks exactly the way it did before. It is a miracle.

Caroline has been saved. Her father will never even know.

"Thank you," she breathes. "You're the most wonderful person in the world."

Then she flushes. She thinks with shame about how badly she has been behaving to Laura lately. There are no words to explain or apologize with, and she flings her arms around Laura's neck.

"I love you better than anyone."

"Thank you, honey." Laura pats her on the back.

Caroline does not let go. "Laura?"

"What is it, baby?"

Caroline finds she is too shy to come right out and ask the question. "I need to whisper."

Laura leans closer. "Yes?"

"Are you my mother?"

Laura gives a sad little smile.

"No, baby, I'm not."

Disappointed, Caroline nods. Then she ducks her head and pulls away.

Later that night, she is in bed. Laura comes into the room. She is holding something in her hand. She sits on Caroline's bed and turns on the light.

"You don't have to tell your daddy I showed you this," she says.

She is holding the photograph of a woman, the prettiest woman Caroline has ever seen. She loves the woman's hair; it is fluffy and flipped in little waves. She likes her mouth, too. It seems to be saying something, something teasing, something to make you laugh. Only the woman's eyes are disappointing. They are looking down, so you can't see into them. Caroline tilts the picture up, trying to see if she can get a glimpse of the open eyes that way, but she can't.

"That's your mother, baby," Laura tells Caroline.

CARO

Caro's first memory is of the little girl cutting her hair.

She is three—it's one of her first auditions. Her mother dresses her in her purple party dress, and she keeps talking all the way to the studio.

"Be happy in this one," Zoë tells her. "It's for a doll commercial. If you get it, they'll let you keep the doll. You can be happy for that, can't you? Sure you can!"

Caro is sure that she can. If she gets this commercial, then there will be more money. They can go to more restaurants. Caro can have a hamster. And maybe she and her mother can even move out of their apartment in Westwood, and into Beverly Hills, where all the beautiful houses are.

She and Zoë go into a small office. There is a lady who signs Caro in and takes the big photograph Zoë gives her.

"Go right on in," she says.

Caro and Zoë go through the office into a big room filled with little girls and their mothers.

"All right if I leave you for a few minutes?" Zoë asks Caro. Then she adds in a louder voice, "I want to have a word with the casting director."

The other mothers do not look happy when they hear this.

Caro isn't happy, either. She doesn't want to be left alone with those other little girls, all in their party dresses, all acting happy about the doll. But she sits down. She likes two other dresses better than hers, and one other girl has prettier patent-leather shoes, but Caro knows she has the best hair of anyone in the room. She was at the beauty shop yesterday, and no one else has curls quite as round and yellow.

Next to her, a skinny little girl with mean eyes is sitting with her mother. The mother stands up.

"I'm going to get a drink of water," she says. "Wait right here and behave until I get back."

When her mother is gone, the little girl turns to Caro.

"What's your name?" Her voice is sharp.

"Caro Andrews."

The little girl keeps watching Caro. Her little eyes get littler. Then she goes over to her mother's purse and pulls something out. It is a pair of manicure scissors.

Caro is frozen. She sees the scissors coming, but there is nothing she can do. None of the other mothers is watching. The scissors dart forward. A curl is cut from Caro's head. The little girl looks stern and sorrowful. She lifts the scissors again.

"Oh, my God!"

The mother has come back. She knocks her daughter away from Caro. She takes away the scissors. She takes away the little girl.

All the mothers crowd around Caro.

"Are you all right?"

"Are you hurt?"

"I'm fine," she says politely.

But when it is Caro's turn to hold the doll and say how beautiful it is, she is still upset. She is not happy enough, and she does not get the commercial.

"Your fault," Zoë tells her on the way home.

"She cut my hair," Caro whispers.

Zoë sighs. "That's no excuse."

She pulls the car over to the side of the road and stops. She looks at Caro for a long moment.

"You might as well learn it now," she says. "People are always going to be jealous of you. It's going to be like that for the rest of your life. And if you hold your head above the crowd, you can be sure that someone's going to take a shot at it. That's the way it is, sweetheart. Get used to it."

Caro fingers her curls all the way home.

* * *

Caro loves little things. Tiny glass animals, an owl carved from a peach pit, fairy-sized chairs and tables. She has a collection that she keeps on her windowsill. It is a perfect world—something the big world can't possibly touch or spoil.

She wants a dollhouse more than anything, but Zoë tells her she can't have it for a while, even though her fifth birthday is coming up. There are a lot of things Caro can't have for a while. This is because the business is in a slump.

"Only temporarily," Zoë always adds, "but you know how it is—casting directors have no memories, and clients are not exactly famous for their loyalty."

Caro doesn't know what much of this means, but she nods and frowns.

She does understand a few things. She knows that her mother is an agent, and that her job is to help find parts for children in movies and television. She works at home a lot, but she also has an office in Hollywood; sometimes, when a baby-sitter can't be found, Caro goes in to work with her.

The office is called Zoë's Babies. Caro used to get upset by the name because she wanted to be Zoë's only baby, but now she understands that it's just pretend. None of those other children matter to Zoë in the same way she does.

"But one of those little darlings is going to make us rich someday!" Zoë always says. Then she casts a look over at Caro. "Maybe it'll be you."

But it doesn't look like it's going to be Caro. Though she tries out for commercial after commercial, so far she hasn't gotten anywhere.

She doesn't particularly mind. It would be nice to move into Beverly Hills and have a dollhouse, but it's not that important. Things are fine as they are now.

But she worries about Zoë. Usually, when the business gets bad, Zoë just shrugs and says, "Don't worry, baby, things will pick up." But sometimes she gets low, very low, and Caro doesn't know what to do about it. She rubs her mother's head and brings her glasses of ginger ale, but this doesn't really help. And then things get worse, with Zoë just lying in a dark room for hours.

It has been like that all morning now, Zoë not dressing, Zoë not making any food, Zoë just lying there.

Finally she comes out of her room. She looks very pale. She goes into the kitchen, and sees that there is nothing in the refrigerator.

"Come on, Caro," she says. "We're going grocery shopping."

Caro reminds herself not to ask for pineapple and cookies. Those are things that are bought only when the business is not in a slump.

The Brentwood Mart is small and smells of clean, fresh, cheerful things. All the checkout girls know Zoë, so do the deli man and bakery lady. They tell Caro how pretty she is, how she is going to be a big movie star one day.

As Caro and Zoë are leaving the store, they pass a vending machine. Caro knows better than to ask her mother for a penny today, but she looks in the machine anyway, and she sees, halfway up the pile of toys, a tiny pink roly-poly teddy bear, the size of her fingernail.

She gasps; she cannot move.

"Chop, chop," Zoë says. "Let's get going. I need to be in Burbank by three."

Caro bursts into tears.

Zoë hates tears. And she especially hates tears cried by children in front of vending machines. Caro knows she will be pulled away and scolded, but she does not care.

She points with a shaking finger. "Look at the little bear, Zoë."

And, amazingly, Zoë looks. She looks at the bear, she looks at Caro and Caro sees a strange smile, almost like crying, come onto her face.

"What the hell," she says quietly, and calls the manager over.

"We need this bear," she tells him. "Would you mind taking apart the vending machine so that we can get to it?"

"I'm afraid I can't do that," the manager says. "It's not my property—I don't even have a key."

There is a long pause.

"Well, then," Caro hears her mother say, "in that case, please change these into pennies."

Grandly, she hands him two dollar bills.

Caro stares. Two dollars! And the business in a slump!

The manager does not have that many pennies, and he has to go to the florist's next door. Caro stands absolutely still. She sneaks little glances at her mother, waiting for her to get impatient, to change her mind. But Zoë continues to smile, that tender, slow smile.

The manager comes back with the change, and Zoë and Caro start putting pennies into the machine. They are there for half an hour. They pull out balls and rocket ships and stickers and beads and plastic jewels. Caro keeps looking at the clock on the wall. She can't tell time, but she knows that her mother has to be in Burbank at three. Surely it's nearly three now—maybe even past three. She shoves more pennies in, afraid that Zoë will notice what time it is and say they have to leave.

But at last the bear comes out of the slot; the perfect, wonderful bear.

Zoë grabs it from Caro. "My bear," she says, but Caro knows she is kidding and holds out her hands in stern joy. Zoë's hands are warm and scented with lotion, and now the bear is warm and scented, too.

Zoë looks down at the half-empty vending machine, and the pile of treasure they have pulled from it.

"Do you want any of this?" she asks.

Caro shakes her head.

Zoë goes over to the butcher. "I know you have grandchildren," she says. "Please give them these with our best wishes." And she hands over the tiny toys.

As they walk out of the store, Zoë glances down at Caro.

"Sometimes you have to live a little," she says.

She tweaks Caro's ear and smiles.

Caro is seven. She is the best reader in her class, as well as the best kickball player. She has grown tall and her hair is prettier than ever. She loves to wear a crown in it and pretend she is a princess, or a garland of leaves and pretend she is a fairy. She thinks she'd like to be a nurse when she gets older, now that Zoë seems to have given up hope that she'll ever get a commercial.

One Friday night, she is sitting on the living room floor doing a jigsaw puzzle, when Zoë rushes in from the kitchen.

"Was that the phone?"

"No," Caro tells her. It is the second time she has asked.

Zoë seems very nervous. All afternoon, she hasn't been able to stop fidgeting. She keeps applying bright red lipstick to her mouth, then biting it off with quick little nips, then spreading it on again. And she has three pale brown drinks after dinner, instead of two. Caro asks her mother if the drinks taste good. Zoë says no, they taste like medicine, but she's tense and she needs them to relax.

"I'm tense, too," Caro tells her. "Can I have a drink?"

Zoë is shocked. She says no, and then pours her own drink down the drain.

The next afternoon, Caro is sitting in the living room, watching *Engineer Bill.* Zoë comes in. She is pale, with bright spots of red on her cheeks.

"We're going out to dinner tonight, at a new place."

Caro sits up. "Who's taking us?"

"A man called Jack. He's a director," Zoë says, and adds, "I want you to wear your yellow dress."

The restaurant they go to is in Beverly Hills, and it's called The Luau. It is decorated like a Polynesian village, with grass shacks and spears and waterfalls and rain forest flowers. Caro thinks it's the most exciting restaurant she's ever been to.

Zoë's friend Jack turns out to be funny and nice.

"How old are you?" he asks Caro.

"Seven."

"Well then, you must be married. Do you have any children?"

Caro laughs. She feels like showing off, so she sings a song and does her Annette Funicello imitation. Jack calls her princess and makes her sit in the big wicker chair and orders her spare ribs, an egg roll, and an ice-cream snowball for dessert.

When the meal is over, he turns to Zoë.

"I think I've found my angel," he says.

Zoë looks pleased and relieved. Caro is very surprised. Where did he find an angel?

Before she can ask, he turns to her. He says, "Caro, how would you like to work for me in a television commercial?"

She squeals and says yes, yes. Then she thinks maybe he won't like her to be so excited, so she says primly and angelically that yes, she would like that very much, thank you. And he and Zoë both laugh.

The commercial is shot the following Friday. Caro enjoys everything about the day. She loves getting up at five in the morning, when the sky is still dark and secretive. She loves the drive to the studio, and her name being on the special admittance list. She loves to see the wooden bar rising, letting their car go through.

Mostly, she loves being in the studio. The silence of the soundstage makes her shiver—no one has to tell her to be quiet. She tiptoes around the sets, gingerly touching false walls, props, camera cables. It seems somehow holy, like going to church.

Jack is there. He introduces Caro around. Everyone is nice to her, tells her how pretty she is. A young woman comes to take her into the makeup room. Caro's hair is washed and her curls are set and fluffed and her face is sprinkled with sweet-smelling blush-on. Then she is put into a soft white dress with gold-tipped wings. Caro looks into the mirror and smiles. Behind it is another mirror, and she can see dozens of pretty little Caros, all looking like angels.

It is easy to do the commercial. All she has to do is sit on a cotton cloud and wait for the blond man by the camera to say "Speed!" and for Jack to call "Action!" Then she waits a moment, looks straight into the camera, and says, "It's heavenly soft." Finally, she picks up the toilet paper and spins it away from her so that it unrolls.

Spinning the toilet paper well is the hardest part. The first two times she does it, it catches on the cloud, and Caro is afraid Jack will be angry with her. But it seems it's not her fault. A short, perspiring man comes up and says he will fix everything. And he does. He makes a little cut in the cloud, so the toilet paper can roll free.

Caro has to say "It's heavenly soft" quite a few times before Jack is happy, but finally he is, and then it's time to go home.

"Could I keep the angel dress?" Caro whispers to Zoë, but Zoë tells her no. It is not like a birthday party. There are no favors.

When she and Zoë come out of the soundstage, it is dark. Caro is amazed. When they arrived at the studio it was before dawn, and now it is after sunset. Hidden in that dark stage, she has missed one whole day of her life. She decides she likes that.

When they get back home, Caro is in a very bad mood. She hates being a regular person again, only Caro. Zoë is in the bedroom, talking on the telephone, telling someone about the day.

Caro goes into the kitchen. She sees the bottle, the one her mother always pours the pale brown drinks from.

"I need to relax," Caro says out loud.

She pours a little of the drink into a glass, and takes a taste. It is horrible, and she spits it out. Then she rinses out the glass and stares out the window.

The next day, when Caro comes home from school, Zoë is on the sofa, smoking furiously.

"Your father called today," she tells Caro. "I told him about the commercial."

Caro frowns. Her father calls from New York once a month, and he always seems to make her mother upset.

"He thinks I'm ruining your life," Zoë bursts out. "Putting you on television. Do you think I'm ruining your life?" she demands.

Caro shakes her head.

"I don't, either," Zoë tells her

A few weeks later, Caro is taking a bath when she hears her mother's voice screaming from the living room.

"Caro! Come here! Hurry!"

Caro jumps from the bathtub and rushes in, dripping. Zoë is on the couch, stabbing a finger at the television set. Caro turns and looks. There, on the screen, is a pretty little girl with blond hair. She is dressed in an angel costume and sits on a cloud. "It's heavenly soft!" she says, and throws down a roll of toilet paper, which turns magically into a sparkling rainbow bridge.

Caro stares at the television, at this girl who is and isn't herself. How had she done that? How on Earth had she made the toilet paper turn into a rainbow? She watches herself with awe.

* * *

The next morning at school, Mrs. Valdez, the second grade teacher, comes into class a few minutes late.

She smiles at Caro.

"Children, before we start the day, I have a special announcement to make. I have just been told that our own Caro Andrews can be seen on a television commercial—playing an angel."

Caro is red with embarrassment. She will kill her mother for telling her teacher. But when she looks around the room, she sees only interested faces, impressed faces. Even Adrianna Holmes, who hates Caro, doesn't have a thing to say.

Caro gets a lot of money for the commercial.

"Can we buy anything we want?" she asks her mother.

"No," Zoë tells her. "We're putting that money straight into your bank account. I don't want you dragging me into court someday on a child exploitation charge."

Then, seeing Caro's face, she laughs. "Okay, okay," she says. "We'll get you something."

She takes Caro to the F.A.O. Schwarz toy store in Beverly Hills. "Choose anything your heart desires," she tells her.

Caro finds what she wants immediately. It is a dollhouse, a beautiful two-story dollhouse with red velvet furniture in the living room, and a four-poster bed and an old-fashioned bathtub. And most precious of all, in the den, there is a tiny television. Caro wonders if she will be able to see herself, a miniature Caro angel, on the screen.

During the drive home, she sits in the backseat, with one hand on the big box. At last she has a dollhouse, and she has earned it herself. She sighs with pride. She has ended the slump. She is in a television commercial. She may not remember how she turned that toilet paper roll into a rainbow, but she has still done magic.

Caro is standing outside of school, waiting for her mother to pick her up. It is a hot day, and Zoë is late.

A car the color of lime sherbet comes along the street. The man inside slows the car and smiles at Caro. He beckons her over. He doesn't look like other men she knows; his face is very thin, his clothes are sad.

"Hi, Caro," he says. "I have a message from your mother. She got tied up with work and asked me to pick you up."

Caro hesitates. Zoë has done this once or twice before, sent someone else to bring her home. Finally she decides to get in, mainly because of the color of the man's car. It is such a hot day, and the pale green looks so cool.

Caro gets in the car. It isn't cool at all.

The man smiles at her as they drive away.

"I told you a little fib just now. It wasn't your mother who asked me to pick you up. It was the Lord."

His breathing starts to get faster.

"God has special plans for you," he tells her. "You were such a good angel on television, and God wants you in heaven, to be an angel for Him all the time."

Caro frowns. If God wants her in heaven, doesn't that mean she has to die first? But that can't be what the man means.

They are driving into a strange neighborhood. The houses are small and dirty and there are no gardens anywhere.

"Where are we?"

The man doesn't answer.

"When is my mother coming?"

The man doesn't answer that either. When she looks over at him, she sees that there are tears running down his face.

They pull into a driveway near the end of the street. The concrete is old and stained, and weeds are growing through all the cracks. The man reaches into the backseat and pulls out a blanket. He puts the blanket over Caro. It is hot and smelly, and Caro is angry. She kicks and tries to yell, but the man's arms are very strong.

He carries her into the house. He lets her out of the blanket, but it hardly makes a difference, the house is so dark and hot. The windows have all been boarded up and there are no lights. The room is almost empty—there are no sofas, no chairs, only a big table covered with a cloth. The walls are covered with crosses; some are made of wood, some are made of stone. On the biggest one of all, there is a statue of a man. Caro can't bear to look at him because he is bleeding.

"Who is that?" she whispers.

The man turns around. "That's the Son of God," he tells her.

He sounds angry that she doesn't know.

Caro backs away from the bleeding statue. She thinks about what the man said, about God wanting her in heaven.

She goes into a corner and stays there. The man kneels before the big covered table and starts talking to himself. Caro cannot understand what he is saying.

Caro's mind does something strange. It leaves the dark house and the bleeding statue and the man. It travels far, far away. She is at Disneyland, going on the Peter Pan ride. She is at school, playing tetherball. She is at home with her mother, watching Zoë paint her fingernails. And then she is back in the room once again.

The man is coming toward her. He has a white towel in his hands with something under it. He pulls the towel away and Caro sees that he is holding a knife.

Then suddenly there are loud running steps and the front door is shattered open.

Zoë is there, crying, rushing to Caro, holding her. Policemen with guns come in, and lead the man away. He looks small and harmless now, like a bewildered bug. Caro calls good-bye to him, because she has always been taught to be polite.

It is on the local news that evening. There are pictures of the kidnapper, Harvey Benedic, aged fifty-four, who worked as a garage mechanic, and, according to a fellow worker, had always been something of a recluse. Caro's teacher is also interviewed—she explains how, when she saw Caro get in the strange car, she wrote down the license plate on the playground with hopscotch chalk, then called the police. Greg Altman, the policeman who had first burst through the door, confirms the story.

"Luckily, we got there in time."

"How come I didn't get to be on television, too?" Caro complains.

"This is not the kind of publicity we want," Zoë tells her.

She bursts into tears and hugs Caro so hard that her ribs hurt.

CAROLINE

Caroline thinks a lot about the photograph Laura showed her. Especially at night, when she is about to go to sleep, she can't get the image of her mother out of her mind. She sees other mothers at school, or at the park, and tries to guess which of them hers is most like. Is she a good sport like Eleanor's mother? Does she have a high, squeaky voice or a low, runny one? Does she laugh a lot? Caroline knows she could ask someone—Laura, even her father—but she doesn't want to. She figures that she'll find out someday, when the time is right.

Laura has gone out onto the balcony, to water the plants. Caroline hides behind the drapes. She plans on jumping out and yelling "Boo!" when Laura comes back inside. It's one of their best games.

Then she hears a voice call, "Hey, girl," and Laura calls hello back. It is her friend Janet, the maid from across the way.

Laura and Janet start talking. Mostly, it's uninteresting stuff about Janet's new boyfriend. Caroline is about to leave the curtains and go back into her room, when she hears her own name.

"Oh, yes," Laura is saying, "such a good girl. Never gives me a day of trouble."

Caroline is pleased to hear this, but then she hears Laura sigh.

"There's no getting around it, though. I keep telling Mr. Andrews—that child's at the age where she needs a mother."

"What's been heard from her lately?" Janet asks.

Caroline holds her breath, waiting.

Laura whistles. "Oh, this and that. You know how she is."

Caroline bites her lip. No, she does not know how she is.

* * *

Caroline does not want Laura to find her now. She sneaks back into her room and plays all afternoon with her dollhouse built from shoe boxes. But today she plays a new game. Today, in the bedroom, a mother sleeps in the cardboard bed. In the bathroom, a mother washes her face at the tiny sink. In the dining room, a mother tells her children to eat their cereal. There are kisses from a mother. There are smiles from a mother. The house has been taken over by a mother.

That night, Caroline cannot sleep. Far past her bedtime, she hears her father's key in the lock. She jumps out of bed and runs to the front door.

"Boo!" she cries.

"What are you doing up?" her father asks. He seems pleased to see her.

"Tell me about my mother," Caroline says.

"Oh." The pleased sound has gone out of his voice. "Why do you want to know all of a sudden?"

"I just do."

He takes her back into her bedroom, tucks her in bed, and sits beside her. He looks like a mountain in the semidarkness.

"What do you want to know?" he asks.

"What's her name?"

"Zoë."

She giggles. "Zoë." She has a mother called Zoë.

"Where is she?"

"California." That word doesn't mean anything to Caroline.

"Why isn't she with me?"

Her father is silent for a long moment.

"Well, Caroline," he says carefully, "when your mother and I were married, we weren't happy together, so we decided to live apart. She stayed in California, and you and I moved back here."

"Will I ever get to see her?"

"Yes," her father says. Then he stops; then he starts again. "In fact, when you're seven, you're going to spend a whole month with her in the summer."

Caroline gulps. A month with her mother. This is too much to think about.

"Why can't I go now?" she asks.

Her father sounds a little hurt.

"I think seven is early enough," he says. "Zoë can be a little overwhelming. Besides, aren't you happy with me?"

Caroline ignores this last question. "What does overwhelming mean?"

"A bit much to take."

There is silence. She changes the subject.

"What does she look like?" she asks, although she already knows.

Her father stands up.

"I think I have a picture," he says.

He holds out his hand. Caroline takes it and follows him into the den. He opens a drawer, and there, underneath some papers, is the picture Laura had showed her.

It is as bewitching as ever.

Until Caroline meets her mother in California, there are other women. Women who appear for a night, or a weekend, or a month.

The first one was Diane. She had short black hair. The day Caroline met her, Barton took them all to a movie, and afterward they walked down Fifth Avenue, window-shopping. Diane spent a lot of time in front of the jewelry stores, pointing out all the things she liked best. "I'll make a note of that." Barton smiled.

Caroline thought this was very clever, and when they reached F.A.O. Schwarz, the toy store, Caroline pointed to the window and began to talk about what *she* liked best. Diane smiled a squeezed little smile and asked if someone was a teeny bit spoiled?

Tall, red-haired Evelyn was not much better. When she met Caroline for the first time, she shrieked and squeezed her hard; and then she paid no more attention to her.

But Jackie was the worst. Jackie was tiny, but she had big ideas about changing everything around. She didn't like the way Laura served dinner. She didn't like Barton's ties. She said Caroline should be sent to boarding school.

None of the women lasts long.

Every few months, Caroline sneaks into the den and looks at the photograph of her mother. One day Laura catches her, but doesn't scold.

"What's she like?" Caroline asks.

"I don't really know, honey. I only met her once. Your father's the one who could tell you."

That night at dinner, Caroline asks.

"What's my mother like?"

Barton frowns, then puts on a strange little smile.

"Well," he says, "let's put it this way. There is no one in the world like Zoë."

She cannot tell if this is good or not.

"How did you meet her?"

"About eight years ago, I was sent out to Los Angeles on an assignment; it was my first time there. One night, I was invited to a party, and there was Zoë." He shakes his head. "I don't think I've ever seen anyone quite as animated."

Caroline isn't sure what animated is, but from the way her father is looking, she knows it isn't bad.

"She came over to me, and we got to talking. She offered to show me around town."

"Did you think she was pretty?"

"Oh, yes," he says. "Very pretty." He studies Caroline. "She looked a little like you."

This is overwhelming.

"Did you get married right away?"

"Pretty much."

"And then you had me."

"Yes."

"And then you started not getting along."

"That had nothing to do with you."

Caroline swallows and looks down. "After you got a divorce, didn't my mother want to keep me?"

"Yes," Barton says slowly. "Of course she did. But she got a job in Europe and she couldn't take you with her. It made more sense for you to stay with me." He reaches over and tips her face up. "Hope that's okay."

Caroline is silent. "Why hasn't she ever—called me or anything?" she asks at last.

Barton considers this. "I think she didn't want to—confuse you," he says.

Caroline nods. "But I'm seven now. This is the summer I'm going out there, right?"

He frowns slightly. "If you want to."

"Oh, yes," Caroline tells him. "I want to."

When the plane lands in Los Angeles, one of the stewardesses walks off the ramp with Caroline, and asks if she needs help finding her mother.

"No, thank you," Caroline tells her.

She knows immediately who her mother is—the tall blond woman in the red stretch pants, the red-and-white striped top, the large floppy hat tied with a scarf, and the sunglasses. She thinks of what her father said, that there was never anyone like Zoë.

"Caroline? Caroline!"

She is being hugged. There are a dozen edges to absorb all at once. Her mother's smell, a musky perfume. Her red-painted toenails. Her laugh, so loud it attracts the attention of everybody around. Her voice, the words loaded and popping, as if fireworks were going off.

"Caroline!" Another hug. "My baby!" Another hug. "You're absolutely gorgeous!"

Caroline is a little shy about being hugged so hard in front of everybody at the airport. She pulls back a little.

"What do you want me to call you?" she asks primly.

Her mother looks surprised.

"Zoë," she says. "I think it would be phony-baloney to call me anything else, don't you?"

Then she takes off her dark glasses and smiles, and Caroline finally gets to see what Zoë's eyes look like. They are dark brown and slightly slanted.

Caroline takes a good look at her mother. She is a little sad to see that Zoë no longer much resembles the photograph in the drawer, but in a few minutes she gets over it.

"That picture's just phony-baloney," she tells herself.

The two of them lug Caroline's suitcases through the airport parking lot, and into Zoë's car. It's a wonderful car, huge and white.

"A Mercedes 600," Zoë says proudly. "My baby." Then she hugs Caroline. "No, you're my baby."

Caroline sees, wrapped around the rearview mirror, a medallion on a chain.

She points. "What's that?"

"That's St. Jude. The patron saint of lost causes."

Caroline is puzzled. "Do you get lost a lot?"

Zoë laughs. "You might say that."

On the drive home from the airport, Zoë takes a roundabout route, and gives Caroline a tour of the city.

"This is Brentwood, nice but a little Republican . . . And here's Westwood, where the smart college kids and the struggling show-business types like me live. And this is Beverly Hills, where I fully intend to move someday . . ."

Caroline loves Los Angeles right away. She loves the swaying palm trees, the unnatural green of the lawns, the pink buildings, the warm wind. It doesn't seem like real life at all.

She also likes her mother's apartment complex on Midvale Avenue. It's completely different from the big stiff building in New York where her father lives. The other tenants wave when she and Zoë come up the walk. Caroline can't get over all the friendliness and all the flowers. She can't get over the white sunlight. She can't get over the swimming pool in the center of the courtyard.

They climb the stairs to the apartment. Everything in it is relaxed and fun. There is wicker furniture with tropical print pillows, and bright rugs from Mexico. There is a papier-mâché parrot on a perch, and sticks of incense scenting the air.

It is strange to think that her mother has been living here all these years, with these blazing couches and colorful curtains, and that Caroline never knew.

"Your room is over there." Zoë points. "It has to double as my office. I have another one in Hollywood, but I do a lot of work at home. Hope you don't mind."

Caroline likes being part of an office. It makes her feel important, not like her babyish room in New York.

"What do you do?" she asks her mother.

Zoë seems a little upset.

"Didn't Barton tell you?" she asks. "Well, never mind. I'm a children's theatrical agent."

"Oh," Caroline says blankly.

"You've seen kids on commercials and TV shows? Well, I get some of them the parts." Her glance fastens on Caroline. "You've got the right look, as a matter of fact—how would you like to be on television?"

Caroline thinks Zoë is joking. She smiles nervously.

"Can I see my room now?" she asks.

Her room doesn't look like an office. It's as bright as the rest of the apartment, with a yellow sofa bed, potted plants at every window, and Indian hangings on the walls.

On the bed is a pile of presents. Zoë has bought Caroline cute sundresses and dark glasses and a little straw purse that looks like a watermelon. She has bought her flippers and fins for the swimming pool and a skateboard for the sidewalk. She has bought her Bobbsey Twins books and—best of all—a Troll doll in an angel costume.

Caroline is awed. "I wanted one of these more than anything," she says. "How did you know?"

Her mother only smiles. "Zoë magic," she tells her.

Caroline wonders if her mother has been secretly getting to know everything that has been happening in her head since she was born.

That night, Zoë comes into Caroline's room to kiss her good night.

"I can't believe I've lived without you this long," she says.

Caroline is silent for a moment. Then at last she asks, "How come you never called me or anything?"

Zoë sighs. She sits down on the edge of the bed. Then she picks up Caroline's hand and strokes it.

"Honey, I thought it was the best thing. You were three thousand miles away, living an entirely different life. I didn't want you to be—"

Caroline remembers her father's word. "Confused?"

"Yes," Zoë says. "That's it, exactly." She leans over and gives Caroline a rough hug. "But now that I know you, my darling, just *try* to keep me out of your life!"

Within a few days, Caroline is used to California. She starts to take for granted the huge oranges and the bright sunshine. She makes friends with the children in the building; they meet every morning to play in the pool. She tells them about New York, about Broadway plays and Central Park. Caroline, shy in Manhattan, is not shy in California. It isn't real life, not her real life, so it doesn't count.

Mornings, after her swim, she sits in the living room and reads *The Bobbsey Twins,* or watches television. Sometimes, Zoë has to go to her office, so Clarice, an older woman from downstairs, keeps an eye on Caroline while she's away. Other days, Zoë stays home; she spends the morning behind closed doors, talking on the phone. Sometimes Caroline can hear her screaming. She hopes Zoë isn't screaming at the children she gets into television shows. But she thinks it can't be anything too bad, because Zoë always comes out smiling.

"Brought another producer to his knees," she says.

Then, in the afternoons, the two of them go on adventures.

"Got to get you a little California culture," Zoë tells her. "Make you see what you've been missing."

The adventures are great. One day they go to the Farmers' Market, where they each eat a bagful of chocolate-covered peanuts. Another day they go to a miniature golf course, a tiny world with dollhouse-size windmills and castle and church. Another day, they go to Marineland, where Caroline watches huge, dark, finned fish circling the glass tanks.

"Are those sharks?" she asks her mother.

"Directors," Zoë corrects her.

She laughs, as if this is an old joke, and Caroline laughs, too, as if she has heard it a thousand times.

One Saturday morning, Zoë wakes Caroline up early.

"Prepare yourself," she tells her.

They have a quick breakfast. There is no swim, no television, no talking on the phone. They get in the car and drive and drive, until they come to roads lined with orange trees.

"Where are we going?" Caroline keeps asking.

"You'll see," is all that Zoë will say.

Finally, Caroline looks up and is amazed to see a huge snow covered mountain right ahead of them.

"Look!" she cries.

Zoë laughs. "Welcome to Disneyland!"

Disneyland is fantastic. Disneyland is a dream. They go on all the rides—Peter Pan, Alice in Wonderland, Mr. Toad's Wild Ride, but their favorite of all is the Matterhorn. Zoë and Caroline go on the bobsleds four times, and Zoë screams and screams. The last time they ride, her scarf is suddenly whipped away by the wind. They watch it slowly float down and disappear into the entrails of the dark mountain.

"I'm sorry about your scarf," Caroline says when the ride is over.

"Oh, never mind." Zoë smiles at her. "For the rest of your life, whenever you go on the Matterhorn, you'll think of me."

One afternoon, Zoë says, "Today is a buying day. What would you like?"

Caroline knows exactly what she would like. She has been seeing a commercial for a tiny baby doll called Little Darling, which comes in its own pouch, complete with crib and high chair.

"Sounds absolutely nauseating," Zoë tells her. "Let's get it."

They set off for the toy store. Caroline scans the shelves. Finally, she finds Little Darling, but the pouch has been ripped apart. The doll is still there, but the high chair and the crib have been stolen.

"There's another toy store a few blocks away," Zoë tells her. "We'll get one there."

But Caroline is holding Little Darling in her hands. It is the doll she wants, more than the pouch or the crib or the high chair—who could say for sure if it would be in the other toy store? And what if it wasn't, and Zoë got tired and didn't want to come back to this one? Caroline couldn't take that risk.

"It's all right," she says, holding up the vandalized pouch. "This Little Darling is fine."

Zoë looks at her curiously. "Are you sure?"

"Yes."

They buy the doll. They continue down the street and pass the other toy store. In the window is a whole display of Little Darlings, each one perfect, each one with its pouch and crib and high chair.

Zoë stops and looks at Caroline.

"I think there's a lesson to be learned here," she says.

•

Every night before bed, Zoë comes to tuck Caroline in. She straightens the chair cushion, she smooths the spread, she draws the curtains. Then she sits down on the edge of the bed, and pulls out a cigarette. Caroline enjoys watching the lit red tip wave back and forth in the darkness.

"Tell me about Barton," Zoë says one night.

Caroline is not sure what she is expected to reply.

"Still the same, I imagine?"

Caroline does not know what Zoë remembers. "I guess."

"Does he work all the time?"

"Yes."

Zoë sighs. "That man. I couldn't do a thing about it. Any women?"

Caroline is startled.

"No. Not really."

Zoë shakes her head. "He needs someone. He's not a man who does well alone. But of course he doesn't know that."

She looks carefully at Caroline. "Are you happy living with him?"

"Yes."

"Good," Zoë says abruptly.

Caroline wonders what her mother would have done if she had said she was unhappy with her father. Would Zoë have made it so that Caroline would live with her from now on, in the apartment in California?

Caroline wonders if she would have liked that. No father or sledding in winter, but she would always have the sunshine. No Central Park or Laura, but there would be Zoë and Disneyland.

She imagines what it would be like if she lived with Zoë always. It is too much even to wonder about.

* * *

Caroline likes the way Zoë talks to her, as if she were a grown-up. She tells her about her boyfriends and her work and about all the children she handles, what brats they are, and how ungrateful.

"They want the moon and a pair of orange ice skates—then, the minute I get them booked, they're off to the William Morris Agency." She regards Caroline gloomily. "Would that I could have you. I could do great things for you, kiddo."

One day, Zoë has to go into her agency to sign a new client, and she takes Caroline with her. It's a long drive into Hollywood. Hollywood isn't Caroline's favorite part of town—it's sad and dark compared to Westwood—but the agency is on a quiet side street, which Caroline likes. She also likes the small, old-fashioned building, with its brick walkway.

She and Caroline walk up the slick marble stairs, down the corridor, and toward a door decorated with a bright orange sign: Zoë's Babies.

The agency reminds Caroline of Zoë's apartment—it is full of bright colors and wall hangings. Phones are ringing, people are rushing around.

"Attention, everyone!" Zoë says. She puts her hands on Caroline's shoulder. "This is my daughter, Caroline. She's madly talented, and mark my words, she'll be a big star someday."

Everyone applauds. Caroline is embarrassed, and a little pleased. Then she sees another girl, around her own age, standing in the doorway, looking at her. This is the girl whose contract Zoë has come in to sign. The girl is not applauding.

On the drive home, Zoë asks, "So what did you think of the agency?"

"It was great."

"What I said about you in there—I was kidding of course. But seriously, baby—*do* you ever think about being an actress?"

Caroline draws in her breath. Being an actress, being on television—that's her biggest, most secret dream.

Zoë is looking at her curiously. "Do you?" she asks again.

Caroline gives a tiny nod.

Zoë smiles with satisfaction. "Would you like me to try to get you something?"

This nod is a little bigger.

The next afternoon, Zoë comes into the living room where Caroline is watching television. She seems pleased about something.

"A friend of mine is taking us out to dinner tonight. Wear your checked sundress."

The restaurant is in Beverly Hills, and it's called The Luau. It is decorated like a Polynesian village, with grass shacks and spears and waterfalls and rain forest flowers. Zoë's friend, Jack, turns out to be funny and nice and he makes Caroline laugh. She feels like showing off, so she sings a song and tells him jokes she's heard in school. He calls her princess and makes her sit in the big wicker chair and orders her spare ribs, an egg roll and an ice-cream snowball for dessert.

When the meal is over, he turns to Zoë.

"I think I've found my angel," he says.

"It's a commercial for toilet tissue," Zoë tells Caroline on the drive home. "You'd be an angel who sits on a soft cloud and says how great the toilet tissue is. Do you think you can do that?"

They both smile because they know that Caroline can do that.

When they get back to the apartment, Zoë pours herself a drink from the decanter on the sideboard.

"Well, that's about it," she says. "Except for calling Barton."

Caroline frowns. "What do you mean?"

"Well, I can't put you in a commercial without his approval," Zoë tells her.

"Why not?" Caroline's voice is high and nervous. "He doesn't watch television. He won't ever see it."

Zoë sighs. "We've still got to call." She eyes Caroline. "He might go for it, if we catch him in the right mood—what do you think?"

Caroline has her doubts. She thinks about the way her father likes her to be, sitting up straight, going to the Clark School for Girls, eating with beautiful table manners. She is not at all sure that this goes along with being an angel in a toilet paper commercial.

"I think he'll let me do it," she says stoutly, nevertheless.

Zoë nods. "When you tell him how much it means to you, I'm sure he will."

Caroline doesn't hear the phone conversation. But the next morning, when she wakes up, she sees that Zoë's face is pale and her eyes are red.

"Well, your father didn't exactly go for it," her mother says. Then she laughs, like a bark. "In fact he hated the idea so much that he's pulling the plug on the visit. You're going back to New York tomorrow."

Caroline and Zoë stare at each other.

"Oh, well, baby," Zoë says to her. "Never mind. Talent will out. Someday you'll get your chance. You wait and see."

Caroline doesn't want to wait and see. And she doesn't want to go back to New York. But the next morning, there she is at the airport, and her mother is hugging her good-bye.

"Next summer?" Zoë asks. "Do you want to come for another visit next summer?"

Caroline can only nod.

And she gets on the plane, crying, and behind her is her mother, calling out "Don't lose that gorgeous suntan!"

It's hard to be back in New York again. The streets seem so noisy and the fruit is so small and there is no Disneyland. Still, it's good to be back with her dollhouse, and with Laura. Caroline is cold to her father at first, because he wouldn't let her do the commercial, but after a week, she forgets about it. California is starting to seem unreal.

One of the first things Caroline does when she returns home is to take away that phony-baloney picture of her mother from the drawer in the den. By her bedside, she puts another—a picture of Zoë and herself eating ice-cream cones, taken the day they went to Marineland. That one is a real picture.

One night, a month after Caroline returns to New York, she and Laura are watching *Route 66.* A commercial comes on. A little golden-haired girl dressed as an angel is sitting on a cloud, holding a roll of toilet paper. "It's heavenly soft," she says.

"That could have been me," Caroline almost tells Laura, but in the end she says nothing.

Caroline is ten. She is tall and her hair has grown past her waist. She takes piano lessons and ballet lessons, and she has learned how to crochet.

Her life goes in nice straight lines. Fifth grade isn't too bad, and after school she likes to spend time reading and going to the park and playing with her dollhouse. And there are still card games with Laura, though now they play War instead of Old Maid. She doesn't really have any friends, but that's all right. She enjoys being by herself.

Zoë calls her often now, and sends presents, and every summer, Caroline goes to spend a month with her. She comes back with cute new clothes and a suntan.

Her father is still busy, still traveling a lot. There hasn't been a new girlfriend in over six months. Caroline thinks that he has given up trying. That's fine with her. She's happy with things the way they are.

Then, one Saturday night, her father gives a dinner party. He doesn't often give parties, so it is exciting to Caroline and Laura.

The day of the party, Caroline helps Laura shine the silver and get the buffet napkins ready. Caroline takes an extra-long bubble bath and dresses in her favorite green pantsuit. She practices being hostess and shaking hands with all the guests.

She has a good time at the party. All the women say how pretty she is, and how lucky Barton is to have her for a daughter. Just before the guests sit down for dinner, she says good night and goes to her room. At nine o'clock, Laura tells her it's bedtime.

As Caroline is finishing brushing her teeth, she hears a soft knock on her bedroom door. She opens it. One of the guests, a tiny blond woman, is standing outside.

"Hello," she says softly, "I'm Meg. Can I come in for a little while?"

"Aren't you enjoying the party?" Caroline asks her.

Meg sighs. "I'm not very good at parties."

Caroline invites her in.

"May I look through your books?" Meg asks.

"Sure."

Meg goes over to the bookcase. With a little cry, she pulls out the stories of Hans Christian Andersen.

"These are my favorites!" She flips through the book. "Do you know "The Christmas Tree?"

Caroline says she doesn't. So Meg sits down in the easy chair and reads her the story, even though Caroline can read perfectly well, and it's nowhere near Christmas. But Caroline likes the way Meg reads; it's as if she really cares about the little tree.

"Would you like to hear "The Wild Swans" now?" Meg asks her.

Caroline loves "The Wild Swans," but she knows that Meg is just putting off going back to the party.

"I think you'd better go in the other room now," she tells her.

Meg's face falls. "I guess you're right."

Caroline sighs. She rises from the bed and puts on her robe. She takes Meg by the hand, and leads her down the hall to the party.

"You can do it," she says encouragingly, and gives Meg a little push.

Caroline is glad when Meg becomes Barton's girlfriend. She is wonderful—not like a grown-up at all. She doesn't tell Caroline to wash her hair, she doesn't remind her to do her homework. She listens to the Beatles and she even has chocolate cake for breakfast.

She loves dollhouses, and the second time she comes to visit, she plays with Caroline's for almost half an hour.

"Do you have any miniatures at home?" Caroline asks.

"I have one," Meg tells her.

And that is how Caroline finds out about Adam.

Adam is Meg's little boy.

"I want you two to meet," Meg says. "I think you'll like him."

Caroline is not so sure. All the little boys she knows are messy and loud. But she says she would be happy to meet Adam, and they all go to the zoo the following Saturday.

Adam is three years old. He is lumpy and jolly and fun to drag around. He puts his hand in Caroline's, and she likes that. She also likes it that he's a good sport. He doesn't cry when his Popsicle drops, or when a twig pokes him in the face.

She starts to want to be with Adam every Saturday.

* * *

Adam and Meg visit Caroline even when Barton is not home. They always have a good time. They go to the park, and the zoo, and ride the bus down to Washington Square. Caroline teaches Adam to play War, and they play it out on the balcony. Every Saturday they go out for ice cream at Rumplemeyer's. Adam always has a caramel sundae, and Caroline has the "Flaming Robin Rose Glow with Lisa Delight." Usually, she stays away from foods with silly names; it's too embarrassing to order them. But Adam laughs so hard every time she says the magic words, that she keeps on ordering it.

"Flaming Robin Rose Glow with Lisa Delight!"

She and Adam sing out the words together, in harmony, and the waiters laugh.

Caroline's class is due to go to Plymouth Rock on a three-day school bus trip. She is half dreading it, half excited.

The day before she leaves, she tells Adam, "I'm going on a trip tomorrow."

She hopes he will cry and tell her not to go, but he is too little to understand.

"I'm going to be away a long time," she says.

There are still no tears. He just looks at her with a smile.

Caroline can't stand that.

"I'm never going to see you again!" she cries.

And Adam wails and screams.

Caroline feels comforted. She holds Adam in her arms and says that she was only kidding, that she will see him again in just a few days.

"I couldn't really leave you for longer than that," she tells him. "I love you better than anything."

CARO

Zoë has a new boyfriend—Greg Altman, the policeman who helped rescue Caro from the kidnapper, the one who was first to break through the door.

Caro is not grateful that Greg saved her life; she does not wish to remember that it needed saving.

At first Greg is over at the apartment a lot. And then Greg is over practically all the time. And then Greg is always there.

Caro can see that Zoë is serious about Greg. She can tell by the way her mother dresses, and by the way she looks at him. Sometimes Zoë even says things to her like, "Wouldn't it be a relief to grow up in a nice normal family, eating meat loaf?" For some reason, it is always meat loaf.

Caro says no.

She does not like Greg. He pretends to be friendly, but she knows that he's mean inside. She knows he doesn't like her, either. He offers to play games with her, but they're never the games Caro is good at. She thinks basketball and baseball are stupid, and she tells him so. He never offers to play anything with her again.

Zoë tries to make it better.

"Greg had such a hard time as a child," she tells Caro. "His father used to hit him and his mother ran away. That's why he seems a little strict sometimes. He just doesn't know any better. But he loves you, baby. Really he does."

Caro doesn't say anything.

Greg wants to take them all on a road trip to Oregon during Caro's spring vacation. Caro has no interest in going. She doesn't like the sound of Oregon, and she doesn't want to spend hours in the car with Greg.

To make herself feel better, she packs all her toys. When Greg sees the pile, he slams his fist down.

"You're spoiled rotten," he says. "You've got enough toys for ten kids in there."

Caro dumps out all of her toys; the only thing she ends up taking is her most precious possession, the tiny pink teddy bear her mother got for her, years ago, from the vending machine.

The first night they stop at a Travelodge motel. It's right by a truck stop, and the big rigs keep Caro from sleeping. Greg wakes her early the next morning.

"You have ten minutes to be dressed and in the car, or we're leaving without you."

Caro gets her clothes together and rushes to the car. They drive for fifteen minutes. Suddenly Caro realizes that she has left her pink teddy bear in the hotel room.

"We've got to go back!" she cries, but Greg won't listen.

"Please! Please!" she screams, and she beats on Greg's shoulders.

Greg keeps driving.

"Honey, don't you think we could go back?" Zoë steps in. "It's her favorite—"

Greg tells her to shut up.

The trip lasts nine days. Caro and Greg do not speak at all.

The final morning, they are in Andersonville, getting ready to leave their motel. Caro finds a vending machine in the lobby and buys a Mars bar. When she passes Greg in the corridor, he sees the chocolate in her hand.

"Don't you go spoiling your breakfast," he says. "I pay enough for these goddam meals."

Caro walks off as if she hasn't heard. She finds her mother, who is starting to pack the car.

"Zoë," she says, "I'm starving. Can I eat my candy bar?"

Zoë laughs. "What else are candy bars for?"

Caro goes back into the room. She takes a big bite of the chocolate. But it doesn't taste right. It tastes of guilt. She throws the rest of it in her underwear drawer.

She does not know how Greg finds out about the candy. But in a minute there is a knocking on the door.

"Caro, did you eat that candy bar—after I told you not to?"

"I only had a little." She hates how scared her voice sounds. "Honestly."

"Let me in. Now."

He is pounding on the door. She remembers how he broke down that other door, the kidnapper's door.

She opens the door and Greg is in the room. He is breathing hard.

"Where's the candy bar?"

"I put it in that drawer."

He jerks the drawer from the bureau. He is pulling out her nightgowns, her panties.

There is no candy bar.

Caro cannot believe it.

"But I put it in there. Really. I promise."

He looks at her.

He is quiet as he hits her, she is quiet as she is hit.

The first sound is Zoë's scream as she comes into the room.

The removal of Greg from their lives is swift.

"I thought I was doing what was best for you," Zoë keeps saying. "I thought it would be such a relief, being a real family."

"With meat loaf," Caro adds.

For a few weeks, Caro is even allowed to sleep with her mother in the big bed with pink satin sheets. There will never be another man allowed there, Zoë promises her.

As awful as Greg had been, he has started Caro thinking.

Up until now, she has never been particularly curious about her father. She likes it that he sends money for her every month—with extra for birthdays and Christmas—but she doesn't like it that his phone calls always seem to upset Zoë. On occasion, Caro has spoken to him herself; his voice sounds pleasant but very far away, and she never quite knows what to say.

She always supposed she would meet him one day, but she's never imagined what that would be like. Now, though, she finds she's thinking about him a lot. She looks carefully at other girls' fathers, and wonders which of them is most like her own.

"What was my father like?" she asks Zoë one night when they are in bed.

Zoë seems a little taken aback.

"Well," she says finally, "he's nothing like me, that's for sure. I guess that's what drew me to him. He's reserved, very New York, very business suit."

"How did you meet him?"

"At a party. He had come to L.A. on business. He seemed so ridiculously out of place; I took pity on him. We ended up falling for each other. Opposites attracting, I guess." She gives a phony-baloney little laugh. "But you can judge all that for yourself. You're going to be seeing him in August."

Caro sits up in bed. "What?"

"You'll be going to New York and spending a month with him."

Caro can't keep the excitement out of her voice.

"Why didn't you tell me?"

"I thought surely I'd mentioned it." Caro can tell that Zoë is trying to sound airy. "It was an agreement we made when we were divorced. You'd live with me all the time until you were seven, and then, after that, you'd go visit him for a month every summer."

Caro flops down on the bed again. "I can't believe it."

"You'll probably have a very dull time," Zoë tells her. "I doubt if Barton has changed much."

Caro can hear the hurt in her mother's voice. She props herself on one elbow and leans over Zoë.

"I promise not to love him more than I do you," she says.

"You better not."

Zoë tickles her. Afterward, Caro turns over and pretends to go to sleep. But the sentence repeats and repeats in her mind: She'll be seeing her father in August.

* * *

During the drive to the airport, Zoë gives Caro instructions. She must remember to behave beautifully. She must remember that things are a little more formal in New York. She must keep in mind that Barton isn't a fan of show business—perhaps it would be better not to talk too much about the angel commercial. And it would definitely be wise not to mention the kidnapper. Or Greg.

Caro nods impatiently. She is off to see her father.

As they are saying good-bye at the airport, it occurs to Caro for the first time that she won't be seeing her mother for a month.

She hugs Zoë hard.

"Don't forget your promise," Zoë says, trying to smile.

"I won't," Caro says earnestly.

She tries to remember which promise that was.

Caro guesses who Barton is the moment she sees him at the airport. He is handsome enough, stylish enough, but she feels let down. She has imagined her father with so many faces; he wears only one. She has imagined him wearing so many different types of clothes, giving her so many different greetings. But he wears only one blue suit, and he utters only one word when he sees her. He says "Caroline?" He does not use her nickname.

They drive into New York. Caro looks up at the crowding, crushing buildings. She feels uneasy—small and shadowed underneath the skyscrapers.

"Our firm designed that one," Barton tells her. "And that one's ours, too." He points up and up.

"Wow," Caro says in a small voice.

They arrive at the place where Barton lives. Caro wonders if she will ever recognize it from the buildings on either side. They go up in a swooping elevator that makes her feel sick.

Her father's apartment is very different from her mother's. There are no bright colors, no wicker to put your feet on. Nothing is stained, everything matches.

"Better be careful," Barton tells her. "This place isn't really designed for children. I don't want you hurting yourself."

He shows her her room. This is much better. There is a pretty flowered comforter on the bed, and the closet is full of toys. Most of the toys are things Caro was interested in a year or so ago, but that's all right. Her father has tried.

"I hope you'll be very happy here," he tells her.

"I like it already," Caro says, in the brilliant voice she uses for auditions.

Her father coughs.

"How is your mother?" he asks.

He uses the exact same phony-baloney voice that Zoë had put on when she told Caro, "Give my regards to your father."

"Fine," Caro says.

"Has she put you in any more commercials?"

"Oh, no," Caro says quickly. "No more commercials. She wants me to be an architect like you when I grow up."

Her father looks at her skeptically.

"I see." Then he smiles at her. He has a nice smile. "Now tell me about yourself. I want to get to know you."

Caro is careful. She tells her father about school, and how much she likes art class, and who her friends are. She says she can play "Ode to a Mouse" on the piano, and that she'd love to come see Barton work in his office one day.

She is finished, waiting for his response.

"I can tell you're a great kid," her father says.

She has passed the audition. She is a great kid.

Caro sleeps well that night, although the sheet is cotton and not satin. By her bedside, there is a framed picture of a man holding a little baby. It takes her a while to realize that the man is her father, and the baby is herself. It makes Caro sad to think that she once knew this man and sat on his lap, and then forgot about him for so many years.

The next morning, when Caro wakes up, she finds a large, dark woman sitting on the edge of her bed.

"Hello, honey," the woman says, with tears in her eyes. "I'm Laura. I'm your daddy's housekeeper. I'm going to be taking care of you."

Caro is embarrassed by the way the woman is beaming at her.

"Hello," she says.

Then Laura reaches out and grabs Caro in a huge hug.

"I've been looking forward to doing that for seven years!"

Caro does not know what to say. She cannot pretend that she has been looking forward to being hugged by Laura; up until today, she had not known that there even was a Laura.

But Laura is nice, and Caro soon learns that Laura will do anything she wants. If Caro wants creamed corn and canned peaches for dinner, that's what she has. If she wants to wear the same dress three days in a row, Laura lets her. If she wants to play hide-and-seek, they play, even though it hurts Laura's back to hide behind the sofa.

And Laura cannot hear enough about Caro's life in California. She wants to know about everything—all about Zoë, and what kind of clothes people wear in Hollywood, what it's like in a studio, and if she's ever seen Doris Day or Hayley Mills.

Caro enjoys hearing about Laura's life, as well. Laura tells her all about Dale, her daughter, and her granddaughter, Yvette—"my other little princess."

Caro is jealous that there is another little princess in Laura's life besides herself.

"Would you like to come with me to visit them? Next time your daddy's out of town?"

"Yes," says Caro primly. She wants to keep an eye on this other little princess.

A week later, Barton has a trip to Atlanta.

"Why do you have to go?" Caro wants to know.

He seems pleased that she will miss him.

"It's an assignment I can't pass up," he tells her. "There's going to be a new civic center, and I've been asked to design it. But Laura will take good care of you while I'm gone."

"Ready to go?" Laura asks Caro the next morning.

"In just a minute," Caro says.

She brushes her hair extra carefully. She makes sure her teeth are extra clean.

They walk down the block and get on the subway. The long, hot ride in the swaying car makes Caro queasy, but she does not tell Laura.

They get out at their stop and walk through the lively, littered streets. Caro likes Harlem. It is filled with the bright colors of her mother's apartment.

Several blocks later, they turn a corner and reach a small blue house.

"Here we are," Laura says.

They climb the front steps and knock on the door. It is opened almost immediately by a tiny woman with huge hair, and a little girl a year or two older than Caro.

Laura hugs them while Caro stands back.

"Caro, I'd like you to meet my daughter, Dale, and my granddaughter, Yvette."

The other little princess. Caro studies her carefully. She is tall and too skinny, but her hair is wonderful. It flies around her face in tiny braids tied with ribbons that match her dress. For a moment, Caro is almost jealous; but then she remembers her own blond curls and how good they looked on the angel commercial.

Laura pats Yvette on the bottom. "Why don't you show Caro around, honey?"

Caro would rather stay with Laura, but she follows the little girl down the hall.

"This is my room," Yvette tells her.

Caro thinks at first that it is a not-very-interesting room; then she notices the huge pink teddy bear on the bed.

"I won that," Yvette tells her proudly. "All by myself. Playing the throwing game at Playland."

It is definitely an interesting bear. Even though it's a million times bigger, it makes Caro think of the tiny pink teddy bear from the vending machine that she had loved and Greg had made her lose.

"Did you ever go to Playland?" Yvette asks.

"No."

"You should. You should get your daddy to take you."

Yvette tells Caro all about Playland, and the throwing game.

"And if you throw the rings around three bottles in a row, then you can win a bear. Wanna try?"

"Sure."

Laura is pleased that Caro and Yvette have found an interesting game. She helps them set up a row of milk bottles, and cuts three rings out of cardboard.

They play for an hour. Laura tells them they are so good they should win a dozen bears apiece.

Afterward, while they are having cookies, Yvette asks, "Is there anything like Playland where you live?"

Caro smiles. "Well, we do have Disneyland."

Yvette frowns. "I thought that was just something on television."

"Oh, no." Caro tells Yvette all about Disneyland—all about going to Never-Never Land in a pirate ship, seeing mermaids on the submarine ride, twirling on the teacups, and going to Wonderland in a pink or purple caterpillar.

Yvette puts down her cookie. Her mouth sags.

"Really?" she asks in a little voice.

Caro knows she should not go on, but she can't resist. So she tells Yvette some more—about riding bobsleds down the Matterhorn, and seeing Tinkerbell flying across the night sky.

Yvette swallows hard.

"That sounds better than Playland," she says finally.

Caro is ashamed.

"Oh, no," she says quickly. "Playland sounds much better."

But Yvette does not look up.

Caro is reading in her room when her father knocks on the door and opens it.

"Caro, come here a minute; I want you to see something."

She follows Barton into the den. There, resting on a board atop the big glass coffee table, is a tiny, perfect building. There are miniature walkways and trees around it, and minuscule people on the paths. Tears prick Caro's eyes.

"Is it for me?"

Her father laughs. "I'm afraid not. This is what we call an architectural model—it's a miniature version of that new civic center we're doing in Atlanta. Tomorrow I'm showing it to the people in charge."

"Can I have it when you're done?"

"Sorry." Then he looks more closely at her, and his eyes grow watchful. "And Caro, I don't want you going anywhere near this. Understand? It's very delicate. Touch it the wrong way, and weeks of work will be down the drain." He smiles. "You wouldn't want that to happen, would you?"

"No," Caro says.

He goes out, a few minutes later, for a meeting. Within seconds, Caro is back in the den.

Of course she isn't going to hurt the model; but how insulting to be told that she can't even touch it—Caro, who has starred in an angel commercial; Caro, who has turned toilet paper into a rainbow bridge.

She leans in to play. She reaches toward one of the tiny people, meaning to move it closer to the building. There is glue holding the figure down. Caro works at the figure. The glue still holds. She pulls harder. The glue gives way and the figure comes up with a jerk. Caro loses her balance. She falls backward, and her knee catches on the edge of the model. The civic center tilts, then flips, then crashes upside down on the floor.

It is completely ruined.

Caro's lips tremble.

"Laura!" she starts to call, and then she stops. No. Laura works for her father. He's her boss. No matter how much she cared for Caro, no matter how she might want to help her out, she'd have to tell the boss what had happened.

She can't call Laura.

Caro runs from the den. She goes into her own room, closes the door silently, and plays with her paper dolls.

She waits and waits all afternoon. Finally she hears her father come back into the apartment; a few minutes later, there is a commotion, footsteps, a knock at her door.

"Caro?" Barton looks very grim. "Did you go back in the den after I left?"

"No," Caro tells him with surprise. She really is an excellent actress. She points to the paper dolls spread around her. "I've been playing right here."

"The architectural model I brought home," he says, "it's been destroyed. Do you know anything about that?"

Caro stares at him. She knows she should tell the truth. Flossie Bobbsey would tell the truth. Rebecca of Sunnybrook Farm would tell the truth. And Caro is about to tell the truth, too—but then she thinks of Greg. *Did you eat that candy bar—after I told you not to?* And his hand raised, coming toward her face.

Caro swallows.

"No," she says again. And then she looks thoughtful. "But I did hear something crashing. And then—" she cannot stop herself. "I'm not sure, but I think—I think I saw Laura coming out of there."

She can't get to sleep. She can't stop trembling. She hadn't meant to—really, she hadn't. She didn't know why she had lied like that. She didn't know there would be a big fight. She didn't know Laura would quit.

Laura is leaving the next morning. Caro locks herself in her room. She is too scared to come out. She knows, up until the front door finally closes and Laura leaves, that she still has a chance to tell the truth, to make it all right. But she can't do it. And then Laura is gone.

Caro herself is gone three days later, back to California.

Zoë picks her up at the airport.

"Well," she says. "Did you have a good time?"

The phony-baloney brightness in her voice is dazzling.

Caro knows that all she has to say is "I'm glad to be home," and her mother would be perfectly happy. But she doesn't say it.

Why *should* her mother be perfectly happy? Who in the world is perfectly happy? Laura isn't, because she has lost her job. Yvette isn't, because the best thing in her life is only Playland. Her father isn't, because he cried saying good-bye to Caro at the airport. And Caro isn't, because she told a lie. So she says to Zoë, "I had a great time. I can't wait to go back next summer." And she watches, with satisfaction and with sorrow, the pain on her mother's face.

Caro is in art class when the principal comes in. He is crying. He says the president has been shot. The children assemble in the auditorium. They are to be sent home early because of the tragedy. Caro cannot help but feel a little happy. If she gets to go home early, she will miss her multiplication quiz.

It is not so much fun once she is home. Everyone is crying, her mother, the neighbors in the building, even the reporters on television.

She watches the broadcast all afternoon. A picture of Kennedy's little girl comes on. Caro is uneasy, thinking how quickly the life of a little girl called Caroline can be destroyed. One minute it's perfect, the next minute it's ruined, like an architectural model. But then she reminds herself that her own name is Caro, not Caroline, and that nothing bad will ever happen to her.

CAROLINE

It is the last day of fifth grade. There is a party and afterward all the girls assemble in the great hall for the prize-giving. Caroline sits in the back row. She tells herself she is not going to win a prize, that it would be foolish to expect anything.

But then she hears her name being called.

"The award for Best Manners—the winner is Caroline Andrews."

Caroline stumbles up onto the stage. Her face is a dull red. Best Manners. That was not an award. That was something a loser got, someone who did not deserve anything better.

She takes the ribbon, and tries to smile. Then she hurries back to her seat and slumps in her chair.

"And now, the award for the girl Most Likely to Succeed."

The headmistress holds out the next ribbon. This is the one Caroline had wanted, the one she had secretly been longing for.

She listens as another name is called, watches as another girl walks up onto the stage.

CARO

It is the last day of summer camp. There is an awards ceremony, held out by the pine knoll. The campers sit in a big circle and one by one, the awards are read out by the head counselors.

Everyone has won something. Some are serious—Best in Crafts, some are funny—Worst Bed-Maker.

Finally it is Caro's turn.

"And now we have Caro Andrews," the leader of the Wolf Cubs announces. "Caro has been unanimously voted the girl Most Likely to Succeed."

Everyone yells and applauds. It is the award that Caro has been expecting to win. She stands up, walks up to the pine knoll, takes the ribbon, and gives a little curtsy.

PART TWO

RED BALLOON

CAROLINE

Caroline is coming home from another bad day in the sixth grade. Sixth grade is a terrible year, the worst she's ever had. Up until now, she's been mainly ignored at school; suddenly, she seems to be hated—she's not sure why. The girls laugh at everything about her—her handwriting, her hair, the way she talks. Sometimes, riding the bus home, she thinks of Zoë and California. She remembers the palm trees and the beach and she wants to cry.

But at least today is Thursday, and *A Tree Grows in Brooklyn* will be on at eight o'clock.

A Tree Grows in Brooklyn is Caroline's favorite television show. She thinks about it whenever things get bad, during lunch when no one wants to sit with her, in gym when everyone snickers at her cartwheels. It makes up for a lot.

Thursday nights, at seven fifty-five, Caroline leaves her homework, hurries into the den, and turns on the big television set. She always worries that, for some reason or other, the program won't come on that week, but this has never happened. At eight o'clock, the show begins. The theme song starts to play, and Caroline imagines she can never be unhappy again.

The opening credits come on, with photographs of New York as it looked at the turn of the century. There are carriages instead of cars, street vendors instead of stores, cobblestones instead of paved streets. How lovely, Caroline thinks, to have lived in New York back then, back in the days when her school wasn't even a building yet.

Then the episode begins. The show is about a family—the Nolans—and every week they get into a different adventure. Sometimes the adventures are scary, like the time Neely got run over by a horse, and sometimes they are funny, like the time Aunt Sissy pretended she was a doctor, but they always turn out well. By the time the credits come up at the end of the show, everyone in the neighborhood is hugging and everything is happy again.

Caroline's favorite character is Flossie Gaddis. Flossie isn't one of the Nolans—she's a neighbor, the little girl who lives down the hall. Flossie is always thinking up ideas, and getting herself and Francie Nolan into trouble, but she's never sneaky or unkind. She takes care of all the stray animals in the neighborhood, and stands up to Jack when he bullies Annie-Laurie.

Caroline wishes she could be just like Flossie Gaddis. Once, she even wrote a letter to the girl who played Flossie. She told her how wonderful she was, and how she wished they could be friends. But she didn't send it. Caroline knew that Flossie and the girl who played Flossie were not the same thing. The girl would think she was stupid for writing.

"Oh, God, not again," Barton shakes his head every Thursday evening at eight o'clock. "When is this show going to get canceled, so I can have my den back?"

Caroline knows he is kidding, but he will not watch the show. He calls it sentimental tripe.

But Meg and Adam love it. They do not miss a week. Sometimes they come over and watch it with Caroline.

Meg always says she wishes she were more like Katie Nolan, "Mama" on the show. "How does she do it?" she wonders when Mama charms the landlord into forgiving that month's rent, or talks Neely out of quitting school. And Caroline always comforts her by saying, "Oh, Meg, it's just a show."

But of course it is not just a show.

Meg loves to give Caroline *A Tree Grows in Brooklyn* surprises. One day Caroline comes home from school to find an antique patchwork quilt, in a Grandmother's Flower Garden pattern, on her bed.

She bursts into happy tears. "It's just like the one Flossie Gaddis has!"

Another day, there is a novel lying on her pillow, *A Tree Grows in*

Brooklyn by Betty Smith, with a picture of a brownstone house on the cover.

"This is the book the show is based on," Meg tells her.

But the book is nothing like the show. It's very depressing. Mama doesn't charm the landlord, and Papa is a drunk. And Flossie Gaddis is only four years old and she dies.

Caroline is too upset to finish the book, and she hides it at the back of her underwear drawer. But it doesn't take away the joy of the television show, not at all. That's the real *A Tree Grows in Brooklyn.*

It is Halloween. Halloween is a big deal at the Clark School. The girls wear costumes and there is a parade and prizes.

"What do you want to go as?" Meg asks Caroline.

"I'm not going as anything." She does not want to be ridiculous. She does not want the other girls to laugh at her.

Meg says nothing. But the night before Halloween, there is a big package waiting on Caroline's bed.

"What's this?" Caroline asks.

"A little something to wear tomorrow."

Caroline opens the box. She draws back and gasps. Inside is a copy of one of Flossie's dresses—the most beautiful dress of all, the one she wears in the opening credits of the show. There is the scalloped white petticoat, the rosebud-covered pinafore, the lace-trimmed blouse.

She cannot believe it.

"Oh, Meg, how did you do it?"

"Well, I found this incredible dressmaker down on 14th Street. And she and I—"

But Caroline is no longer listening. She is seeing herself at school the next day, a perfect Flossie in this lovely dress. She imagines the faces of the other girls, stunned, seeing a Caroline they had never suspected existed.

She imagines the headmistress beaming at her.

And the winner of the costume contest is—Caroline Andrews!

To huge applause, Caroline goes up on the stage and accepts the blue ribbon.

* * *

Caroline is up early the next morning, and Meg comes over after breakfast to help her get dressed. She braids Caroline's hair in the special way that Flossie wears hers, looped across the back of her head and tied in two big bows.

"I only wish I could have found you some high-button shoes," Meg says.

Caroline hugs her and says her shoes are fine.

"Come home with the blue ribbon!" Meg calls as she puts Caroline on the school bus.

Caroline arrives at school and walks self-consciously toward her classroom. Amanda Waverly, dressed as a princess, eyes her.

"Who are you supposed to be?"

"Flossie Gaddis. From *A Tree Grows in Brooklyn.*"

Amanda chokes.

"You watch *A Tree Grows in Brooklyn?* I didn't know *anyone* watched that show! Hey, guys!" Her voice rises. "Guess who Caroline is—the girl from *A Tree Grows in Brookyn.*"

And the whole hallway is exploding with laughter.

Most of the girls haven't seen the show, but those who have sing the theme song and do mincing little dance steps around Caroline.

She tells herself it does not matter. It does not matter that the girls are laughing. It does not matter that she does not win the prize ribbon. She will always love *A Tree Grows in Brooklyn.* And she will always love her beautiful costume.

Meg is not there when Caroline gets home from school. Caroline is grateful for that. She will tell Meg that everyone admired her dress and the only reason she didn't win the blue ribbon was because they canceled the costume contest.

She goes into her room and quickly pulls off the Flossie dress. As she is putting it away in the closet, she sees that someone has written "Go to Hell" on the hem.

Caroline rushes to the sink and scrubs at the writing, but it has been written in indelible ink and does not come off.

* * *

One cold November afternoon, Caroline comes home after school to find her father, Meg, and Adam all waiting for her in the foyer.

"Caroline, we have a surprise for you," Barton says. He puts an arm around Meg. "Meg and I have decided to get married."

Meg throws out her arms to Caroline. Caroline rushes into them, grabbing Adam on the way. They are in a big octopus hug, all laughing and happy.

"When?" Caroline asks.

"We thought we'd do it in March," Meg tells her. She looks anxious. "And I'm going to need your help. You know how hopeless I am at things like that."

Caroline says that she will be happy to do it all.

She cannot get to sleep that night. She rehearses the new words, "wedding," and "my stepmother," "my brother," "my family." She will be complete now, just "one of a family." It no longer matters that sixth grade is bad. At the end of the day, Meg will pick her up. Adam will rush into her arms. She will not even look back at the other girls. On weekends, it will not matter that she is not invited over anywhere to play. She will have picnics in the park with Meg. She will have games of War with Adam, out on the balcony.

It is a lot of fun, planning the wedding. Almost every afternoon, Caroline and Meg go off to do an errand for the big day. They choose the caterer, audition the musicians, select the china pattern. Meg always gives in to Caroline's choice.

At the pastry shop, there is a little disagreement. The cake is ordered, and they need to find figures to go on the top. Meg is thinking about a traditional bride and groom, but Caroline finds something much more wonderful. It is a pair of tiny porcelain mice, dressed in wedding clothes.

"I don't know what your father would say to these." Meg sounds anxious. But Caroline looks so hurt that she gives in, as Caroline knew she would.

There is only one bad moment, when the guest list is written out.

"And of course we'll invite all the girls in your class," Meg tells Caroline.

"No."

Meg frowns. "But, darling, we have to. It's only polite."

"If they come, I won't."

Meg knows how mean the girls are.

"But, Caroline, don't you see—it'll be such a beautiful wedding, and there you'll be, the junior bridesmaid . . ."

Unexpectedly, Caroline smiles.

"Okay," she says suddenly. "But it's silly to send them all invitations. I'll just take one to school tomorrow, and the teacher can put it up on the bulletin board."

Meg is delighted. "And we'll invite her, too."

"Oh, yes," Caroline agrees.

Meg gives her an invitation, which Caroline carefully puts in her schoolbag. The next morning, when the bus reaches the school, she rips the invitation into tiny pieces, and throws it into the trash can.

"I can't understand it," Meg says, two weeks later. "Twenty-five girls, and not one R.S.V.P. Do you think I should call the parents?"

"Oh, no," Caroline tells her gravely. "I told you—they're just very, very rude."

Zoë has been invited to the wedding. She sends back a note, written with a gold pen on lilac stationery, and thick with perfume.

Dearest Barton and Meg!

I'm afraid that a Busy Network Season will prevent me from attending your Very, Very Exciting Day, but please know that my Best Wishes are with you.

Meg, you are a Courageous Woman—only joking, of course.

Love,
Zoë

Along with the note is an expensive crystal bowl from Tiffany, which Meg immediately places in the spot of honor on the dining room table. Caroline wants to shout with pride in both her mothers, old and new.

Finally, it's time to choose the wedding clothes.

"Saks," Caroline says firmly.

"I can't," Meg tells her. "You know I hate department stores."

Caroline relents, and they scour Lexington Avenue and Third Avenue, hunting in thrift shops.

"What do you think of this?" Meg asks. She holds up a white lawn Edwardian dress.

Caroline looks at it critically. "It doesn't look very much like a wedding gown."

"Yes." Meg sighs. "That's why I like it. All that veil and train stuff scares me to death. This way, I can pretend I'm going down the aisle to a tea party."

Caroline laughs, and Meg buys the dress.

Her own outfit is easier to find. Caroline, who has no problem with department stores, heads directly to Saks. She finds almost immediately the perfect junior bridesmaid dress—pink, with a full skirt and a petticoat. For a moment she is almost sorry that the other girls at school won't be there to see how beautiful she looks in it.

There is some talk about whether, after the wedding, they should all move to a new apartment. This is Barton's idea.

"No," Meg is definite. "I think we should stay here. This is where I got to know you, this is where I met Caroline. And it's her home."

Caroline is very pleased with that.

The lease on Meg and Adam's apartment isn't up until April, but in early March, they start moving in some of their things. Caroline helps them unpack. With every outfit of Meg's that is put into the closet, with every toy of Adam's that is placed on the shelf, she feels happier and happier. Meg and Adam are safe now, wedged in behind all these possessions. They are not going anywhere. She will have them forever.

Things get busier and busier. Wedding presents start arriving. Meg waits to open them until Caroline gets home from school.

"This is a nice one," Caroline will say. "We'll put it on the hall table." Or, "This one's awful. It'll have to be exchanged."

Occasionally, Meg sticks up for the awful present.

"Let's ask Daddy," Caroline tells her, and Barton always agrees that the gift is awful and needs to be exchanged.

A week before the wedding, Caroline goes out to buy her own gift for the couple. While Meg is away getting her hair cut, she sneaks off and rushes to the shop on Lexington where Meg found her wedding dress. She looks in the window for the small antique petit point purse that Meg had loved—yes, it's still there.

"How much is this?" she asks the salesman.

"Seventy-five dollars."

Caroline has saved up all her birthday and Christmas money since she was born. She has a hundred fifty-eight dollars. She gives the man the seventy-five.

To Daddy and Meg. Best Wishes on your Wedding Day, she writes on the card. It occurs to her that the gift is really all for Meg, but she's sure her father won't mind.

It's the day before the wedding. Everyone is very excited, and making silly jokes. Only Laura seems sad.

That afternoon, she comes into the den, carrying a package.

"Here's a present for the bride and groom," she says. Inside the box is a new coffeepot. Meg hugs her.

"Well, I guess I'll be saying good-bye," Laura tells them.

"Good-bye?" Meg echoes blankly.

"I know married couples want a fresh start," Laura says proudly. "You'll have your own ideas about running the house, and you know what they say about new brooms."

Meg bursts into tears.

"I'm not a new broom!" she cries. "If you think I could run this place without you, you're crazy—Barton and the kids would be dead in a week."

Caroline and Adam clamor around Laura, screaming that they need her, they need her.

So of course Laura promises to stay forever, and beams and beams and Adam puts the new coffeepot on his head, and the jokes get sillier and sillier.

* * *

On the wedding day, the weather is clear and tingling. Caroline takes a slow, sweet-smelling bubble bath, then she puts on her pink dress and stares at herself in the mirror.

She is awed by how grown up she looks.

She and her father take a limousine to St. Bartholomew's Church. People try to peer into the car; their faces look friendly, satisfied.

The church is already starting to fill up. Caroline's father kisses her and goes to the altar where he will wait for his bride. Caroline goes back to the changing room to be with Meg and Adam.

Meg is nervous and pale. She looks beautiful, but she keeps pulling at her dress and biting her nails.

"Caroline," she says.

Caroline knows that Meg is going to make some sort of speech. Some embarrassing speech that she probably spent all night composing.

"I know," Caroline says quickly, "you love me and you'll try to be a great mother."

She gives Meg a shut-up hug. Meg hugs her back, hard.

"When this damn thing is over," she whispers in Caroline's ear, "you can have the mice from the top of the wedding cake."

It is the final drop of happiness. The organist puts his hands on the keyboard. The wedding march has started.

CARO

It seems as if every week there's another audition, and Caro gets them all. She's constantly seeing herself on television, on the commercial for speak-and-wet dolls, life insurance, the J.C. Penney Memorial Day Sale, canned fruit. She is no longer surprised when the calls come, telling her she has gotten the job.

One night, Zoë overhears her talking to a friend from school.

"I'll stop by on Friday if I can, but Mars bars wants me, and I think they're shooting that day." Caro gives a sigh. "God, what a drag. I don't even like Mars bars."

Zoë is suddenly in the room. Caro straightens up at the look on her mother's face, and hastily hangs up the phone.

"You arrogant little brat!" Zoë sputters. "How dare you speak like that? Do you have any idea how lucky you are to get these commercials? Or how soon it could all be over? You're ten now; all it takes is one growth spurt, one pimple, and nobody will ever want you again."

Caro apologizes meekly. She tells her mother that she knows how lucky she is, that she knows it could all be over tomorrow.

But she is sure that isn't going to happen.

Caro learns quickly. She soon picks up all the right moves. She learns how to shake hands with just the right pressure. She learns how to say "Sir" without it sounding phony-baloney. She learns how to smile shyly at the directors.

Zoë is told repeatedly what a pleasure Caro is to have on a set.

"Well, I've obviously taught you something," Zoë snorts, but she is delighted.

* * *

One day, she comes home, her eyes blinking with excitement.

"Red alert," she tells Caro. "A new show. Hour-long. CBS. Could be a part for you."

"What is it?"

"It's called *A Tree Grows in Brooklyn.* Terribly old-fashioned, but who knows? It might be a hit. It's about an Irish-German family, living in New York at the turn of the century." She inspects Caro's profile. "You could pass. I think your father had some cousins from Munich or Stockholm or something."

"Is there an audition?"

"I'm working on it. Of course every kid in town is after this one. But my friend Rick is the A.D., so that's a help."

Zoë goes into immediate action. She visits Hunter's Bookstore and buys everything she can find about immigrants, as well as a copy of Betty Smith's novel *A Tree Grows in Brooklyn.*

Caro does no homework that evening. She sits on the couch while Zoë reads portions of the book aloud to her. It's tender and bitter and very sad. They both like it. And whenever Zoë reads about the little girl Francie, it is Caro's face they both are seeing.

The following day, Zoë calls her friend Jasper at MGM.

"I wonder," she says, "if you could dig up an old film for me. An old Dorothy McGuire movie. It was a favorite of mine, and I was telling my little girl about it. I can't remember the title, though—something about a tree in Brooklyn."

Jasper laughs. He knows Zoë. He also knows about the new television show that is being cast. But he is amused by her tactics, and he agrees to find the film.

The following afternoon, Zoë and Caro settle down in an MGM screening room to watch the movie.

"Peggy Ann Garner," Zoë reads the name off the credits. "She's the one with your part."

Twenty minutes into the movie, Caro shakes her head. Peggy Ann Garner is the best child actor she's ever seen. No one could be Francie after her. Caro doesn't even want to try.

The movie ends; both Caro and Zoë are crying. The lights come up, and briskly Zoë wipes away a final tear.

"Well, you're not going for Francie," she tells Caro. "That's for sure. But maybe there's something else I can find."

Zoë asks her friend Rick at CBS if she could possibly take an advance peek at the television script. Rick says he'd get into terrible trouble. Zoë asks him out to dinner. She gets the script. She is up half the night reading it, and in the morning, she wakes Caro.

"They've killed the story," she tells her. "Taken out the edge, made it sentimental mush. And Francie's a horror—such a little goody-goody. Completely wrong for you—a real career killer. However"—she smiles—"I think there's another part for you."

"Who?"

"The little neighbor girl—Flossie Gaddis."

"Flossie Gaddis? But she's four years old and she dies!"

"Well, she doesn't die in this script. She's eleven and she's Francie's best friend. I'll see if I can arrange an audition."

Once more, she goes to see her friend Rick. An audition is set up for the following Wednesday.

Zoë is not normally inclined to overkill, but she makes an exception in this case. She goes to Western Costume and rents an old-fashioned dress, pinafore, and high-button boots. Then, the morning of the audition, she keeps Caro home from school. She takes her instead to Elizabeth Arden in Beverly Hills, and shows Roberto the hair stylist a photograph from the book on immigrants.

"Make her look like this."

The show's producer and casting director are having coffee on the soundstage when Caro arrives. When they see her standing in the doorway in her old-fashioned dress and hairstyle, they put down their coffee cups. Caro gives a little curtsy.

She has gotten the part before she even opens her mouth.

"We'll have to call your father," Zoë says, a week before shooting is about to begin.

She and Caro look at each other.

"You call," Zoë tells Caro.

"No," Caro says. "You call."

They both call. Barton is not happy with the news.

"Why didn't you tell me earlier?" he demands.

"I honestly never thought she'd get a part," Zoë says meekly, winking at Caro. "It was such a long shot—it didn't seem worth bothering you for. And then afterward, well, things have been so crazy here . . ."

"And I notice you've left it too late for me to do anything now."

Barton goes on to ask a lot of questions: where would Caro go to school? Who would look after her on the set? Was her salary being properly invested?

Zoë answers everything, and finally she puts Caro on the phone.

"Do you really want to do this show?" Barton asks her.

"Oh, yes, Daddy."

"Won't it bother you not being at school with the other kids?"

"No."

"It'll be a lot of hard work, learning those lines."

"I know."

"Well," he says doubtfully at last, "I suppose you and your mother know what you're doing." He sighs. "I really should be proud, I guess, having a daughter who's on television."

Caro smiles. "Thank you, Daddy. I love you."

She hangs up the phone. She looks at her mother.

"There's an old proverb, my darling," Zoë tells her. " 'It is better to apologize later than to ask permission before.' Never forget that."

She grins at Caro.

A Tree Grows in Brooklyn is due to air at the beginning of September.

"It's a tricky season," Zoë admits, scanning the trades, her reading glasses atilt on her nose. "*Flipper, Pistols and Petticoats, The Beverly Hillbillies,* and those damned *U.N.C.L.E.* shows. What we're betting on is the women. That they're getting sick and tired of all that stuff, and that they'd love nothing better than a nice, sentimental family drama."

The women are, and they would. And not only the women.

The show starts off slowly, but word of mouth is good. By the third week, it is starting to build an audience, and by the sixth week, it has won its time slot. Its popularity spreads in a soft, friendly fog. People like it. They laugh about it, but they watch it. There is a story in *TV Guide* saying that *A Tree Grows in Brooklyn* may usher in a whole new era of television.

Flossie Gaddis is one of the most popular characters in the show. Soon, Caro's picture is on the cover of *Good Housekeeping* and *Family Circle.* Fans wait with open autograph books every morning as she enters the studio, and every evening as she comes out. And she starts getting letters from girls all over the country.

"Listen to this one," Zoë says. "Dear Flossie, I wish I lived like you do. I wish my mother was like yours. We just learned that my older brother is missing in Vietnam, and I don't know what to do."

"Well, neither do I." Zoë tosses the letter down, and then adds, "Poor kid."

She picks up another. "Dear Flossie, I love to watch your show, and how wonderful everything is with you. My name is Ellen. I am ten years old, and I have leukemia—"

"Oh, God," Zoë says. She tosses this one away also, and stares at the pile.

"No more fan mail," she announces. "We're having everything sent to the studio publicist. They'll hire someone to take care of it."

Caro is relieved, but at the same time she feels as if she is letting these girls down.

She wishes she could write a letter to them. You don't understand—it's all pretend, she would say. My life isn't like Flossie's, and, believe me, you don't wish you had my mother. I don't really wear those dresses; I wear blue jeans like you do. I like Herman's Hermits and James Bond movies, and pepperoni pizza. And I can't help it that your brother's missing, or that you have leukemia. I'm just a kid, I'm just like you.

But sometimes Caro doesn't think that. Sometimes she lies in bed and thinks, *I'm a star.* She is a star like Shirley Temple, a star like Jerry Mathers in *Leave It to Beaver* or Margaret O'Brien in *The Secret Garden.* She is special, she is famous all over the country.

It's fun being a star. It's fun being on the show. Everyone is friendly to her, everyone does what she asks. It's like being on

Pleasure Island in *Pinocchio,* except that since she still goes to school, she won't turn into a donkey. But this school is wonderful. There's a tutor, and he teaches in the dressing room between takes. Half the time, though, just as they're starting to study, an A.D. or makeup person will tap on the door and say, "Sorry to interrupt, but Miss Andrews is needed on the set."

Caro also enjoys being with the other kids on the show. They don't get as many fan letters as she does, but they're still friendly to her. Diana, the girl who plays Francie, teaches her how to make Troll doll clothes out of felt. And Robert, the boy who plays Neely, does great magic tricks. Only Pam, the girl who plays Aunt Sissy's daughter, Christina, is a pain. She's always forgetting her lines in Caro's scenes—when it's her own scene, she can remember them perfectly—and she's constantly fussing for more close-ups. Caro, Robert, and Diana can't stand her. They start an "I Hate Pam Club," and play tricks on her. They put pepper in her food and spiders on her shoulder. They hide her makeup and cut chunks out of her script.

This is a lot of fun until the director finds out what they are up to and threatens to tell their various fan clubs.

Caro also likes hanging around the soundstage between takes. The other kids go into their dressing rooms and watch television or read comic books, but Caro stays on the set. She listens to what the soundman and the grip have to say. She watches the camera shots being prepared. She decides she would like to be a director someday. It would be wonderful never to have to leave the studio, never to have to go back in the real world.

The moments on the set Caro likes the least are those in which she is actually acting. When she is being dressed by wardrobe, or having her hair done, or being made-up, she is still Caro. When she is filming, she is Flossie. It is a little scary to put her real self away, even for the few minutes it takes to film a scene. She does not like losing herself in that way, blending into someone else. It is a little like dying.

And Caro is not sure she likes being Flossie Gaddis. In a lot of ways, Flossie is a nicer person than Caro Andrews. Flossie always stands up for the underdog, Flossie always tells the truth, Flossie is never jealous or mean. It makes Caro feel phony, putting on her brave, kind, Flossie smile, saying those wise, lovable Flossie words. It is like looking in a mirror, and seeing a reflection that is a lot prettier than your own.

One morning in December, Zoë seems unnaturally cheerful as she drives Caro to the studio.

"No overacting today," she says. "I'm coming to the set."

"Really?" Caro is surprised. Her mother hasn't been to the set since the first few weeks of shooting. "Why?"

Zoë smiles over at her. "Have I ever mentioned Hans Lasky to you?" she asks softly.

Caro gasps.

She has heard about Hans Lasky all her life. He was a fairy-tale prince in her mind, except, she always had to remind herself, he wasn't young and handsome, he was really an old man.

Hans Lasky was a photographer; his work was in museums; he had photographed all the great beautiful stars in the great beautiful days of movies. Years ago, when Zoë had just come out to Hollywood, she had met him. He had admired her courage, this young woman who wanted to be a children's agent, and later, when she started Zoë's Babies, he did her a great favor—he photographed all her child actors, photographed them as seriously as if they had been great beautiful stars. And what did he charge Zoë for the sessions? "Nothing! Not a penny," Zoë would always say triumphantly, making a "zero" with her fingers. "Hans Lasky got me started. My whole career. If it hadn't been for Hans Lasky . . ." and she would shake her head and sigh.

"Well, he called last night," she tells Caro. "He's in town for a day or two, and I'm taking him to your set."

It is hard for Caro to be Flossie that morning; all she can think about is meeting Hans Lasky. At noon, they break for lunch. Caro is starting toward her trailer to take off her costume when she hears her name being called. It is her mother's voice, but she sounds very young and excited and happy.

With her is Hans Lasky. Caro is introduced, shakes his hand.

"I've always wanted to meet you," she tells him. But the truth is, Hans Lasky no longer matters in the least. The one who matters is the young boy standing beside him.

"This is my grandson, Steven," Hans Lasky says.

Steven is about twelve. He has the most wonderful hair, thick and curly as a doll's. He has white skin with cheeks as red as strawberry Kool-Aid. His eyes are slanted, teasing, heavy with dripping lashes. This is the prince. There is no doubt about that.

Caro stares at him. She can always think of something clever and funny to say to casting directors or producers, but she can't think of anything to say to Steven Lasky.

They all have lunch together in the commissary. Caro sits next to Steven.

"Do you live in Los Angeles?" she finally manages to ask.

"No," he tells her. "In Boston. I'm just visiting."

"Oh," is all she can think of to answer.

They are joined by other people. Horrible Pam is there, and her four-year-old brother Jackie, who visits the set often. Caro can tell that Pam likes Steven. She sits on his other side, and asks him all kinds of questions. Caro is afraid that Steven will like her back, but he doesn't seem to. He seems more at ease with her little brother.

"Who's that on your T-shirt?" he asks.

"Frankenstein."

"I just read a book about Frankenstein," Steven tells him. "Would you like to hear the story?"

"Sure!"

Caro gets great pleasure hearing Steven tell *Frankenstein.* He tells it beautifully, using his hands with a lot of enthusiasm.

Jackie is enjoying the story until it starts to get scary. When Steven describes the townspeople going around with torches, wanting to kill the monster, the little boy starts to cry.

Steven breaks off. He looks bewildered for a moment. Then he holds up his hand.

"But just at that moment," he goes on brightly, "just as they're about to kill him, another monster, a beautiful girl monster with golden hair, comes out of a cave and rescues him."

He goes on to tell how the monster is saved and given chocolate cake to eat. How the monster finds friends and happiness. And how, at the end, he is made king of the whole country.

Jackie is happy. Caro is awed. She thinks Steven Lasky is the kindest, most grown-up boy she has ever met.

And then Steven turns to her and smiles and winks. Caro feels the wink in the pit of her stomach.

After lunch, they go back to the set. Caro walks beside Steven Lasky. She is braver now.

"Do you like Los Angeles?" she asks him.

"Sure," he tells her. "I'll probably move here someday. I want to be a photographer like my grandfather. I love to take pictures." Then he coughs, and his voice suddenly sounds strangled. "I even brought my camera today." He does not look at Caro. "Would it be all right if I took your picture?"

"Sure," Caro says in a high, unnatural voice.

She poses for him by a tub of artificial flowers. She hopes he does not want her to look perky, like Flossie, for she feels very serious inside.

Steven takes the picture. His grandfather and Zoë come up behind him.

"Did you get your photo?" Hans Lasky asks. And then he says to Caro, "I think that's the real reason he wanted to come out to California."

Steven's cheeks turn ever redder.

"If you like, I could send you a copy," he tells Caro.

"Will you sign it?" she asks.

The grown-ups laugh.

"You've got it wrong, sweetheart," Zoë jokes, as if Caro doesn't know better, "it's the actress who's supposed to sign the picture!"

"But he took it," Caro says doggedly, "and he should sign it."

"I'll sign it," Steven promises.

Soon it is time to film. Caro plays her scene, aware that Steven is behind the director, watching her. She wonders if anyone realizes that Flossie is not herself today. Today she is a grown-up woman, only pretending to be a little girl. And the prince is watching her.

A few weeks later, a manila envelope arrives from Boston. Inside is an eight by ten photo of Caro, standing seriously beside a tub of artificial flowers. At the bottom, it has been signed with black ink. *To Caro, with love from Steven Lasky.*

CAROLINE

When Caroline wakes, her first thought is *school.* And then she relaxes. It is Saturday morning.

She sits up in bed, smiling. There is blue spring sky to be seen from her window. There is Adam, sleeping in the next room. And there is no school for forty-eight hours.

The door opens. Meg, her hair tousled, comes in and hops on her bed.

"Guess what!" she says. "We're all going on an adventure today!"

"Daddy, too?"

"Absolutely. I told Barton he hasn't paid us any attention in weeks, and he's coming along whether he likes it or not."

"Where are we going?"

"I'll tell you at breakfast."

She kisses Caroline, and leaves to wake up Adam.

Caroline stays behind in bed a moment longer. She sighs with happiness, then races to get dressed.

As she is putting on her shoes, she can hear Adam's sleepy voice in the next room, and once again, Meg saying the word "adventure."

"So where are we going?" Caroline demands at breakfast.

Meg smiles at her. "A place called Playland."

For a moment, Caroline is disappointed. The name Playland sounds like something for Adam, not something for her.

But then she remembers. Playland. Playland! Of course. *Playland.* Suddenly she is four years old again, back in Laura's house, visiting her granddaughter, Yvette. They are throwing cardboard rings around milk bottles, practicing to win a huge pink teddy bear, like the one Yvette won at Playland.

Caroline has a little twist of guilt. She hasn't been to Yvette's house since she stole the television set from her dollhouse. Laura could never understand why she never wanted to go back, and Caroline could never explain. But that was years and years ago—she really ought to ask Laura about Yvette now, find out how she is doing. Maybe even go for a visit again.

"Playland's great," she tells Adam quickly. "I've never been there, but I knew someone who just loved it. She always played this special game. You throw rings around the tops of milk bottles, and if you get three in a row, you can win a big teddy bear."

Adam is grinning with excitement, and Caroline finds herself getting excited, too. After all this time, she is finally going to Playland.

It's a long drive and Barton is not in the best of moods. When they finally pull into the parking lot, he stares around the crowded, raucous park, then turns and looks ironically at Meg.

"This is what we've come for?"

Meg flushes. "I think it will be fun."

Caroline rallies instantly to Meg. "I like it. And look, Adam—there's a roller coaster, and a Ferris wheel."

"Wow!" Adam cries happily.

Barton laughs. "I guess I'm outnumbered."

He buys them all tickets, and they go inside Playland. They ride through the Tunnel of Love and the Haunted House, and try to knock down bandits at the shooting gallery.

Caroline keeps laughing and saying what a great time she is having. She sneaks little glances at Meg. Meg looks flushed and happy. Her adventure is going well.

"I'm hungry," Adam says after half an hour.

He and Caroline and Meg buy corn dogs and French fries. Barton says he will pass.

They sit down at a sticky table to eat. The day has become very warm, and Caroline notices that Meg is looking pale.

"Are you okay?" she asks.

"I'm fine," Meg says quickly. "It's just the heat. It's making me a little dizzy."

Adam has finished his lunch.

"More rides," he announces.

Meg sighs.

"Don't worry," Caroline tells her grandly. "Why don't you and Daddy rest here, and I'll take Adam on some more rides."

"Are you sure?" Meg asks gratefully.

"Yes, yes!" Adam clutches Caroline's hand.

"Well, be back in half an hour," her father says. "I don't want to spend the rest of my life in Playland."

Caroline leads Adam away.

"What do you want to go on first?"

But Adam doesn't answer. He is hopping up and down and pointing to the balloon vendor by the Tilt-A-Whirl.

"Oh, please, please, can I have a balloon?"

He spends a long time choosing, and finally decides on a big red one.

Caroline brings out a dollar from her purse. It gives her satisfaction that she is buying Adam a balloon with her own money. That is the sort of thing big sisters do, and she is a good big sister.

They head toward the Ferris wheel. On the way, they pass a row of arcade games, bright and colorful.

Caroline stops suddenly, and points.

"Oh, look, Adam—there it is. The game I was telling you about."

It is the throwing game, just as Yvette had described it. And yes, hanging from the net ceiling and along the sides, are the big teddy bears.

"Do you want to try winning a bear?"

Adam shakes his head. "No. Let's go on the Ferris wheel."

But Caroline can't go just yet. The bears may not look as good as they used to—well, to be honest, they don't look good at all—but it's a thrill to see the throwing game at last. She can't go away without playing it just once.

She squeezes Adam's hand.

"Well, I'd like to try this," she says. "Just one turn."

She gives the man behind the booth a dollar, and he hands over a set of rings.

As she takes them, Caroline has an idea—she decides that if she wins a bear, she will give it to Yvette. That will make up for stealing the little television set, all those years ago.

Adam is scowling.

"Now I need you to stand by me and watch," she tells him. "Don't move—okay?"

Adam says okay.

It feels so familiar, holding the rings in her hands. Caroline throws them carefully, but misses all three. They are heavier than the cardboard ones she and Yvette played with, and the milk bottles are much farther away.

She'll try again. She hands over another dollar, and is given more rings. The first one misses, the second one glances off a bottle, and the third one—yes!—rings it!

One more time should do it. Caroline digs into her purse and hands over another dollar.

The first ring settles easily over a milk bottle. Cautiously, Caroline holds the second ring and throws. It goes right over another bottle. She's almost there. A few people in the crowd around her are watching. She leans forward, and tosses the final ring. It nears the milk bottle, then bounces off at the last second.

The watchers groan sympathetically.

"One more time?" the vendor asks.

Caroline has two more tries, then she gives up. She shrugs her shoulders—Yvette had probably outgrown teddy bears, anyway.

The vendor gives her a little plastic yo-yo as a compensation prize.

Caroline is pleased; Adam will like that.

At that moment, she hears someone scream. It is a woman's voice, not a little boy's, but she looks down anyway. Adam is not beside her. Caroline keeps looking down, stupidly, because Adam must be there. But he isn't. She runs up and down the row of arcade games. She does not see him anywhere.

"Adam!" she calls. He does not answer.

She pushes her way through the crowd. He can't have gone far. Probably he went back to Meg. Yes, of course that's where he was. He got tired of waiting for her to throw the rings, and he went back to his mother.

Caroline is pushing her way to Meg. She hears the scream again. She wishes that woman would stop screaming. It's making her nervous. It is a light and sharp scream, like a steel thread. It is coming from the direction of the Ferris wheel.

People are rushing over. Caroline looks over to see why they are running. She sees, caught halfway up the scaffolding, a red balloon.

It all happens very slowly. Caroline does not actually see Adam fall. She only sees the faces of the people. She does not hear any thud, only voices.

". . . balloon got caught . . ."

". . . trying to get his balloon . . ."

She wants to explain that it was a gift, something a good big sister would give, that she never, never meant to hurt him.

She pushes her way to the front of the crowd. Adam is lying facedown, twisted and still. He looks very small. No one is moving forward to touch him. Caroline is told to get away.

She says, "I'm his sister."

The voices stop instantly. There is no sound. She kneels beside Adam. It is the thing a sister would do.

A man is now standing beside her. Helplessly, he holds out to Caroline the rescued red balloon.

The first thing Caroline does when she gets home is go into Adam's room. He is not there. She had somehow thought he might be. The room is dark, and she turns on the light. On the floor are his pajamas, tossed in a heap, shed quickly for his day at Playland. On the floor is his dinosaur collection, one pterodactyl on its side, interrupted in mid-flight.

She opens Adam's drawers. She sees his ironed shirts, his folded shorts. In the corner of one drawer she discovers a Moon Unit doll crammed under some underwear. It was hers, and Adam had always wanted it. He must have taken it from her room.

"You can have it," she whispers. "It's all right. I'm not mad."

Under the bed, she finds a little dusty sock. It is heaped at an odd, broken angle. Caroline tries to remember where she has seen something else that looked like that. Oh, yes; it was Adam.

Caroline picks up the little sock and holds it crushed in her palm. Its little soft lump feels like a hand being held in hers. Caroline sits on the bed. She strokes the little sock.

It is a Saturday morning in late July.

"Well," said Barton. "Ten o'clock. Time we got started."

He and Caroline ride the elevator down in silence. They go into the parking garage and find the car.

"A father–daughter outing?" the attendant asks.

"Something like that," Barton tells him with a pained smile.

They are going to visit Meg in the special hospital. That is the only name they call it.

"Are you sure I should go?" Caroline asks as her father pulls onto the street.

"Yes, honey. It's important that she sees you."

The last time they went, Meg was sitting in her room, staring out a window. At first, when she saw Caroline, she smiled; but then a slow pucker came over her face. Finally, she began to point to Caroline and scream. The nurses came running. They took Meg into another room. Caroline could still hear her screaming.

Caroline's father had hugged her. "I'm sorry about that," he said. "It's still hard for her. But there's progress—big progress," he added. "She knows it wasn't your fault, honey. We all know that. It was an accident, just an accident."

But Caroline remembers Meg's face, as she was taken away by the nurses. There was terror on it, as if Caroline were bound to kill everything she looked upon.

She gazes at her hands. Her killer hands.

"Today should be fine," her father is saying. "Dr. Reynolds said she's doing better and better. We should have her home in a few months."

The road up to Westchester is very twisty, and Caroline makes a deal with herself. If she gets to the special hospital without throwing up, the visit will be a success.

The nausea shakes in her throat, but she does not throw up.

They reach the hospital, park the car, and go into the front lounge.

"We're here to see Mrs. Andrews," Barton tells the receptionist.

"They're just tidying her room," she says. "I'll send you back in a minute." She smiles confidently at Caroline as if Caroline isn't a killer at all.

"Why don't you go into the garden?" her father asks. "I'll call you when they're ready."

Caroline steps out into the garden. There is an old man in a wheelchair sitting by the flower beds. She tells herself that if she is nice to him, makes him happy, then the visit with Meg will go well.

"Would you like me to pick you a flower?" she asks loudly.

The man stares at her and starts to mutter. Caroline backs away.

"Here they are!" the nurse says gaily. They go into Meg's room. It is small and bright, with a sunflower quilt on the bed, and framed Impressionist posters on the wall. Caroline imagines that this was like Meg's room when she was a girl, in the days when she went to college, in the days before there was an Adam.

Meg looks well. Her hair has been freshly washed and she has gained a little weight. She wears a soft-looking pink dress, and she has even put on earrings.

"Barton!" she says. He goes to her, wraps protecting arms around her shoulders.

"How are you?"

She pulls back and smiles at him. "Fine," she says, very brightly. "Just fine."

Then she looks past him.

"Caroline!" she says. She smiles. Then, deliberately, she lifts up her arms and holds them out for a hug.

Caroline rushes across the room for the hug. She is almost there, almost in Meg's arms. But as she draws near, Meg's face crumples.

Her arms drop and her hands cover her eyes. They are knotted in fists.

She is bent over, retching.

"Get her away," she moans. "Oh, get her away."

On the drive home, Barton has to pull over to the side of the road so that Caroline can be sick.

"You know she doesn't mean it," he says when Caroline gets back in the car. "It's just that, seeing you . . ." The sentence dies away. "Not that she blames you," he adds hastily. "She knows it was an accident."

Caroline needs to be sick again.

"But I think maybe it would be a good idea if we gave her a little more time," Barton goes on. "The doctor said she could come home for a long visit next month. I was thinking maybe that would be a good time for you to go visit Zoë. You'd like that, wouldn't you? You always like going out to California."

Caroline opens the window and puts her head outside. The air is damp and warm, like breath. Caroline catches a glimpse of herself in the side-view mirror. Her face looks white, silly, weak. *Get her away,* she thinks. *Oh, get her away.*

CARO

One Tuesday night in November, Caro is sitting on the rug, learning her lines for the next day's scenes. Zoë comes into the room.

"What is it?" Caro asks, seeing her face.

"It's your father," Zoë says. "He's getting married." She shoots a look at Caro. "What do you know about this?"

"Nothing," Caro says. "The last time I saw him, he didn't even have a girlfriend. Who's he marrying?"

Zoë snorts. "A fast worker, evidently. I think her name is Meg. And," she goes on irritably, "he wants you to be a junior bridesmaid."

"Oh," says Caro. She is charmed by the idea. "When's the wedding?"

"In March. It's completely ridiculous, asking you to fly out for it," Zoë adds coldly. "*Brooklyn*'s not on hiatus then. I'll call Barton and tell him it's impossible."

"Please don't," Caro tells her. "Just leave it to me."

She goes to the producer the next day. With a few tears, she asks him if something could possibly be done—if she could work extra hard, finish her scenes early—she would be willing to do anything so that she could be in her father's wedding.

The producer confers with the show's writers, and two scripts are rewritten. Flossie Gaddis goes to visit her grandmother in Philadelphia, and Caro is free to go to New York for two weeks.

Zoë tries not to show how interested she is in Barton's bride-to-be, but Caro knows better. She suspects that her mother has made secret calls to friends back in New York, to find out everything she can about Meg.

"I hear that your new stepmother's very young," she says, and adds with a delicate little smile, "I'm sure Barton will enjoy molding her."

A young stepmother. Caro imagines running down Fifth Avenue with her, hand in hand, and the two of them doing something daring and foolish, like jumping in a fountain.

"And apparently, she's got a little boy. That'll be quite a change for Barton, having a child to think of."

This isn't such welcome news. The little boy will surely be the favorite. Still, Caro likes the idea of being a big sister; she will take the little boy for walks, buy him toys. It could work out just fine.

Zoë goes to Tiffany, and sends an elaborate, expensive, cut-glass bowl for a wedding present.

"Never let it be said that I do things by halves," she says to Caro, delighted by her own generosity.

She is even more delighted with the thank-you note that Barton's bride-to-be sends—she calls up all her friends and tells them about it.

"It's written on stationery that must have come from Woolworth's," Zoë cackles, "and her handwriting looks like she's in the fifth grade. Anyway"—she scans the note—"Listen to this. 'Dear Zoë, thank you for the generous gift. The bowl is just beautiful, blah, blah, blah . . . ' But here's the part that just kills me. She ends it with, 'I hope you're as happy as I am.' Can you believe it? It was all I could do to keep from writing back, Dear Meg, or whatever your name is, I have had the experience of being married to Barton Andrews and I have also had the experience of not being married to Barton Andrews, and take it from me, darling, I am a lot happier than you are, or ever will be."

Caro stops listening. She is eager to meet Meg, or whatever her name is, and she thinks it is very sweet of her to have written to Zoë like that.

A week before the wedding, Zoë puts Caro on a plane to New York.

"Well, have a good time," Zoë says grudgingly.

Caro takes pity on her.

"Are you sure you don't want to come? I know they'd love to have you."

"No, thank you," Zoë says loftily. "I'm not really very interested."

Caro gives her a look, and Zoë laughs. "But make sure you call and tell me absolutely everything that's going on."

As Caro walks into the terminal in New York, she sees a knot of strangers waiting by her exit gate. When they catch sight of her, they rush over.

"There she is!"

"Flossie, you're my absolute favorite character on the show—"

"You're even prettier in real life—"

They thrust autograph books and fan magazines and scraps of paper toward her.

Caro smiles, as she has been taught, and begins to sign her name. The crowd grows larger.

She keeps looking up. Where is her father? Isn't anyone going to come for her? What is she supposed to do now?

She smiles and signs and signs and smiles.

Suddenly, she sees two figures flying toward her, a tiny blond woman and a little boy.

"Caro! Oh, Caro!" The woman throws sweet-smelling arms around Caro's neck. "The traffic—you've no idea—and the parking—I've just been dying—your father will kill me when he hears I was late. I'm Meg . . . this is Adam."

They move through the crowd of fans.

Adam is tugging solemnly at Caro's hand.

"They said that once you got here we could go to the zoo in Central Park," he says. "But only if you want to. Do you think you'll want to?"

Caro smiles down at him.

"I know I'll want to," she says.

Preparations for the wedding are quite scrappy. Meg is not very good with details, and she has left a great deal to the last minute. Caro is afraid that Barton, always so orderly, will be annoyed by the chaos, but, surprisingly, he isn't. He doesn't seem to mind anything, only smiles indulgently at all the dramas and the mixed-up plans. Caro guesses he must be very much in love.

It is Caro who helps with everything. She goes the rounds with Meg, helping her make final decisions about music, flowers, and where to put the wedding presents.

Three days before the wedding, Meg still doesn't have a gown.

"Let's go to Saks," Caro tells her.

"Oh, no," Meg says. "Department stores scare me to death."

They visit a secondhand shop on Lexington Avenue, and there Meg finds an Edwardian tea dress.

"I love this," she says, "but I'm not sure your father would approve."

"Who cares?" Caro says. "If you like it, buy it. You can tell him it was my idea."

Meg buys the dress.

"And what about me?" Caro asks patiently. "I can't be your junior bridesmaid in jeans."

Fortunately, Caro has no problem with Saks. A pink extravaganza is bought, which costs three times as much as Meg's wedding dress. Caro is very pleased with it.

When she is not helping Meg with the wedding plans, Caro spends time with Adam. She teaches him to play Tarzan, and tells him scary stories and takes him to the park. She thinks she will soon get tired of his company, but she doesn't. On the one afternoon when he has a play date and is gone for two hours, she finds she misses him.

"It's so wonderful to have you here," Barton tells Caro the night before the wedding. "Being a family again. Meg loves you so much—and Adam's just crazy about you. I'd like you to give some thought—when your series is over, maybe—to coming to live with us. On a permanent basis."

Caro is pleased by the offer. She thinks maybe she'll even take her father up on it. Someday.

The morning of the wedding, Meg is in a state of shock.

"Don't worry about anything," Caro tells her soothingly. "Just go back to bed and rest for a while. I'll get Adam ready."

She gives Adam a bath, brushes his blond hair straight back, and dresses him in his little blue suit.

"You look like a movie star," she tells him.

He squeezes her hand. "I wish you and I could get married."

Caro smiles down at him. "Oh, we're something much better than married," she says.

Barton has already left for St. Bartholomew's. Caro gets herself dressed, and helps Meg on with her gown. Then at last it is time for Meg, Caro, and Adam to get into the waiting limo.

"What I really wanted," Meg gasps, "What I really wanted was just a little ceremony in Central Park, and a picnic afterward."

"Well, you've got this instead," Caro says, and they both laugh. She hopes that Meg will be happy with her father.

The limo pulls up to the church.

"Oh, no," Meg whimpers.

The sidewalk is alive with people. Photographers are circling, waiting for the car to stop.

"Don't worry." Caro sighs. "They're here for me, not for you."

She steps from the car. Flashbulbs go off; she is shot from every angle. Caro knows she looks lovely. She has, of course, chosen her dress with this moment in mind.

For a second she feels sorry for Meg; this is her wedding day, and none of the photographers are interested in her. But she knows that Meg prefers it that way. Really, things are exactly as they should be.

It is Saturday morning, the day before Caro is to fly back to Los Angeles.

Meg comes into her room, and sits on her bed.

"Wake up, sweetheart. We're going on an adventure today."

Caro stretches. "What is it?"

"A place called Playland."

Caro is suddenly very silent.

Meg goes on quickly, "It's for Adam, mostly. He's so upset you're going home, we thought this would cheer him up. But I hope you'll enjoy it, too. It's supposed to be fun."

"I'm sure it'll be great," Caro says hastily.

Meg leaves, and Caro remains in bed. Playland. There was something about the name Playland . . .

Then she remembers—a dark little girl talking about Playland in a shrill voice. And a game they had played—throwing cardboard rings around the tops of milk bottles, to win a big bear. She was the granddaughter of that maid, the one who quit because of the broken architectural model.

Caro frowns. She has not thought about that night for years.

It takes a long time to get to Playland. Barton is not a good driver, and keeps changing lanes. Caro feels queasy as she leans against the window.

Adam is wild with excitement. He takes off his seat belt and sticks his head out the window, and sings, and points out all the red cars he sees.

Finally they arrive. Adam is thrilled by Playland, but Caro has grown up with Disneyland. She pretends to like Playland, of course, to please her father and Meg and Adam. She goes in the Tunnel of Love, and screams in the Haunted House, and eats cotton candy that is too sweet and pink.

"Please, please can we go on the Ferris wheel?" Adam begs.

"In a little while, honey," Meg tells him. "Let's sit down and have some lunch first."

They sit down at a sticky table to eat. Caro notices that Meg is looking pale.

"Are you okay?"

"I'm fine," Meg says quickly. "It's just the heat. It's making me a little dizzy."

Adam has finished his corn dog.

"More rides! More rides!"

Meg sighs.

"Don't worry," Caro tells her grandly. "Why don't you and Daddy rest here? I'll take Adam on some rides."

"Are you sure?" Meg asks gratefully.

"Yes!" Adam clutches Caro's hand.

"Well, make sure you're back in half an hour," her father says. "I don't want to spend the rest of my life in Playland."

"What do you want to go on first?" Caro asks Adam.

"The Ferris wheel."

They start in that direction, then Adam stops and pulls at Caro's hand.

"Look! Look!"

There's a balloon vendor up ahead, the bright globes bobbing above him.

"Oh, please, can I have one?"

Caro smiles.

"Of course," she says. "That's what big sisters are for." She remembers with a pang that she is leaving tomorrow. "Keep it in your room and think of me."

"I'll keep it forever," Adam promises.

They go over to the vendor, and Adam chooses, with great deliberation, a big red balloon. Then they head toward the Ferris wheel.

On the way, they pass the arcade. The first game Caro sees is the one she and the little girl had played, the throwing game. And sure enough, the huge teddy bears are still pinned invitingly to the top and sides of the booth. Caro hesitates—maybe she should play the game; she could win the girl another bear, and send it to her without saying who it was from. But then she remembers hiding in her room, the morning when the maid left, and hearing the front door slam shut. No; she does not want to be reminded of any of that.

Caro turns deliberately away from the booth.

"Let's go," she says.

But Adam is no longer by her side.

Caro looks quickly around. He is nowhere to be seen.

"Adam?" she calls. There is no answer. She heads in the direction of the Ferris wheel and finally she spots him.

"Adam!" She grabs the back of his shirt and shakes him. "What do you think you're doing?"

Adam is sobbing.

"My balloon! My balloon!"

Caro looks up. The red balloon is caught high in some scaffolding.

"I don't care!" she scolds. "You never should have run off like that. You could have gotten lost. Someone could have stolen you!"

"But my balloon!" Adam is roaring. "It can't be in my room now! It can't make me think of you!"

Caro kneels down. She hugs him. She begins to cry also.

"Don't worry," she says. "We'll get another balloon."

She stands up and takes Adam's hand, and they make their way back through Playland. They pass by the throwing game, and again Caro hesitates a moment in front of it.

She decides that it's silly to feel bad. All that business with the maid happened years and years ago. She was probably doing just fine now, and so was her granddaughter. By this time, the girl probably had five giant teddy bears on her bed.

Yes, everyone was doing fine. And Caro was a good person—wasn't she going to buy her little brother another balloon?

Sunday evening, Caro returns to Los Angeles. Barton and Meg and Adam take her to the airport.

"You're the greatest daughter ever," Meg says. "I couldn't have made it through that wedding without you."

"Come back soon," her father tells her, "or I may have to go out to California and steal you."

"I don't want the balloon," Adam is shrieking, holding on to her leg. "I just want you to stay."

Caro cries. She hugs them all and promises to return, and when she reaches the gate, she turns and blows kisses.

This is mostly because she is going to miss everyone so much, and only a little bit because a group of fans is watching her.

CAROLINE

Caroline is sitting by the swimming pool in Zoë's apartment complex. She has a book in front of her but she is not reading it. She stares into the pool. A ripple of wind has come up, and the water shakes gently.

She has been here a week, and she has done nothing but sit by the pool. She has not wanted to stay inside. The apartment seems less wonderful than it used to—dingier and smaller. And although her mother has bought her new clothes, as usual, and new toys and books, they seem too young for Caroline now.

Zoë has been kind. She has not once mentioned Adam or what happened that day at Playland. She asks Caroline if there is anywhere she would like to go, anything she would like to do, but there is nothing. Caroline thinks she will keep sitting by the pool until it is time to go back to New York.

Zoë has come out onto the balcony of her apartment.

"Caroline! Phone call for you!"

Caroline jumps to her feet. It can only be her father. He is calling to tell her that Meg has forgiven her, and that they want her back home as soon as possible. She is sorry to disappoint Zoë, who has been so welcoming, but she must go.

She rushes into the apartment and takes the phone.

"Hello?"

"Caroline." Her father sounds far away.

"How are you? How's Meg?"

"We're fine, but the thing is, honey . . . the doctors say Meg's well enough to come home permanently next month."

"That's great."

"Yes. But they think, well, it might be a little rough on her, your being there. Just at first."

Caroline listens, numb, as her father tells her of his plans to send her to boarding school in New Hampshire.

"Just for a semester or two. Till we see how things are working out. I've talked to the headmistress; she'd love to have you. I'm very impressed with the sound of their program—and in winter, you can learn to ski."

Finally the conversation is over, and Caroline hangs up the phone. She goes back downstairs to the swimming pool. The wind has come up—it is whipping the water into frantic blue patterns. Caroline stares at the pool—she is sure there's a secret message for her in there somewhere, but she has no idea what it could be.

CARO

A *Tree Grows in Brooklyn* has been canceled. There is a big scandal concerning Barbara Ann Fleming, who plays Katie Nolan. She is involved in an ugly divorce suit and loses custody of her children. After this, it is hard to pretend that she is the ideal mother, and ratings for the show quickly drop.

Caro is not especially upset. She is sure that another series will come along next season. And, this way, she will not be forever typecast as Flossie.

After the final day's shooting, there is a farewell party on the set. Everyone is joking and hugging and laughing, but there is an air of despair underneath it all.

Toward the end of the party, the actor who plays Steve, Sissy's husband, comes up to Caro. He is very drunk, and smiles broadly.

"Remember tonight, little Caro," he coos. "Your last cast party."

"Why will it be my last one?" she asks him, smiling also.

"Because you have no talent," he tells her, the smile growing even broader. "No talent whatsoever. You have just been one very lucky little girl."

Caro goes into her dressing room and starts to clear it out. She takes down her posters of Robert Vaughn and Herman's Hermits, she folds the Grandmother's Flower Garden quilt that her fan club made her. She packs the collection of paperbacks and puzzle books she has collected through the years. It is strange to see how little there is.

* * *

Caro spends most of the summer sitting by the swimming pool in her mother's apartment complex. She doesn't know what to do with herself. She is ready to go back on the set, but there is no longer a set to go to.

She wonders what will happen next. She holds her breath and waits for an answer. The wind has come up. It ruffles the water of the pool and seems to make a pattern. Caro is sure that, somewhere in there, is a message for her—but though she stares and stares, she can't imagine what it could be.

PART THREE

PLUM VELVET

CAROLINE

The worst times come at night. At two o'clock in the morning, Caroline wakes to the dark dormitory room around her. She can't get back to sleep. She looks at the white curtains at the window, at her desk and bookcase. Everything is normal, even nice, but she lies there, frozen, sweating.

She is back at Playland, playing the throwing game. She feels the rings in her hands. She sees the red balloon on the scaffolding. She hears the woman screaming.

She wonders if she will ever have a night where she doesn't wake up remembering these things.

The days are better because they are busier, but even then there are bad moments. Caroline has to be very careful with her free time. She has to plan out every hour of every afternoon. Bath; homework; studying; bed. She finds she can read, but not everything. Some books have little boys in them that remind her of Adam. *Little Women* used to be her favorite book, but she can't stand it now, because of the sister called Meg. Doing needlepoint is fine; counting stitches fills her head. But she can't listen to music.

In general, though, the days are safe. Caroline likes the order and routine of boarding school. She likes it that there is always something to do next—a class, lunch, a daily walk. It is relaxing not to have to think.

She also likes the school itself, the red brick building with its crisp white shutters and neat flagstone paths.

Caroline has her own room, but she always keeps the door to it open. She likes hearing the other girls' voices down the hall. Sometimes she thinks that when she leaves boarding school she might become a nun, so she can hear women's voices around her always.

The girls here are different from the ones at the Clark School. They're easier to be around. A lot of them have fathers who are in the army; they've lived in a lot of places and they don't take anything very seriously.

She hasn't made any real friends. It would take too much effort. But she does nice things for the girls, secret things. She puts autumn leaves on their pillows, or candy bars. The girls talk about their friendly ghost, but they never guess who it is.

She has told no one about the accident.

One night Caroline is going down the hall to take a bath. Fiona Marshall's door is open, and eight or ten girls are inside the room, sitting on the floor. Fiona catches sight of her.

"Hey, Caroline! Come on in!"

Caroline comes into the room.

"What are you doing?"

"Playing Truth or Dare."

"How do you play?"

"Sit down and you'll see."

Caroline sits down on the floor.

Charlene Perry goes first. Her dare is to raise her skirt all the way up past her waist, her truth question is "Describe your perfect wedding night."

Three other girls go after her. Nobody takes the dares—it's the truths that everyone is interested in.

Finally it's Caroline's turn.

"Truth or dare—tell us the worst thing you've ever done in your life, or jump out the window."

Caroline's face grows hot. It is so hot she feels like it's bleeding. She looks around the circle of faces. Somehow they found out. They must have found out. And this is the trap they have laid for her.

But when she looks again, she sees that they really don't know. They are innocent faces, simply curious, waiting for her answer.

Caroline decides that she will tell them. They are friendly girls—they would understand what happened that day at Playland.

She starts to tell them, but the words will not leave her throat. The worst thing she has ever done is so bad that it is choking her. She swallows and smiles nervously at the girls. Then she walks over to the open window, steps onto the sill and jumps out.

The phone rings and rings. As Caroline waits for someone to answer, her hands grow sweaty.

At last the receiver is picked up. "Hello?"

"Daddy?"

"Caroline." He sounds surprised. "Is everything all right?"

"Yes."

"How's your ankle?"

"The doctor says I can take the bandage off next week."

"Good. No more nonsense about jumping out of windows."

"No, Daddy."

He has never asked why she did it. Maybe he thinks she will do anything for attention. Maybe he is afraid she is going crazy like Meg.

"Daddy, I was wondering about Thanksgiving."

There is a long pause.

"I'm sorry, pumpkin. It's just a little too soon. Meg's making real progress, and we don't want anything to slow it down. I've asked Mrs. Talbot and she says you can stay at school—lots of the girls are doing that."

She bites her lip and nods.

"And Christmas? What about Christmas?"

She clutches hard onto the phone. There is an even longer pause.

"We'll have to wait and see."

"Sure," she says.

She hangs up the phone. Her hands hurt.

Caroline realizes that she has forgotten to say "I love you" to her father. She has never let a conversation end without saying "I love you." She picks up the receiver again and quickly redials.

"Hello?"

This time it is Meg who answers. Caroline is so startled to hear her voice that she cannot speak.

"Hello? Hello?" Meg repeats in a loud and frightened screech.

Caroline hangs up the phone.

* * *

It is an icy night. Caroline is in her room, but she does not feel like studying. She pushes open the window, and closes her eyes to the bitter air. She can hear music—something swift and sweet. She wonders if she is actually hearing the stars. Then she realizes it is just a record being played down the hall.

She closes her window, then sits on her bed and listens to the song in the darkness. She can't hear any words, just a voice. She gets an image of clear water running through white woods.

She sits very still until the song is finished.

"Come in!"

Janice Pearlman is at her desk, wearing flannel pajamas and curlers in her hair. She seems surprised to see Caroline.

"Sorry to bother you," Caroline says, "but were you playing some music just now?"

Janice nods. "Was it too loud?" She gestures for Caroline to sit down. "My sister sent me some brownies. Want some?"

"No, thank you." Caroline takes a breath. "What was the record you were playing?"

"Songs from Camelot."

Janice reaches for the cover and shows it to Caroline. On the front is a watercolor picture of a lake with a castle rising from the mists.

"It's by a new guy from England—his name's Tristan. My sister says he's going to be bigger than Donovan. I don't know about that."

She turns the record over.

"He's kind of cute, though."

Caroline looks at the face on the back of the jacket. It is not at all cute, but it is the face she has waited all her life to see.

"You want to hear the song again?" Janice asks her.

"No, thank you," Caroline says hastily.

"Well, come back later—around ten. I'm having a little party; we'll eat the brownies and listen to the whole album."

"That sounds great."

But Caroline has no intention of coming. She does not want to be in a roomful of people, listening to Tristan sing.

* * *

Every Thursday afternoon, there is a trip to town scheduled. Caroline has never been interested before, but today she puts her name on the sign-up list.

At two o'clock, the girls set off down the hill.

"Stay in pairs," the head of house tells them when they reach the main street. "And no going beyond Cross Avenue. Meet back at this corner in an hour and a half. A demerit if you're late."

Caroline is paired with a fat, shy girl called Marigold.

"Where do you want to go?"

"The bookstore," Marigold says instantly. "Jean Plaidy has a new novel out." Marigold is addicted to historical romances.

They go into the bookstore. Marigold finds her Jean Plaidy, and leans against the wall, reading. Caroline waits until she is completely absorbed, then she edges to the front door and slips out onto the street. She'll be back in five minutes—Marigold will never even know she's gone.

The record store turns out to be several blocks away. Caroline doesn't see *Songs from Camelot* at first, but at last she finds it and takes it to the counter. She stares at Tristan's white face as the record is purchased and put safely into a plastic bag.

Caroline looks at her watch. Two forty-five—she'd better get back to the bookstore. She hurries down the street, and then when she reaches the final block, she stops. There on the corner is a small green shop she had not noticed before. It is a store that sells dollhouses.

Caroline hesitates. She looks down the block toward the bookstore, but there is no frantic Marigold standing outside. She was probably still reading Jean Plaidy. Five minutes. Caroline will give herself five more minutes.

She walks into the dollhouse shop.

"Hello, there." A plump woman is in the window, setting up a Thanksgiving display. "Sorry we're in a bit of a state here."

Caroline smiles. "It looks great," she says. "I wish I could help you set it all up."

"Why don't you?" the woman asks her. "You have nice small hands."

Caroline shakes her head. "I'm afraid I don't have time."

The woman starts to pick up a tiny banquet table. It slips from her fingers, and the miniature cobs of corn and turkeys roll all over the floor.

Caroline hurries to pick them up. Carefully she rearranges everything on the table and hands it back to the woman.

"Do you have any kegs of cider?" she asks. "They might look good next to the benches."

"Right here," the woman points. And in a moment, Caroline is in the window, helping to place the tiny barrels.

The two of them assemble a wonderful banquet. They seat half the adult dolls at the trestle table, and stand the others alongside, holding platters of food. Caroline arranges a game of tag with the doll children, both Indian and Pilgrim, and underneath the table, she places a little black dog and gives it a plateful of turkey to eat. She sits back on her heels, and looks at the scene, smiling. She is very happy. She loves making Thanksgiving for the tiny dolls.

Suddenly there is a rapping on the window. Caroline looks up. All the girls from school are standing outside. Tears are falling down Marigold's face. The head of house has almost no lips, they are pressed together so hard.

Caroline stares at the faces. Then slowly she climbs down from the window.

"I have to go now," she says. "Thank you for letting me help."

"Thank *you,*" the woman tells her cheerfully. "We could use you anytime."

That evening, Caroline is summoned to the headmistress's office.

Mrs. Talbot is standing behind her chair. She does not offer Caroline a seat.

"I understand that you broke a very important rule this afternoon."

Caroline nods, her head heavy.

"Do you have any idea how much concern you caused?"

"I'm sorry. I didn't mean to. I just got—involved with something, and forgot about the time."

There is a silence.

The headmistress is looking at her keenly. "What did you get so involved with?"

Caroline finds herself telling Mrs. Talbot all about the dollhouse shop. She tells her about the window display, and the miniature Thanksgiving dinner, and the little dog having his plateful of turkey under the table.

"And then I looked up, and—there everyone was," she finishes.

"I see," Mrs. Talbot says.

She walks to her chair and sits down. Then she looks thoughtfully at Caroline.

"I know you meant no harm, Caroline, but it was a silly thing to do and you caused a lot of needless anxiety. And unfortunately, the school rules are quite clear about cases like this. You must make an apology to your head of house, and you've got Study Hall detention for two weeks."

Caroline bites her lip. "Are you going to tell my father?"

"No," Mrs. Talbot says. "It was thoughtlessness, not malice. I see no reason your father should be told. And frankly, Caroline, I like the idea of your helping out at this shop. I know you haven't had—an easy time lately." There is a pause. "I hope you'll go again—I'll tell your head of house that you have my permission."

"Thank you, Mrs. Talbot," Caroline breathes.

The headmistress smiles. "I'm looking forward to seeing the Christmas window."

December is sharp and beautiful. Caroline tries not to think about Christmas, and where she will be spending it. She thinks instead about the window at the dollhouse shop, and what still needs to be done for the display. She has been spending a great deal of time at the shop—Mrs. Talbot lets her go there not only Thursday afternoons but on Saturday mornings as well.

Caroline adds a few final touches to the scene, then goes outside to see how everything looks. The window is filled with glittery cotton snow, Christmas trees, and reindeer. On the far left is the workshop where Santa surveys his long, ink-spattered list, and on the right is a knot of Victorian carolers. And in the middle is a big dollhouse, full of wreaths and ivy, mistletoe and stockings.

Caroline smiles. The Christmas in the window is perfect. But the days are going by, and soon she can no longer shut out the real Christmas. The other girls are all going home for the holidays; suitcases are brought out, clothes are being sorted.

"Caroline, I'm going up to the attic," the head of house says. "Do you want your suitcase?"

"No," Caroline tells her shortly. Then, seeing the girl's curious look, she changes it to, "Not yet."

She waits to hear from her father, but he does not call. Finally, on the eighteenth of December, a telegram arrives.

CAN'T DO WITHOUT MY BABY FOR CHRISTMAS STOP TICKET ARRIVING STOP LOVE, ZOË

It is a golden rescue. Now Caroline can take her suitcase down from the attic. Now she can go into town and buy a present for her mother. Now she can be envied because she, alone among the girls, is going to sunny California for the holidays.

Christmas in Los Angeles is terrific. Although it is eighty degrees outside, every house gleams with decorations, and surfers wear Santa Claus hats as they ride the waves.

Caroline has fun. She does not think about Adam or her father or Meg. She goes with Zoë to pick out a tree, and they decorate it with golden balls. They take a horse-drawn carriage ride in Pasadena, attend the Christmas brunch at the Beverly Hills Hotel, and go to the Music Center to see *The Nutcracker.* Zoë flirts with all the Santa Clauses.

On Christmas Eve, Caroline and Zoë put up their stockings, and in the morning they find them filled—Caroline's with makeup, stationery, and hair clips, Zoë's with a bottle of champagne and a tin of caviar.

Then they start on their presents.

The first package Zoë opens is the music box from Caroline.

"It's the most beautiful thing I've ever seen," she says softly.

Caroline flushes with pleasure.

Zoë tosses over a big package. "Here's something from your father. It came last night, Special Delivery."

It is an elegant red coat, but Caroline puts it aside. She does not want to think about her father today.

She goes on to her other gifts from Zoë. There are skirts and blouses, a sweater set with matching beret, the cast album from the new show *Hair,* turquoise earrings. And in the final box there is a dress—an evening gown of plum-colored velvet.

"This is really a present for me," Zoë tells Caroline. "You're getting your picture taken in it on Thursday. I can't believe you're twelve years old, and I don't have a single decent photograph of you."

Thursday morning, Caroline is sent to Elizabeth Arden, to have her hair cut and styled.

"Roberto's doing you—he's a genius," Zoë tells her.

Roberto kisses Caroline's hand when she comes in.

"You look like a young Catherine Deneuve, only prettier," he says, and he gives her a long fifties-style bob.

Zoë picks Caroline up at noon, with the plum velvet dress on a hanger in the backseat, and they drive into Hollywood.

Zoë is shimmering with excitement.

"You'll remember this day for the rest of your life." She beams at Caroline. "It's not every girl who gets to be photographed by Hans Lasky."

Caroline tries to respond with the proper enthusiasm, but Zoë looks sharply over at her.

"You don't know who he is, do you?"

"Not exactly," Caroline confesses.

Zoë sighs. "Well, you probably wouldn't, growing up with Barton."

She tells Caroline all about Hans Lasky. How he was one of the greatest photographers in the world. How his work was in museums, and how he had photographed all the great beautiful stars back in the great beautiful days of movies.

"I met him at a party, when I had just come to Hollywood. And you know what he did when I started the agency? He took headshots of all my kids—for free." Mistily, Zoë smiles. "It's sheer luck he's here now—he lives in Boston. But when he told me he was coming out, and I told him *you* were coming out, you know what he said? "It's time I photographed your real baby."

They arrive at the studio, a brick building not far from Zoë's office. Hans Lasky is waiting for them. He is old and small and creased. Zoë kisses him and introduces Caroline. Hans Lasky looks at her with wise red eyes. Caroline feels awkward. She knows she is not beautiful, not worth being photographed.

"Why don't you change behind the curtain?" is all he says.

Caroline comes out wearing the plum velvet dress. Hans Lasky seats her on a stool, adjusts the lights, arranges her hair. Then he gets behind the camera and starts to take pictures.

"Head tilted," he tells her rapidly. "No; the other way. Eyes up. Not so high. Relax your hands."

Caroline feels ridiculous. Her gestures are awkward, her smile unnatural. She looks toward Zoë, who is standing off to the side, and reminds herself that this is a present for her mother.

Toward the end of the session, she hears the front door of the studio open; another person comes into the room. The lights are so bright that Caroline cannot tell who it is, only that it is a man or a tall boy. The figure moves forward to Hans Lasky and touches the old man's shoulder.

"Grandpa."

"Steven," The old man turns around. "Is it time already?"

Hans Lasky leaves the camera and puts his arm around the young man.

"This is my grandson, Steven," he says. He pats the boy's cheek and goes back to the camera. "I'm almost ready—just give me one little minute more."

Another picture is taken, and another. Caroline knows that Steven is watching her. Then he moves forward, to the side of the room, and now she can also see him. He is thirteen or fourteen. His hair is fascinating, thick and curly as a doll's. And he has white skin, erupting into red cheeks. His eyes are slanted, with thick black lashes. She finds she is heating up, reddening.

Hans Lasky turns the lights off at last.

"A little warm," he says kindly.

They all leave the studio together.

Zoë kisses Hans Lasky on both cheeks. "Thank you, my darling," she tells him.

Caroline is too embarrassed to say anything. Especially, she cannot think of words to say to Steven Lasky. She only jerks her head and whispers "Merry Christmas," then realizes to her chagrin that Christmas is already over.

Zoë has to go out that night, to a business dinner. After she leaves, Caroline wanders around the empty apartment, savoring the silence for a few moments. Then she goes into the hallway and looks into the big silver-framed mirror. She stares for a long time at her reflection, scrutinizing the face that Steven Lasky had seen that afternoon. It seems to her a plain face, unformed, uninformed.

She goes to her mother's record cabinet and looks through the albums. To her surprise, Zoë has a copy of Tristan's *Songs from Camelot.* Caroline puts the record on the turntable, and Tristan sings to her while she dances around the room. She pretends that Tristan has Steven Lasky's face. And she pretends Steven Lasky has Tristan's voice. She is dancing with him; he is singing to her. She stops dancing and goes to look in the mirror again—this time she looks flushed and beautiful. Caroline puts her hands over her eyes.

During the spring semester, Barton telephones to say that he and Meg have decided to move. The doctor at the special hospital suggested the change—he thought it would do Meg good. It doesn't take them long to find an apartment, and they are soon moved into their new building on 62nd Street. Caroline will love the place, Barton tells her. She'll see it in the summer. Both he and Meg are looking forward to her spending her vacation with them.

When Caroline first walks into the new apartment, she is stunned. She does not recognize anything. The furniture, the rugs, the paintings on the wall—everything has been changed. Even the books in the library look different.

And when she goes into the room Barton points out as hers, it is the room of a stranger.

"Where are my things?" she asks her father, trying to keep her voice from sounding shrill. "My bed, my dresser. My doll collection."

"Everything's safe," he says. "It's all in storage."'

Caroline tries to be philosophical. It is like Sleeping Beauty—her things are only resting until the day when she has her own life and can wake them all up again.

She looks around the new apartment once more. On the whole, she is rather glad to be in a place without a past.

Laura has also gone. Instead, there is a Korean woman called Kim who doesn't speak English.

Meg is looking well. She has put on more weight, and her hair has grown long again.

When she first sees Caroline, she says, "Welcome!" She walks over and hugs her. "We're so glad you could spend the summer with us."

It is strange to feel like a guest.

It is a long summer. Caroline does not know what to do with herself during the day. She is too young to get a job, and she does not want to force her company on Meg. She ends up going out as much as possible, to the park and to museums and galleries.

Meg never leaves the apartment. She sleeps late and stays in her room all afternoon.

It is a relief when Barton gets home from work.

One morning, when Caroline comes into the kitchen for breakfast, she is surprised to find Meg sitting at the table, waiting for her.

"My watch is broken," she tells Caroline, with large frightened eyes.

Caroline cannot understand why she is so anxious. Meg never goes out; she doesn't even need a watch.

"I have to get it fixed."

"Don't worry," Caroline tells her soothingly. "There's a jewelry shop right on Lexington."

Meg's voice is small. "That's so far."

"I could take it in for you, if you want."

"No," Meg says after a long silence. "They say I should go out more."

"Why don't I come with you?" Caroline suggests. She smiles at her stepmother. "We'll have a good time."

They walk along Lexington Avenue. Whenever a bus goes by, it hurts Caroline to see the way Meg flinches. She remembers how Meg used to love walking around New York.

They pass an antique shop. In the window is a pair of worn, silk high-buttoned shoes.

Meg stops and points. "I tried to get shoes like that for you once."

"That's right. For the *Tree Grows in Brooklyn* dress."

"Yes."

"That was a wonderful surprise," Caroline tells her gently.

"You never wore that dress," Meg says, frowning. "I guess you didn't like it."

Caroline can laugh at the memory now.

"I loved it. It's just that one of the girls at school wrote 'Go to Hell' on the hem."

Meg looks at her, and nods.

"Yes," she says thoughtfully. "After what you did, of course you're going to hell."

She puts her hands over her face and begins to wail.

"I'm sorry about this, honey," Barton says as he puts Caroline on the train back to boarding school the following afternoon.

"I know," she tells him.

"I'm sure you'll enjoy the summer session. And we'll be seeing you for Christmas. The doctor said he's going to change Meg's medication a little. She'll be much better by then."

Caroline kisses him good-bye.

It is March of her sophomore year. Caroline is in the school library, working on an English essay.

There are footsteps behind her.

"There you are!" It is Pam Allbright, one of the seniors. "Mrs. Talbot wants to see you right away."

Caroline puts her book down, and walks toward the headmistress's office. She is curious, but she can't think of anything she has done wrong.

"Caroline, sit down," Mrs. Talbot says pleasantly. She gestures toward a chair across from her desk.

"I've just received the most charming note from a friend of yours—a young man named Steven Lasky."

For a moment, Caroline cannot remember who Steven Lasky is. When she does remember, she is filled with confusion.

"He's not actually a friend of mine—he's more a friend of my mother's. Or rather, his grandfather's her friend. I only met him once."

"Well, he writes to say that he saw your mother, and she asked him to look you up. He's going to be in the area, and he'd like to take you to tea next Wednesday."

Mrs. Talbot is looking at her drily.

"Would you enjoy having tea with this young man, Caroline?"

Caroline remembers Steven Lasky's hair, and his eyelashes.

"I can't," she says quickly. "I have a French class on Wednesday afternoon."

"I can give you an excuse slip," Mrs. Talbot tells her.

"So, Caroline—what's he like?"

All the girls are excited that shy little Caroline Andrews is being taken to tea by a boy.

"I haven't any idea," she tells them coolly. "I haven't seen him since I was twelve. I barely remember him."

On Wednesday afternoon, the taxi pulls up in front of the school. All the girls in the dormitory watch Caroline greet Steven at the front door. The lashes, the cheeks are the same. He has grown up to be very handsome.

"You really didn't have to do this," Caroline tells him.

"That's all right," he says. "I'm in the area anyway—looking at a few colleges in New Hampshire. This is a nice break." He smiles at her. "Do you want to go into town for tea? I saw a bakery shop as we drove up."

They walk into town. Steven is easy and friendly. He comments on the houses they pass, and points out little details—a door here, a window box there. He wants to be a photographer someday, he says. That's why he notices all these things.

It's hard not to enjoy being with Steven. And impossible not to laugh as they eat cakes in the tea shop and he gets chocolate cream all over his chin.

"Your mother sends her love," he tells her. "She says she can't wait for your next visit."

"I can't either," Caroline says.

"I wish I had your setup. I wish I could spend my summers in California."

No, you don't, Caroline wants to tell him. You don't wish for my setup. You don't wish that your father won't let you come home because you made your stepmother insane.

She changes the conversation. "Well, maybe you'll live there after college," she says.

That gets them talking about college and where Steven is applying. And then they talk about their present schools, and what subjects they like, and which teachers they hate. Finally, the waitress brings the check.

"Let me pay half," Caroline tells Steven.

"Don't be ridiculous," he says. "It's been a huge pleasure."

As they walk back to Caroline's school, they pass the dollhouse shop. In the window is an Easter scene, with miniature dolls hunting for colored eggs and the Easter Bunny hiding behind a bush.

Steven stops and studies the window display. "I wish I'd brought my camera. I'd love to have a picture of this."

Caroline smiles. "Thank you."

He looks up questioningly.

"I put the display together," she says, blushing. "At least most of it."

"I'm very impressed," he tells her.

It is like being drenched with a hose of happiness.

* * *

Steven says good-bye at the front door.

"I really enjoyed the afternoon," he tells her. "If I end up going to college here, let's do this often."

Everyone is watching from the dormitory windows as he leans over and kisses Caroline on the cheek.

CARO

In the last two years, business has been so good that Zoë is finally able to buy a small house on Linden Drive in Beverly Hills. True, the house is south of Sunset and not north, but for now, she is satisfied.

Caro will be a sophomore at Beverly Hills High School.

"It'll be a fresh start," Zoë tells her. "No excuse for not getting A's anymore. You're bright. It's just that you don't work."

Caro hasn't felt like working since *A Tree Grows in Brooklyn* ended.

At first, she and Zoë had kept hoping there would be another series, but there wasn't. And Zoë didn't want Caro doing commercials anymore—after the show, it would be a comedown.

"You're at that awkward age, honey," Zoë kept telling her. "Just wait a few years—when those braces come off your teeth, and you get a bit of a bosom; you wait and see."

The braces came off, the bosom arrived, but still there were no parts. Caro kept remembering what the actor at the cast party had said to her. *You have no talent. No talent whatsoever.*

But now she is starting a new school. She has all kinds of plans. She will work hard and get grades good enough for Stanford. She will be popular. She will be voted president of a club. She will find a best friend.

And even more important, she will find a boyfriend.

On the first day of school, Caro is up at six o'clock. She dresses very carefully, in the flowered skirt and white top she and Zoë had bought the week before at Judy's.

She goes into her mother's room to say good-bye.

"Knock 'em dead," Zoë tells her sleepily.

The school is on Moreno Drive, not a long walk at all. Classes start at eight eleven, but Caro gets there forty minutes early. She walks around the buildings, up and down the tiered patios. She visits the Swim-Gym, made famous by the dance scene in *It's a Wonderful Life.* She treks up to the cafeteria at the top of the campus—it pleases her that one of the walls has been painted in bright rainbow colors. She finds her locker and practices her route to classes.

Finally, the first bell rings. Caro hurries to her English class and sits down. She glances at the other kids taking their seats around her. None of the girls looks like the best friend she hoped to find. None of the boys looks like the boyfriend. But it's only the first day.

Caro hears a sound coming from behind her; a sort of insect buzz. Then she hears a giggle. The buzz grows louder. It is coming from all over the room now. She realizes it is not a buzz; it is a tune. The tune is so familiar that she barely registers it at first, but then she realizes—it is the theme song from *A Tree Grows in Brooklyn.*

The tune grows louder and louder, accented by laughter now.

The teacher comes in.

"Quiet!" he shouts. "What's going on here?"

His eyes fall to Caro's reddened face.

Caro is not popular. She is not sure why, but no one seems to like her.

"It's because you're better than they are," Zoë says. "What have I always told you? If you raise your head above the crowd, someone's going to take a shot at it."

But Caro hasn't raised her head above the crowd. Not in years, anyway. Nowadays, her head is not worth taking a shot at.

She tries to be friendly, but the girls don't respond. When they have study groups before a science test, Caro is not asked to join. When they sit at the benches for lunch, Caro's place is not saved. When they come to school on Fridays carrying sleeping bags, it is for a party Caro has not been invited to.

It is as if they are all real girls, and she is not. It is as if they have received some special instruction, read some special book, know some secret code, that no one told her about. Caro gives up on the idea of having a best friend.

As for a boyfriend, there is nobody she is interested in.

And then, one Friday in mid-October, a boy transfers into Caro's Spanish class. He is a junior. He looks like a character from a Celtic myth, with pale skin and greenish-blond hair. His name is Brian Sheffield.

Brian sits in the chair in front of Caro, and smiles at her. From the moment she sees him, things become easy. Once again, Caro has a script to act in, and a character to play.

She is a girl in love.

All that weekend, Brian is the only thing Caro thinks about. She takes long walks and imagines Brian beside her. She buys a new dress and dances in the darkness.

At last it is Monday morning, and time for Spanish class. Caro sits behind Brian once more. She likes his shirt, a soft plaid of several blues. She watches him take notes. His handwriting is appealing—straightforward and large. She imagines what a love letter from him would look like. His fuzzy gray sweater is hanging on the back of his chair. Caro drops a pen on purpose so that she can lean forward and touch it.

She finds out that he plays basketball. That Friday, she stays after school and goes to the Swim-Gym to watch him practice. She pretends she is just doing homework, but she watches everything Brian does. She likes the way he moves, ducking, twisting lightly. She imagines herself going up to him after he has won a game, imagines him throwing an arm around her shoulders, giving her a careless kiss.

After a week or two, Zoë starts to notice.

"So what's going on with you?" she demands. "All this mooning, all this secrecy. Is it some boy? It has to be. Well, congratulations, baby." She laughs. "Feel free to pick my brains if you need help. I'm good with boys."

Caro cannot keep the disdain out of her smile. She thinks of Greg, bursting into the motel room and hitting her. No, she doesn't think she'll go to her mother for any tips.

"Well, just be careful," Zoë warns her. "A guy will promise you the moon and a pair of orange ice skates to get what he wants."

Brian has not promised Caro the moon, ice skates, or anything else. He has never even spoken to her.

But Caro can wait. She knows that everything will come about in time. And in the meanwhile, she talks to Brian in her mind. She tells him little stories about her childhood, and her days on the *Brooklyn* set. He tells her not to worry—that she will be a star again someday. Sometimes they just hold hands and do not talk at all. They are happier together than any other couple at the school, possibly happier than any other couple in the world.

But sometimes Caro feels lonely. Sometimes she wishes things would move a little faster. One day she gets Brian's phone number from the Spanish teacher, saying she needs it for help on a project. Lots of girls did that sort of thing. It would be so easy to call. But in the end, she throws away the number. This is not how she wants the relationship to begin.

The weeks go on. It is January now.

One Friday afternoon, Caro stays after school to watch Brian in a basketball game. He scores the winning shot and is carried around the court on the shoulders of his team.

Caro is thrilled to tears. It is just like the poem she read for English class, "To an Athlete Dying Young."

The athlete in the poem was given a laurel wreath, and Caro decides to make one for Brian. She spends all evening with ivy vines, wire, and gold paint.

"Well, this is intriguing," Zoë says, coming into Caro's room and seeing the mess. "Would you care to explain?"

Caro shakes her head.

She decides to put the wreath on Brian's desk, anonymously, on Monday morning. And then she changes her mind—she will give it to him herself. The time has come.

* * *

Monday morning, Caro walks up to Brian after class. He is bent over his desk, organizing his books.

"I made this for you," she tells him, handing over the wreath. "It's what they used to give to all the Greek heroes."

She can see that he has no idea what she's talking about, but he seems pleased by the gift.

"Hey, thanks!" he says. "That's really great."

They walk together down the hall.

"You're the one who was on television, right?"

She nods.

"That must have been something."

He is smiling at her.

He smiles again later that day when he sees her in the cafeteria, and again, after school lets out.

The next morning, before Spanish class, they talk about the homework. And the following morning, they talk about the quiz.

On Thursday afternoon, Brian comes up to Caro as she is getting her books from her locker.

"Hey," he says. "If you're not doing anything tomorrow night, maybe we can get together."

Caro can't hear her own voice; the blood is pumping too hard in her head.

"All right," she says carefully.

Friday afternoon, Caro goes home from school and does all the things that girls in books do when they're getting ready for a date. She manicures her fingernails. She washes her hair. She gives herself a facial. She borrows Zoë's Joy perfume.

"So what exactly is going on here?" Zoë wants to know.

"I have a date tonight," Caro tells her.

"So I gathered. Well, I have one myself." She watches Caro. "Nothing worth doing my nails for, though. You be careful."

"I will."

There is a discussion about when each of them will be home, and who will leave the porch light on. Caro feels like a woman, an equal.

Finally it is time to get dressed. Her dress is new—flowered with the same shades of blue that are in Brian's plaid shirt.

She waits outside the house. She does not want Brian coming in and meeting Zoë.

At seven fifteen, his green Volkswagen pulls up to the curb.

"Hey," Brian says. He is wearing the plaid shirt.

"I'm starved," he tells her. "Let's get something to eat."

They drive into Westwood. Caro keeps staring at Brian's hands on the steering wheel. She imagines them, skillful, light, on her shoulders.

They have dinner at McDonald's. Caro is too nervous to eat. She drinks a glass of water while Brian finishes a hamburger and French fries. They talk a little about school and teachers, but really there is not much to say.

Finally, Brian pushes the tray away and gives Caro a tousled, easy smile.

"So," he says. "What do you want to do now?"

They end up going to see the movie *Concert for Bangladesh.* The film starts at eight. Caro had told her mother that she would be home no later than nine thirty, but she can't worry about that now.

They go into the theater. It is nearly filled.

"That's okay," Brian says. "I like sitting in the back row."

He points to the far corner, and they sit down in the red leather seats. The instant the houselights dim, Brian reaches over and takes Caro's hand. His hand feels warm and solid in hers, and she settles herself contentedly. But Brian is suddenly in front of her, coming nearer. And then his face is pressed on hers and his tongue is in her mouth.

Caro freezes. Her heart is thumping uncomfortably. She does not want Brian's tongue in her mouth.

But Brian goes on. One hand is squeezing Caro's breast now; the other is sliding down the blue flowered dress, lifting the hem, traveling up her thighs.

Working away with both hands, he gives a soft groan. Caro tries pushing him away, but the hands return instantly. She doesn't know what to do.

"Brian," she whispers. "Wait." The hands stop. "There's something I've got to know," she falters. "Do you—love me?"

"Sure," he tells her. "Sure I do."

"Really?"

"Of course."

Caro sighs with joy.

"I love you, too."

Everything is all right then. Everything is most wonderful. She closes her eyes and starts to kiss Brian back.

The movie is over, and they leave the theater. They walk to Brian's car and get in. They are both silent during the drive.

Zoë is waiting for Caro by the front door.

"You told me you'd be home by nine thirty." Her voice is quaking with anger. "It is nearly eleven o'clock."

"I'm sorry."

"Do you have any idea how worried I've been?"

Caro puts her arms around Zoë. "It'll never happen again. I promise."

It is an odd sensation, feeling like the mother and not the daughter.

The next school morning, Caro wears the blue flowered dress again, even though it is wrinkled. It is her secret message to Brian.

When she gets to school, Mindy Peters and her group are waiting.

"I hear you and Brian had a lot of fun at the movies."

"*Quite* a lot of fun, from what Brian says."

"Hey, Caro, how about coming with me to see *The French Connection* next week?" a boy with pimples calls, and he makes kissing noises.

They all start laughing.

Mindy put her arms around two friends. "Let's go, girls." She looks meaningfully back at Caro. "This is a contaminated zone."

Caro's face is so hot and red that she feels it is going to bleed.

When she goes down the hall, there are wolf whistles all around, and scattered applause.

During Spanish class, Brian stares down at his textbook. He does not look up at her.

Caro excuses herself. She goes into the girls' bathroom, and is sick before she can reach the toilet.

She calls home and asks Zoë to pick her up.

"What's the matter?" Zoë keeps asking, but Caro won't say.

When she gets to the house, she rushes into her room. With shaking fingers, she pulls off the blue flowered dress. She sees that someone has written the word "SLUT" on the hem.

She throws the dress in the sink and rubs soap on it. She scrubs until she has blisters, but the ink is indelible.

* * *

Caro comes home from school, throws her books on the sofa, goes into her bedroom and locks the door behind her. She changes into her nightgown and puts *Songs from Camelot* on the record player. Then she turns off the lights, lies down on the bed, and listens to Tristan over and over again.

She has been doing this every day since January. It is March now. Caro sees no reason why things should ever change. What's the use of even trying? There's simply no point. School is a nightmare, everyone thinks she's a slut; Brian is a bastard, her life is a complete waste.

"I hate you," she mouths the words into her pillow.

The only time she doesn't feel in pain is when she is lying in the dark, listening to *Songs from Camelot.*

One day Caro comes home and finds Zoë standing in front of the door, her arms crossed.

"I've had just about enough of this," she says. "Just about enough of you and your teenage angst. I've had it to here with nightgowns at three in the afternoon, and that miserable music over and over again. Listen here, young lady." She points a finger, and Caro can tell that she has had a few drinks. "You are going back to work."

"What are you talking about?"

"I mean you are going back into acting."

Caro is filled with both fury and deep relief. She lets Zoë see only the fury.

"Are you crazy?" she says icily. "I never want to act again in my life. I only did it because you forced me, but I'm too old for that now—so just leave me alone."

Zoë is quiet a moment. When she speaks again, her voice is casual.

"Nothing's going to happen overnight," she says. "I'm just asking one thing of you now. Just one thing. Go and have some more stills made. The last batch you did was—what?—two years ago? You've changed so much since then; gotten even prettier."

She smiles at Caro.

Caro scowls. "You're nuts," she says, but inside her is a little excitement at the thought of having new stills made.

"All right," she says finally, "but that's all I'm doing. You're not running my life anymore."

The next afternoon, when Caro comes home from school, a big box from Saks Fifth Avenue is waiting on her bed. She opens the box and finds an evening dress inside; it is velvet, plum-colored with lace at the collar. It is utterly beautiful.

Zoë comes into the room. Caro does not want her mother to see how much she loves the dress.

"You have a three o'clock appointment at Elizabeth Arden tomorrow," Zoë tells her, "and the shoot is at four thirty."

Caro makes a face.

She is still sulky the following afternoon at the beauty shop. Roberto asks her what she wants done, and Caro only shrugs.

"I was thinking of a long bob," Zoë tells him, ignoring Caro. "A fifties ingénue look."

Roberto starts to work.

When he is finished, he claps his hands.

"A young Grace Kelly," he cries, and turns the chair around so that Caro can see herself in the mirror.

Caro finds she likes the new hairstyle a lot. She can't help smiling.

Next is the shoot.

"I've got a surprise," Zoë tells her. "Hans Lasky's in town—he's doing the photography."

"He must be a hundred and thirty by now," Caro only says, but she is thrilled.

They drive to the studio in Hollywood, and Caro changes into the plum velvet dress.

Hans Lasky is as tiny and wrinkled and scuttled as ever.

"You're even more beautiful than you were before," he tells Caro, and kisses her hand. He reminds her that they met several years ago, when she was acting in *A Tree Grows in Brooklyn.*

"And do you remember my grandson Steven? He came with me to the set and took your picture."

Of course Caro remembers. As she listens to Hans Lasky talk about that day, her throat grows tight. His remembering is making her remember. She remembers those days on the set, the fan letters, the feeling of being somebody important. She wasn't always a despised, ignored, high school girl. She did not always have to get in her nightgown at three o'clock in the afternoon because there was nothing better to do.

As Caro poses for the pictures, the tide rises and rises. She sees Zoë standing behind the camera, smiling with pride. She hears Hans's voice saying she looks like an angel with sex appeal. Her body takes over; she knows just how to pose, knows just which angle of the face to present. How could she have forgotten all about this for so long? It is incredible. How could she have forgotten herself like this?

Caro makes herself remember Brian, and "SLUT" being written on the hem of her dress. It seems so trivial now, so completely unimportant. All that matters is the way she is turning her head, the way she is smiling while the camera clicks.

On the drive home, Zoë suggests that Caro audition for the school's spring musical.

Caro pauses for only a moment.

"Okay," she says.

* * *

The musical is *Bye, Bye, Birdie.* Auditions are held the following Tuesday after school.

Zoë goes into immediate action.

"Try out for Kim," she tells Caro.

"But Rosie's the best part."

"For a grown-up, sure; not for you. A high school girl can never be convincing as an adult—but you'll be adorable playing a high school girl. And look what the part did for Ann-Margret."

So Caro is to try out for Kim. She has been given a three fifty audition time, but she arrives early. The auditions are private, but the classroom door keeps opening, and Caro finds she can hear almost everything that goes on. She hears Tessa Armbrister sing "Somewhere Over the Rainbow." She hears Mimi Carruthers do Rosie's soliloquy. She hears Mindy Peters perform "I Got Rhythm." These are some of the girls who have been the meanest to Caro, and none of them has an ounce of talent. Caro can't believe she ever could have cared what they thought about her.

It is three fifty.

"Caro Andrews!" Mr. Stein, the drama teacher calls.

Caro comes into the room and smiles. Zoë has dressed her carefully. She is wearing a cashmere sweater and pleated skirt, bobby socks and saddle shoes—all the clothes that Kim would wear. And the new hairstyle is perfect.

Caro sings "Just the Way You Look Tonight." She sings it to Mr. Stein. She can tell by the way he straightens up in his chair that she has made the proper impression.

The next morning, when Caro goes to the bulletin board to see the cast list, her name is at the top—she is to play Kim.

Rehearsals begin. By the end of the first read-through, Caro can see that the show will be dreadful. The boy who plays Albert keeps changing pitch. Rosie gives a one-note performance. Hugo has a lisp. But none of it matters. The moment Caro reaches the auditorium, the moment she steps up onto the stage, all her problems fall away. She is her best self here, doing what she does better than anyone.

* * *

Zoë is full of plans.

"We'll send out some letters to casting directors. Very polite, very professional, simply telling them about your show. And I'll get a few extra tickets. We'll invite Hank Bloom from Universal, and Dana Fellows. Oh, and I ran into Marge O'Connor the other day—she says there's a new pilot floating around NBC that has a part for a girl your age. So we'll invite some NBC execs as well. Can't hurt."

The show is to open the night of May twenty-third. That afternoon, as soon as her eighth period class is over, Caro walks into the auditorium for the last time before the performance.

The atmosphere is hectic. Stagehands and prop people are racing around. Parent volunteers are putting out ice chests and a coffee machine. The foyer is being set up for refreshments at intermission. And the bulletin board at the entrance has been covered with pictures of the cast. Caro looks at her photograph—a full-length shot of her in the plum velvet dress.

She becomes aware that there is a girl standing behind her. It is Lindsay Sanders, who also tried out for the part of Kim.

Lindsay is staring at her.

"I guess some people would do anything for a part."

Caro frowns.

"What?"

"We all know," Lindsay tells her. "We all know about you and Mr. Stein."

Caro's face freezes.

"You two in the drama lab." Lindsay shakes her head. "God, you're a tramp. But it's not going to do you much good in the long run," she adds with a smile. "Everyone in the play says you stink."

She walks away. Caro waits until she is gone, and then she goes into the empty auditorium. Slowly, she sits down in one of the seats.

She looks around, imagining the room as it will be that night, filled with an audience, all of them coming to see her play Kim.

Everyone in the play says you stink.

The seats are filled with people. The kids she goes to school with. The ones who made fun of her. The ones who hate her. The ones who call her "slut." They would love her to trip, to miss a note, to come out for the final curtain call and be met with no applause.

Caro knows she's being ridiculous. She knows Lindsay's just jealous. She knows she's good in the play. But there is perspiration starting on her temples. She remembers the actor's words: *You have no talent. No talent whatsoever. You have just been one very lucky little girl.*

Everyone in the play says you stink.

Caro jumps up and leaves the auditorium. She will go home and tells Zoë what has happened. Zoë will hold her and say she is the most talented person she has ever known.

Caro runs the six blocks back to the house. Zoë is not there.

Caro goes into her bedroom. She puts Tristan on the record player, but he does not make her feel better. She takes a bath, but the steamy water cannot relax her. She sits, stiff in the tub, wondering how she will be able to play Kim tonight.

Finally she gets out. She dries herself off and goes naked into the living room. She walks over to Zoë's bar, and sees the crystal bottles filled with pale gold. All her life, she has been watching Zoë use these to get calm. Tonight Caro has to go onstage; surely she has a right to get calm, too.

She pours a drink into a crystal glass. It looks beautiful. It tastes terrible. She sees if she can still hear Lindsay's voice after she finishes the drink. It is still there.

Caro pours another drink. She closes her eyes and gulps it down.

Everybody in the play says you stink.

You have no talent. No talent whatsoever.

The drinks haven't helped. Angrily, Caro pours a third. All those warnings about alcohol, what it can do to you—and what it does is absolutely nothing. Another set of lies grown-ups tell.

Caro goes over to the couch to lie down, and that is when she sees the note her mother has left her.

"Darling," in Zoë's huge scrawl, "I won't be home before your show—crisis at work. Get yourself to school, and I'll be there, front row center, at seven. Can't wait to see my little star. Break a leg."

Caro wonders what time it is now. She turns to look at the clock, and to her surprise, a group of invisible people won't let her up. She tries again. Suddenly her stomach is heaving—she is sick all over the coffee table. And dizzy. The furniture in the room looks like blown paper, scudding this way and that.

She lies back on the couch and breathes slowly. After a few minutes, she sits up carefully and looks at the clock. There is less than an hour and a half before she is supposed to be onstage.

She had not thought being drunk would feel like this. She does not know what to do. Then she remembers coffee.

She gets to her feet. She did not know she could feel this ill. She goes to the kitchen and pulls the instant Folgers down from the cabinet. She boils water and pours in three, four teaspoons of the coffee. She has one swallow, and is sick again.

She goes into the living room and lies back down on the sofa. It does not help.

She sits up. She will try water. Water will make her feel better. She drinks the water, but it's no good either.

She goes into her bedroom. She tells herself that once she is dressed, she will no longer be drunk. She pulls on a dress, but feels the same. She tries to brush her hair, but gives up because the motion makes her queasy.

Fresh air. That's what she needs. Caro leaves the house and starts to walk to school. She tells herself that every breath is clearing her head. With every block, she is feeling better and better. And by the time she gets to school, she will be able to play Kim.

Caro reaches school. She goes backstage.

"Hey, Caro." Mr. Stein smiles.

Caro thinks of what Lindsay said, about her getting the part by diddling Mr. Stein. Mr. Stein with his big gut and wild hair. The very thought is hilarious—the most hilarious thing ever. Caro starts to laugh. She cannot stop herself. She laughs louder and louder.

Mr. Stein is staring at her in a strange way.

He comes up to her, uncomfortably close. Caro wonders if he is going to kiss her. Instead, he only smells her.

"My God," he says. "You're drunk. Completely smashed. You're out of the play."

Caro is huddled backstage. She has been told she will be suspended from school, maybe even expelled. She doesn't really care. What she minds is the thought of Zoë—Zoë sitting in the audience, front row center, surrounded by all her friends from NBC and Universal, waiting for Caro's entrance, and seeing the understudy coming on in her place.

That never happens. When Zoë comes into the auditorium, she is met by Mr. Stein. She is told what has taken place, and that she is to take Caro home immediately.

Zoë goes backstage. She does not say a word. She only folds Caro in her arms and leads her away.

But Caro dreams of that scene—Zoë sitting, waiting, in the auditorium—for the rest of her life.

CAROLINE

I grew up in New York City. Caroline writes in her college essay. *It's a big city, but I've always thought I've had a little life. I feel comfortable with little lives. Maybe this is because my father is an architect; he used to bring home models that were like dollhouses, little worlds.*

I went to a very proper school when I was small. They inspected our fingernails to make sure they were clean. We wore uniforms and had to polish our shoes every night. And then I went to a very proper boarding school in New Hampshire. By this time, it was in my nature to polish my shoes.

When I finish college, I will probably live in New York. I will probably be an architect and bring home little models of my own. I will probably marry a proper man and live in a tidy apartment, and have a baby whose fingernails I will inspect.

And that's why I want to go to college. Before that future gets hold of me, I want one chance to make my life bigger.

She leaves for Yale on a sultry brown day. Her father takes her to the station.

"You sure you don't want me to drive you?"

"I'm sure," Caroline tells him. "The train will be fine."

Taking the train means that it is her own decision to go. It will not be like boarding school, where she was sent away. This time it is she who is leaving them. The train will pull away, and she will see her past get smaller and smaller in the window.

"We're very proud of you," Barton tells her.

He reaches into his pocket and gives her a folded piece of paper.

Caroline is curious—could he have written her a letter? She puts the note into her purse.

"I'll come up and visit if I can," Barton says, "and we'll see you for Thanksgiving."

"That'll be great."

She kisses her father and gets onto the train. She sits alone on the worn seat, her two suitcases making a barricade around her.

She unfolds the piece of paper. It's not a letter after all. Her father has written down the name of a Yale professor he knows; someone in the Spanish department. If Caroline is interested in taking Spanish, she should see this man. Caroline crumples the paper and drops it on the floor.

A plump, middle-aged lady has come up beside her. "Excuse me, dear—is this seat taken?"

Caroline shakes her head. She pulls her suitcases closer to her, and the lady sits down.

"And where are you off to?" she asks.

"I'm starting college," Caroline says carefully.

"How exciting! I remember when I first went away from home . . ." She gives Caroline a lot of advice. Caroline does not tell her that she has been at boarding school since she was twelve.

"You're so lucky, " the lady ends wistfully. "You're so young."

Caroline considers this.

"I don't know," she tells the woman. "I'm not really very excited. Actually, I'm kind of tired of it all—and it hasn't really even started."

She leans back on the seat and closes her eyes.

Yale turns out to be not bad, though it does not make Caroline's life much bigger.

It is not all that different from boarding school. She likes it that every day has certain things she can count on. She gets up at seven, and has breakfast with her roommate, Delores. Delores is black, from Virginia. She is sleepy in the mornings, and doesn't talk much, but it is reassuring to have her there across the table.

Then there are classes. Caroline is taking English, psychology, French, art history, and a seminar on French Impressionism. The seminar is her favorite class, with its daily feasts of beautiful paintings.

It is a joy to fall into each work, making up stories about the people in the pictures. Sometimes she leaves the classroom almost giddy.

After classes, she goes to the art library to study. She has the building almost to herself. At the beginning of the year, a notice was handed out, saying that the library was a health hazard—asbestos had been discovered in the insulation. This problem will be fixed, but it will take time. In the meantime, students are still permitted to use the building, but at their own risk.

Caroline rather enjoys the idea that she might literally be killing herself over her work. As she sits in the art library, she takes in an occasional, purposeful, deep breath. It is a flutter on the edge.

After studying, she takes a walk. Most days, she goes down Connecticut Avenue. The students have been told not to walk too far past the co-op, but Caroline goes there anyway. These are some of her favorite streets. She notices things: a window box full of flowers, a child's toy, little efforts to make the dilapidated houses prettier.

On Mondays, though, she goes in the other direction. Near the Yale theater, she has found an obscure little store that sells art prints. Every week, an imaginative new display is in the window. Caroline finds all that work, all that effort for no audience, very beautiful. She makes it a point to pass by and admire.

On Sundays, she visits the cemetery. She goes to the older, ignored graves, and reads their inscriptions. They remind her of the print store—all that effort, and now no audience.

And then it is late afternoon and time for dinner.

Dinner is the most difficult part of the day. Delores has her friends from the soccer team, and she generally eats with them. Caroline goes early to the commons, before the crowds come. She brings along a book and eats alone.

Delores calls her the hermit crab.

"I'm poking you out of that shell," she threatens, and periodically drags Caroline to a movie or a college production. Caroline enjoys these evenings, but in general she prefers to stay in her room. It is as if there is a slow leak somewhere, and energy needs to be conserved.

Once a week, she calls her father. He is always interested to hear what she has been learning in her classes. He ends the conversations by saying that he is eager to see her for Thanksgiving. He does not invite her to come home before then.

* * *

Caroline is in the art library, preparing for an assignment; the following Wednesday she has to deliver a presentation in front of the class, analyzing a painting according to the principles of art.

She has been worrying so much about the speech that she has not yet chosen a painting. Time is running out—she needs to decide today.

She opens a guide to the National Gallery in Washington and begins flipping through the book. When she reaches Manet's painting *The Railroad,* she stops. It is a strange picture—a young woman sits on the bench of a train station, her gaze mysterious and sad. Next to her, facing the departing train, is a little girl, also dressed in blue. She is oddly painted—flat and insubstantial, as if she is not quite there.

Caroline stares at the picture for a long time.

She is standing in front of her art history class, pointing toward the projected slide of *The Railroad.*

"I think this young woman is remembering a day when she was a child. She'd gone to the train station and stood by these railings and waited for her father to come back from a trip. But he never came. He had been killed. And this little girl standing beside the lady—the reason she doesn't look real is because she's a ghost."

There is a smothered snort.

Caroline looks down. Her voice slows, grows uncertain. The roomful of faces in front of her are skeptical, hostile.

She flushes. She grows damp all over. She finishes the rest of her speech staring at the floor. Then she puts down the pointer and hurries from the room.

It is a gray November evening. Caroline is having dinner in a corner of the commons.

"Mind if I join you?"

She looks up. A boy with dark blonde hair and a blue jean jacket is standing behind her with a tray.

"I'm Graham Moss." He sits down and holds out his hand. "We have art history together."

"Right."

"I haven't seen you in class lately."

"No. I dropped the course."

He frowns. "That's too bad. I really enjoyed your presentation of the Manet picture."

She scowls, thinking he is making fun of her. But he doesn't seem to be.

"I don't know if I agree with your theory, but I think you had some really good points. It's just that people here tend to take themselves so seriously—and there you were, telling us a fairy tale." He smiles. "Though, as I said, I really liked it."

Caroline shrugs. "Well, thanks."

"I always see you eating alone," he goes on. "Is that on purpose?"

"I guess so," she tells him. "But you can sit down if you want."

By the end of the meal, Caroline knows all about Graham. He's a sophomore, and he's majoring in art. He's from Philadelphia, his father died two years before, and he goes back home to visit his mother whenever he can. When he finishes college, he hopes to be an art critic—but if that doesn't work out, he'll settle for becoming an architect.

"And what about you?" he asks finally.

The thought of going into it all makes Caroline weary.

"Let's keep that for another time," she tells him.

There is a pause.

"The Pierson Dramat's putting on *Our Town* tonight," Graham says finally. "The director's on my floor, and I sort of promised I'd go. Want to come?"

"All right," Caroline says.

The play is over. Caroline cannot stop crying. She thinks of Emily coming back to Earth for just one more day. She thinks of the little print shop. She thinks of the cemetery.

"It's all so beautiful," she weeps. "It's all so sad."

Graham is amused. "Look at you," he says, and he puts his arm around her shoulder. "You're such a baby." He gives her a quick hug. His blue jean jacket feels warm.

They leave the theater and go out into the cold night. His arm is still around her.

"What do you want to do now?" he asks. Then he says, "My room's right up this staircase. I have a single."

Caroline stares at the ground. She isn't sure what this means. But, "All right," she says. "Let's go there."

At first it seems that Graham just wants her to see his room. He shows her photographs of his parents, and the house he grew up in. He shows her some sketches he has been working on. Caroline compliments their good points, but she does not really think he's very talented.

She is sitting on the bed, because it's the only surface in the room that is large enough to accommodate the sketches. When Graham puts them away, he sits down beside her and puts an arm around her shoulders once again.

"May I kiss you?" he asks.

Caroline stiffens.

"No."

Graham looks surprised.

"It's just—I can't."

He frowns.

"Okay."

Caroline is sorry to have things end like this. He is a nice boy, and he looks so hurt. She has no idea why she said what she did; especially since a part of her really wanted to kiss him.

Caroline goes home for Thanksgiving. Meg tries hard—she greets Caroline at the door and gives her a hug and asks all about college. But, through the bright voice, Caroline can tell how much Meg wishes she were not there.

Caroline spends as much time as she can away from the apartment. She goes to museums and walks through the park. She sees a lot of couples—sitting on benches, holding hands, kissing. Caroline thinks of Graham, and that night in his room. She is sorry she acted the way she did.

Saturday afternoon, her father calls her into his den.

"We haven't really had a chance to talk," he says.

Caroline sits down self-consciously in the overstuffed chair.

"So," he says, "you like college?"

"Yes. I guess so."

"Any idea what you want to do when you graduate?"

Caroline has a very clear idea. She hadn't planned to tell her father yet, but he has asked, and he is smiling at her.

She takes a deep breath and says, "I'd like to be an architect. Like you."

She waits for his reaction.

Barton is silent. He does not say that this is great news. He does not say that it is what he has always dreamed of. He does not say that someday they will design a building together.

"I'm not so sure that's the best plan for you," he tells her at last. "I don't think your math skills are up to it. It's also a very competitive field—I'm not sure you've got the determination."

Caroline brings up the subject of the art library to show him how much determination she has. She tells him how she studies there almost every day, even though there is asbestos in the ceiling.

Barton smiles. "I wouldn't worry about it too much," he says. "Not with the amount of time you probably spend there."

"I'm going back to New Haven tonight," she tells her father and Meg at dinner.

"So soon?" Barton asks. "I thought you were staying till tomorrow."

"I'd like to go now, if that's all right."

He and Meg tell her they're sorry they won't have her longer, but do not insist she stay.

When she gets back to Yale, Caroline finds she is almost alone on campus. She walks, as a ghost might, through the deserted quads and colleges. She is empty; she has no plans, she is no longer going to be an architect. She sees it was a pointless dream, anyway; just a way to please her father, and it hadn't pleased him. She sits on a stone bench and watches her breaths smoke into the air.

"Caroline?"

She looks up. A figure in a green corduroy coat is coming toward her.

It is Graham.

They go to a coffee shop. He asks about her Thanksgiving and she cannot stop crying. She tells him about Meg forcing herself to be friendly, and her father laughing about the asbestos and saying she shouldn't be an architect.

"They don't want me," she keeps saying. "They don't want me."

Graham doesn't say much in response, but he holds Caroline's hand.

Dinner is over. They look at each other.

"What do you want to do now?" he asks her.

There is a pause. "I'd like to go up to your room," she says finally.

They go up to Graham's room, and they sit on the bed. Graham asks again if he can kiss her. This time Caroline lets him. He does not say anything about the time before, and she is grateful.

After a while, he asks if she wants to make love.

Caroline can't think of a good reason not to.

Afterward, he asks her, "How are you feeling?"

She is feeling nothing. Not guilty, not happy, not particularly closer to Graham. But a step needed to be taken—a step in some direction, and this seemed as good as any.

Having a boyfriend isn't what Caroline thought it would be. She thought it would make more of a difference. She thought it would make her giddier, more optimistic about the world. But it doesn't do any of those things. She guesses it's her own fault—after all that's happened in her life, she's outgrown that kind of innocence.

"Bullshit," Delores tells her. "The bottom line is he's just not doing it for you, girl."

"You're wrong," Caroline says quickly. "Graham's just fine."

And he is just fine. Friendly and sweet and funny. She's honestly very lucky to have him.

* * *

As the weeks go on, Caroline finds herself wondering, without too much anxiety, how things will progress. She guesses she should tell her parents about Graham, but she somehow doesn't. And Graham never mentions taking her home to Philadelphia.

Then, in March, to her surprise, he says he is going to visit his mother, and he asks her to come along.

"It's time you two met," he says solemnly.

"So you're Caroline."

Nina Moss is a tiny, fluffy woman, with sharp heels and a tight dress over her still-well-tended figure.

"Graham's Caroline," she adds slowly.

She pats the damask sofa next to her, and draws Graham down. "Sit next to me," she tells him. "I haven't seen you in so long."

She tells Graham all the news. She talks about neighbors and dinner parties and cousins. The name "Arlene" keeps coming up. Graham looks uncomfortable every time it is mentioned. Caroline guesses that Arlene is an old girlfriend.

"Now," Nina says brightly, "enough about me. What's been happening with my boy?"

Graham tells her. He tells her the story about his economics professor, and the mix-up about the test, and what the guy across the hall did with the stereo. Nina is fascinated.

Caroline sits stiffly in the chair. She waits to be mentioned, to be included in one of the anecdotes, but her name doesn't come up. She looks out the window. Graham and his mother laugh and talk.

Caroline and Delores are drinking beer. Caroline is on her third bottle. She has never drunk so much before; her head is filling with thick gray dust.

"It was so strange," she says over and over. "So completely incredible. The moment he got around her, it was like I wasn't there at all."

Delores nods. "You got to get rid of him. I keep on telling you."

Caroline shakes her head. "No. Honestly, Delores. He's got some wonderful qualities."

Delores rolls skeptical eyes. "You could do so much better."

Caroline finishes the third beer. She is silent for a long time.

"The thing is," she says finally. "The thing is, I don't think I could."

"You're crazy."

With great deliberation, Caroline puts the beer down.

"Let me tell you a story," she says. It is hard to get her tongue to move. "Once upon a time I was seven years old. I went to see my mother out in California. I wanted this doll. This Little Darling doll."

"I had that doll!"

"Yes, but listen. We went to the toy store, and there was the doll. But the crib and the high chair had been stolen. My mother said we should go to another toy store, but I was scared it wouldn't be there. So I made her buy me the broken one. And then we came to the other toy store and there were about a hundred perfect Little Darlings in the window. And I remember my mother said, "I think there's a lesson to be learned here."

Delores shakes her head. "Well, girl, you sure haven't learned it." She reaches over and lightly punches Caroline's arm. "This time you've got to wait."

They sit in silence.

"There was a boy once," Caroline says suddenly. "I met him when I was twelve. And then, when I was fifteen, he took me out to tea. I never heard from him again. But I still think of him sometimes."

Delores raises an eyebrow. "And the point being?"

Caroline shrugs. "I guess there is no point."

Caroline is finishing her junior year of college. She is still with Graham. He has graduated and is working at a firm in New York, but he comes down and sees her most weekends.

She knows they are sliding toward marriage. Even his mother knows it. The last time Caroline visited, Nina asked her all about her family and her classes. And, when she makes her daily call to Graham now, she has started sending Caroline her love.

In May, Graham proposes. He takes Caroline to the 21 Club one Sunday night and asks her to marry him.

She is not sure what she will say, but yes seems the easiest answer.

All of a sudden, there is champagne and clapping from the waiters. Caroline wishes that Graham hadn't been quite so sure.

"Graham and I are getting married," she tells her father and Meg the following morning.

"Congratulations." They seem happy and unsurprised.

"He'll take good care of you," Barton adds.

Caroline hasn't seen much of Delores in the past year, but when she gets back to Yale, she goes directly up to her room to tell her the news.

"Hey, girl!" Delores hugs her. "What's going on?"

"Well," Caroline says, "Graham and I have decided to get married."

Delores sits slowly down on the batik bedspread.

"You sure?" she asks.

And Caroline discovers that she is sure. "Yes," she says slowly. "I think it'll be fine. We get along very well."

Delores shakes her head. "Well, I just hope that someday a guy doesn't come along who really does it for you."

The idea of losing her head over a guy makes Caroline smile.

"I promise you that won't happen."

There is a silence.

"Am I invited to the wedding?" Delores asks.

"You bet."

"Will there be those little hot dog things?"

Caroline gives her a hug. "Just for you."

Caroline is on the train to New York for the weekend. Someone has left a copy of the *New York Times* on the seat beside her, and she glances through it. She comes to the society page, and sees a large studio portrait of a pretty blonde girl; the caption underneath says, "Marjery Chalmers to marry Steven Lasky."

Thoughtfully, Caroline puts the paper down. So. Steven Lasky was getting married. And she was getting married herself.

She wonders which of them will be the happier.

CARO

Zoë comes into Caro's room and sits on the bed.

"That was the principal on the phone," she says. "You've been suspended."

Caro nods. It is the morning after *Bye, Bye, Birdie.* She has been throwing up all night. She did not know her head could hurt so much.

"And there's going to be a hearing," her mother goes on with a sigh. "That idiot drama teacher wants to expel you." She lights a cigarette. "Might be the best thing," she shrugs. "You could go to a theater academy."

"I don't want to go to a theater academy," Caro tells her mother through the beating of her temples. "I'm fifteen years old. I just want to go to high school."

Caro and Zoë make an appointment to see Mr. Stein that afternoon. Caro apologizes and weeps. Zoë assures him that, before last night, Caro has never tasted liquor in her life. Caro weeps some more.

In the end, Mr. Stein agrees that she may remain in school.

"But don't ever try out for one of my plays again," he tells her.

At last it is summer. Caro is going to New York, to spend a month with her father and Meg and Adam. She can't wait to get out of Los Angeles. She can't wait to forget about *Bye, Bye, Birdie.* In New York, she can let all that go.

But when Caro gets off the plane and sees her father, she realizes it isn't going to be that easy.

Barton does not say much during the drive. He doesn't mention what happened, and Caro hopes that maybe he isn't ever going to.

But then, when they get to the apartment, he comes into her room while she is unpacking, and sits down on the bed.

"Caro," he says. "We have to talk."

He talks for an hour. On and on about how disappointed he is in her, about how she let not only herself, but her whole school down, about how drinking could ruin her entire life.

Caro sighs and looks out the window.

At last Meg comes in, but she isn't much better.

"Oh, Barton," she interrupts, putting a hand on his arm. "Caro doesn't need to hear all this. I'm sure it will never happen again. Let's all just have a great summer together." But her voice is anxious, and higher than usual.

Even Adam is not as much fun as he used to be. He is seven now. All he wants to do is play space monsters with his friends and watch television.

For the first few days of the visit, they all try. Barton comes home early from work. There's a trip to the movies and shopping excursions and a day out in Southampton. But for some reason, none of it is much fun.

Gradually, everyone stops trying so hard. Barton goes back to his usual hours. Meg goes back to helping at the women's shelter. Adam goes back to space monsters and television.

Caro spends a lot of time alone, wandering around New York. She thinks how much the city has changed. It used to be so exciting; now it's just crowded and dirty. But maybe she's the one who has changed.

She doesn't like to stay in the apartment, but there's nothing she really wants to go outside for. She ends up hanging around the building, going up and down stairs, looking into the electrical rooms, sitting on the balcony.

One day she goes out onto the roof, and finds that there is someone already there. He is a boy around her age, maybe a year or two older, with long blonde hair and ripped blue jeans.

"Hey," he says. He holds out a cigarette. "Want a smoke?"

Caro sits beside him and takes the cigarette. Even though his clothes are dirty, he smells clean.

"Do you live in this building?" he asks her.

"My family does."

He nods. "I know what you mean. Them, not me."

He shakes his head. "I'm splitting as soon as I can. Maybe by the end of the summer."

"Where will you go?"

"Montana. I'm going to work on a ranch."

For a moment, they are both silent, thinking of sunsets and red dust and the sound of cows.

"What's your name?"

"Caro."

"I've never seen you around here before."

"Well, I'm only here certain times."

"Lucky you."

"Yeah. This summer's been a drag."

He takes a long draw on his cigarette.

"I could—give you something. If you want."

"What do you mean?"

"So you'd have a better time."

"Oh."

Caro has never done drugs. She doesn't like the idea of being out of control. But now, if she got high, there would be nobody around to see her, nobody except this boy. She shrugs.

"What's your name, anyway?" she asks.

"Jordan."

She laughs. Jordan is also Mr. Stein's first name.

"All right," she says.

She and Jordan start meeting regularly on the roof.

"What kind of stuff do you want?" he asks her the second time they get together.

"Nothing that's going to fry my brain," she says. "I'm an actress."

So he gives her pot.

She likes it. She gets along fine on the skinny, sweet cigarettes. And if her eyes are glassy, if she says stupid things, she doesn't care.

When she's smoking out, New York seems beautiful again. There is wit and style all around her. One day she brings her portable record player up to the roof and plays Tristan's *Songs from Camelot.* The music is brittle and fragile and completely beautiful. Caro weeps and weeps.

Jordan tells her that his cash is running low—that if she wants to keep smoking, she'll have to come up with some money of her own. It isn't hard to get what she needs. She goes into her father's office one morning when everyone is out and finds a fifty at the back of a drawer.

At the beginning of July, Jordan tells her that he's going away for the long weekend.

"My parents are taking me camping." He makes a face.

"Well, have a good time," Caro says.

"I've got a present for you." He hands over two joints. "These should keep you going while I'm away."

Caro hides the joints in her room, in the bookcase behind the Monopoly game. She decides not to smoke them; for the days Jordan is gone, she will be the way she used to be. She will go on errands with Meg and play chess with her father and watch television with Adam. She won't go up to the roof at all.

The next morning at breakfast, Barton tells Meg, "I'll be home early tonight—we have to be at the Abbots' by seven thirty."

"Right." Meg says brightly. Caro can tell she had forgotten all about the date.

Sure enough, as soon as breakfast is over, Meg hurries into Caro's room.

"Oh, Caro," she says, "This Abbott thing completely slipped my mind—and there's no time to get a sitter. Would you be a doll and watch Adam while we're out? We won't be late, I promise."

"Of course I don't mind," Caro tells her.

The first hour is fun. Caro and Adam eat takeout pizza and watch two old *I Love Lucy* shows back-to-back.

Then Adam leaps up, face alight, the instant the second episode is over.

"Now can we play space monsters?"

Caro sighs. "Okay."

She does her best. She screeches and sneers, leaping out from the asteroid belt and chasing Adam all over the universe with her intergalactic sword. But after they've played for forty-five minutes, she falls back on the sofa.

"That's enough for me."

"Oh, please!" Adam wails, tugging at her sleeve. "Please! Just one more game!"

Caro jerks her arm away.

"No!" she says crossly. "I've had enough."

Adam looks crushed.

Caro sighs. "All right, all right," she tells him, more gently. "I'll play some more. But just give me a minute first."

She walks into her room and closes the door. She goes over to the bookcase and pulls out the Monopoly set. She feels for the joints she has hidden, pulls one out, and lights it. With a long sigh, she inhales.

There is instant peace; she can feel her whole body stretch and purr. She is ashamed that she yelled at Adam. But now she's relaxed; now she's calm. She can handle anything. She can play space monsters until midnight.

She hears the click of the door, but doesn't realize until she turns around that Adam is in the room.

"Caro?" he says softly.

Quickly, she hides the joint behind her back.

"Is that pot?" he asks matter-of-factly.

Caro's eyes fill with tears. What an incredible kid he is. No squealing, no prissiness. Just "Is that pot?"

"Yes."

He steps closer.

"What's it like?"

"Never mind." She laughs. "You'll find out soon enough."

He is laughing also. "Oh, please, Caro. Just one puff. Just one tiny little puff."

He pretends to be smoking a cigarette, and Caro giggles. He is so adorable—how can she say no?

She looks at him fondly. One puff wouldn't hurt him. It would do him good; make him relax. And it would make space monsters a whole lot more fun.

"All right," she says.

She holds out the joint to him.

The next few minutes happen in patches, in flashes of lightning. There is the door opening. There is Meg. And there is a lot of screaming.

The next day, Caro finds herself on an airplane, headed for Los Angeles.

Zoë sends her to counseling once a week. The counselor asks a lot of questions. What did Caro imagine that drugs would give her? What is it that she's missing from her life? Sometimes Caro tells her the truth. Other times, it's more fun to make up answers.

"Your daughter has a lot of issues she isn't willing to face," the counselor tells Zoë after the third session. "I don't think she's quite ready for this."

"What am I going to do with you?" Zoë bursts out.

Caro shrugs. "I'm not asking you to do anything."

She hangs around with kids at school she never hung around with before. They get high in the locker room. They get high behind the cafeteria. Caro doesn't often get high with them—she doesn't like the things it does to her head. But she still likes hanging around with that crowd. It's relaxing to be with people who don't expect anything of her.

"You're going to flunk out of school," Zoë rages. "You know that, don't you? And then what? What college is going to want you?"

"Maybe I don't want to go to college."

Zoë snorts. "Your father would kill you."

"It is better to apologize later than to ask permission before," Caro reminds her with a smile.

Caro is not invited to New York that summer.

* * *

It is February of her senior year. Caro is sitting in the cafeteria, staring at the rainbow wall. She can hear a group of kids behind her, talking about college—where they're applying, who was accepted early admission, who's going after a scholarship.

Caro is not applying to college. Her advisors say they could get her in somewhere—maybe a junior college—but she isn't interested. If she goes to college, she wants it to be the best—Harvard or Yale or Princeton. Otherwise, it's better to go nowhere.

"I'm taking some time off," she tells Zoë.

"Oh, you are, are you?" Zoë says tightly. "Well, you'd better plan on making some money while you're doing it. I'm not going to support you forever."

"Don't worry," Caro says haughtily. "You won't have to."

She thinks about getting a job. She watches salesgirls at Judy's and waitresses at Hamburger Hamlet. She wonders if, six months from now, that's what she'll be doing, too.

It is depressing to realize that the most interesting thing about her was *A Tree Grows in Brooklyn*—and that happened six years ago. Maybe, six years from now, that will still be the most interesting thing about her. Maybe that will be the most interesting thing about her for the rest of her life.

A boy comes into the cafeteria, a transfer student. Caro is always seeing him around. She's not sure why she notices him—he isn't particularly handsome. Maybe it's because he always looks so angry.

He sees her looking at him. He hesitates, then walks over to her table.

"Hi," he says. "I'm Daniell. Spelled with two ls."

"Was that your idea?"

He nods.

"I'm Caro."

"Like the syrup."

She makes a face. "I'm not so sweet."

He sits down. "I don't know what I'm even doing in this fucking place."

She shrugs. "It's only four months till graduation."

"Then the real shit begins."

"College?"

He rolls his eyes. "My father's funded a building in just about every goddam school in the country, so that I can have a choice."

Caro smiles sourly. "Pretty cool. And what's your choice?"

"Not college."

She looks at him quickly, interested.

"Really?"

"Yeah. I want to do something that's worth a damn. I'd like to join the Peace Corps. Or go off somewhere. Maybe join a commune."

Caro nods, but she knows exactly what Daniell's future will be. He will go to college. He will probably become a banker. And by the time he is thirty, there will only be one l in his name.

Caro does not want to go to her graduation.

"You're going," Zoë informs her. "This is a big deal."

Caro snorts. "No, it isn't."

"It is to me," Zoë tells her with dignity. "I never graduated from high school."

Caro agrees to go to the graduation.

Barton and Meg and Adam do not attend.

As Caro stands in the line to get her diploma, she remembers her first day at Beverly, and Zoë saying happily, "It'll be such a fresh start for you."

She wonders how she managed to ruin it all.

Caro looks around at the other girls in her class. Some are weeping because they hate to leave; others are calm, with the prospect of a wonderful college to go to in September. She looks away.

When she is handed her diploma, it feels unreal, like a joke, like a theater prop.

She spends the summer sitting around the house.

"My God!" Zoë explodes. "You're driving me crazy. Every time I see you, you're on your behind. Get up—do something! What about some acting?" she demands. "Maybe a little theater? Do you want me to try to set something up?"

"No!" Caro screams.

Everyone in the play says you stink.

You have no talent—no talent whatsoever.

She doesn't want to act ever again. She isn't good enough—she simply isn't good enough.

"What about the agency?" Zoë goes on. "How would you like to work with me?"

Caro puts her hands over her ears and runs out of the house.

She hitches a ride to the park on Beverly Glen. She goes to the playground and stays there all afternoon, swinging slowly on the swings.

"Hey!" A voice is calling her.

Caro turns to look. It is Daniell. She hasn't seen him since graduation.

"Hi," she says. "What are you doing here?"

"I was driving by, and I saw you. How's your summer going?"

She makes a face. "Yours?"

He smiles. "It's been great. A friend of mine from San Francisco's starting a commune. Up near Oakland."

"Terrific," she says.

"And I'm going to join it."

Caro gapes. "Really?"

"Yeah."

"But weren't you going to U.S.C?"

He shrugs. "Not anymore."

Caro stares at him respectfully.

"I never thought you'd really do something like that."

He smiles self-consciously.

"Neither did I."

There is a pause.

"So what's your commune going to be like?"

He thinks about this for a moment.

"Like paradise," he finally says.

Caro starts swinging again. She swings higher and higher. Then, at the very top of the arc, she calls down to him.

"Can I come, too?"

CAROLINE

Caroline and Graham choose the first Saturday in June for their wedding. They'll go to Hawaii for a two-week honeymoon, and then Graham will start his new job at Steiner & Ross. Caroline does not yet have a job; she isn't sure what she wants to do. Graham says there is no rush to decide.

They plan a simple ceremony at a justice's office in midtown Manhattan. Caroline buys a white ankle-length silk dress at Bonwit Teller. It does not look like a wedding gown.

Only immediate family and close friends have been invited.

Zoë arrives in town, with tears and presents, in time for the wedding rehearsal.

"My darling!" she cries, embracing Caroline.

She kisses Meg gently. "We meet at last."

Then she turns to Barton. "You're looking ridiculously handsome."

It is the first time Caroline has ever seen her mother and father together.

Zoë invites the entire wedding party for drinks at the Waldorf-Astoria, where she is staying. Afterward, she asks Caroline and Graham to dinner at the Russian Tea Room.

"I think we're supposed to be seeing Graham's mother tonight," Caroline says.

"Well, cancel it," Zoë tells her. "This is my first chance to get to know my son-in-law."

* * *

Zoë is charming during dinner. She tells wonderful stories and drinks a great deal of vodka.

When the meal is over, she gives Graham a playful push. "Now go on back to your mother," she says. "Shoo." She kisses his cheek. "I want a few minutes alone with my daughter, while she still is my daughter."

Zoë and Caroline walk arm-in-arm back to the Waldorf-Astoria. They talk about the wedding, and New York, and Zoë's latest batch of child actors.

When they reach the hotel room, Zoë sits down on the couch. She pulls out a cigarette.

"Your Graham is absolutely adorable, by the way," she says. "Such a sweetie."

"I agree." Caroline smiles.

"But he's completely wrong for you."

Caroline stares at her mother. Zoë sighs and looks blandly at her fingernails. "And if you marry him, my darling, you're going to ruin your life."

CARO

"You must be absolutely mad," Zoë says flatly.

"No," Caro tells her. "This is what I want to do."

"You want to act," Zoë insists. "*That's* what you want to do."

"No," Caro says through gritted teeth.

"You're a coward. That's your problem. And this ridiculous commune nonsense—it's just a delaying tactic."

Caro puts her hands over her ears.

"I'm not listening to you!" she screeches. "Don't you get it—I'm doing this whether you like it or not."

Zoë sighs. She is silent for a long moment.

"Well," she says at last. "You're eighteen years old. If this is really what you want, I'm not going to stop you."

"Thank you," Caro tells her stiffly.

Zoë's eyes fill with tears.

"But, darling, it kills me to see you ruining your life."

PART FOUR

SONGS FROM CAMELOT

CAROLINE

Caroline is lying on a lounge chair by the hotel pool, wearing her red bikini. Almost no one else is around—no one but the couple Graham has nicknamed "Jack Sprat and his wife." The husband is small and skinny, the wife enormous. Caroline likes them. They have all smiled at one another in the hallway and the dining room. She knows that they are newlyweds, too.

Graham is in the pool. Caroline drinks her piña colada and watches him. He is a beautiful swimmer. Anyone can see, looking at his crisp and even strokes, all the years of country club instructions he has received.

His last lap finished, he pulls himself onto the ladder and grins at her.

I am a married woman, Caroline tells herself, and this handsome man who swims so well is my husband.

Caroline is not a tropics person. She had hoped they could honeymoon in London or Rome, but Graham preferred to go somewhere peaceful. Nina suggested Maui, where she and Graham's father had gone on their honeymoon, and Graham liked the symmetry of that.

He gets out of the pool and sits on the chaise beside Caroline. "Give me twenty minutes to shower and get dressed, then we'll leave for Lahaina."

Caroline nods, hiding a smile. Graham is having a hard time relaxing. Every day, he has been organizing excursions—to the volcano, to the aquarium, to the whaling village. He has snorkeled, played golf, and rented a speedboat. By now, they have almost run out of things to do. It is perhaps a good thing that the honeymoon will be over in two more days.

"Aw, come on! It's not that cold!"

Caroline looks up. Jack Sprat is trying to drag his wife over to the pool.

"I just had my hair done!" she squeals.

They get to the lip of the pool, lose their balance, and fall in with a splash. They come up, sputtering, laughing. She mock hits him. He dunks her. She comes up. They look at each other for a long moment, and then they kiss.

"God," Graham murmurs. "That was something I didn't need to see."

But it gives Caroline shivers, the way that fat young woman was looking at that tiny freckled man.

The honeymoon is over. Caroline and Graham have returned to the mainland. Caroline shakes out her red bikini to find Maui sand still in the crevices.

She and Graham spend a few days at Nina's house in Philadelphia. It is the first time, in all the years that she has visited, that Caroline has been allowed to sleep in the same room as Graham.

Now she knows she's really married.

Sunday afternoon, they take the train to New York, and a taxi to their new apartment on West 54th Street.

The apartment was Graham's find. Back in the spring, he had given the job to Caroline, and she had spent her Easter vacation looking for the perfect place. On the last day, she had found it.

"It's this wonderful little walk-up in the Bay Ridge area of Brooklyn," she told Graham. "Owned by the dearest old couple. They said they'd—"

"Ah, but I've got something even better," Graham interrupted her. "Something came up at work today. One of the guys in the office is going to let us in on a building we've just finished. West side, terrific address, and renovated by the greatest firm in town." He grinned at her. "So what do you have to say to that?"

"Sounds great," she told him lightly.

She does not much care for the new apartment.

They ride up in the elevator. Graham carries Caroline over the threshold. The boxes they have stored line the living room. Caroline begins to unpack, but Graham stops her.

"This is not the way I want to spend the first night in our new home." He kisses her on the neck.

It is one o'clock in the morning. Caroline can't sleep. Finally, quietly, she gets up.

"What are you doing?" Graham asks in the darkness.

"Trying to find some paper and a pencil."

"Why on Earth?"

"I need to make a list."

"A list of what?"

"Everything I've got to do."

There is laughter in his voice. "And what have you got to do?"

She doesn't like the laughter. "Buy a sofa, get some curtains. Have the shower door fixed, find a dining room set—"

"Oh, boy," he says.

"And then I've got to think about getting a job."

"You know what you remind me of?" She can see his dark shape sitting up on the mattress. "A top. One of those old-fashioned humming tops. Flying around all over the place."

Caroline likes the image. It is pleasing to see herself in motion like that—to think that she is going so fast that there are no individual colors left, only an intriguing blur.

"Now come back to bed," he says.

The humming top spins on. Caroline is out all day, every day. She buys decorating magazines and checks out library books and visits designer showrooms. She brings home wallpaper samples and swatches of fabric and color wheels. But she can't pull the apartment together. She can't get a focus. She can't make any choices.

Graham is getting impatient. He is tired of living out of boxes. "Just pretend it's a dollhouse," he groans.

From then on, it's easy. She knows exactly what dining room set to buy, what carpet to choose, what color to paint the walls.

Finally, there is only one task left to do. Caroline telephones her father and arranges to have all the things from her old room taken out of storage.

The furniture and sealed boxes arrive and are piled up in the hallway. Caroline goes around, lightly touching the painted headboard, the scarred chest of drawers, the little step stool. Then she kneels by the boxes. For a moment, she doesn't allow herself to open them, but finally she cuts the tape on the first box and starts to pull out the contents. There is her flowered tea set—all her books. Her chessboard, her Madame Alexander dolls. The photo of herself and Zoë eating ice cream. Her Sambo. Her Jumbo. A painted paper tortoise Adam made.

She sits down on the carpet and hugs the things to her.

The apartment is finished. There is no more reason for Caroline to spend her days looking at fabric swatches and Florentine end tables.

It is time now to find a job, but she still doesn't know what she wants to do. Maybe in a year or two, she'll go back to school and get a master's, but not right now. For now, she just wants something that will help with the rent—nothing too ambitious.

One day, she is walking along 59th Street. She sees a HELP WANTED sign in the window of a small architectural bookstore. The sign has been done in beautiful calligraphy, with the W drawn to look like an upside-down flying buttress. Caroline goes inside. She comes out, half an hour later, with the job.

She works at the store four mornings a week. She catalogues books, shelves new arrivals, assists the shop's few customers. The boss is Laszlo, a middle-aged European man with sad gray eyes. He is kind to Caroline; he sometimes brings her back to his office for a glass of tea and a hard biscuit. She wonders, amused, if he might have a small crush on her.

She also gets on well with Gina and Peter, the two other employees. Gina can be a little remote, preoccupied with a thesis paper, but Peter is a lot of fun. He's only killing time here, he tells Caroline, just waiting to inherit a fortune from his billionaire grandfather. He and Caroline often have lunch together at a coffee shop around the corner.

Caroline likes her job. It's safe and sleepy in the bookstore—it reminds her of being back in the art library at Yale.

The spinning top hums on. Now that the apartment is decorated, Graham has started bringing home friends from the office. There is Mike and Oliver, Glenn and Sandra. They meet for brunch on Sundays and attend gallery openings on Friday nights. It is a busy social life.

Caroline makes trays of hors d'oeuvres, fixes drinks, defrosts miniature cheesecakes.

She notices that all the men seem to be a version of Graham. And their wives, or girlfriends, remind Caroline of the girls she went to boarding school with. She finds this ironic. She had supposed her life to be going forward—she had not expected to double back on the same people.

Fall comes. It must have come last year, too, but Caroline had been so busy that she didn't particularly notice. This year, she notices. All around her are "Back to School" sales, store windows full of clunky oxfords, sharp pencils, empty notebooks. She goes into a dime store and buys a binder, but she has nothing to put in it.

"I want to go 'back to school,' too," she tells her friend Peter with an embarrassed laugh. "Whatever that means for me now. But I feel like I've reached the top class with nowhere to go."

"God, you're depressing me," he says.

Caroline tries to get herself energized. She buys guidebooks to New York, and pretends she is a tourist. She visits hidden little corners of the city. After that, she gets involved in the Three Mile Island crisis, and joins an organization to stop the building of nuclear power stations. After that, she starts taking classes. She takes calligraphy, watercolor, Chinese cooking. Now she is thinking of joining a gym.

One day, on her way home from work, she walks down Lexington Avenue and passes a shop that sells antique toys. She goes inside. The proprietor is showing a customer an old-fashioned spinning top. The top is whirling busily on the counter; Caroline smiles at the speed and the blur of color. But then the top slows down—and when it finally stops, Caroline can see that the wood is old and cracked, and that the colors are faded and streaked.

* * *

While reading the newspaper at breakfast, Caroline notices that a production has just opened off Broadway, a stage version of *A Tree Grows in Brooklyn.*

She gives a cry. "I'd love to see that!"

"It got lousy reviews," Graham tells her.

"I don't mind. When I was a little girl, that was my favorite television show in the world."

She thinks of those Thursday evenings, that hour of perfect safety, sitting in her father's leather chair, watching those sweet stories with their happy endings.

"I can't tell you how much I loved it."

Graham can see that Caroline has her heart set on seeing the play, and her birthday is coming up. He buys two tickets.

As the reviews had warned, *A Tree Grows in Brooklyn* is blandly directed, and the performances are mawkish and predictable.

"Well, that was a complete waste of an evening," Graham says as they leave the theater.

"Not for me." Caroline sighs. "It was absolutely inspiring. If I could play any part in the world, I think I'd choose Katie Nolan."

He is looking at her curiously.

"If you could play any part in the world?" he repeats.

She flushes. "What a strange thing to say."

A few days later, Caroline is doing some inventory work at the front of the bookstore. A scruffy young man walks in, carrying a bulging satchel.

"I was wondering if I could put a flyer in your front window."

"I guess that depends on what it's for."

"It's for a new theater company my friends are starting—the

Eastside/Westside Playhouse. We're having our first meeting on Thursday."

"Sure," Caroline says. "You can put that up."

After he leaves, Peter sidles over.

"Papa Laszlo's not going to be happy," he tells her. "You know how he feels about flyers in his window."

But Caroline does not hear him. She is studying the piece of paper.

Thursday afternoon, Graham calls to say that some out-of-town clients have asked him to dinner, and that he probably won't be home till midnight.

Caroline makes herself a sandwich, takes a bath, gets in her nightgown, and settles down for a quiet evening reading. Then all at once, she puts the book down. She gets up, gets dressed, and takes a taxi to the first meeting of the Eastside/Westside Playhouse.

The meeting is being held in what seems to be an abandoned dance studio. It is filled with men and women all wearing jeans and dark turtlenecks, and talking intensely. They seem very young—Caroline is startled to realize that most of the group is actually around her own age. She sees the boy who put up the poster in the bookstore, and gives him a little wave.

A dark man with a beard claps his hands and calls for attention. Everyone sits down on folding chairs or on the floor.

"First of all, thank you for coming," the man begins in a hurried, clipped voice. "I'm Chad Levitt, the director of this would-be enterprise."

He goes on to tell them his goals for the theater: to find meaningful, resonant plays—consciousness-raising scripts by Symboliste masters or modern works by talented new playwrights—and to present them in an atmosphere of integrity and supportiveness. Everyone applauds, including Caroline. The goals seem dreamy and naive to her. Still, she likes them, and she likes the young man.

"And for our first play, my committee and I have decided to put on Neil Simon's *Barefoot in the Park.*"

There are outraged boos from the audience.

Chad holds up a hand.

"Not so fast," he says. "It's all part of our strategy. We're a new company, and we want to get this theater on its feet. We need to start building an audience. Bring the people in with the surefire hits, and then next season, we give them Strindberg."

Several people stand up and stalk out.

Caroline stays. She has nothing against *Barefoot in the Park.* She saw the play once, and thought the story was cute—newlyweds who find out that marriage isn't quite what they had been expecting.

Chad is passing out a stack of xeroxed pages.

"This is the audition packet," he says. "It's pretty self-explanatory. If you want to try out for Corie or Paul, you'll be auditioning with the first scene. Valesco and Mother, that's the second. Minor characters, you'll read the part of the repairman—that's scene three."

When the stack of pages gets to Caroline, she takes a set. It's a lot easier than explaining that she's only here out of curiosity.

She glances through the first scene, the one between the young couple. It's not Neil Simon at his best, perhaps, but the line about the mother being dragged to the harbor for a bowl of sheep dip makes her smile.

"So," Chad is calling as the people rise to leave. "Auditions tomorrow night, same time, same place. Sign up on the sheet if you're interested. Read the material over tonight. You don't have to make up your mind until tomorrow who you want to read for."

Caroline stands up to go. A crowd is gathering around the sign-up sheet; everyone is talking excitedly.

The scruffy boy comes up to her. "Hi."

"I'm sorry," she tells him, "I don't know your name."

"It's Tim."

They shake hands formally.

"Who are you auditioning for?" he asks.

"Nobody," Caroline says. "I'm not an actress. I'm just here out of curiosity."

"I'm going for the repairman," Tim tells her.

"Well, good luck."

He studies her. "You're really not going to audition?"

"No. I'd never get a part, and even if I did, I wouldn't have the time for it. Things are so busy."

After Tim signs his name and leaves, Caroline lingers. She goes over this "so busy life" of hers. A part-time job at the bookstore. Waiting for Graham to come home from work. Weekends with his friends.

She hesitates. She goes over to the sign-up sheet. It would be fun to write her name, to go for the audition.

She remembers something Zoë had once told her a long time ago, when her father hadn't let her do that television commercial: Never mind. Talent will out.

It would be interesting to find out if she did have any talent.

Caroline reaches for the pen, and starts to write her name. She gets as far as "Caroline," and then she stops. She doesn't want to write down "Caroline Moss." Auditioning for a play isn't something Caroline Moss would do. Finally she writes "Caroline Andrews."

She finishes the signature with a flourish.

The following day, she makes a deal with herself. If Graham doesn't call to say he'll be home late, she won't go to the audition—if he does call, she'll go. At five o'clock, Graham telephones—there's going to be another dinner with the out-of-town clients. At six o'clock, Caroline is back at the dance studio.

She decides to audition for the part of Corie. Chad gives her the cues for the test scene. When they're finished, he tells her to do the speech about the mother again, this time showing a little more concern. Caroline does it again, trying to show a little more concern.

"Thank you," is all he says when she's finished.

She doesn't get a phone call that evening. Though she tells herself she isn't disappointed, she is. Then, the following morning, as she is about to leave for the bookstore, the phone rings. It is Chad, telling her that she has gotten the lead in *Barefoot in the Park.*

Caroline hangs up the phone and sits back down on the sofa. She has a vision of herself, putting, with great deliberation, a big black spanner in the wheel of her life. But she knows she is going to do the play.

Caroline is completely distracted at work that day. All she can think about is *Barefoot in the Park.* She tells Peter the news, and he gives her shoulder a delighted little punch.

"I always thought you had that prima donna thing going."

After work, Caroline is too restless to go home. She stays in midtown, window-shopping, wandering through Central Park. At five o'clock, she goes down 58th Street. She passes a bar called The Parrot. She's walked by it before, but has never been inside—she does not go to bars. But this afternoon, it looks warm and bright. And her feet hurt.

Caroline walks up to the bar and sits down on a stool.

The bartender smiles at her.

"What'll it be?"

She likes the look of him. He is middle-aged, heavily built, with thick, curling gray hair and a peaceful face.

"I'll have a glass of white wine." Caroline laughs a little awkwardly. "I don't usually drink, but I got some good news today. I'm going to be in a play—*Barefoot in the Park.*"

"Well, well, well. Congratulations." He pours the wine and gives it to her. "This is on the house."

Caroline takes the glass. "That's very kind. But I don't know that it warrants much of a celebration—we're talking about a show that's opening in a warehouse. Probably one that's been condemned."

"It's still wonderful news."

She goes on to tell him more—about Chad, and the company, and the play. The bartender listens, nods. When she finishes the glass of wine, he tells her to come in again.

"I'd love to hear how rehearsals are going. I'm Mike, by the way. This is my place."

He smiles at her.

Caroline is suddenly aware that she would like to come back to the bar and tell this man Mike how rehearsals are going.

She stands up quickly.

"I don't really live near here," she says. "But thanks, anyway. And thanks for the wine."

When Caroline gets back to the apartment, Graham is already home. She makes herself kiss him with real focus.

"To what do I owe this honor?" he asks.

"Sit down," she tells him. "I've got some really crazy news." And she goes into the whole story, about the Eastside/Westside Playhouse and auditioning and getting the part of Corie in *Barefoot in the Park.*

Graham is silent. Caroline can't tell from his face what he is thinking.

"Well, that's great," he says at last. "I've always thought you had a secret yen to act."

But she can tell that he is just being a good husband, that he is not terribly pleased by the news.

"Are you really okay with this?" she asks him in bed that night. "Because I can always say no."

"Of course I don't want you to say no," he tells her quickly. "I think it's great."

"And the rehearsal schedule isn't that bad. It's only a few nights a week, and I shouldn't get home later than nine. Except for the week before opening; that'll be crazy."

"Don't you worry," he pats her shoulder. "Listen—you've been great about all my late nights; the least I can do is be supportive about this. I'll bring the whole office down to see your opening."

Caroline is grateful for Graham's reaction. She turns toward him and starts to stroke his arm. But he rolls onto his other side.

"I've got an early meeting tomorrow," he tells her.

Rehearsals begin. There are fights every night. Chad screams. Caroline screams back. They argue endlessly over the "fuddy-duddy" speech in act 3. When Caroline goes home afterward and thinks about what happened, she cannot believe she has let herself get so upset. But at the next rehearsal, it happens again.

"I don't know what's wrong with me," she says to Tim one evening.

He looks at her in surprise. "Nothing's wrong," he says. "You're just an actress."

Caroline is taken aback. An actress?

Never mind. Talent will out.

As the weeks go on, rehearsals start running later and later; often, by the time Caroline gets home at night, she finds Graham already in bed. Chad has also begun scheduling weekend rehearsals, so she is no longer able to go to the brunches and the art gallery openings.

"I'm sorry," Caroline tells Graham repeatedly. "I never dreamed it would take so much time—but once the play opens, things will calm down, I promise."

He only nods.

At last, it is opening night. Caroline has overheard Graham making a call to a florist, and she knows that he has done the nice husband thing.

"Now don't expect too much," she tells him for the fifth time. "Remember, it's just an amateur production."

"I know you'll be great," he says brightly.

As Caroline is about to come onstage for her first entrance, she sees Graham in the second row of the audience. She can tell from his face that something is wrong. It must be the tiny theater, or the rickety set. She had warned him, but he hadn't listened. He is embarrassed that she is in this play. She has shamed him in front of his friends.

Caroline takes a breath, forces her look away, and makes her entrance.

After the play is over, Graham and his buddies come backstage. Mike and Oliver, Glenn and Sandra all tell Caroline she was wonderful; Graham is silent. He carries a bunch of flowers in his arms, but does not give them to her.

They say good-bye to everyone and walk away from the theater.

"What's wrong?" Caroline finally asks Graham.

He says nothing.

"I warned you it wasn't going to be exactly professional."

"I don't give a damn about how professional it was," Graham says coldly. He pulls out a crumpled program from his pocket, and opens it to the cast bios.

"Caroline Andrews," he reads. "This is Caroline's first appearance onstage. But theater is in her blood—her mother, Zoë Andrews, has had a long career as a children's agent." Not only don't you mention me, not only haven't you given me a thought since this damned play began, but you don't even use your married name in the program."

Caroline is speechless. She reaches up and puts her arms around Graham.

"Oh, darling," she says finally, "I'm so sorry. I just thought it would be more appropriate. I'll write a new bio tomorrow. And I'll use my married name from now on, I promise—I'm very, very proud of being Caroline Moss."

Graham shrugs her off.

They walk another block in silence, and then he adds that he's sorry if he's overreacted. Stiffly, he hands her the bunch of flowers.

The show runs for another six weekends. Caroline is relieved when the last performance comes up. The play has taken too much of her time, too much of her attention. In an odd way, it's even taken too much of her personality. Sometimes when she's talking to Graham, she realizes she's answering him not as herself, but as Corie.

Well, all that was ending now. And she won't do any more plays.

There is a cast party after the final performance. Chad makes an announcement.

"Good news. We let the world know we're here, and now we can afford to move up the food chain a little. Our next production will be Shaw's *Arms and the Man.*"

There is jubilant applause.

"Let's drink a toast!"

"To *Arms and the Man!*" everyone cries.

"To *Arms and the Man!*" Caroline echoes, but her hands remain at her sides.

* * *

In May, Zoë comes for an unexpected visit. She is in town for a long weekend, to recruit some young performers for a revival of *Oliver!*

Caroline shows off her busy new life for her mother. She brings her to the bookshop and introduces her to Laszlo and Gina and Peter, she cooks her a Chinese meal, she shows her everything she's done with the apartment. Zoë is full of praise and lack of interest.

The morning of her return flight, she comes over to say good-bye.

"Won't you stay for a cup of tea?" Caroline asks her.

"I'm sorry, darling—I wish I had the time."

"But I've got Petit Ecolier cookies!"

Zoë smiles. "In that case, I'd be a fool to refuse."

Caroline goes into the kitchen. When she comes out with the tea tray a few minutes later, she sees Zoë standing by the desk. In her hand is a crumpled copy of the *Barefoot in the Park* program.

"Why didn't you tell me about this?"

Caroline puts down the tray.

"There really wasn't anything to tell," she says. "It was a terrible little production."

Zoë nods. "Where's the script?" she asks.

Caroline laughs with embarrassment. "Zoë, what are you doing?"

"Get the script," Zoë tells her.

Caroline goes into the bedroom and finds her copy of *Barefoot in the Park.*

Zoë takes it and sits down on the sofa. She puts on her reading glasses.

"Let's hear your first scene," she says.

"This is ridiculous. You have a plane to catch."

"The first line is yours," Zoë rides over her. "You come into the apartment, put your flower in the paint can, and the downstairs buzzer rings."

Caroline goes over to an imaginary intercom.

"Hello?"

With her mother giving her the cues, she does the scene.

Zoë puts down the script, takes off her glasses. She looks thoughtful. Her voice is sad.

"You could have been an actress," she says.

She leaves soon afterward to catch her plane. Caroline stands in the empty living room a moment. Tears run down her face.

You could have been an actress.

She picks up her purse and walks quickly over to 58th Street, to The Parrot.

CARO

Smoothly, Caro lifts two cans of soup from the supermarket shelf and drops them down into her large raffia purse. After four months in the commune, she's become quite expert at stealing.

She does it as if she's playing a part—she's a young housewife learning to shop on a budget. Hesitantly, she'll pick up a can or a vegetable, and weigh it in her hand as if she's not sure she's chosen well; then, when no one is looking, down it goes into her bag.

She moves to the front of the store, to pay for the lentils and orange juice and cookies in her grocery cart. Nelle will make cracks about the cookies, and say that Caro shouldn't be trusted to do the shopping; but these are Petit Ecolier cookies, Zoë's favorite.

Caro leaves the market and goes back to the street where the dented blue truck is waiting.

"That took long enough." Nelle, sitting in the driver's seat, makes a big production of rubbing her arms. "It's freezing out here."

"Sorry," Caro says.

She is amused, more than anything else, by Nelle. Nelle is in love with Daniell, and Daniell has a crush on Caro.

It would be so easy to tell Nelle not to worry, that she isn't in the least interested in Daniell, but Caro doesn't do it. The whole point of this commune is supposed to be about sharing; besides, Nelle is a bitch and deserves to suffer a little.

Caro hums the theme song from *Mission, Impossible* as they ride along the dusty roads. She misses television a lot.

"Do you mind not doing that?" Nelle snaps.

"Sorry," Caro says again, and stops.

"It makes me nervous. I'm worn out getting the place ready for your visitor."

Caro remembers a favorite old joke:

Who was that lady I saw you with? That was no lady, that was my wife.

"That's no visitor," she tells Nelle. "That's my mother."

Nelle is not amused. "I still don't think she should be coming," she bursts out. "Our first rule is no contamination."

They are pulling into the commune now. Caro looks around at the small faded house, the rusty iron fence, the yard furred with weeds.

"My mother won't stay long enough to contaminate anything," she tells Nelle. "Believe me. She'll take one look at this place and run away screaming."

Zoë's train isn't due until four o'clock; Caro feels restless all afternoon. She goes outside and brings the ancient lawn mower into the shed. She tidies the living room, picks Colleen and Nelle's underwear up from the floor. She goes into the bathroom and starts scrubbing out the toilet.

Joey comes in and laughs. "What are you doing? Trying to impress your mother?"

Caro flushes. "Of course not," she says. "Toilets do need cleaning occasionally."

He unzips his fly and pees into the bowl.

Caro looks down at the yellow stain. She decides she'll leave it there after all.

She walks outside into the gray, sullen day. A headache is starting at the back of her neck. She very much wishes that Zoë weren't coming.

"But, darling, you're my daughter," Zoë had pleaded. "I need to know you're all right."

"Honestly, I'm fine."

"But I want to make sure. You've got no phone, I haven't heard your voice in weeks. I just want to see you. Please. Just for the weekend. An overnight, even. I could take the train up. Please."

"I need to talk to the others. We have rules here."

The most important rule was the "no contamination" one, but Daniell had said Caro could break it, just this once. She wished he had said no—now her mother would be here in less than an hour.

It was going to be awful. Zoë would be absolutely horrified. She would never be able to see beyond the filthy house and weed-filled lawn, never be able to understand how Caro could live in such a place.

But Caro would take her mother by the shoulders and say, "Listen to me, Zoë; I am happier than I have ever been in my life."

And it was true. Living in this filthy house, working in this beat-up yard, living with this group of people who didn't care a damn about money or fame, Caro had found contentment.

She stretches in the frigid air. The headache is a little better now. She remembers the girl who had come to this commune four months ago—useless, unhappy, bitter. Then she pictures herself now. She has learned to plant a garden and drive a stick shift and use a sewing machine. She has learned to plan menus and to cook and to steal from grocery stores.

Her mother will just have to understand—Caro has finally grown up.

Zoë is the first one off the train. Caro had been expecting her to be wearing the usual silk dress and high heels, but Zoë is sporting blue jeans and a corduroy jacket. She holds out her arms and kisses Caro warmly.

"I think this life agrees with you," she says. "You've never looked more adorable."

For some reason, Caro is a little disappointed by the praise.

Zoë hops into the old pickup truck.

"How absolutely marvelous!" she cries, patting the dashboard. "It's just like the one my Uncle Oliver had when I was little. Oh, do let me drive!"

She drives it well—better than Caro. They head back toward the commune. Zoë raves about everything she sees.

"Will you look at that elm? Utterly beautiful. Do you have any at your place?—we must get a cutting.

"Oh, and, my God, that fence over there! It's sheer Norman Rockwell."

Caro's headache starts up again. At last they arrive at the commune. Zoë pulls up in front and slowly gets out.

"So this is where my baby lives." She stares in silence, and then nods. "I can see it," she says. "I can definitely see it."

Caro takes her inside. Zoë seems surprised by nothing—not the holes in the living room ceiling, not the dirty mattresses on the floor.

"I can't get over the air." She thumps her chest and beams at Caro. "I feel a week being added to my life every time I take a breath."

At five o'clock, it is time for dinner. The gong is sounded and the members of the commune come in to sit at the long pine table.

"This is my mother, Zoë Andrews," Caro says formally.

Daniell and Frank and Colleen smile at her. Nelle and Joey and Marcia only nod.

Zoë motions toward the soup. "This looks absolutely delicious."

"We help ourselves here," Nelle tells her. "We don't have servants."

Zoë picks up her cracked bowl and takes a large portion.

"It's wonderful!" she exclaims, taking a spoonful. "I'd love to have the recipe—who made it?"

"Caro," Daniell tells her.

Zoë stares at Caro. "You? Honey, I had no idea! You're just blossoming in all directions. Honestly, if you could have seen her six months ago," she smiles at the others. "Couldn't make herself a cup of tea."

Caro flushes.

The soup is eaten, the bowls are taken away.

"There's only fruit for dessert," Nelle informs Zoë, before Caro has a chance to mention the Petit Ecolier cookies. "We don't believe in refined sugar here."

"That's fine with me," Zoë tells her. "I've been trying to cut back."

Suddenly, Joey speaks up.

"Uh—Zoë? Are you really a Hollywood agent?"

"Yes."

He gives a shy little shrug. "It must be fun, working with all those hotshots."

Zoë considers. "Well, I don't know that 'fun' is exactly the word I'd use. Yesterday, I had a meeting with some ABC execs, and you wouldn't believe what happened . . ." And she is off.

She tells story after story, about Hollywood and actors, and the bratty child stars she works with. Caro grows more and more embarrassed–why won't her mother stop talking?

But when she looks covertly around the room, she sees, to her surprise that everyone seems to be riveted by Zoë's stories. Even Nelle.

"Have you ever met Clint Eastwood?"

"Sure." Zoë shrugs. "As a matter of fact, Clint and I dated for a while. But I make it a rule not to get too serious about actors—even though I must say, Clint does have a brain in his head."

"And what about Robert Redford? Did you date him?"

"Alas, no. The man's far too faithful for his own good. But let me tell you about Richard Burton!"

The group leans in to listen. Caro stands up abruptly. She cannot stand any more of this.

She stalks into the bedroom. This is reality, these lumpy beds and rusted headboards; this is what life is—not the sham, overblown Hollywood world her mother is talking about. She sits down, takes some deep breaths, and feels better.

When she comes back into the living room, she finds her mother sitting behind Nelle, fixing her hair in a pompadour.

"Actually, you have the face for it," Zoë is telling her. "Have you ever considered modeling?"

"Well, actually," Nelle simpers, "I've always wanted to be an actress."

"Fancy that," Zoë says. "And why on Earth, with your looks, would you let a dream like that get away?"

Caro leaves the room again. She goes outside, sits on the front steps, and bursts into tears. Zoë has ruined everything. She has Daniell laughing at her stories. Nelle sitting at her feet. Colleen asking questions about Steve McQueen. It is absolutely sickening. The whole ethos of the group has been shown up. They have all been seduced, demeaned.

She realizes she will never be able to think of them in quite the same way again.

Caro stands up. As she goes back into the house, she knows that her days at the commune have come to an end. And she understands something else as well—that it is not the group who has been changed. Zoë's siren song has not wooed the others at all—it has called only to Caro.

She is given a farewell party with a homemade applesauce cake, but she suspects that nobody will miss her very much. Nelle, sitting close to Daniell tonight, seems especially unmoved by the prospect of Caro's departure. There is talk of writing letters, but Caro doubts that this will happen.

She gets on the train with her duffle bag, and stares out the window the entire ride back to Los Angeles. She tells herself that the last four months were by no means a waste—she did not make a mistake in joining the commune. She had been mistaken only in her intent. Once again she had been performing a role—this time the role of a girl dropping out of society. And now the season had simply ended.

Her mother is waiting at the train station in her white Mercedes.

"You need a bath," Zoë says.

In September, Caro comes to Zoë and tells her that she is planning to move to New York City.

"Why?" Zoë asks cautiously. "Is some other commune opening up?"

"No," Caro says. "This time it's Broadway."

Zoë claps her hands and hugs Caro hard.

"Well, I must say, it's taken you long enough—but I couldn't be more delighted."

Zoë goes into immediate action. She buys Caro an East Coast wardrobe, and takes her to Roberto at Elizabeth Arden for a more sophisticated hairstyle. She goes through theater guides and culls them for possible agents. Finally, there is nothing left to do but make the plane reservation.

"Do you want a one-way ticket or a return trip?"

"A one-way ticket," Caro says.

Zoë is satisfied.

"It sounds like you're serious."

"I am."

"Good."

At the airport, Zoë gives Caro money for her first six months' rent.

"Now knock 'em dead."

She hugs her good-bye, and Caro starts for the gate.

"When you get your first lead, I'm coming to see you," Zoë calls after her. "But I'm not flying out for chorus."

"Are you going to New York on business?" the woman in the seat next to Caro asks. She is in her seventies, with hands cupped into stiff Cs from arthritis.

"In a way," Caro says. "I'm moving to Manhattan. I want to be in the theater."

"How exciting," the woman tells her. "Do you have family there?"

"Yes," Caro says, after a pause. "My father and stepmother and stepbrother."

"They must be thrilled you're coming."

"Actually, they don't know."

"It's a surprise?"

"Something like that."

She has not called her father with the news, and she had made Zoë promise not to tell. It was partly that she wanted to make it on her own, and partly because the last time she had left New York, her father had turned his head and not even said good-bye.

The plane is landing. Under muggy clouds, the city looks formidable, mysterious.

"Well, good luck," the old woman says to Caro. "I'll look for you on Broadway."

Caro gets off the plane. The airport is loud and bright. The area around the gate is gyrating with people. They catch sight of the passengers they're waiting for, wave, shout, rush over.

Caro waits for a voice to call her name. She realizes that, ridiculously, she had expected her father to be there.

She waits for a few minutes longer, then walks to the baggage claim.

She checks into a hotel on Sixth Avenue. She is shown to her room—it is as brown and impersonal as a coffin.

She unpacks quickly and goes to sleep.

The next morning, she walks over to Park Avenue. She stops in front of the building where her father and Meg and Adam live. The plantings have been changed, and there is a new doorman. She does not go in.

She knows she could. She knows that she has probably been forgiven for what happened that summer—it was three years ago, after all. She knows that, if she went up there, Meg would doubtless give her tea, and help her find an apartment. Just as if she were the old Caro.

But she isn't the old Caro anymore. That's just it. She is nobody's daughter, nobody's child now. She is a woman starting a new life alone.

That is much more pleasing.

Still, Caro crosses the street, and sits down on a nearby bench. She waits there for fifteen minutes. She does not see her father or Meg, but at seven forty-five, Adam comes outside.

He has grown taller, and his hair is curly and wild. The way he walks is exactly the same. And his hands, holding his school satchel, are still delicate and small.

Caro almost waves to him. She almost runs across the street. She knows he would throw down the satchel and hug her the way the travelers in the airport had been hugged. She would tell him that her being here was a secret, and that he was the only one she wanted to tell.

But she does not do it, and in a moment the school bus comes and takes Adam away. Caro stands up and walks back down Park Avenue. In a year, she'll be in touch. In a year, she'll send them all house seats to her Broadway show. For the moment, it is enough to know that Adam is still there—and that his hands are still so small.

* * *

The first thing on the list is to find somewhere to live. Caro has no interest in sharing with a roommate; she has had enough of that at the commune. She would rather be in a dive, and have it all to herself. She finally finds a place—a walk-up in Hell's Kitchen. It is a single, tunnel-like room with one tiny window, its light obscured by a fire escape. The kitchen area doubles as the bathroom, with a flimsy curtain screening the toilet, and a piece of wood converting the tub into a dining room table. It could not be worse. Caro is tickled by the place and she signs the lease. She likes it that there is no telephone, and she decides not to have one installed.

The apartment will make a marvelous set for act 2, "Caro's Struggle," in which she becomes a famous actress.

She moves her suitcase from the hotel and hauls it up the four flights of stairs to her new apartment. It takes her no time at all to unpack. She puts a photo of Zoë, and one of Adam, on the windowsill. She stacks her books by the floor, awaiting a bookshelf. She folds her clothes into the built-in chest of drawers. The bottom drawer sticks and will not open. She works at it, and finally manages to pull it out. She sees what has caused the problem—a magenta leg warmer has been caught at the back.

Caro unhooks the leg warmer and stares at it. She wonders who left it there; the last tenant, probably—a dancer, by the look of things. One who had no doubt that she was going to be a star someday, too.

Caro suddenly feels restless and uneasy. She gets on the subway and heads crosstown to Bloomingdale's. The store is crowded and comfortingly bright. She goes into the evening wear department and tries on a short red Armani dress. It looks good on her. One day soon, she promises herself, she will get it. In the meantime, she buys a pair of chunky tennis shoes. She has noticed that all the women on the street are wearing them.

When she comes out of Bloomingdale's, it is dusk. She is tired, but she doesn't want to go back to her room yet. She walks a block, and halfway down 58th Street, she spots a bar called The Parrot. She goes inside.

The bartender smiles at Caro as she sits down on the red leather stool. He is a middle-aged man, heavyset with thick graying hair. He looks strong, unsurprisable.

"Hello," he says. His voice is slow and deep.

"Why The Parrot?" Caro asks.

"No particular reason."

"That's the best kind." She smiles back at him. "I'd like some white wine, please."

He pours her the wine and gestures at the Bloomingdale's bag. "I see you've been shopping."

"I needed some grounding."

"It seems to have worked."

"Thanks," she says.

She tells him that she has just moved to New York, that she has come here to be an actress.

"Good for you," he tells her. He does not add that he'll look for her on Broadway one day.

When the wine is finished, Caro reaches for her purse.

"No," he says. "It's on the house."

Caro is unsurprised. "Thank you."

"My name's Mike. This is my place."

"I'm Caro."

"Well, Caro, I hope you'll come back again. I'd like to hear how things are going with you."

For a moment, Caro pictures herself and Mike together in her little room. She has seen the thick gold wedding ring on Mike's hand, but she knows that she could get beyond that.

"Thanks," she says.

It doesn't take Caro long to get a pattern established. She wakes up at six. She goes to the coffee shop down the block, drinks black coffee, and reads the trades. She shows up at auditions. She waits. Then she waits tables at an Italian restaurant at night. It's monotonous, but there are moments. A good audition. An interesting customer.

Nearly a year goes by. Success is not coming as quickly as she had hoped. She does have an agent—one of the men Zoë had recommended—but he wasn't doing anything for her. She also, thanks to a two-week gig playing a bit part in *Oklahoma,* has her Actor's Equity card—but the open calls were getting her nowhere. And now her money was starting to run out.

Twice more, she has gone back to the apartment building on Park Avenue, walked up and down the street, but not gone in.

"I think you're being silly," Zoë complains repeatedly in her weekly calls to the pay phone. "Lord knows I have my issues with Barton, but this simply isn't fair. The man's reduced to calling me up to find out how you are. All that funny business happened years ago, honey; you should go over and see him."

"I will," Caro tells her mother stiffly. "When I'm ready."

But the months go by, and it gets harder and harder. It's more than just what happened that summer—Caro is determined not to appear before her father as a failure.

Still she goes by the apartment building once more and waits. She makes a deal with herself—if she sees Barton or Meg or Adam, this time she would go up to them. But no one comes out of the door.

Caro spends a lot of time walking around New York. Occasionally, she finds herself going into The Parrot. The restaurant where she works is not far from there; it's a convenient place to unwind.

The customers are mostly regulars, and they leave her alone. No men try to talk to her or pick her up. At first this seems strange, but finally she understands. Everyone assumes she is Mike's.

Caro is flattered—he's an attractive man. Whenever she comes into the bar, there is a loud hello from him and a big smile. He has wonderful teeth, white and strong. She settles down on the stool and tells him about her week. He always remembers what auditions she's up for, and asks how they went.

He does not talk much about himself, but one day he opens his wallet and shows Caro a photo. It is of his three-week-old granddaughter. She finds it interesting that he has never shown her a picture of his wife.

* * *

One day, Caro is passing by a men's store. In the window, there is a blue knitted scarf with a rough weave. It makes her think of Mike and she buys it.

"This is for you," she tells him the next time she visits The Parrot.

Mike opens the present. He pulls out the scarf and holds it up for everyone to admire. Then he comes out from behind the bar and wraps Caro in a warm, growly bear hug.

Caro knows that, if she wants to have Mike, this is the moment to let him know. It is tempting—he is a warm man. But she decides that, after all, it isn't what she wants. She likes things better the way they are now. So she hugs Mike back, kisses him on the cheek, and then steps away. They smile at each other. It is good to have a friend.

CAROLINE

Caroline and Graham come into the dark apartment. Caroline flips on the lights and tosses her purse onto the sofa.

"Well, I'm glad to be home," she says. "I'm exhausted."

"I don't see how you can be," Graham tells her stiffly. "You didn't exactly put yourself out."

She makes sure her voice is calm. "I think I did."

"Really? From what I could see, you were in your own world pretty much the whole evening."

"I'm sorry."

"You know, you could try a little harder," he bursts out. "These are my friends. These are the people I work with."

Caroline tenses. "Well, maybe if they weren't around all the time, I could be a little more excited about seeing them."

"I didn't know you disliked them so much."

She sighs. "Oh, Graham, you know I don't dislike them. It's just that we see them every week."

"Fine," he says shortly. "Have it your own way."

He goes into the den. She rushes to follow, rattles the knob.

"Graham?"

There is no answer.

It is two o'clock in the morning but Caroline can't get to sleep. She leans over and touches Graham's back. It feels heavy and warm. At least their bodies are still friends.

They had made up after the quarrel, as they always did—but loneliness makes Caroline ache. She wishes she could shake Graham awake and ask him what is happening; but those kinds of questions cause the worst arguments of all.

It seems like they're never easy with each other anymore. More and more, lately, there have been these fights. He is finding so much wrong with her now; the way she dresses, the way she behaves at parties, the way she talks to his mother on the phone. And now the way she treats his friends.

It's as if he's starting to look for things to dislike.

And Caroline knows she's no better. She's getting good at fighting back. She scratches and picks, and she hates the way she sounds.

She's not sure when it all started—maybe after she did *Barefoot in the Park.* She knew he didn't want her to do the play—and yet she had kept on. Or maybe it had started before.

What had happened? It wasn't like that in college. In those days, they were on each other's side. They were friends. But it was so different then; there were always so many things to do together, always so much to talk about. She assumed it would be like that forever—but it seemed the minute she got married and real life started, she and Graham didn't even seem to share the same life anymore.

Caroline stands up quietly and goes into the living room. She tells herself she's overtired, and overreacting. All young married couples went through adjustments like this—look at Corie and Paul in *Barefoot in the Park.* But it's depressing to compare her life to a Neil Simon play.

It's been nearly two years now—maybe it was time they had a baby. But she had mentioned a baby the other day, as a kind of joke, and Graham had taken her seriously. "Are you kidding?" he said. "We're nowhere near ready."

She wonders if this was his way of telling her he didn't think they were going to last.

Were they going to last? She grows cold at the thought they might not. She remembers Zoë talking about Graham, the night before her wedding: *But he's completely wrong for you.*

Caroline sighs. She's got inventory to do in the morning. She'd better get to sleep. She remembers the day when she first took the train to Yale, and a woman told her how lucky she was. Caroline had replied that she was tired of it all—and that it hadn't really even started yet. She was eighteen then, she is twenty-four now.

She wonders if she will just get more and more tired.

Caroline has started going into The Parrot every Thursday afternoon. She has a glass of white wine—a little treat to celebrate that the week is almost ending. Mike, busy behind the bar, always seems to know when she has come. He straightens, turns, gives her a slow wave over the heads of the other customers. She has noticed that he does everything slowly, with satisfied unhurriedness.

"Hi," he says.

"Hi." She sits on her stool.

"How are things?"

"Great."

She never mentions what is happening with Graham and herself.

She tells Mike little stories about her week. Today, there is one about a customer who was mugged twice in the same day. Mike throws back his head and laughs. Caroline likes the way Mike laughs. It is thorough, like everything else about him.

"Hey," he says, "My son just sent me a picture of my new granddaughter—want to see?"

"I'd love to."

He pulls out his wallet and shows her. His hands are large. She finds she is looking at them instead of the picture.

Caroline flushes to find she has been staring too long.

"What a beautiful baby," she says quickly.

"Want to see more?"

He flips through the wallet. She watches his fingers tease the edges of each plastic photo pocket. Rhythmically, he turns the pages.

Caroline, her eyes still on his hands, does not pay close attention to the pictures. But she has seen that there aren't any of his wife.

By summer, she finds she is stopping by the bar twice a week. By fall, it is up to three times. It is so close to work; it is so convenient.

Mike does not comment on the fact that she is coming more often. He greets her with the same smile and wave. Her stool is waiting for her.

They never discuss anything out of the ordinary. She tells him about what book she is reading; he tells her about his windowsill garden. There is never a word said between them that Graham couldn't have heard.

Nevertheless, she has never mentioned to him that she goes to the bar.

It is the day before Christmas. Graham has a week off from work, so this is the last time Caroline will have a chance to go to The Parrot before the new year. She has a present for Mike—a blue scarf, thickly knitted and a little rough. She has not enclosed a card.

"Hey," she says, slipping onto her stool.

"How's everything?" he asks her.

"Fine." She reaches into her satchel and pulls out the gift.

"This is from Santa," she says.

Mike takes the package very formally. He puts it down for a moment, then wipes his hands on a towel before opening the wrapping.

"Well, what do you know." He pulls out the scarf. He feels the rough wool with his rough fingertips.

"I love it," he says. "Come here, you."

He steps out from behind the bar. Caroline slips off her stool. It is the first time she has seen the whole of him. He goes over to her and wraps her in a huge, growly bear hug.

She finds she cannot breathe.

She does not sit back on the stool.

"Well, I've got to go now," she says. "I just came by to give you the gift."

Her hands shake as she leaves the bar. She feels her heart thudding like an animal under her coat.

Caroline focuses hard on Christmas. She hangs up wreaths and evergreen swags and bakes cookies and buys ornaments for the tree.

Graham praises her efforts. They have a pleasant weekend together, window-shopping, having brunch, seeing a movie. It is like being back in their college days.

Christmas morning, Graham comes up with some very nice good husband gifts—lingerie and a new watch and an antique opal necklace. And she has gone out of her way to buy equally thoughtful presents for him. Things are going well.

Then they stop going well.

Christmas night, Caroline sees Graham searching around the apartment.

"Where did you put the vase from my mother?"

"In the powder room."

There is a pause. "Is that the best you could do?"

"But it's perfect in there," Caroline says quickly. "The colors match exactly."

"Oh, come on," he says. "You just can't stand anything my mother gives us." He points to the inlaid box on the hall table. "I notice your mother's gift is in the place of honor. Even though it's hideous."

Caroline flushes.

"I'll move it, if that's how you feel."

"Do whatever you want," Graham tells her. "I just think you should be aware of your own motives."

He goes into the den and locks the door.

Caroline goes outside. She walks down the cold streets until she is exhausted.

She does not go back to The Parrot for over a month. And then, one bitter afternoon of blackish snow, she cannot hold out any longer.

She walks in. The change from outdoors to indoors makes her face itch and sting. She stands in the cloakroom a moment. She takes off her coat, hangs it up carefully, walks into the bar. Mike is not there.

In that split second, when her heart dives with disappointment, Caroline realizes how far it has gone. She turns to walk out, but then she hears a voice calling her name. It is Mike. He is coming from the back. It is the first time she has ever seen him move quickly.

He reaches her.

She says, "I thought you weren't here."

He says, "I thought you weren't coming back."

He leads her to her stool. His hand on her elbow is calm and sure. He gives her an Irish coffee.

"I'll be right back," he says. He goes over to a table, greets another customer. Caroline watches him—she realizes he is the most attractive man she has ever seen. She remembers something Delores had once said. *I just hope that someday a guy doesn't come along who really does it for you.* And Caroline had smiled. *I promise you that won't happen.*

She shivers, and looks away from Mike. She focuses on the television screen above the bar. The news is on. A young African-American broadcaster is saying something she cannot hear. A photograph comes up on the screen—the face is familiar, but she can't think who it is. Then she realizes it is Tristan.

She taps the arm of the man next to her.

"Could you please turn the sound up?"

He takes this as a pickup line.

"Didn't you hear?" he asks. "He died of an overdose."

"—found dead in a hotel bathroom," the newscaster is saying. "Tristan, the popular songster, dead at age thirty-seven. Back to you, Bob."

The voices go on, but Caroline doesn't hear what they are saying. She bends her head and stares into her lap. Tristan is dead.

She is twelve years old, listening to *Songs from Camelot* at boarding school. She is touching Tristan's face on the record cover. She is wondering if one day she will get to meet him. And now he is dead. She puts her hands over her eyes. Across the room, Mike sees her. He excuses himself to the customer he is with, and returns to the bar. He bends over Caroline.

"What's the matter?"

She looks up. "I just heard Tristan died."

Mike nods. "It's a shame," he says. "He was a nice guy. He came in here once or twice over the summer."

Caroline lets out a breath. Tristan had been here. Tristan had been at The Parrot. If she had only come in on the right day, she could have met him. She could have gone up to him, touched his hand, told him how much his songs had meant to her.

It is unthinkable that she missed the chance.

She feels the tears hot behind her eyes.

"I'm sorry—I'm being ridiculous," she pants. "But all those years I was at boarding school . . . You can't imagine . . . He was . . . the one bright thing."

Mike calls out to John, the other bartender.

"Cover for me for a few hours, will you?"

He comes from behind the bar and holds his hand out to Caroline. She takes it and gets down slowly from the stool. They emerge together into the dark afternoon.

They turn and look at each other.

"My brother's away in Canada for a few months," Mike says. "He has an apartment near here."

Caroline did not think that having an affair would be this difficult. The first day, it isn't. She leaves Mike, tender, grateful, renewed. She hurries home and waits for Graham. When he comes in, she is glad to see him. She wonders how she ever could have snapped, ever could have criticized. She makes him dinner, listens to him talk about his day, and kisses him as if she were giving him a gift; just as Mike had given her a gift earlier.

Her mood lasts until the morning, when she wakes to find the wrong man sleeping beside her.

Work is endless that day. She cannot wait to get to The Parrot. She runs the block and a half. When she comes in, Mike looks up. He smiles and waves as usual, just as if nothing had happened the afternoon before.

He gives her an Irish coffee, and goes off to talk with other customers. Caroline can't believe it. She sits, cold, on the stool.

But when her drink is finished, he comes back.

"Cover for me, will you, John?" he says again, and once more, he holds out his hand to Caroline.

They go back to his brother's apartment.

It has been a month now. Caroline is constantly irritated, constantly on edge. She messes up the inventory at the bookstore. She cannot concentrate. She can't hear much over the screaming of her own nerves. She doesn't know where to go from here; she only knows that she doesn't like herself very much.

She goes over the options obsessively.

Stop seeing Mike. Never go into the bar again. And make things right with her husband.

That is the sanest plan, but she knows she can't follow it. She cannot be left with only Graham—not now. It is too late. Everything between them has putrefied—it is like a dried-up lake, with only silt and decomposing fish remaining.

She could leave Graham. Divorce him for Mike. But Mike is middle-aged. He has lived too much of his life without her. If he married her, cut himself off from all his past, there would be too little of him left. There would be only empty spaces in his wallet. And she could never make it up to him.

She hunts for the third option, the right option, but in her head there is only noise and more noise.

Graham has noticed. He has watched the changes in Caroline. He has seen the new blouses, observed the restlessness. One morning he finds he has an hour or two free. He decides to surprise Caroline at the bookshop and take her to lunch.

"She's not here," Gina tells him. "She left half an hour ago."

Graham goes down the street, into stores, into restaurants, looking for Caroline, but he doesn't find her.

"How was your day?" he asks when she comes in at five.

"Wonderful," she says quickly. "Sorry I'm a little late. I've been at the shop all afternoon—I wanted to catch up on some bookkeeping."

The following day, Graham leaves the office on his lunch hour and goes by the bookstore again. This time he waits across the street. He sees Caroline come out. He follows her to The Parrot, waits outside, sees her leave with Mike, and follows them to the apartment.

Caroline comes home at six. She finds Graham in the living room.

"You slut," he says. "You fucking slut." Tears are pouring down his face.

"Graham, you're drunk," is all she can say.

"How could you do this to me?"

She watches him, helpless, filled with pity.

"You're sick, you know," he tells her. "Carrying on with that old man."

Caroline sighs. "Maybe," she says.

"You can't have it both ways—I won't stand for that. You have to choose—between that old man and me."

And for the first time in months, the noise in Caroline's head stops.

The third option is finally there. It is to have neither Graham nor Mike. It is to be alone.

It is three o'clock in the morning. Graham has gone. He is staying at a hotel for a night or two. He says that when he returns, they will talk some more, try to work things out.

Caroline sits alone in the living room. She makes herself a cup of tea. She begins first to laugh and then to cry.

When she stops crying, she goes to the window and looks down at the city. It is a clear night, and the lights of ten thousand windows are blinking at her. They are sending out a message, but she does not know what it is.

She knows she will never get back with Graham; she also knows he will not suffer long. By next summer, he will have found someone lovely, someone who will truly enjoy the soccer games and the friends and the Sunday brunches.

She has no idea what will happen for her. But next time she will make sure she waits until the next toy store.

Caroline walks over to the stereo cabinet. She puts on *Songs from Camelot* and dances to the music.

CARO

It has been a bad day. Caro went down to audition for the part of Raina in *Arms and the Man,* but when she got to the theater, she overheard another actress say that the whole thing was a put-up job—the director was planning to cast his girlfriend.

She leaves the theater and walks through the hot and dusty park. She hasn't landed a job in months; it's scary to realize that she's been in New York almost four years now. Caro thinks of the magenta leg warmer—the one she found her first day in the apartment. How much longer is it going to take?

"You'll make it," Zoë says confidently in her weekly phone call. "Just give it a little more time." But the words are starting to sound more and more like gibberish.

The days have gone by, gray and unsubstantial, like a puff of dust. She has done so little; made no progress, no real friends. She sees her mother occasionally, when Zoë has a business trip to New York, but she has not been back to California. Caro is afraid that once she gets back there, she will want to give up and stay.

She hurries into the restaurant. She is late to work. The manager tells her that if this happens one more time, she'll be out of a job. She changes into her uniform.

The day is finally over. Caro checks her wallet. She has only seventy-five dollars left, and the month is not even half over. She's not going to make it. She's going to have to get another job, or write Zoë for a loan.

She decides to walk home and save the bus fare.

As she is going down 58th Street, she passes The Parrot. It looks warm and cheerful. There is music coming from inside. Caro pauses. She hasn't been in there for a while. She doesn't have to spend any money—she could just sit for a minute and talk to Mike.

He is at the bar, fixing a drink. She sits down at her stool.

"Hi," she says.

"Hey." He is pleased to see her. "It's been a while. How's the acting going?"

"Terrible," she tells him. "And I'm too broke to buy a drink."

"On the house," he says. "You'll pay me back when you're a star. Speaking of which," he adds, "we've got a celebrity in here tonight."

"Man or woman?"

"Man."

"Who is it?" Caro asks. "I'll see if he's worth turning around for."

"Well, I don't know," Mike teases. "He was a big deal a few years back. I don't know about now so much."

Caro turns.

The blood roars through her.

He is with two other people; they are in shadow, but the light falls straight onto Tristan's face.

Mike sees Caro's expression and laughs.

"Oh, it's like that, is it?"

She flushes. "He meant a lot to me when I was in high school."

She is lying in the darkened room at three in the afternoon, and listening to *Songs from Camelot* over and over again.

"You should go on over there," Mike tells her. "Introduce yourself."

"I couldn't."

"Sure you could."

Caro gets off her stool and walks over to the table where Tristan is sitting. She stands there, silent. As he glances up, his expression is wary. Then, when he sees Caro, it changes into a strange look—one almost of wonder.

Caro stares down at him.

"I just wanted to tell you . . ." She cannot go on.

He smiles. "What's your name?"

"Caro Andrews."

He stands up. "I'm Tristan Michaels." He bows. "And this is Zak Petrie and Rob Levinson."

Zak clears his throat.

"Uh, miss, we're in kind of a business meeting here."

"I'm sorry." Caro does not take her eyes off Tristan. "I just wanted to tell you," she begins again, "how much you've meant in my life."

He smiles. "Thank you."

She turns to go.

"Wait a minute," he says.

She stops.

"We're here until Friday. We're staying—" He turns to Rob. "What's the hotel?"

"The Helmsley Palace."

"The Helmsley Palace," Tristan says to Caro. "Maybe you could come up."

Caro shakes her head.

"Please," Tristan tells her. "Come if you can. I'll put your name on the list." He smiles. "Caro Andrews."

It is still light outside. Caro leaves the bar and goes to Central Park. There are grandmothers feeding ducks and little boys climbing rocks and young executives roller skating. She does not see any of it.

For two days, Caro hesitates. She takes long walks and tries to decide.

She is aware of what going to the Helmsley Palace would probably mean. She knew a girl once—a waitress at the restaurant—who had met up with the Doors and gone with them on tour for a couple of weeks. She had told Caro all the stories.

Caro is not interested in anything like that. She is no one's groupie; she is no one's one-night stand.

But she wants to see Tristan again.

She enters through swinging doors into the lobby of the Helmsley Palace.

She goes up to the front desk.

"Could you please tell me which room Tristan Michaels is in?"

The concierge is too well-trained to give her the look she senses he would like to give her.

"And your name, miss?"

"Caro Andrews."

If Tristan has forgotten to give her name, that will be the end of it. She is prepared for that.

The concierge looks at a list. "Ah, yes, Caro Andrews. Please go right up. Room 2104."

The elevator is so swift that Caro gets giddy. The hallway is tasteful and discreet. She walks along until she comes to room 2104.

She knocks softly. If the door doesn't open by the count of ten, she will go away. Zak opens it by the count of four.

When he sees Caro, he looks at her in the way the hotel manager hadn't.

"Hey, Tris," he calls in a high, false voice.

Tristan walks in from the other room and sees Caro.

"You came," he says.

With him is a thin, dark-haired man. He is like a ragged edge.

"This is Harper. Harper Joely, Caro Andrews."

Harper glances briefly in Caro's direction.

"We're ready to go, Tris. Are you coming?"

Tristan looks at Caro.

"Interested in going to a reception?"

"No."

"No," he tells Harper. "But you go on."

Harper shrugs. "Allen's not going to be pleased if you don't show up."

"Tell him I'm sorry."

Tristan and Caro are alone in the hotel room. They stand awkwardly, saying nothing. Finally, Caro takes a few steps forward and touches the delicate upholstery on the couch.

"My father would like this. He'd say it has clean lines. He's an architect."

"And what about you?"

"I'm an actress."

He smiles. "I would have guessed that. Have you had any luck—or is that rude to ask?"

"No. Well, I had a lot of luck when I was a little girl. I was in a television show—*A Tree Grows in Brooklyn.*"

"*A Tree Grows in Brooklyn,*" Tristan repeats. "That sounds rather sweet."

"It was. Maybe too sweet."

Caro tells him about the show. She tells him about what things were like when it ended, and how there had been all those years when she hadn't acted at all. She has meant to make it all sound light and funny, but she finds there are tears in her eyes.

"But you'll get to act again," he says.

She nods. "I think I'm meant to. I was hooked early, anyway. I did my first commercial when I was seven."

"That must have been great."

She laughs. "It was. I played an angel. I rolled some toilet paper out of a cloud, and it turned into a rainbow. When I saw myself on television, I actually thought I had done the trick."

Tristan is looking at her strangely. "That was you?"

"What do you mean?"

"That was you in the advertisement?"

"Yes. But it was on American television."

"I saw it," he tells her. "I came to New York on holiday. I saw you on television."

"That's amazing."

"And I put you in a song."

She laughs. "What?"

"Yes. Years later, I was writing 'Nimbus.' There was a line—'Cloud angels carrying—"

"—bridges of rainbow,' " Caro breathes.

"Yes. That was about you."

They stare at each other.

Caro is the first to break away. She walks around the room, slowly, gently touching things. Finally she stops in front of the silver-framed photograph of a woman.

"Who is that?"

"My mother. Margaret. She died when I was twelve. She was killed in a traffic accident."

There is a tap on the door, and the maid comes in. When she sees Tristan, she goggles and nearly drops the towels she is carrying.

"Oh, excuse me, Mr. Tristan," she says. "I didn't mean to disturb you."

She flees, clutching the towels.

Tristan glances at Caro. His eyes are amused and a little sad.

"Promise me you'll never look at me like that," he says.

Caro laughs. "Don't worry," she tells him.

He walks over to her. He takes his hand and puts it up to her face. Then he kisses her.

It is past midnight. The other members of the band return from the reception. Zak has been drinking; he swaggers up to Caro, and puts his arm around her. At Tristan's look, he removes the arm. Rob is quiet, stoned. Harper is manic. He goes around the suite, doing hurtful little things. He dirties a chair with the sole of his foot, he punctures a lamp shade with his fingernail.

"Stop it," Tristan tells him, but he keeps on.

"I'd better go," Caro says.

The eyes of Tristan's band are driving her away.

Tristan walks her to the door of the hotel room.

"Can I see you again?"

"Yes."

She gives him the number of the pay phone down the street.

"Would ten o'clock be too early to call?"

"No."

Gravely, he kisses her once more.

Caro does not sleep that night. At ten o'clock the next morning she waits, pacing by the pay phone. If he does not call, she is prepared.

The phone rings.

They meet at a nearby coffee shop. Caro is waiting in the booth and sees him through the window, crossing the street. The other customers pretend not to stare, but she can hear the whispers. Tristan sits down in the booth across from her.

They smile at each other.

"I couldn't sleep," he says.

She does not tell him that she couldn't either.

"I wanted to get you something." Tristan reaches into his pocket. "I saw this. I hope you like it."

Inside the small box is an enameled eighteenth-century button. A tiny lady dressed in pink sits on a bench while a troubador kneels before her and plays his mandolin.

"Thank you," Caro says after a long moment. "I will keep it for the rest of my life."

The words come out somehow ominous, sad.

Tristan is taking out his wallet. "And I wanted to show you something else."

He pulls out a photograph.

"This is where I live."

It's a large Victorian house, painted pale gray with dark blue trim. A porch runs along the front, and there are stained glass windows on the upper level. Beside it is a tangled garden.

"How beautiful."

"It's on an island."

"How wonderful to live on an island."

"It's quite a tiny one. It's near Maidenhead—about an hour from London. Mine is the only house on it. It *is* wonderful, but a little inconvenient. The only way to get there is by boat."

"Not really."

"Yes. I have a small motorboat. But mostly I like to row."

Caro smiles at the thought.

"I'm quite good at it, actually," Tristan tells her. "But it gets a little difficult when you've got bags of shopping."

She laughs.

"I'd love you to see it. I think you'd like it." Tristan coughs, looks down at the tablecloth. "I've got to go back to England day after tomorrow. I was wondering if—you would consider coming with me."

* * *

"Caroline Jane Andrews!" Zoë explodes over the phone. "You have gone completely mad. I refuse to let you do this idiotic thing."

"But I want to do it," Caro says gently.

"Do you have any idea what you're getting yourself into? My God—that I'd live to see my only child cheapening herself—becoming a groupie! And just when things were starting to happen with your career!" she adds in a wail.

"It isn't like that, Zoë. Really. I'm not a groupie. I'm just going with Tristan." There is a pause. "Zoë—don't you understand?"

"I understand," Zoë says grudgingly. "I've lived with his posters stuck up in my house for years. But what's going to be the end of it, baby? What's going to happen when the tour is over?"

"I don't care," Caro says.

Zoë sighs. "I suppose I have no choice. You'll do as you like, as usual." There is a pause. "Well," she says at last, "if he should happen to play Buckingham Palace, be sure to wear the white Halston I gave you."

The band is staying at the Hotel Marcliffe at Pitfodels. The concert tomorrow is in Aberdeen, and Tristan, Harper, and Zak have gone to check out the hall. Caro said she would remain in the hotel.

The room is lovely—old-fashioned and serene. Caro unpacks the suitcases and puts the clothes away. She pours potpourri into all the ashtrays. She takes out the photo of Margaret and polishes the silver frame.

Several times Tristan has mentioned that he would like to have a picture of Caro to put beside it. She always refuses. She is superstitious about that. If Tristan has her picture, it will mean that, for some reason, she herself is no longer there.

Caro sits down on the sofa and closes her eyes. She is lapped by happiness.

And yet it is an odd kind of happiness because it bears no relationship to anything that came before. It is rare that Caro even thinks about the old life. She might see a woman in a flowered scarf who reminds her of Zoë. She might see an old movie poster for *Bye, Bye, Birdie* and briefly remember high school. A middle-aged man in the park makes her think for a moment of Mike, the bartender. But it is no more than that. The new life has washed everything else clean.

But it is tiring. And the touring doesn't seem real. On tour, there are only interiors. The insides of hotel rooms and buses and limousines and concert halls.

Tristan and the band stay indoors, playing cards, giving interviews, watching television. But Caro can't stand to do that. She goes out every day, she feels the weather, she walks around the towns. She goes into churches, buys fresh flowers, bread. But even so, the days blur and dull.

Concert nights are sharp. Before each show, the band is brittle. Fights break out over nothing. Caro makes a point of staying away from Zak.

Tristan is very quiet on concert nights. Caro sits beside him backstage before the performance. At the last possible minute, she takes her seat.

When he comes onstage, the audiences stand up and scream. She can see him become happy again.

The first song is always "Nimbus."

"Cloud angels carrying bridges of rainbow." When he sings the words, he looks down at her.

She cannot believe the fineness, the delicacy of him. He is a light pouring onto the stage.

After the concerts, they all go out. Caro sits next to Tristan, but it is Zak who talks to him. They go over the flaws in the show, plan for the next one.

On these nights, Caro talks to Harper and Rob. She knows they don't particularly like her, but that's all right. Their dislike is only mild. Zak is the one who hates her.

The door of the hotel room opens and the band shuffles in.

"Pretty little Caro."

She knows instantly that Tristan is high. It is Zak's doing. He is the one who gives him the drugs.

She cannot stand the shine in Tristan's eyes. She turns away.

* * *

They travel to France, Holland, Italy, Germany, Finland. Sometimes they fly, sometimes they take trains. Sometimes, traveling between towns, they hire a bus. These are peaceful times. Caro looks at the scenery outside, and is without thoughts. Occasionally, Rob comes over to sit next to her. He asks about Hollywood. Caro tells him about surfing at Malibu and eating hamburgers at the Brentwood Country Mart. She tells him all about Zoë. She can imagine her mother and Rob having lunch together at the Bistro Gardens, both laughing and smoking madly.

"You two would like each other."

Talking about Zoë makes Caro miss her. When they reach Antwerp, she sends her mother a postcard, and Tristan and Rob and Harper all add a message.

Tristan writes songs on the bus. One day he asks Caro to sing the melody line.

"Again."

She sings it again.

He looks up at her. "You've got a pretty voice."

"I know," she says drily. "I almost got to play Kim in *Bye, Bye, Birdie.*"

"Now the second verse."

She sings the lyric while he harmonizes.

"Hey, listen," he calls out to the band. "I want you to hear this."

"No," Caro says.

But he makes her sing the song with him.

"I was thinking, we might do this one. Let Caro sing with the band."

Zak walks abruptly to the front of the bus.

"No," Caro tells Tristan again.

"Oh, come on. It'll be wonderful."

The next concert is in Brussels. Caro is going to sing the song. She waits backstage instead of going to her seat in the audience. Halfway through the set, Tristan gestures for her to come out onstage.

When the concert is over, Tristan hugs her.

"You were fantastic."

She shakes her head. "Never again."

"Why?"

"She's too shy," Rob says.

Caro smiles. "Not exactly. When I perform," she tells them, "I don't want to be part of a group. I want to be the star."

She can see that Tristan is puzzled, even a little hurt, but she knows Zoë would understand.

There are always girls around after the concerts. Fans who hang around the stage door, groupies who come back with Zak and Rob and Harper to the hotel. Caro doesn't have much to do with them.

But one night there is a very young girl. She can't be over fifteen. She waits for Harper while he changes in the next room.

"I can't believe I'm here," she says happily to Caro. "Harper says he's going to get me an acting contract when the tour is over."

"Go home," Caro tells her. "You don't know what you're doing."

The girl stares at her.

"But you're here," she says finally.

"It's different for me."

The girl flushes. "I think you're jealous."

Caro goes over to her wallet and holds out some money.

"Take a taxi," she says.

The girl bursts into tears, but she takes the notes and leaves.

Harper comes out of the bathroom. "Hey, where's what's-her-name?"

"I sent her home," Caro tells him.

The tour is finally over. There will be another one, a local one, in the new year, but for now she and Tristan are free.

He takes her home, to the gray Victorian house on the island. Caro would like to stay here, walking around this garden, forever. The only sounds are the ducks and the moorhens and the busy little stream. She spends her days taking care of the house, giving it all the attention it needs. She darns the antique linen tablecloth. She polishes the heavy silver candlesticks.

She would not have believed that she would love doing these things so much.

She leaves the island as little as possible. She does not even like having to cross the river to get groceries. Until it gets too cold, she spends hours sitting in the rowboat moored to the bank. She looks up at the willows reflected in the water and knows herself to be utterly happy.

It is a week until the next tour begins. Thursday afternoon, Caro goes into Windsor to do some shopping. When she comes back to the dock, she hears a little cry. She looks down and sees a stray cat standing by the boat. It is tiny, hardly older than a kitten.

Caro brings the cat home with her. She carries it inside the house and puts it on the library table where Tristan is working.

"See what I've got."

It is the first time he has ever been angry with her.

"That was incredibly thoughtless," he says. "We're going on tour in a few days. Who do you expect to take care of it?"

Caro says nothing, only picks up the cat and leaves. She goes into their bedroom, sits on the bed, and looks out the window.

Then she stands up and goes back into the library.

"I want to keep the cat," she tells Tristan. "We can board it at the vet while we're away, and then afterward, I want you to stop touring. I want us to stay here. And," she adds, "I want to have a baby."

He stares at her. She has no idea what he is going to say.

The transatlantic connection is full of static.

"Zoë?" Caro calls. "Zoë?"

"Caro?" A voice at last. "Where are you?"

"Still in England."

"What's the matter? Are you all right?"

"Zoë, can you come over here? Can you come in two weeks?"

"Why? What's wrong?"

Caro smiles. "Nothing's wrong. But can you bring a dress that you might wear to a wedding?"

"What?" Zoë is screaming. "You're getting married?"

"That's right."

"My darling, this is wonderful! Absolutely wonderful."

"But, Zoë, it's a secret," Caro says. "No one must know."

"I understand; I won't tell a soul. I think I still have the garter I wore when I married your father," Zoë goes on happily. "For 'something borrowed,' you know. Oh, I'm absolutely—"

But the static rises and rises, and all Caro can hear are a few more faint, happy screams.

The night before they leave for the tour, Caro cannot sleep.

"What's the matter?" Tristan asks.

"Nothing. I was just thinking—if we ever do have a baby, I'd like to name him after you."

Tristan shakes his head. "Let him be someone new."

"Do you have a middle name?"

"Alexander."

"Then we'll call him Alexander."

Caro imagines Tristan on one side of her in the bed, the baby Alexander on the other, her arms around them both.

The tour is winding down. There are only four more days. The band will drive through the Midlands, playing in Liverpool and Manchester, and end up in London for the final concert. Then, the following week, Tristan and Caro will be married. The secret has been kept—Zoë is still the only one who knows. Tristan feels it would be a mistake to tell the others now—there is no point in upsetting anyone, disrupting the tour. After the final concert, he will announce the news—first to the band, and then to the press.

There are three days left.

They are staying at the Chester-Grosvenor Hotel in Chester. Dusk is falling. Caro pulls back the curtains, and together she and Tristan look out onto the main square. The street has been closed to traffic, and the only sounds they hear are the church bells ringing. Caro stands with Tristan's arms around her and closes her eyes.

"Can we have dinner together tonight?" she asks him. "Just the two of us?"

"I'd like that."

Caro calls the concierge and he makes a reservation at the Blue Bell, the oldest restaurant in the city.

The doorbell rings. It is Zak. He ignores Caro, turns to Tristan. "Want to go to the pub?"

Tristan looks at Caro.

"Our reservations's at eight," she says.

He smiles at her. "I'll be back by half past seven."

Caro goes into the bathroom. She starts to run a bath, watching the water flow into the creamy Edwardian tub. She touches the antique soap dish, the old-fashioned porcelain faucets. In this small room, she counts eighteen things of beauty around her.

She dresses in her blue silk dress. She brushes her hair a hundred times while she waits for Tristan.

He does not come. It is seven thirty, then seven forty-five, then eight thirty.

At five of nine, he comes in.

"I'm sorry I'm late," he says. "I'm sure we can still get a table."

He is very quiet during the walk to the Blue Bell.

"What's wrong?" she asks.

"Nothing."

But she can guess what it is. He has told Zak that they are going to be married.

The Blue Bell is enchanting, with its ancient beams and tables, but neither of them notices. Tristan works hard for Caro not to see that he is distressed; he holds her hand, strokes it. She does not make him talk.

They go back to the hotel. They go into their room, undress in silence, and get into bed. Caro turns to Tristan and holds him, but his body feels oddly abandoned.

At last she falls asleep. And then suddenly she is awake. Tristan is not in the bed. A light is on in the bathroom, and she gets up slowly in the darkness.

* * *

He is lying on the bathroom floor. The needle is still in his arm. She knows he is dead. She stands very still. She counts the eighteen beautiful items in the bathroom again. Then she kneels by Tristan. She touches his hair. She touches his cheeks, and his lips. She straightens out his robe around him. He was a modest person and would not like to be seen, crumpled, by strangers.

Then at last she stands up and makes the call to the hotel manager.

CAROLINE

In the days after Graham leaves, all the novocaine wears off.

Caroline is panicky. She doesn't know what she should do. She makes plans all day long. She cannot stay in the current apartment; she cannot carry the rent on her salary from the bookstore. She is not sure she even wants to remain in Manhattan. She considers moving to Brooklyn—or Los Angeles. She could live near Zoë and try her luck at little theater.

When she isn't working, she spends her time at home. She has not been by The Parrot. She has not seen Mike at all.

At the beginning of March, she starts to suspect—finally she goes to the doctor. He tells her to call back the next day.

The nurse keeps her waiting on the phone for a long time. At last she comes back on the line.

"Yes, Mrs. Moss," she tells Caroline brightly. "Yes, you're going to have a baby."

CARO

"Rock Star ODs."

"Singer Found Dead in Hotel Bathroom."

The headlines blaze in her mind. The press is worse than she could have believed. They call after her like a siren.

"Hey, Caro! Did you know he was on drugs?"

"Are you on drugs?"

"Did he have a death wish?"

"What were his last words?"

She speaks to the doctor who signs the death certificate. She tells the police what happened. She asks if she is free to go back to America. They tell her she is.

As Caro is leaving the police station, she starts to feel dizzy. She sits down and sees the smear of blood on the front of her dress.

She is taken to the infirmary.

"I'm sorry," the doctor tells her. "If it's any comfort, it wasn't very far along."

Caro goes back to the hotel. She calls the vet and arranges to have the little cat put up for adoption. Then she packs her suitcase, taking with her only her clothes, the photograph of Margaret, and the little enamel button with the painting of the troubadour.

PART FIVE

LITTLE WORLDS

CAROLINE

Every day before work, Caroline takes a walk in Central Park. She grows to know certain trees, certain banks of flowers. Day by day, she watches them come into bloom. Time is passing.

She must do something. She must come to some kind of decision. Every morning, she promises herself that it will be today. She will walk around the park, and there, in front of a pond or a bench, the answer will come to her. But the days pass.

There are a lot of babies in the park, dressed in their soft spring parkas. Caroline stops and looks at them. She puts it into the simplest terms. Does she want a baby? She tries to imagine her hands pushing a carriage. She tries to imagine holding a baby up to her shoulder. But she cannot make it real.

Every day she passes a sign advertising a family planning clinic. Superstitiously, Caroline averts her eyes. But she finds she has memorized the telephone number.

She has told no one about the baby. She thinks about telling Graham. He had said they weren't ready, but now that a baby was coming, he would act responsibly. He might even be pleased. She knows he would want to get back with her for the baby's sake. They would continue to live in the nice apartment, they would buy the baby beautiful designer clothes. But Caroline reminds herself that this is never going to happen.

She has done the math, again and again.

The baby is Mike's.

* * *

One morning when she gets dressed, she finds she is having trouble buttoning her skirt. She realizes that there is no more time.

That evening, before the crowd comes, she goes into The Parrot. She hasn't been by since the night Graham left. As she stands in the cloakroom, she watches Mike. He is as expansive as ever. Not having her there hasn't diminished him at all.

He catches sight of Caroline.

"Well, well," he says slowly.

She moves to her stool, sits down.

"Hi."

"You haven't been by for a long time."

"No. A lot's been going on." She takes a breath. "My marriage is—" She makes a crumpled gesture.

"Sorry," he says.

"Mike, I came to tell you something." Sharp streams of perspiration prickle her underarms. She could not have imagined it would be this difficult. "I'm going to have a baby."

Deliberately, Mike lays down the glass he is holding. He looks up at Caroline. She has never seen such coldness in anyone's eyes.

"Congratulations," he tells her. His lips make a white smile. "Your husband must be delighted."

Caroline turns red. "Mike," she says, "It's not his baby."

"Sure it is." He keeps smiling at her.

"Please—Mike—"

"Yes, a baby's a wonderful thing," he says in a louder voice. "I have grandchildren of my own. I should know."

Then he comes around the bar, goes over to Caroline, and escorts her down from the stool.

"But you shouldn't be here," he tells her. "Babies and alcohol don't mix."

A man at a nearby table has heard this. He raises his glass.

"Listen to Mike," he says. "He's a helluva guy."

Caroline walks slowly home. An old song is stuck in her head, "The Men in My Little Girl's Life." It occurs to her that she is now without any men in her life at all.

Then she stops in the middle of the sidewalk. All at once she knows her baby will be a son. And she can feel his weight on her shoulder.

Graham comes by the following evening. It is strange to have him back in the apartment. She offers him his old chair, but he does not take it. He sits on the company couch.

"How are you doing?" he asks her formally.

"I'm fine."

She is not sure why he has come. He does not mention anything about wanting a divorce. He stays a few minutes and talks about how things are going at work.

"I just wanted to say," he tells her finally, "the lease is coming up on this place in a few months, and I need to know what your plans are."

She nods. "I understand. I'll let you know soon."

He nods in return.

He looks suddenly very young, the way he did when she first met him. She almost tells him about the baby, but does not.

After Graham is gone, she walks around the apartment. Of course she can't stay there—she has known that for weeks. But she has put off making any kind of decision.

The fear starts to rise in little waves. She has a savings account, and most of her earnings from the bookstore, but that won't last for more than a few months. And then there will be the baby. She needs to make the decisions now. She needs to find somewhere cheaper to live. Maybe in Brooklyn. Or down in Hell's Kitchen. And she needs a new job. Something that will support a child. But what can she do? She sees girls from N.Y.U. and Columbia walking around, and their youth and confidence are frightening. She should have gotten a job right out of college. Something that would have given her a future. But now it was too late to start anything new. And yet she was having a baby—so everything in the world would be new.

The following afternoon, she is passing the Citicorp Building. She notices a small, brightly painted sign by the side of the street. It says Little Worlds, and an arrow points down to a basement-level store.

Caroline likes the name. She goes carefully down the wrought-iron stairs.

Little Worlds is a dollhouse shop. Caroline stares into the window, decked out for spring. She goes inside the store and looks around the shelves full of tiny furniture and smiling doll families.

The proprietor, a woman in her fifties with frizzy graying hair, comes in from the back.

"Anything in particular you're looking for?"

Caroline shakes her head.

"No," she says. "Not anymore. But a long time ago, I used to spend a lot of time in a shop just like this. Looking around here brings it all back."

The woman smiles. "Glad to have reminded you."

Caroline picks up a tiny plastic television. She remembers the one she stole from Yvette when she was four years old. She remembers the dollhouse Laura made her from shoe boxes. The curtains fashioned from scraps of lace. The carpets banded with blue ribbon. And Meg and Adam sitting on the floor with her and playing for hours.

Caroline picks up a tiny wooden cradle from the counter and rocks it gently in her palm.

"I guess it would be good to have a dollhouse again," she tells the store owner finally. "I'm going to have a baby."

This is the first person, besides Mike, that she has told.

"Congratulations! And of course you need a dollhouse." The woman walks quickly about the shop, looking at the stock. "What about building it from a kit?"

"Oh, no. I'm terrible with my hands."

Caroline regrets having said anything. She had forgotten that she needs a new place to live and a new job and that her money is running out. She cannot afford a dollhouse.

"What about this one? It's a beginner's kit, but it's quite effective."

Caroline looks at the dollhouse pictured on the front of the kit. Her mouth waters. Her eyes prickle. It is a three-story Victorian house. A porch wraps around the first level, supported by delicately filigreed pillars, and upstairs on the topmost floor, there are stained glass windows.

She forgets again that she needs to find a job and a place to live, and that her money is running out.

I'll paint it pale gray, she decides. With dark blue trim.

"I'll take it."

She wants to carry the kit home with her, right that moment, but the woman will not hear of it.

"You're pregnant," she reminds Caroline. "Tell me where you live—I'll bring it by after I finish work."

Caroline goes to some trouble for the visit. She gets English Breakfast tea from the grocery, a carrot cake from the bakery, and she arranges everything on an antique wooden tray. It has been a long while since anyone has come to visit—she cannot even remember the last time the visitor was a friend of hers. Not that the store owner is a friend, exactly—Caroline is embarrassed that she does not even know her name.

At six o'clock, the doorbell rings. The woman is there, carrying the dollhouse kit. Together she and Caroline maneuver it into the hall closet.

"Thank you so much," Caroline pants. "I had no idea it would be so heavy—I can't believe you brought it all this way."

"Not a problem. You needed to have it." The woman reaches into her tote bag. "But as I was leaving the store, I started thinking—what's a dollhouse without a few dolls to go in it?" She pulls from the bag a miniature family—a father, a mother, a little girl, and a baby—and hands them to Caroline.

"These are for you."

Caroline sighs. "You've been so lovely to me," she says, "and I don't even know your name."

"I'm Trina Gellis."

"Is that short for Katrina?"

"I wish. Actually, my real name's Tina, but I'm not exactly the Tina type. Not Tina Turner, not even Tina Louise. So I changed it."

Caroline smiles. "I can understand. I always wanted to be 'Chantal.'" She pats a chair. "Well, sit down and I'll get us some tea."

"Oh, no," Trina protests. "It's much too late—I'll get out of your way. I'm sure your husband will be home soon."

"No," Caroline tells her. "My husband's not coming home. I don't mean just for now—I mean forever. We're separated." She gestures awkwardly. "And I've got the tea all ready in the kitchen."

"Well, then, sure," Trina says. She sits down on the sofa. "I'd love some."

Caroline knows she is talking too much, but she cannot seem to stop herself from saying more.

"Everything's pretty much up in the air right now," she babbles on, as she brings the tea tray in. "It was crazy of me to have gotten the dollhouse. I'm not even sure where I'll be a month from now."

She tells Trina about her life; about going to Yale and meeting Graham, and how things had fallen apart. And Trina tells her about her own husband and her own divorce. Caroline has not talked this much, or listened this much, in a long time.

"And what are your plans now?" Trina asks finally.

"I'm not sure. I've got to move soon. And I've got to get another job. But I don't know what else I can do."

Carefully, Trina picks up her teacup. She asks Caroline, "How would you like to work for me?"

By the time Trina leaves, it is dark. Caroline goes over to the window and looks out at the city below her.

Monday afternoon, she will start work at Little Worlds. She will be in charge of the window displays, doing the inventory, and helping the customers. She'll find a cheaper apartment, and between the old job and this new one, she'll be able to manage.

Relief flows through her.

As Caroline turns to go into the bedroom, her glance falls on the little family of dolls that Trina brought over. She stops and walks over to them. She picks up the baby doll, and fits it into the mother's arms. She takes the father doll and seats him on the edge of the table. Then she lifts the little girl doll and puts it onto his lap. She stares at these last two figures for a long time.

Barton seems pleased to hear her voice on the phone.

"Caroline! How's everything?"

"Everything's fine," she says. "I just haven't seen you in a while—I miss you. I was hoping we could have lunch."

"That would be wonderful. Let's say Tavern on the Green, Thursday, one o'clock. I'll have my secretary make the reservation."

When Caroline arrives at the restaurant, the maitre d' informs her that Mr. Andrews is already there. Caroline can see him sitting upright at the table, jotting down a note in his leather memorandum book. He seems very spare, very gray, and she feels a sting of anxious guilt. Her own worries have kept her so busy—she's let too much time go by without seeing her father.

She hurries forward now.

"Father." She bends down and kisses him.

"Caroline—it's been too long." He studies her, nods. "You're looking well."

He calls over the waiter. "My guest is here. We'd like some water and some rolls, please."

Seeing him sip water, seeing him carefully break a roll, fills Caroline with tenderness. This is her father.

They talk casually. Barton tells Caroline about what's going on at his firm, she tells him about her job at the bookstore.

"And I'm doing something else as well, now. I'm working at a miniatures shop—I started this week."

He frowns. "Graham isn't making enough money? You have to have two jobs?"

She hesitates. She has put off telling him that she and Graham are separated.

"I enjoy them," she says.

"Not much of a career, though."

She does not remind him that she once wanted to be an architect.

They order, the meal comes, the waiter goes away.

"Father," Caroline says, "I have something to tell you. I'm going to have a baby."

His face grows pink. He cannot keep a surprised smile away.

"Oh!" he says. "That's wonderful. Boy or girl?"

She laughs. "The doctor doesn't know—but I'm pretty certain it's going to be a boy."

"A grandson," he says thoughtfully. "Well, well."

Caroline can see how excited he is. She glows with satisfaction. Her father has had so much tragedy in his life—but now she will be giving him a grandson.

"Graham must be thrilled."

Caroline takes a deep breath.

"Actually, Graham and I are separated," she says. "And I don't think we're going to get back together."

There is a pause. "What happened?"

Caroline does not tell her father about Mike, only that she and Graham had stopped getting along.

Barton is silent.

"But surely you can do something. You've been married such a short time. What about a marriage counselor? That might help."

Caroline remembers how hard he has worked all these years on his marriage to Meg.

"No, I don't think it would," she says.

Barton sighs. "I wish you had told me about this earlier. But I suppose I'm not the first person you'd come to." There is regret in his voice. "I can understand that."

"Oh, Daddy." Caroline hasn't called him that in a long time. "No one could have done anything."

"Well," he goes on briskly, "can I do anything now?"

"No. But thank you."

Barton is shaking his head. "It'll be hard on the baby—his parents not being together."

Caroline knows all about children whose parents are not together.

"I'll see that he'll grow up fine," she tells him.

"And I'm sure Graham will do his part."

Caroline swallows. "Actually, I haven't told him about the baby."

Her father frowns. "But he has a right to know."

She shakes her head. "No, he doesn't."

"Caroline, of course he does. He's the father."

Caroline hesitates. She still cannot bring herself to tell him about Mike.

"I'll think about it," she promises.

"Do that."

They sit in silence for a few moments.

"And what does Zoë have to say about all this?" he asks finally.

"I haven't told her yet. I wanted you to know first. I was planning on calling her tonight."

Barton rolls his eyes. "She'll have that baby on television before he's a month old."

They both laugh. Caroline is surprised that her father has said that, that he has mellowed enough to say something like that.

The sun moves out from behind a cloud. The rush of light picks out the lines around Barton's eyes and mouth. Caroline puts her hand over his and strokes it gently. She remembers how he used to tickle her when she was little, and how much fun it was.

"How's Meg?" she asks.

He considers this. "She's leveled off. I don't think it's going to get much better at this point."

"I'm so sorry."

Her father adjusts his shoulders. "Well. It can't be helped. She'll love your news, though."

Caroline isn't so sure. She can hear Meg screaming at the sanatorium, "Get her away. Oh, get her away."

"Well, anyway," she says, "she'll have a new grandson in October."

The lunch is over. When Caroline rises to go, Barton stops her.

"I'm going to drop by the bank this afternoon. I'm setting up a trust fund for the baby and starting an allowance for you. That should take some of the pressure off."

Caroline goes over and puts her arms around him.

"Thank you so much," she says, "but I don't need it. I think I'll be okay on what I'm making."

"Are you sure?"

She nods. "But if I'm wrong, I'll come crawling."

"Promise?"

"Yes."

"But the trust fund—this is my grandson we're talking about."

Caroline smiles at him. "We'd both be very grateful."

She hugs him hard.

* * *

She calls her mother that evening.

"Zoë, I've got some news for you—I'm having a baby."

"Oh, my darling!" Zoë whoops. "How splendid, how absolutely splendid. You'll make a marvelous little mama, and what a delicious grandmother I shall be. I do hope it's going to be a boy."

"I think it will be." And remembering what she and her father had laughed about, she adds, "Maybe he'll be an actor. You can handle his career."

"Yes, wouldn't that be nice?" Zoë says brightly.

Caroline is about to tell her mother the other news, the news about Graham, but Zoë cuts her off. "The other phone's ringing, my darling; I'm expecting a call from the studio. We'll talk soon."

The following week, an exquisite wicker cradle arrives from Los Angeles, accompanied by a card covered in Zoë's explosive handwriting. "For the New Little Star."

On Friday night, the doorbell rings. It is Graham.

"Your father contacted me," he says solemnly. "I understand that we're going to have a baby."

Caroline's hands clench. How just like her father—to ignore what she had said; to assume he knew what was best, without knowing anything at all.

"He shouldn't have done that."

"He was thinking of the baby."

"But, Graham—"

He holds up a hand.

"This changes everything, of course," he says. Once more, she tries to stop him, but he will not be stopped. "At this point, we've got to put the baby first." He talks quickly on about how they have an important responsibility, how they owe something to this new life they have created, how they have an obligation to lay aside their differences and make a fresh start.

He is sincere, and his eyes are earnest. Caroline imagines stepping into his arms and agreeing to the fresh start. And she senses she could make a go of it this time—she is older now, with fewer illusions. The baby would have a father. Graham could take him to baseball games, buy him little Yale T-shirts. But this is all fantasy.

Caroline steps back. She cannot look at him.

"Graham, I'm pretty certain it's not your baby," she says gently.

He takes in a breath. She realizes how excited he has been about becoming a father. It is horrible to have to cause him this pain.

His face reddens. "It's the old man's?"

"Yes."

"Your father didn't mention that little detail."

"He didn't know."

Graham turns away. "I wish you'd told me sooner—stopped me from making a fool of myself."

"You didn't make a fool of yourself."

There is a silence. "Is he going to take care of it?"

"No. I'm on my own with this."

"I see." He starts for the door. "Well, I guess there's nothing more to say."

"I'm so sorry, Graham."

He pauses at the door. Awkwardly he adds, "But if you ever need anything . . ."

Caroline walks over and puts her arms around him.

"You are a very nice man."

He pulls away, shakes her hand, and says good-bye.

Caroline loves working at Little Worlds. She soon learns the inventory and the bookkeeping system, and she stays awake late at night, planning the windows. She remembers a shop she had admired at Yale, an obscure little print shop, which always had a grand new window display on Mondays. Every week now, in its honor, she arranges a different scene in the window of Little Worlds.

People notice. There is always someone coming down the stairs to the shop. And business has increased.

Trina says that hiring Caroline was the best thing she's ever done.

When closing time comes, Caroline hurries home and spends the evening working on her dollhouse. It is coming along well. She has sanded all the floors. She has painted the outside with four coats of shiny gray enamel. There is nothing about it that isn't perfect.

When the shell of the house is completed, she starts to decorate the rooms. She begins with the nursery. She stencils minute ducks in a frieze, paints scenes from Beatrix Potter on the chest of drawers.

Caroline imagines holding her son on her lap.

"Now touch it gently," she'll say, and his wondering finger will reach out and make the tiny cradle rock back and forth.

Caroline is in the bay window of Little Worlds, working on a Mother's Day display. As she places baby dolls in bassinettes, she hears Trina sigh. She turns and sees her pick up a brochure from the mail and toss it aside.

"What's that?" Caroline asks.

"An ad for the London Dollshouse Festival."

"Why are you throwing it away?"

"Because I want to go."

Caroline laughs. "Well, why don't you?"

"Don't be ridiculous."

"It's not ridiculous. It's only for a few days—I'd watch the shop for you. Trina, you've talked about this dollhouse festival ever since I've known you—do yourself a favor and go."

Hesitantly, Trina looks toward the brochure.

When Caroline comes in to work the following afternoon, Trina grins at her.

"I'm going to London," she announces.

"Good for you!"

"Well," Trina says sheepishly, "Good for us, actually."

She reaches down and puts two airline tickets down on the counter.

Caroline stares at the tickets.

"Trina," she says, "I'd love to, but I can't. It's completely impossible. Who would mind the shop? And there's my job at the bookstore . . . and I'm having a baby."

"All the more reason to go now," Trina tells her.

"Anyway, there's no way I could afford it."

"It's a gift," Trina says. "It wouldn't be any fun at all, being there on my own. You'd really be doing me a favor." She puts the tickets in Caroline's hand. "We leave May seventeenth."

* * *

London is too rich, too much to take in all at once. Instead, Caroline concentrates on little things, turns the city into a series of tiny, bright etchings. The leaves of a plane tree falling over thick wrought iron. Amber tea in a translucent white cup. A charwoman polishing a brass door knocker. A freckled schoolboy in a red-and-gray uniform.

Her mornings are spent at the dollhouse festival, walking around the booths with Trina, talking to the artisans, buying tiny Elizabethan beds and Georgian caps and silver candlesticks. The afternoons and evenings are spent exploring London. Trina begs to go back to the hotel and rest, but Caroline won't hear of it. They visit the docklands, the bridges, every museum in the guidebook. They take a boat ride to Greenwich, attend a session of Parliament, go to the theater, and see a puppet show on Lavender Hill.

"God, I wish I'd never brought you," Trina groans.

The final afternoon of the trip, she rebels.

"You do what you want, but I'm not budging from this room."

Caroline decides to spend this last afternoon walking down the King's Road. The weather is windy and blue; the street winds like a path in a fairy tale. Every block or so, she stops, making more little etchings in her mind.

At last, she comes to a large building—the name Antiquarius is tiled in fading circus letters above the door. Caroline goes in.

She has found Sleeping Beauty's castle. Dusty sofas, antique four-posters, battered carriage clocks gleam dully against dark corners. Shredded tapestry reticules, filigree jewelry, heavy, blackened books peep out behind thick glass.

Caroline tiptoes around. She touches a pair of frayed mauve gloves, and wonders whose hands had last worn them. She fingers a wicker high chair, imagining the baby who once sat in it.

And then, high upon a wall near the exit, she spots a painting—a small painting of a Victorian dollhouse. It is the most enchanting thing she has ever seen.

She must have it. It is not an option. She has not brought much money, but she will charge her credit card to the maximum, she will borrow from Trina, she will sell all her furniture when she gets home.

Caroline looks around for someone to help her. She sees a man sitting on a stool in a nearby booth. He smiles at her. Something about him seems familiar—he looks remarkably like someone she knows, but she cannot think who it is.

"May I help you?"

Caroline tries to sound casual. "I was wondering about that painting of the dollhouse."

"Ah, yes. It's a lovely one."

"How—how much is it?"

He names the sum. It is not that great; Caroline will not have to sell her furniture. She finds herself a little disappointed that the sacrifice is to be so small.

"I'd like to buy it."

The man stands up on the stool and pulls the painting gently down from the wall.

"I'll miss this one," he says. "It doesn't pall on you, the way some do." He starts to wrap the picture. Caroline watches hungrily as the dollhouse begins to disappear beneath layers of cardboard.

"It's always made me think of that Katherine Mansfield story," he goes on. "The one about the doll's house."

"I'm afraid I don't know it," Caroline says.

She counts out the money and gives it to him.

He takes it with a little bow. Again, he makes Caroline remember someone else—she cannot imagine who.

But what does it matter, anyway? She has the painting, the most glorious painting in the world, in her arms.

CARO

Caro returns to New York. She goes back to her apartment in Hell's Kitchen. She doesn't leave it.

She puts the picture of Tristan's mother in the bottom drawer of her bureau. She does not let herself think about the baby or the gray Victorian house with the stained glass windows. She does not let herself think about Tristan.

She has no plans for her future, but this does not worry her. It is as if she were standing on a completely white space. She can stay there as long as she likes, and when she is ready, she will step off into any future she chooses.

Zoë writes to her, but it is too tiring to read letters. Caro throws them, unopened, under her bed.

It is also getting too tiring to eat.

Caro is sitting on her bed. She cannot remember how long she has been there. There is a sudden noise; someone is banging on the door.

She does not want to open it, but the banging won't stop. Finally, she pulls the door open.

A woman is standing there, someone familiar, though Caro can't quite place who it is.

"My God," Zoë says.

She rushes into the room, a tangle of scent and flowing clothes. "My darling, you're killing yourself."

Caro smiles. Yes, that's exactly what she is doing. She had just not put it into words before.

The voice goes in and out. ". . . never answered my letters . . . knew there was something wrong . . ."

Caro is being put to bed. She goes to sleep. When she wakes up, Zoë is sitting beside her, holding a bowl of soup.

"This is incredibly selfish of you," she tells Caro as she props her up and feeds her the broth. "There are other people who love you, you know. It wasn't only him."

Caro turns her head away. Zoë puts down the bowl.

"I'm sorry I couldn't come to England," she says. "I know I would have liked him."

"Yes."

Zoë's white hands with the long red nails stroke Caro's hair.

"This would have made him miserable, darling. He wouldn't have wanted to see you doing this to yourself."

Caro shrinks away.

"We were going to get married," she says tightly. "We were going to stay on the island and have a baby."

Zoë nods rapidly.

"Yes," she says. "I had something like that, too, once." Her voice is thin. "With a man named Max. We were going to move to Paris. But he was killed in a car crash."

There is a long silence. Caro did not know that there was a story like that in her mother's life. Zoë's color is high. She smiles at Caro with hard brightness.

"So, believe me, darling, I understand. But you've got to let him go."

Caro clenches her hands.

"How can I let him go? I never had him. It was only a few months. I never really knew him at all."

She is aghast at the pain. She puts her head in her hands.

"He was going to show me everything—all the places he'd lived. All the people he loved. But we never got to do any of it."

"Well," her mother says, "maybe you should do it now."

Caro looks up. "What?"

"Go back to England. Go to those places he wanted to show you. Meet the people."

"But I don't know where they are."

"You could find out easily enough. Go to the library. There must be so much written about him. Where he grew up, where he went to school. Go visit those places. Even if you don't get it exactly right, at least you'll come close."

Caro turns away impatiently. "But what would be the point?"

Zoë straightens. "The point would be that you're doing something he wanted. Go back to England, baby," she says. "I'll pay for the trip. And when it's over, I want you to get on with your life."

Caro prepares. She reads everything available about Tristan, every review, every article, every interview. At the Museum of Television and Radio, she finds taped performances, early concerts. She tries to contact Harper and Rob, but they do not write back. It doesn't matter. She will find the places without them.

She has her list. The house Tristan was born in. The primary school he went to. The first bar he played at. The address of his brother's shop in London.

She finds out so much about Tristan she had not known. She wishes she had talked with him more. Sometimes, when she goes to bed, she feels him beside her with soft yellow hair and warm hands. She talks to him now, but he does not answer.

She arrives in England on a morning in May. She spends three weeks. She takes the train to York where Tristan grew up. She visits the school he went to. She sees his desk, and the peg where he hung his coat.

She goes to see the house where he was born. It has been torn down, but she walks the streets where Tristan used to walk. There are two neighbors, an old man and his wife, who knew him as a child. They tell her how he used to ride his red scooter up and down the road.

She takes the train south. She goes all over. She meets a lot of people, and listens to all their stories.

The day before Caro is to fly back home, she goes into London.

Tristan's brother owns an antique shop on the King's Road. Caro takes a taxi to the address. It turns out to be a large building, with the name Antiquarius tiled in faded circus letters above the door. She goes inside. The building is dark, filled with stalls and corridors.

She turns a corner and there is Tristan standing behind a counter. She draws in a breath. The man looks up. She sees that he is not Tristan.

"Are you all right?"

Caro smiles brightly. "Oh, yes. I just turned my ankle."

She cannot bring herself to tell Tristan's brother who she is. She keeps looking at him, staring at the hair which is the same, and the hands.

She can't bear it—she has to leave.

She walks down the King's Road, crying.

When she comes back, he is ready for her.

"I know who you are," he says. "I recognized you from the newspapers."

"I know who you are, too."

They smile bleakly at each other. Caro has her list of questions all ready to ask him, but she doesn't take them out of her purse. She will leave his memories alone.

They make small talk; they are respectful of each other. They do not even mention Tristan.

She looks around the shop.

"You have some lovely things."

"Thank you."

And then, high up on the wall, she sees a painting—a small oil painting of a Victorian dollhouse.

Caro gives an exclamation.

"What a wonderful picture."

"Isn't it, though? There's such marvelous detail. It's always made me think of that Katherine Mansfield story—the one about the doll's house."

Caro hesitates. "How much are you asking for it?"

He looks up.

"It's not for sale. It's a gift."

He pulls the painting down from the wall and starts to wrap it up.

"Thank you," she says.

He hands the package over the counter. She leans forward and kisses his cheek. Then he kisses hers.

Caro knows the trip has come to an end. She has done all she needed to do for Tristan—she has even been given a gift and a kiss to start a new life upon.

Caro goes back to New York. She calls Zoë from the pay phone down the street.

"I want to thank you for the trip," she says.

"Did it work?"

"I think so."

"Good," Zoë tells her briskly. "Well, now that all that's over, we can get cracking on your career."

Caro closes her eyes. "No," she says.

"When you're ready," Zoë tells her. "When you're ready."

Caro hangs up the phone and walks back to her apartment. She doesn't think she will ever be ready.

She finds another waitressing job; this time in her neighborhood. Not many people come into the coffee shop, and the work is light. She stays close to home, goes to work, wanders along hot summer streets.

One Saturday in July, she takes a walk downtown and ends up at the Barnes & Noble bookstore on 18th Street. She looks around for a few minutes, but doesn't find anything of interest. Then, as she is about to leave, she sees a thick paperback high on a shelf; it has the picture of a woman on the cover. Her expression is extraordinary. Caro stops. She cannot take her eyes from this woman's face.

The Collected Stories of Katherine Mansfield. The name is familiar, but Caro can't remember from where.

It's always made me think of that Katherine Mansfield story—the one about the doll's house.

Caro buys the book. First she reads "The Doll's House"—it moves her almost unbearably. Then she reads the rest of the stories. It takes her all day and most of the night. The stories are about little things.

The gift of a pineapple. A garden party. An almond in a cake. When she finishes the book, she reads it again. And when she finishes it the second time, she leaves it face up on her desk, so that Katherine Mansfield is always looking at her.

One muggy evening, Caro is finishing up at work. A customer has left a folded newspaper on the booth, and an ad catches her attention.

> AUDITIONS: A Tree Grows in Brooklyn. The Eastside/ Westside Playhouse, August 15th, 8:00.

The Eastside/Westside Playhouse. Caro remembers seeing one of their shows, *Barefoot in the Park,* a year or two before—it had been an awful little production. with a dreadful black-haired actress playing Corie. Still, she does not drop the newspaper. *A Tree Grows in Brooklyn,* of all things. She had not thought to see that title again. She rips out the ad and stuffs it into her pocket.

The auditions are being held in midtown, in an old dance studio. The room is filled with young actresses, and children watched by anxious mothers. There seem to be two men in charge—one is dark and bearded, the other scruffy and bespectacled. Caro is handed a sign-in sheet. She fills it out, and hands it to the man with the glasses. He looks down at what she has written, and hurries over to his partner.

They both come over to Caro.

"Are you really Caro Andrews?"

"Yes."

One of the mothers looks up. "Oh, my God—it *is* you!"

"It's Flossie Gaddis from the show!"

The whisper is beginning to go around. The other actresses hear it. They do not look happy.

Caro auditions for the lead, the part of Katie Nolan. The following day she receives a call at work, saying she has gotten the part.

* * *

Zoë goes into immediate action.

"I'll call Ted Frankenheimer at the Martin Beck, and I'll think of some way we can get Joe Papp to come see you."

"Zoë, I don't want anyone to come see me," Caro tells her. "Including you. I can't tell you how dreadful this show is going to be. Why I'm doing it, I'll never know."

"I do," Zoë says instantly. "Because you're an actress, that's why. Do you have a script yet?"

"Yes."

"Send it to me, and I'll write down your through-line."

Caro sends her mother a copy of the script, and three days later it is returned to her, covered with notes in Zoë's red felt pen. It is good to see her mother's writing on a script again. It is good to be acting. It is good to be Katie Nolan.

A week before the show opens, Caro takes a subway up to the apartment building on Park Avenue. She goes inside the lobby, gets into the elevator, and pushes the button for the eighteenth floor.

She remembers the first time she ever did this, the first time she visited her father, and how queasy the ride made her feel. It makes her feel queasy now.

She walks down the hall to the apartment and knocks on the door.

"Just a minute!" cries a voice. It is Meg's.

The door is opened on the chain. Meg's face appears, and the door is quickly closed again. For a moment, Caro thinks she is not going to be let in; but a moment later, the door is flung wide.

"Caro! I can't believe it!"

She is hustled inside.

"Barton! Adam! Come here!"

"Caro!"

Adam is fifteen now, unbelievably tall. He rushes to Caro and hugs her hard. His hair smells different than it used to.

She looks at his hands. "They've grown," she says accusingly.

"Well, sure," he says. "I'm on the basketball team at school."

Barton hurries into the hall.

"My God. Caro."

She is amazed to see that he is weeping. And now Meg is starting to cry. They beam through tears and pat Caro and lead her to the sofa. Adam lopes by her side.

"I want you to come see me play. We've got a game on Wednesday against the Ratpackers—I'm the point guard. Will you come?"

They are all talking, all jumping happily over one another's sentences. No one mentions what happened the last time they were together. No one mentions that it's been years since they have seen one another. Caro is spared any embarrassment, any recriminations, and she is grateful and relieved.

She wonders if maybe Zoë had been right. Maybe she should have come up here a long time ago—she might have been welcomed like this all along.

But it didn't really matter. The way things are happening now is perfect. They are a family again.

Meg takes her hands. "Caro, we were so sorry about Tristan."

Caro nods.

"We tried to get in touch with you," Barton says, "but Zoë told us you wanted to be left alone. We figured you'd come when you were ready."

"And here you are." Meg glows. "I can't believe it. Tell us everything."

"Well, for starters, I'm opening in a play next week. It's going to be awful, but I'd like you to see it."

While Meg and Adam exclaim, Barton takes out a little leather book from his pocket and writes down the information. It is good to see the little leather book again, good to see his minute, precise handwriting. They will be there, he tells her, the second Sunday matinee.

"And don't forget my game!" Adam cries. "It's Wednesday at four."

Caro stays fifteen minutes more and then she says she has to leave.

"Rehearsal," she explains.

They hug her again as she goes out the door.

The rehearsal isn't, in fact, for another two hours, but this short visit was enough for now. It is a little strange, after all this time, to be part of her father's family once again.

* * *

The day before the show opens, cast photos are put up outside the theater. Caro is startled to see that she is no longer Flossie Gaddis, wearing a pinafore and boots, her hair braided in a coil. Now she is Katie Nolan. Now she is Mama.

She realizes that she has grown up.

Zoë is flying in for opening night; her plane is due in that evening. Caro has the visit all planned. She'll pick Zoë up at the airport, and spend tonight with her at the Waldorf. Tomorrow, they'll go shopping. Then after the performance, she has made reservations at 21, Zoë's favorite restaurant. She has been saving all month so that she can pick up the check.

But when Caro arrives at the theater for the dress rehearsal, Chad hands her a telegram.

> SO SORRY BABY STOP DAMN NUISANCE HEALTH PREVENTS MY BEING THERE STOP NOTHING SERIOUS—NOT TO WORRY STOP GO AHEAD AND ACT YOUR HEART OUT—I'VE GOT THE CRITICS BRIBED STOP

Caro leaves the theater and goes down the street to a pay phone.

The phone rings six times before Zoë picks up.

"What are you doing?" she screeches when she hears Caro's voice. "You should be in makeup!"

"Are you all right?"

There is a small pause.

"Of course I'm all right," Zoë says. "Just a little indisposed. And that idiot doctor doesn't want me flying right now. But I'll be out before the show closes—that's a promise. Now get off this phone and knock 'em dead at the dress rehearsal."

With such competition as *Sweeney Todd, Chicago,* and *A Chorus Line,* Caro doesn't hold out much hope for *A Tree Grows in Brooklyn.* But opening night goes better than expected. *Variety* calls it "a charming confection," and the *Village Voice* is almost affectionate. Caro's performance is praised by everyone. All the critics agree that she has successfully made the transition from child star to adult performer.

Caro sends Zoë the notices.

"Brava," Zoë says, but she does not mention when she is flying out to see the show.

Barton and Meg and Adam come, as promised, the second week. After the show, they go backstage.

"I'm the brother!" Adam tells everyone.

Meg hugs her. "You were just wonderful."

"The best thing in the show," Barton says, and adds slowly, "Your mother would be very proud."

"What are we going to do now?" Adam asks. "We can't just go home."

They decide to have ice cream at Rumplemeyer's. Caro hasn't been there since she was eleven years old, in the days before her father and Meg were even married.

"Remember how we used to sing 'Flaming Robin Rose Glow with Lisa Delight?'" she asks Adam. But he shakes his head.

For some reason, conversation is a little awkward. There is the play to discuss, and Caro's future plans, and then there is suddenly nothing to talk about. They all eat their ice cream.

The maitre d' comes by. "How was everything?" he asks.

"Great," Adam tells him. "But you should get my sister's autograph, and put it up on your wall. She's the star of a Broadway show."

Caro laughs. "Hardly Broadway."

"It's close." Adam sighs. "I'd like to be an actor, too."

Out of the corner of her eye, Caro can see Barton stiffen. She is amused, a little hurt.

"I don't think that's for you, Adam," he says.

When they leave the restaurant, there are hugs and promises to get together soon. Caro watches her father and Meg and Adam walk down the street to the taxi stand.

This is her family. Caro wonders if it is a little bit sad that she doesn't feel something more.

The final Saturday of the show, Caro goes backstage after the performance to find a man standing in front of the dressing room. He is tall, with a dark, generous face.

"Caro," he says, and extends his hand.

He speaks as if he knows her, but Caro has no idea who he is.

"I'm Steven Lasky," he tells her. "We've met once before—I wonder if you would even remember. My grandfather and I came onto the set one day when you were shooting your television show."

"Oh, yes," Caro says. "I remember." She smiles at him. "You wanted to be a photographer."

He laughs. "That's right. It turned out I had no talent whatsoever—I ended up as a publicist."

"Very wise," Caro says. There is a pause.

"How's your mother?" Steven asks.

Caro frowns. "I'm not sure. She tells me she's all right, but she never came to see the play."

"You were wonderful, by the way."

"Thank you."

"Do you know what you'll do next?"

"I've no idea. I've been practicing living in the moment."

He nods. "I try to do that, too," he says. "It's damned hard."

Two little girls are coming shyly up the corridor. Steven gestures toward them.

"Well, I won't keep you. You have other fans waiting."

He pulls out a business card and gives it to Caro.

"But I'd love to have lunch with you sometime. If you're free. Perhaps I could be of help. Not, obviously, that you need help," he adds quickly.

As Katie Nolan, Caro smiles at the two little girls. Then she smiles at Steven, as herself.

"I'll give you a call," she says.

Caro is no longer interested in love. She has already had it. She has been squeezed dry by it. But it is something to be standing here with Steven Lasky, the lost love of her childhood.

CAROLINE

Caroline has had no luck finding a new place to live. For a month now, she has spent every weekend apartment-hunting, but everything is either too expensive or too small. One Saturday morning, she takes the subway down to the Bay Ridge area of Brooklyn and sees a FOR RENT sign in front of a grand old brownstone. The building seems somehow familiar.

Caroline climbs the steps, and the landlady shows her around. "An older couple lived here," she tells Caroline. "The husband died a few months ago, and the wife moved to Phoenix."

Caroline can only nod. It is the apartment she had looked at before she and Graham were married, the one she had wanted so badly. She wonders if it has been waiting for her all this time.

She moves into the new apartment on a Sunday. Eric, Trina's brother, has a truck, and the three of them go back and forth through the city, bringing furniture down the elevator of one building and up the stairs of the other. Caroline leaves a lot of things in the apartment on the Upper West Side, things she imagines Graham might like to have.

At last there are no more trips to make. The three of them sit on boxes and eat cold, bad, takeout pizza. Caroline cannot remember ever being happier.

The apartment is small: a living room/library, a dining alcove with a pull-out sofa bed where Caroline will sleep, a minute kitchen, a bathroom, and a glorified closet, which is to be the nursery. The pared-down furniture just fits. The area rugs seem to have been ordained for their new spaces. There is just enough room for the kitchen utensils. The painting from Antiquarius goes perfectly in a niche above Caroline's bed. But try as she will, she cannot find room for her dollhouse.

"I want you to have it," she tells Trina.

"I couldn't," Trina protests. "Not your dollhouse!"

Caroline smiles. "That's all right. It's time I let it go."

Trina puts the dollhouse on display in Little Worlds, and Caroline is pleased by how many compliments it receives. Many of the customers buy kits for themselves. It is fun being an inspiration.

She decides that her life is small, but that, as far as it goes, it is very good.

Toward the end of the summer, Caroline starts to prepare the nursery. She paints the room a sunshine yellow, and turns the ceiling into a cloud-filled sky. She finds a rocking chair perfect for bedtime stories, and puts a pillow at the back, embroidered with the words, "There's nobody like my son."

"So it's going to be a boy," the saleslady says.

Caroline smiles. "I hope so."

She spends a great deal of time in the room, sitting in the rocker and reading aloud—Beatrix Potter and *Goodnight, Moon* and Shakespeare's sonnets. Bach is always on the record player, along with Tristan's *Songs from Camelot.* She wants her son to get used to the best.

It seems to her that the baby's spirit is there, even before his body has come. Once, by the pantry, Caroline sees a shadowy little boy dressed in a dark-green coverall. Once she finds him climbing up the stool in her bathroom. And when she sits in the rocker and reads the stories, she can feel him breathing.

"You are the most loved child in the world," Caroline tells him.

It is late August. The baby is due in two months. Caroline is beginning to find her work situation impossible. The forty-five-minute commute to midtown is tiring but manageable, but going from one job to the next is becoming more than she can handle.

When Trina offers her a full-time position at Little Worlds, she accepts it gratefully.

The next day, Caroline tells Laszlo that she is sorry, but she must quit her job at the bookstore. He is desolate to see her go.

"And you are leaving us for dollhouses?" he asks incredulously. "This cannot be possible."

She is given a farewell party. Peter brings beer and Gina brings pizza and Laszlo makes his strudel. Caroline is presented with an umbrella with a Degas motif—and for the baby, there is a huge and terrifying volume of Goya's prints.

But even with the full-time work, there is still not enough money. Caroline doesn't know what to do. She considers asking her father for help, but decides against it. And then one night, she gets a call from Laszlo.

"A friend of mine—he has started to publish," he tells her. "Volumes of architecture. But he needs someone who can go through the books, make changes, make them spruced."

"An editor?"

"Yes. I tell him all about you. It will be good work for you with the baby. But I warn him, you cannot work all the time—and you are very expensive."

"Bless you, Laszlo."

Caroline hangs up the phone. Miniatures and manuscripts. It sounds wonderful.

Two weeks before the baby is due, Caroline is walking home from the Park Slope Food Co-Op. In a sudden sharp earthquake, the ground begins to tilt and slide. The grocery bags drop. Caroline falls onto the pavement.

When the shaking finally stops, Caroline finds people starting to gather around her. She understands that there has been no earthquake. She looks down and sees the rich stain spreading from her legs.

Trina is holding her hand in the ambulance.

"It's going to be all right," she keeps saying.

Caroline knows that can't be true.

The doctors are waiting. They say there are complications, but she cannot understand what the complications are. She can only feel pain. She had no idea such pain could exist.

She is lying on a bed, and Trina is beside her.

"The baby?" Caroline whispers.

Trina squeezes her hand. She smiles and nods.

Caroline holds her sleeping son in her arms. He is the child whose shadow visited the apartment. He is the baby whose breathing she knows. Caroline looks down at the pale cheeks, the unbearably minute eyebrows. She wills his life to be straight and simple, but of course it won't be. He will face the tangle of roads, the same as everybody else. One choice and he will be one person, another choice, and he will be someone completely different. She can only stand by and watch.

The one thing she can do is never leave him. That is a promise she can keep. Around the white, confused little body, her arm grows tight.

Then a name comes to her. It is as if it has been whispered in the silence. She will call him Alexander.

Caroline has been sleeping. When she wakes, she finds her father sitting quietly by the side of her bed. He used to do that sometimes, too, when she was a child.

She is embarrassed at being caught asleep.

He smiles at her. "Congratulations. I just saw my grandson in the nursery—he's a keeper." He picks up some packages from the floor. "These are from Meg and me."

There is a Steiff elephant, an embroidered satin blanket, and a set of tiny Lego blocks.

"You can't start an architect too young."

Caroline is glad that her father is letting her son be an architect.

"Do you know what you're going to call him?"

"Alexander."

He tries it out. "Alexander. It's a good name."

"And, if it's all right with you, I'd like his middle name to be Barton."

Her father reaches over and pats her hand.

"Thanks, sweetheart, but no. Let's let him be someone new."

The phone rings four times before Zoë answers.

"Hello?" Her voice sounds sleepy.

"Zoë?" Caroline says carefully. "I just thought you'd like to know—you're a grandmother."

Zoë's scream is so loud that Caroline has to pull the phone away from her ear.

When Alexander is three weeks old, Caroline brings him over to Barton and Meg's for a visit. Meg is in the living room, sitting on the sofa. She smiles and holds out her arms.

Carefully, Caroline gives her the baby. She has a vision of Meg standing up suddenly, walking to the window, and tossing Alexander outside to fall the eighteen stories.

"You killed my son," she would explain, "and I have killed yours."

But Meg holds Alexander gently.

"He looks like Barton," is all she says.

Trembling, Caroline takes the baby back.

When Alexander is two months old, Zoë comes to visit. Caroline meets her at the airport, the baby sleeping in a little sling around her chest.

Zoë gets off the plane. She looks very small. For a moment, Caroline is alarmed—her mother has never seemed small to her before. But then Zoë catches sight of them and everything is all right again.

"Here they are!" she calls, and hurries over, a crowd of passengers following.

"You don't mind, do you, darling? But I told everyone on the plane about my grandson, and they all wanted to meet him."

Caroline pulls down the side of the sling so that the passengers can admire Alexander. He wakes up and wails.

"Oh, darling—he's glorious, absolutely glorious," Zoë gloats as she touches the tiny cheek. "I'm your grandmother, young man," she tells Alexander. "And I plan on spoiling you rotten. You can have the moon and a pair of orange ice skates if you want them."

She laughs and looks triumphantly up at the passengers.

"I told you he looks just like me."

Zoë has booked her usual room at the Waldorf-Astoria.

Caroline is disappointed. "I was hoping you would stay with me."

"And just where would I sleep, my darling? In the sink? No, thank you. But you and the baby must come to the Waldorf."

Caroline is tempted by the beautiful hotel, but she decides to stay at home. She is afraid that Alexander will be anxious if he doesn't have his yellow room with the cloud ceiling.

Caroline is on leave for four months from Little Worlds, so her days are free for Zoë. Mostly, they go shopping for the baby. At Saks, Zoë buys Baby Dior stretch suits, at Bergdorf's, tiny Italian leather shoes. And at Bloomingdale's, she buys Alexander a tuxedo.

"But it's a size eight!" Caroline protests.

"He'll be a size eight someday, darling," Zoë reminds her with a smile.

The day before Zoë leaves, she takes Caroline, Alexander, and six of her cronies to lunch at 21.

"I have great plans for this little boy," Zoë tells her friends. "When he's three, I'm taking him to Hawaii, and when he's five, we're going to Europe."

"And what about his career?" One of the women laughs. "I'm sure you had headshots made the day he was born."

Zoë looks off into the distance.

"Actually, I don't know how much longer I'm going to keep working," she says gently.

A chill comes over Caroline, as it had come over her at the airport.

But in a moment, Zoë is getting to her feet and raising her glass of champagne.

"A toast to my grandson!" she cries.

That evening, Zoë and Caroline take Alexander over to Barton and Meg's apartment.

"Are you really sure we need to do this?" Zoë grumbles.

"Yes," Caroline tells her firmly. "I haven't had my whole family together since the wedding."

"This place terrifies me," Zoë hisses as they ride up in the elevator. It's so conservative—look at all that beige!"

They arrive at the apartment, and Barton opens the door.

"Barton!" Zoë gives him a smacking kiss on the cheek. Then she goes in to Meg, and hugs her gently.

"So what do you think of our incredible grandchild?"

Caroline grins. "I'd like a picture of this," she says, and takes a camera from her purse.

Zoë, Barton, and Meg arrange themselves in a group on the sofa.

"Who'll hold the baby?" Barton asks.

Zoë flashes a glowing smile.

"Meg, of course," she says, and puts Alexander into her arms.

"You were wonderful," Caroline tells Zoë in the taxi on the way back to the Waldorf.

"I know," Zoë says, reaching across for Alexander. "Now give me back my baby."

Zoë leaves for Los Angeles the following morning. Caroline hugs her good-bye for a long time. Then she raises Alexander's hand in a tiny wave of farewell.

Caroline's world has grown very small. It has shrunk to the size of her son.

There is the ritual of every day. Holding him in the white rocker. Feeding him. Dressing him. Brushing the soft blond hair. Taking his picture. Showing him off to the neighbors. Reading him *Peter Rabbit.* Saying "Mama, Mama," hoping he will repeat the words.

She dreads the day she must leave him, but when he is four months old, the call from Trina comes.

"Ready to come back to work?"

Caroline is not ready, but she goes. She hires Jean, a friendly young Jamaican girl, to watch Alexander while she is away.

When Jean arrives for her first day's work, Caroline gives her a long list of instructions. She keeps talking and talking, but finally she can think of no more to say. She bends down to hug Alexander one last time.

She takes the subway into Manhattan. It is the first time in four months that she has traveled without her son. She hates the emptiness of her hands.

The morning is endless. Caroline tries to concentrate, but her eyes keep going to the photographs of Alexander. Every hour, she telephones the apartment—Jean says that he is doing fine.

But when she calls at one o'clock, there is no answer.

"I think something's wrong," Caroline tells Trina anxiously.

"Everything's fine," Trina scoffs. "She's probably taken him for a walk."

"I don't think so; it's very strange." Caroline bites her lip. "Would you mind very much if I went home and just made sure he's okay?"

Trina rolls her eyes. "All right." She sighs. Then she looks out the store window. "But I don't think you really want to."

Jean and Alexander are coming into the shop.

"I thought he might like to visit his mama," Jean says.

Caroline holds her baby so tightly that he begins to cry.

Alexander's first birthday is coming up. Caroline has ordered a special cake in the shape of a dinosaur. She has hired a magician and a man who makes balloons. She has invited every child in the neighborhood, as well as her father, Meg, Zoë, and Trina.

"How are you going to fit everyone in the apartment?" Trina demands. "There'll barely be room for the balloons."

"It'll be fine."

Trina looks around at all the preparations, and shakes her head. "Caroline," she says abruptly, "I'm getting worried about you."

"Why?"

Trina hesitates. "I think you're too focused on Alexander. I mean, he's wonderful, but—look at all this. It's as if he's the only thing in your life."

Caroline stiffens. "I just want him to have a nice party."

Trina backs off. "I know. And I've never had children, so don't listen to me. It's just—I wish you'd think about something else for a change. You never go anywhere. You never do anything. You never meet anybody."

"I don't need to," Caroline tells her with a smile. "I have my son."

It is an afternoon in April. Alexander is two and a half years old. Caroline hurries home from work; a little boy, just about his age, had come into the shop with his grandmother, and it made Caroline miss Alexander even more than usual.

She reaches home and rushes upstairs to the apartment.

Alexander is sitting in his booster chair, about to have his milk and cookies. Caroline smiles at her perfect timing.

"Thanks, Jean," she says gaily. "I'll take over now."

Jean goes off into the kitchen, and Caroline sits on the chair beside Alexander.

"Now, then, sir!" she says, and picks up a cookie. She pretends to eat it herself, but Alexander does not laugh.

Instead, he frowns and turns his head away.

"Gee," he says distinctly.

It is the name he calls Jean.

Caroline feels herself flush.

"Mama's home now, darling," she tells Alexander. "Mama can give you your milk and cookies."

She picks up another one and sails it toward his mouth. He slaps her hand away.

"Gee!" There is a note of hysteria in his voice. "Gee!"

Jean has come back from the kitchen. She giggles nervously.

"Alexander, please—" Caroline says.

"Gee! Gee!" he shrieks, and holds out desperate arms. With a glance at Caroline, half apologetic, half proud, Jean takes the baby.

Caroline goes into the other room. She sits numbly on the sofa bed. She tells herself not to be ridiculous. Everyone knew that children had moments like this. It didn't mean anything. It didn't mean that Alexander didn't love her anymore.

But maybe it did mean that he was no longer a baby. No longer just hers. He was getting to be a big boy now, and there wasn't a thing she could do to stop it. Soon he would be in school. Soon there would be a whole world of Gees for him. And it didn't matter in the least that there would never be anyone else for her.

Tears come to Caroline's eyes. She lies back on the couch. An image comes into her mind—the image of some Japanese paper flowers she had had as a child. They came inside a curved little shell, fastened with a strip of paper. You undid the strip, put the shell in a bowl of water, and left the room. And only a few hours later, when you came back, the shell was open and the flowers had grown, magical and colorful and complete, filling the bowl.

Caroline takes a breath and sits up. She tells herself she must become like those flowers. If she is not to be in pain for the rest of her life, she must learn to blossom—instantly. She must turn into someone who is more than Alexander's mother.

She gets to her feet and walks around the room. But who will she become? She has no idea. It is as if she were standing on a completely white space, and when she is ready, she may step off into any future she chooses.

She takes a few deep breaths and goes back into the living room. Alexander has finished his cookies and milk. He gives her a bright, hard smile.

CARO

Caro sits on her bed, smoking restlessly. Ever since *A Tree Grows in Brooklyn* closed, she has not known how to spend her nights. There is nothing she wants to do, but staying in the apartment hour after hour is making her crazy.

She goes for a walk. Halfway down the street, she sees a woman wearing a bright flowered scarf. She thinks of Zoë and suddenly she is very blue. It is incredible that Zoë didn't come to New York to see her in the play.

Caro pulls out another cigarette. Something must be going on. Something was wrong, and she wasn't being told. But she won't let herself worry about it; it wouldn't do any good.

She remembers talking to someone about Zoë, not too long ago. Who was it? Steven Lasky—the night he had come to her play. How strange it had been, seeing him again after all those years.

Caro wonders if she still has the business card he gave her. Maybe she'll call him; it would give her something new to think about, at any rate.

The following morning, she telephones.

"Steven. It's Caro Andrews."

She can tell how glad he is that she has called.

When Caro comes into the coffee shop on Saturday at noon, Steven is already there. He rises when he spots her. She slips into the chair across from him.

"I'm glad we could do this."

"Me, too," he says. "And I only feel a little guilty. I usually spend Saturday mornings at work."

"Isn't that supposed to be family time?"

He shakes his head. "No family. I was married for a year or two, but it didn't work out."

She nods. He does not ask if she has ever been married. They go on quickly to talk of other things.

It is pleasant, being with Steven. He is funny, quirky. When they leave the restaurant, she asks, "What are you doing this afternoon?"

"I thought I'd go down to the Strand Bookstore and take a look around."

"Mind if I go with you?" Caro asks. "I haven't been there in a long time."

They visit the Strand, then take a walk through Soho. After that, they see *All that Jazz* in the Village. Then they go to Mario's in Little Italy.

It is now eleven o'clock.

"May I take you home?" Steven asks Caro.

She smiles at him and shakes her head.

"No."

Caro does not want Steven to fall in love with her. She's way past that sort of thing. And it's sad, in a way—five years ago, three, even, she knows she could have fallen in love with him, too.

"Well," Steven says. "Thank you for a most amazing day." He smiles at her. "You know, I never once asked you what your plans were. For acting, I mean. Now that the show's over."

She shrugs. "Nothing yet. I told you. I'm practicing living in the moment."

He looks down at the sidewalk. "Can I see you again?"

Caro sees a lot of Steven that winter. He is her good friend. She tells him things. She is never afraid of boring him. She knows she can never fail with him.

Only once does he try to kiss her, and she pushes him away, very gently. He does not try again.

But, as lovers do, they establish their places and their routines. They find the best coffee shops. They find the best paths through Central Park. She does not bring him to her apartment, nor does he bring her to his.

He tells her about the women he takes out on dates. She tells him they all sound awful.

They do not usually meet in the evenings, but one afternoon he calls her at work.

"This is awfully short notice, I know, but I've got two tickets for the new Desiree Kaufman play. Are you free tonight?"

Caro hesitates. She hates seeing plays. If the acting's good, she's jealous. If it's bad, she is frustrated because she isn't up there doing it herself.

"I guess so."

Since she needs to go home and change, Steven says that he will come by her place and pick her up.

He arrives a few minutes early, while Caro is still dressing.

"Make yourself at home," she says. "I'll finish up in the bathroom."

When she comes out, Steven is looking at her photographs of Zoë and Adam.

"I like your place," he says. "I've snooped through everything." He points to the little painting of the dollhouse.

"That's adorable—is it from your mother?"

"No. I got it in England. I went there after Tristan died. I met his brother, and he gave it to me."

"It reminds me of something, but I can't think what."

"It reminded Tristan's brother of a Katherine Mansfield story."

"I read her in college, but it's been a while." He points to the book on Caro's desk. "I see she's a favorite of yours."

"Yes."

She finishes dressing, and they leave soon afterward.

The following week, they meet for their usual Saturday lunch. Steven is a few minutes late. He comes in with a wrapped package, which he holds out to Caro. She takes it slowly. It is the first time either one has given the other a gift.

It is an old book, the *Journal of Katherine Mansfield.*

"I hope you don't have it already."

"No. I didn't even know such a thing existed." She smiles at Steven. "Thank you."

All that afternoon, Caro reads the *Journal.* Dusk comes quietly and does not disturb her. She makes herself some soup, then reads some more. When she finally finishes, it is three in the morning.

She closes the book and puts it down. She feels dizzy. She has the sensation that she is no longer who she was; that there are thoughts in her head that are not her own.

She goes to the mirror. She believes she will see another face, a pale one with dark eyes, staring back at her. But she sees only herself.

The following Saturday, she and Steven meet at the coffee shop.

"Did you have a chance to read the *Journal?*"

"Yes," Caro says. She does not tell him that she turned into the author.

"Well, I reread some of the short stories," Steven says slowly, "and I got kind of an idea." He is very pink. "What would you think about a one-woman show, based on the works of Katherine Mansfield?"

Caro considers. She sees a dark-haired woman in a snuff-colored dress, sitting on a stool, on a small stage, talking.

"I think it's a good idea," she says slowly. The woman onstage picks up a doll and cradles it. "And don't forget to give her a Japanese doll—she took Koko with her wherever she went."

"All right," he says. "We'll get you a Koko."

Incredulously, Caro laughs.

"Me? You can't mean me for Katherine?"

"Of course I do."

She shakes her head. "You're crazy. I'm completely wrong for it. No one would take me seriously."

"You could do it," Steven says.

"And supposing I could? Steven, do you have any idea what's involved with putting on a show? How much money these things cost?"

"Of course," Steven tells her. "I'm a publicist, remember? Now, I figure we have two choices—to get investors or produce it ourselves.

If we produce it ourselves, it'll be our risk, but if it goes over, we'll stand to do very well. We'll find some little theater—or we'll take it to colleges." He is flushing. He is serious.

Caro goes back to her apartment. She sits on the bed and slowly brings down the book of Katherine Mansfield's short stories. Then she goes over to the mirror, holds the book below her chin, and stares back and forth between the two faces.

She calls Steven from the phone down the street.

"All right," she says. "I'll do it. And I want us to produce it ourselves."

Caro calls her mother that afternoon.

"Zoë," she says, "I'm going to put on a one-woman show."

Zoë's scream is so loud that Caro has to pull the phone away from her ear.

Caro starts off by going to the library and reading everything she can find about Katherine Mansfield. She is a mysterious figure, this outsider from New Zealand, this rule-breaker. Sentimental and cynical. Giving and cruel. She loved life more deeply than anyone, and she died when she was thirty-two years old.

Caro rereads, obsessively, the short stories, the journals, the letters to Katherine's husband, John Middleton Murry. She marks certain passages in red, the passages she knows Katherine would want included in the play.

The next step is to get a script. Steven finds Janet, a woman from Columbia who is doing her dissertation on the Bloomsbury Group.

They invite Janet to one of their lunches. She is a plain girl, focused, unsmiling. From her satchel, she brings out her checklist of possible subjects. K.M.: lesbian aspects of. K.M.: relationship with D.H. Lawrence. K.M.: Virginia Woolf's jealousy concerning.

"Well, that was impressive," Steven says when Janet leaves. "I think she'll do a hell of a job."

"I don't want her writing the script," Caro says slowly.

"Why on Earth not?"

She shakes her head. "I'm not sure. I just know she's the sort of woman Katherine would have made fun of."

Steven sounds sardonic. "Well, maybe we've been wasting our time. Maybe you should be the one writing the script."

"With you," she says.

"You're crazy."

It is two o'clock in the morning. They are in Caro's room. She paces around. It takes only five steps to go from one end of the room to the other. Steven sits on her trunk, making notes.

"I want that letter from Lawrence. The 'I loathe you. You revolt me, stewing in your consumption' one."

"And we'll follow it up with a quote from 'Women in Love.' Maybe something from the 'Blutbruderschaft' scene. Let's nail the bastard."

"Then Katherine with the journal entry—"

"Wanting to replace personal love with impersonal—"

"Because the personal has failed me so badly." They say it together. It is their favorite.

He writes it all down. "Do we want to include a passage from 'The Prelude?'"

"She preferred 'At the Bay.'"

"And Kezia?"

"Yes. And something from 'The Doll's House.'"

They work every night. The play is starting to take shape. Entries, stories, quotes leap up to be included. Caro and Steven are amazed to find that in six weeks a first draft is ready. They go to dinner. They drink a toast to Katherine Mansfield and split a bottle of wine to fortify themselves. Then they go back to Caro's apartment and read the script aloud.

The last words of the play are John Murry's, after Katherine has died. His voice is played over a loudspeaker, over the darkened stage:

She loved best these lines from Hotspur:
But I tell you, my lord fool,

Out of this nettle, danger,
We pluck this flower, safety.

Caro and Steven lower their scripts. They put their arms around each other and cry.

"We still need a title," Caro says.

"What about just *Katherine?*"

"No. Everyone will think it's about Katharine Hepburn."

"Epiphanies?"

"Too obscure. We want something simple—she wrote about little, everyday things."

"How about *Little, Everyday Things?"*

Caro laughs. "Let's call it *Little Worlds.*"

The next step is to find a theater. Caro and Steven look all around New York, at every space available. Finally, they find the Van Damm Theatre in Soho. It's intimate, rather mysterious; perfect for Katherine.

Steven comes to Caro with a list of projected expenses.

She shakes her head. "We'll never make it."

"Sure we will. We'll have to pay for the theater, the ads, and the programs, there's no getting around that, but I've got an idea for the rest. We'll hold a backers' audition—see if we can get a stage manager and the sound and lighting guys to kick in for free. We'll give them a piece of the profits."

"And what if there are no profits?"

Steven smiles at her. "Out of this nettle, danger—"

She smiles back. "We pluck this flower, safety."

Caro gets ready for the backers' audition. She tries to find a dark wig in Katherine's hairstyle, but nothing looks real enough. Finally, she goes to a hair salon and shows the stylist the picture on the cover of the book of short stories.

The first sight in the mirror is eerie. Caro is no longer herself, but she is not yet Katherine Mansfield. She is lost between the two.

* * *

Next, she needs a dress. She has gone through all the photographs in Antony Alpers's *Life of Katherine Mansfield,* and there is one dress she keeps coming back to: a simple dark one with half sleeves. Caro is afraid she will have to have the dress copied by a seamstress, but one day, in an antique shop on Lexington Avenue, she finds a dress almost identical to Katherine's. The shop seems familiar. As Caro is leaving, she realizes why—it is the shop where Meg bought her wedding gown all those years ago.

The backers' audition is held at Steven's apartment. He lives in an old building on the Upper West Side—it is the first time Caro has been there. His place is messy. It feels impermanent, as if he is expecting to have to rush halfway across the world tomorrow.

Caro likes that feeling very much.

Steven is in the kitchen, putting out bottles of wine and whiskey.

"Is the show that bad?" she asks him.

"Just giving ourselves every possible break," he tells her. She can see that he's very excited.

"I'm a nervous wreck."

He goes over to her and puts his hands on her shoulders.

"You'll be fine. You'll knock these guys dead."

She hugs him, then pulls back.

"Katherine would have hated this."

He considers. "I don't think so. She was a practical gal. She would have charmed the pants off everyone to get her show done, just like you're going to do."

"Well, well?" Zoë telephones Steven's apartment that night. "How did it go?"

"It was a dream," Caro tells her. "We've got our soundman, our lighting man, a stage manager, and a guy to record the voice of Murry."

"Good for you," says Zoë. "And I guess the rest of this crazy idea is going to be financed from your *Brooklyn* savings."

"Well, yes; partly."

Zoë sighs. "Put me down for one month's theater rental. I've already called the Van Damm. Highway robbery, but what can you do? I've always been one for throwing good money after bad."

"Oh, Zoë," Caro whispers.

She can hardly speak through tears.

The following week, her father invites her to lunch at Tavern on the Green. At first, conversation is a little awkward. Caro has not seen Barton for a while, and it is hard to think of enough things to fill the silences.

"So. How's this play of yours going?" he asks finally.

"We're in good shape. We're almost there, in fact. All we need are some ads—I thought I'd go out with a sandwich board."

"I'd like to help pay for the advertising," he tells her.

Caro looks at him in amazement.

"You don't need to do that," she says at last.

"You're my daughter," he reminds her. "You don't get to tell me what I need to do." He smiles at her. "Besides, I'd like to see this play get some attention. I hear that the girl who plays Katherine Mansfield is pretty good."

The day before *Little Worlds* is to open, Caro goes over to the Van Damm Theatre. She walks inside and stares at the empty seats. Tomorrow night, an audience will be filling them.

She remembers another afternoon, when she went into another auditorium.

You have no talent whatsoever.

She goes outside the theater again and looks at the poster. *Little Worlds* is written in script, and below it is the photograph of Katherine Mansfield. She looks smart, fierce, defying an audience not to respond to her words. Caro makes herself remember that this evening is about Katherine Mansfield, and not about herself. She is completely unimportant—she is only a conduit.

The show is a hit. Opening night, Caro is given a standing ovation and six curtain calls. Afterward, she is congratulated by the stage manager and the lighting man and the soundman. They are all euphoric; money is going to be made.

* * *

Caro and Steven go out afterward, to an all-night coffee shop. When they sit down, Steven takes a wrapped gift out of his briefcase and hands it to her.

Caro finds, framed on a white mat, a handwritten letter dated 1918.

Gently, she touches the glass above the familiar angled handwriting.

"I will keep it all my life," she says.

She goes home and puts Katherine Mansfield's letter next to the antique button from Tristan.

The reviews are excellent. The *Times* calls Caro's performance "mesmerizing." The *Post* praises the show for avoiding pedantry, and adds that Caro has a "boa-constrictor intensity." The *Village Voice* says it's the classiest one-woman show since *The Belle of Amherst.* Caro is besieged by demands for interviews; she finally agrees to have a phone installed in her apartment.

"Why Katherine Mansfield?" is the most common question the reporters ask.

"I like the way she writes," Caro says, "and I like the way she kept remaking her life."

"Do you remake your life, too?" one interviewer wants to know.

Caro is silent a moment. She can see her past, a tangle of roads, all the choices she made instead of all the choices she didn't make. The sight fills her with queasiness.

"Don't we all?" she only says.

The second week of the run, Barton, Meg, and Adam come to see the show. It is not Caro's best performance—she can sense her father's stiff, angular presence all through the evening. But afterward they come back and tell her how wonderful she was.

Barton takes both her hands in his. "I'm so proud of you," he says.

And Meg hugs her. "It's by far the best thing you've ever done. But how come we never see you anymore?"

Adam is inspecting the various bottles on Caro's makeup table.

"How do you think *I'd* look with black hair?"

Caro smiles at them all.

The show is nearing the end of its limited engagement. Everyone is optimistic that there will be a second incarnation.

One day, after a matinee performance, Steven comes backstage, very excited.

"It's all set," he bursts out. "I've booked us a summer package around the East Coast. We're taking this baby on tour."

He kisses her on the forehead.

"It's just beginning," he tells her.

CAROLINE

Her life feels as if it is just beginning. It is exciting not to know what is going to happen, now that she has decided to be Caroline again, and not just Alexander's mother.

What would she do if she could do anything? Be part owner of Little Worlds, perhaps. She could concentrate all her energies, build up the stock and clientele. Maybe she and Trina could even buy up old dollhouses at auctions, and start a museum of miniatures.

Or maybe she could take night classes and work toward being an architect—the job she had wanted since she was a little girl.

Caroline can feel the force of life flowing through her. It does not matter that she cannot predict the direction of the flow.

Then, one Sunday afternoon, she gets a call from Zoë.

The following morning, Caroline goes into Little Worlds. She walks behind the counter and puts her arms around Trina.

"I'm leaving for California," she says. "My mother is dying."

CARO

Zoë flies out for the last Friday performance of *Little Worlds.* Her plane is to arrive late in the afternoon, and Caro offers to meet it.

"Are you mad?" Zoë scoffs. "You'll be in the middle of your warm-up exercises by then. No, I'll be there for the show, and you'd better be good."

Caro does not see Zoë in the theater. But when she says her first witty line, she can hear the laugh. The warm, booming Zoë laugh. Caro flushes with happiness. She gives the best performance of the play that she has ever given.

Zoë comes backstage afterward.

"My darling," she says. "This is the proudest night of my life."

But Caro does not hear a word. She can only stare at her mother, stare at this white, tiny woman. She understands why Zoë didn't come out to see *A Tree Grows in Brooklyn.* She realizes that she has guessed it all along.

She takes Zoë's fine, pale hand in her own.

"Why didn't you tell me?" she asks.

PART SIX

SOMETHING THAT WAS THERE

CAROLINE

They are leaving the doctor's office.

"Good-bye, Yvonne," Zoë says warmly. "And I do think the new haircut is a tremendous success."

The receptionist beams.

Caroline has told herself that when they get out into the hall she will be able to breathe again, but she can't. She drags in air. Red sparks float before her eyes.

There is a chair in the corner. She sits, head clenched in her hands. Her hands are rubbery, icy, like Halloween tricks.

Six months. Maybe a year.

Zoë hurries over.

"Are you all right, darling? Maybe we should go back to the doctor and let him take a look at *you.*"

"No." Caroline stands up. Ashamed, she puts her arm around Zoë.

"I'm sorry," she says. "It won't happen again."

Zoë is walking ahead, a slight smile on her face.

"Well," she says, "What was that Mark Twain line? The reports of my death have been greatly exaggerated? I'm sorry to have brought you out here for nothing, darling."

Caroline's throat closes. She stares at her mother. There is a pale, fixed smile on Zoë's face. She had to be pretending. It wasn't possible that she hadn't taken in what the doctor had said.

Six months. Maybe a year.

"It's rather a bore, though," Zoë goes on. "These doctors are such alarmists." She looks at Caroline sharply. "I wish you wouldn't keep staring at me like that," she tells her. "I'll be fine by summer. In fact, why don't we plan a little adventure? What do you say to a trip to Greece? I'd love to show Alexander the ampitheaters."

Caroline can only nod.

"I'll call my travel agent on Monday. And in the meantime, you can go home to New York and get back to your own life."

For a moment, Caroline is in Little Worlds, opening up the shop for a waiting customer. For a moment, she is in Central Park, watching Alexander run around, chasing pigeons.

"No," she says finally. She tries to make it sound casual. "I'd forgotten how great California is; I think I'll settle a few things and come back to stay for a while."

"Don't be ridiculous," Zoë tells her. "I know what you're doing, and I'm not going to have you sacrificing your life for me. That sort of thing went out in the last century."

Caroline smiles reassuringly.

"I'm not sacrificing anything," she says. "Honestly. I've been getting burned out on New York lately—I'd really like to live here for a while. For six months or a year." The words bring bile into her mouth, but Zoë does not seem to attach any significance to them. "And Alexander would love it, too."

Zoë narrows her eyes.

"And this has nothing to do with me?"

"No," Caroline says. "I really don't have much else going on right now. I'd love to come—please let me."

Zoë rolls her eyes. "Just when you think they're all grown up."

"Honey, guess what?" Caroline tells Alexander. "We're going to be living in California for a little while."

Alexander looks suspicious.

"Why?"

"Because it's such a great place."

Saying that makes it seem for a moment as if that really is the reason they're going. Caroline sees chaises by the pool, rain on palm trees, bright pink shops in Brentwood.

Alexander starts to cry. "No, no, no."

She sets herself to woo him. She draws Alexander onto her lap and tells him about California.

"I went there for the first time when I was seven. Zoë had an apartment in those days, and every morning we'd go on an adventure. One morning, she wouldn't tell me where we were going. We drove and drove, through big groves of orange trees. And then, suddenly I looked out the window, and there was this huge snowcapped mountain rising up in front of us."

He claps his hands. "Disneyland!"

"Disneyland. And we went on that mountain—the Matterhorn—and Zoë lost the big purple scarf she was wearing. It just fluttered down—*whoosh*—into the darkness." She imitates the flying scarf, and Alexander laughs.

"Maybe it's still there," Caroline tells him. "Maybe we'll find it when you and I go to Disneyland."

"I want to go with Zoë!" He laughs. "*Whoosh!*"

Caroline draws in a breath. "I don't think Zoë will be going with us, honey."

Alexander does not hear. He is running around the apartment, chasing scarves into the Matterhorn.

It does not take Caroline long to get out of New York. She is able to sublet her apartment quickly. The young married couple who take it are greedy for her departure, longing to make the place their own.

"Do you mind if we put some of your furniture in the basement?" they ask. "So we can have our own things around?"

Caroline finds she doesn't mind at all.

She holds a sidewalk sale on Saturday morning. She walks around for a few moments before the people come, and looks at the spread of possessions neatly laid out. There is the bedspread she crocheted in high school, the Lalique vase she and Graham received as a wedding present. A poster from *A Tree Grows in Brooklyn,* art books from college. The chair she bought for Alexander's room. She is fond of all these things. These things have all been important to her. It is strange that now she no longer needs any of them.

She imagines what the apartment will be like when she returns from California in six months or maybe a year. It will be almost empty, and perhaps she will keep it that way.

"How much is this?" A young, red-haired woman is holding up a Botticelli poster that Caroline had bought long ago at the print shop in New Haven.

Caroline smiles at her. "It's a gift," she says.

She goes to Little Worlds to say good-bye to Trina.

"I can't believe you're really going." Trina starts to cry. "I keep feeling it's my fault. I was the one who said you needed a change."

Caroline goes over and holds her. "You'll come visit at Christmas," she says. "I'll show you the Farmers' Market. We'll buy you a big basket of dates and mangoes. And we'll have lunch at the best Mexican restaurant in the world."

Trina nods. "All morning I've been thinking about our trip to London. Remember?"

Caroline smiles. "And the night you helped me move. And the first day we met, when you brought over the dollhouse kit."

Together they look at the finished dollhouse, in the window of the store.

"It's scary, how quickly it all goes."

Trina puts her arms around Caroline.

"Just make sure you come back," she says.

Caroline taps on the beige beveled door. Her father opens it.

"Caroline."

His hug feels formal—a hug that a father might give a child who is going away forever.

"Come on in."

Caroline looks around. Since the last time she was here, Meg has once more changed the apartment around. The curtains are different, and the area rugs, and a large glass unicorn rears up on the coffee table.

"I've started collecting them," Meg tells her with pride.

"Very pretty."

They sit down on the new chintz sofa.

Barton clears his throat. "I hope Zoë appreciates what you're doing for her."

"Oh, it's not really like that," Caroline says quickly. "I'm happy to go. I'd do it for you, too," she adds.

"God forbid." There is silence for a moment. "You okay for money?"

"I'm fine."

"Do you have any idea what you're going to be doing out there?"

"Not yet. But I'll find something."

He shrugs. "Well, it's not what I would have chosen for you, but I guess you know best."

Before she leaves, Caroline goes into the kitchen for a glass of water. As she reaches into the cabinet, she sees, on the top shelf, a chipped ceramic flowerpot. It was one from the old apartment—the one she and Adam had always used to store the playing cards for their games of War. Caroline takes down the little flowerpot. She fingers it with a smile, and steals it.

The day before they are to leave for Los Angeles, Caroline takes a final walk all around New York. She passes by her old school. She walks by the church where her father and Meg were married. She goes by the apartment building she and Graham lived in. She passes the warehouse where she did *Barefoot in the Park.* She goes by the bookstore where she worked. She is no longer expected in any of those places. Other people are walking in those doors.

Finally she goes to The Parrot. She presses her face against the large, dim window and looks inside. She can just see Mike, leaning on the bar, talking to a customer. He is such a handsome man; he looks so warm.

She walks past the window. It is time to go.

Zoë doesn't meet them at the airport. Caroline has told herself she would not be there, but still she finds herself looking for the tall figure in the bright scarf.

They take a taxi into Beverly Hills.

"You'll get the big guest room," Caroline says to Alexander as they near Zoë's house. "The one with the zebra wallpaper. That's where I used to stay when I came to visit. And I'll sleep in the room with the orange bedspread."

Zoë seems happy to see them. But, "Oh, no, honey, no," she says, when Caroline mentions the guest rooms. "It simply won't do. It was all very well when you were fourteen, but I'm not about to have you hovering around me now. Not to mention Alexander." She gives her grandson a beaming smile. "Though I adore him, of course. No—you can stay for a few days, but then you're going to have to find a place of your own. I'll pay."

Caroline is embarrassed by how upset she is.

"But I'm here to take care of you," she reminds her mother.

Zoë looks at her coolly.

"You are not here to take care of me," she reminds her back.

Zoë knows a woman, a former client, who has an apartment to sublet in the San Fernando Valley. Within a week, Caroline and Alexander are moved in.

Caroline cannot relax among the alien furniture—in her mind she is always traveling down Coldwater Canyon to Zoë's house. But Alexander loves the apartment. There is an exercise room in the building, and he spends hours there, hitting the pedals on the stationary bicycle, making them go around and around.

Zoë is not driving much these days. Grudgingly, she agrees to lend Caroline her white Mercedes.

"Just make sure you change the oil regularly," she admonishes.

Every morning, Caroline and Alexander drive down to Zoë's house. Caroline tries to fix breakfast, make the bed, but her mother won't let her.

"I have a maid to do that."

"Can I drive you somewhere? Take you shopping?"

Zoë smiles grudgingly. "No," she says. "I've driven everywhere I want to. And I own every damn thing in the world."

Once Caroline asks, "Would you like me to read to you?"

And Zoë blows up. "I'm perfectly capable of reading to myself," she says. "Honey, I think you need to find a job."

Caroline looks around for work. She would like to find a place like Little Worlds, but although there are dollhouse shops in Los Angeles, none of them is hiring at the moment.

"Dollhouse shops?" Zoë sighs. "Never mind, darling. I'll see what I can do."

She calls Caroline that evening.

"You've got a job," she tells her. She sounds terribly pleased with herself. "I called the agency today."

"The—agency?"

"Zoë's Babies? Remember? The agency I spent twenty-five years of my life putting together?"

"But you've sold it."

"Of course. But I still have some clout, darling. The new owner says she'd be happy to try you."

"But what about Alexander?"

"We'll get him a baby-sitter."

"But—"

Zoë cuts her off. "You start work on Monday."

Caroline hasn't been down to Hollywood in years. She is depressed by the littered streets, the boarded-up brown buildings, the men in cheap leather jackets.

Near Vine Street, she passes a corner shop with XXX videos and red filmy underwear in the window. She remembers a photographer's studio being there once, a studio where she went in a plum velvet dress and had her picture taken by Hans Lasky.

She is glad that Zoë's Babies is on a cleaner street. She parks the car, goes into the building, and walks upstairs to the door with the brightly lettered sign.

For a moment she stands in the entry, looking around. She has not been here since she was eleven years old. It is comforting to see that the place hasn't changed at all. The same desks are under the same windows, the same artwork covers the walls.

The receptionist sees her.

"Can I help you?"

"I'm Caroline Andrews. I have an appointment to see Lisa Rodin."

The receptionist presses an intercom button and announces her. After a moment, a young woman comes out. She is chic and pale; although she is smiling, her face is not particularly friendly.

"I'm Lisa," she says. "Come on in."

She leads Caroline to the office that used to be Zoë's. Here, everything has been changed. As of course it would be, Caroline tells herself quickly. Still, it is a shock.

Lisa sees her glance.

"We start the renovation on the rest of the office next month," she says. "It'll be gorgeous."

Caroline nods. "What—what did you do with my mother's things?" she cannot help asking.

Lisa sounds defensive. "Oh, don't worry; they're all boxed and in the storage room. I've been meaning to send them back to Zoë."

Lisa sits down in the white leather chair behind the large Lucite desk.

"Take a seat."

Caroline sits on the small sofa across from her.

"We've met before," Lisa says, after a pause. "Right here, as a matter of fact. I was one of Zoë's babies. She brought you in to visit one day. She said she was going to make you a star." She gives the smile again. "I was so jealous of you."

"Well, my life didn't go that way," Caroline says lightly.

"So now I understand you're going to be working for us."

"Yes."

"Well," Lisa tells her brightly, "let's see where we can fit you in."

Where Caroline is fitted in is in the Xerox room down the hall, copying and filing papers. In a few weeks, Lisa says, when she has learned office routine, maybe there will be a better job. But for now, this is the best she can do.

Caroline doesn't mind being in the little Xerox room. It is easier than seeing Lisa in her mother's old place, in the offices that are going to be gorgeously renovated next month.

At three, she gets off work and drives to Zoë's.

Zoë is talking on the phone when Caroline comes in. She is in her usual stance, body thrown back on a chair, one hand gesturing.

"I've got to go now," she tells the person she is talking to. "My daughter's just come home from work. . . . . At the agency . . . Yes, she's taking over for me. I know. Isn't it wonderful?"

Caroline reddens. She stares at the rug and cannot raise her eyes to meet her mother's face.

The first three or four months, the days are mainly good. When Caroline goes over to visit Zoë, she finds her mother wearing makeup and dressed with care. She does not seem to have lost any more weight. And when Caroline offers to take her out to dinner or to a movie, Zoë often agrees.

Caroline knows that Zoë is having chemotherapy sessions, but her mother never calls them by name.

"I have to go to the beauty shop," is what she tells Caroline about the appointments. "But the blasted girl keeps putting the wrong rinse on my hair. It's all coming out."

But then suddenly there aren't so many good days. Zoë is increasingly tired, and no longer wants to go to the movies.

There are more and more doctors' appointments, but Zoë won't let Caroline come. It is the housekeeper who drives her.

After one appointment, the doctor calls Caroline. He says that perhaps it is time Zoë had a nurse. Not full time, he says, just someone who could be there at night, in case Zoë needed anything.

"Please," Caroline asks her mother. "I could do it for you. Wouldn't you prefer to have me?"

Zoë squeezes her hands. "No, darling. I love you dearly but I don't want my past hitting me in the face every time I turn around."

The nurse is hearty and homely and named Flavia. Zoë calls her "Flatbush" when she is not around.

Caroline is reassured by Flavia's presence. For the first few days, when Caroline comes by, she finds Flavia in the kitchen or the living room, scrubbing or fixing meals. But on Friday, she finds Flavia in

Zoë's bedroom, sitting on the edge of the bed. She is holding Zoë's hands and crying.

Caroline rushes into the room. "Is she all right?"

Flavia looks up with a red, mottled face. "Your mother is a beautiful saint. I was saying her how I miss my family in Prague. Zoë says she sends me to trip there."

She bends and kisses Zoë's hands. Over the prostrated head, Zoë's and Caroline's eyes meet. Zoë shrugs.

"Beautiful saint," she mouths. "What can you do?"

Caroline goes into the kitchen. In the sink is a pile of dishes that Flavia has not washed. She does the dishes herself. In the bedroom, she can hear Flavia and Zoë, their voices confidential and happy, talking about the trip to Prague.

Alexander is almost three; in September, Caroline enrolls him in a little preschool near her apartment. The night before school starts, Zoë invites the two of them over for dinner. On the sofa, waiting for Alexander, is a beautifully wrapped pile of gifts—a slot-car speedway, a motorized robot, and a collection of children's classics.

"To start your education off right," Zoë tells him. She turns to Caroline. "I can still get it together when necessary," she notes with satisfaction.

The next afternoon, when Caroline picks Alexander up from his first day of school, he is very quiet.

"What's wrong?" she asks.

For a long time, he will not tell her.

"Everyone at school has a daddy," he says at last. "Where's *my* daddy?"

Caroline is silent. She is seven years old, sitting on the bed with Laura. *Tell me about my mother.*

She tries to keep her voice light. "Your daddy is in New York,"

"Can I see him?" Alexander asks eagerly.

"I don't think that's possible, sweetheart."

"Why not?"

"It's hard to explain," she says. "Let's wait till you're older."

His face darkens in a frown.

"But you've got me," she tells him quickly. "Me and Zoë and Flavia. And we all love you so much."

But his face does not clear.

"This is how much we love you!" She tickles him under the arm. *"This* is how much!" She tickles his neck.

At last he starts to giggle.

One October afternoon, Caroline goes over to Zoë's.

"Next Friday is Science Day at school," she tells her mother. "There's going to be a special assembly, and Alexander's going to play a bee."

"A bee," Zoë echoes dreamily.

"I'd love you to come," Caroline says. "But let's see if you're up for it."

"Let's see if I'm up for it?" Zoë repeats witheringly. "Let's see if I'm up for watching my only grandson make his theatrical debut?"

The following Friday, Caroline comes over early to help Zoë get ready. Zoë refuses all help, and dresses herself carefully. Over her head is a huge orange-and-green scarf.

Going to Alexander's preschool, it feels like old times, driving with her mother around Los Angeles. Except now it is Caroline who is driving, and Zoë who is in the passenger seat.

They arrive at the school. Zoë is very gracious to the teacher, and accepts two Pepperidge Farm cookies from the refreshment table. When the pageant begins, she sits tensely forward, eyes narrowed. Finally, Alexander comes on in his yellow-and-black felt costume. "I am a bee," he says. "Buzz, buzz. I am the flowers' friend." His antennae hit him in the eye, and the audience laughs.

When the pageant is over, Zoë turns to Caroline.

"He doesn't have an ounce of talent," she says flatly.

Caroline agrees. She is surprised by the relief she feels.

"Oh, well." She smiles. "Maybe he'll find something else to do."

She goes over and hugs her bee, and tells him how proud she is of him.

* * *

The following morning, when Caroline goes over to Zoë's house, she finds her mother in bed, looking through that week's *Dramalogue.*

Zoë taps a paragraph with a long red fingernail. "Have you seen this?"

Caroline laughs. "I don't subscribe to *Dramalogue.*"

"You should start. Someone's doing *They Shoot Horses* at a little theater in Woodland Hills. There could be a role for you."

"Zoë, I'm not an actress," Caroline says firmly.

"Regardless. I want you to try out for this."

Caroline sits on her mother's bed. "It doesn't make any sense. In the first place, I'd never get a part. In the second place, I have a son. In the third place, I have a job. And in the fourth place, I'd like to spend a little time with you."

Zoë sighs. "In the first place, nonsense. In the second place, Flavia can pick Alexander up after school; Lord knows she doesn't have anything else to do. In the third place, your job's only three days a week, and in the fourth place, you can spend time with me when I coach you on your part."

Caroline does get a part—a good one. She is cast as Alice, the actress who has a nervous breakdown and is finally led out of the dance marathon, insane.

Zoë goes into immediate action. Every night, while Alexander plays with Lego on the rug, she works with Caroline on the role.

"Well, the scene with the matron's still an utter washout." She sighs at the end of one session. "I can't believe that a daughter of mine could be so absolutely stiff. But other than that, I guess it's coming along." She gives Caroline a hard little smile. "You're quite good, you know."

Caroline smiles back. "I don't think so. But I'm enjoying working with you."

Zoë sighs. "If I could have gotten my hands on you right from the start, you could have been a star."

Caroline finds she is flushing. "That's all right," she says stiffly. "I'm happy with the way everything turned out."

Zoë looks at her curiously. "What do you want to do with the rest of your life? The big picture."

Caroline hesitates. "I'm not sure," she says. "Sometimes I think about being an architect. But I guess the real dream is to do something with dollhouses. Maybe what I'd like most is to start a museum. A museum for antique dollhouses."

"A museum for antique dollhouses." Zoë repeats slowly. "Very sweet. But Caroline, don't you hear what I'm saying? I'm telling you you're good. You could be an actress."

"Well," Caroline says hastily, "Nothing's settled. I have no real plans."

Zoë shakes her head. "That's your whole problem. Now let's get back to this scene with the matron."

Driving home, Caroline cannot forget what Zoë said. She lets herself imagine what it might have been like if she had grown up with her mother instead of Barton. She might be a famous actress now. She might be on Broadway. She might be starring in a movie.

But that was only the beginning. The past that could have been unfolds like Japanese paper flowers. If she had grown up with Zoë, Adam wouldn't have died. If she had grown up with Zoë, there wouldn't have been Graham. Or Mike. But then she wouldn't have had Alexander. Or worked with Trina in Little Worlds. No. All in all, it was better this way. Her life was just as it should be. Untraveled roads were always intriguing, but surely she was living the life she was meant to be living.

Alexander is looking over at her.

"Why are you crying?" he asks.

They Shoot Horses, Don't They? opens in mid-November and is scheduled to run for six weekends. Zoë says she will be there opening night, but when it comes, she is too tired to go.

"Much less pressure on you anyway," she tells Caroline. "I'll come in a few weeks, when the performances have settled down."

In a few weeks, she says that she would rather go the final weekend of the run.

"Shows always bog down in the middle—the actors are losing their first wind and haven't gotten their second one yet. I'll be there for your last hurrah."

The final night of the show, Caroline comes to Zoë's house to pick her up. Zoë is in her nightgown, in bed.

"I'm afraid I can't make it, baby." She pats Caroline's hand. "But I know how good you are. I don't have to be there to see it."

Caroline bends down, kisses the white hand.

By February, there are almost no good days anymore. Every time Caroline comes over, Zoë is in bed, and usually asleep.

When her mother is awake, Caroline talks to her. She sits on the wicker side chair, pulls it up close to the bed, holds Zoë's hand.

Zoë is full of talk about the future.

"Retirement's a bit of a bore," she confesses. "I think next year, when I'm feeling better again, I'll take on some clients. Just one or two, just the most talented . . ." And she is continually making plans for the summer trip. "We'll go to the Aegean, darling. We'll rent a boat. Alexander will like that. We'll leave the week his school lets out."

It is unbearable to hear these plans.

Caroline wants to tell Zoë how afraid she is. She wants to tell Zoë how much she loves her, how much she will miss her. But Zoë will not listen to that kind of talk.

"Read me something from the *Inquirer,*" she interrupts, pointing a fragile white finger at the magazine rack beside her bed. "I want a little hot gossip."

And the television is on all day; there is always an old movie playing. It is hard to hold Zoë's attention over Katharine Hepburn or Cary Grant.

"Tell me about your mother—my grandmother," Caroline says. "Tell me about when you were a child."

"Oh, come on!" Zoë snorts impatiently. She pushes up the volume on the remote control. "Who on Earth remembers? Who on Earth cares?"

So Caroline gives up and they watch the old movies.

One day, she leaves Zoë's apartment and gets into her car, but she finds she is shaking so hard she cannot drive. She holds onto the steering wheel and screams and screams.

That night, she writes a letter.

> *I love you, Zoë, I love you so much. It's killing me to see you die. It's killing me that you never want to talk about it.*

She doesn't send the letter, but every night, she writes another.

> *I remember the first time I ever saw you. I was seven years old, getting off the plane in Los Angeles. There was a woman in a bright scarf and sunglasses and I knew it was you . . . I remember the commercial I was supposed to be in—the angel on the cloud. Father wouldn't let me do it. I said I didn't mind, but I minded for years and years . . . I remember the night before Graham and I got married. You took me back to your hotel room and said that he was the wrong man, and I knew you were right . . .*

The pile of letters grows thicker and thicker. It is comforting that there are so many memories.

CARO

Caro and Zoë come out of the doctor's waiting room. They pause for a moment in the hallway.

"Well," says Caro.

"Yes," Zoë says brightly.

Caro looks down. "What do you want me to do?"

"What are you talking about?"

"I'll stay, of course."

"Are you mad?" Zoë gasps. "Your show is booked as a summer package. And next year, I expect Broadway."

"Forget the show," Caro tells her. "I'd rather be with you."

"Oh, you would?" Zoë scoffs. "And what on Earth would I do with you?" She reaches over and gives Caro an affectionate little shake. "Honey, these doctors are absolute idiots. And this one's the king of the alarmists. Believe me, baby, if I needed you here, I'd tell you. But I don't. I'll be absolutely fine. I want you to go back and do your show. Make me proud."

Caro swallows.

"All right," she says, "if you're sure."

"I'm sure."

They get into the elevator. Caro makes herself pretend she never heard the doctor's words. *Six months. Maybe a year.*

Steven picks her up at the airport. She catches sight of him before he sees her. His face looks anxious and dear. She hugs him, finding relief in the smell of his aftershave, the smoothness of his cheek, his sweater buttons pressing against her chest.

"Hey, I missed you," he says. "How's Zoë?"

She hesitates, then shrugs elaborately. "Turned out to be a big fuss over nothing."

He smiles. "Well, that's Zoë for you. Loving her dramas."

Six months. Maybe a year.

"She wouldn't let me stay. Said she wanted me to go on with the tour."

"And she's absolutely right. I've got all the final details worked out; you start June fifteenth. Long Island to Toledo—there won't be a little theater in the East that won't fall in love with you."

June fourteenth, Caro leaves for her first stop, the Westbury Music Fair. Steven takes her to Penn Station, helps her with the bags, makes sure the itinerary is folded in her purse.

"I wish I could go with you," he keeps saying.

"You'd hate it. Besides, I do these things better alone. But I'll call."

His face screws up.

"You'd better," he tells her.

The tour is a nightmare. Caro was not expecting that. She had thought it would be like the tour with Tristan. But she was not the star then. Now, she is the star. She is the one in charge. She is the one who must make things work out when the hotel has lost the reservation, when the theater isn't ready. She is the one who must do the interviews, be at the radio stations, rise at five so she can be on the early morning television shows. She is the one who must perform six nights a week, with matinees on Wednesdays and Sundays.

She is always traveling. Buses. Trains. Taxis. Even when she is not moving, she can feel the motion. The summer is humid; it is too hot to sleep. Westbury. Kennebunkport. Sometimes there are hotels. Sometimes there are boardinghouses. A room in someone's home. The purple bedroom. The den with the pullout bed and the broken screen. The whine and itch of the bugs.

The cities, the theaters blur. Cape Cod. Philadelphia. Hershey. The playhouse in the round. The light that crashed down onto the stage. Starting to forget her lines. Starting to forget what she had already told the reporter. Toledo. Beverly.

Sometimes she can stay five days in one place, but most are split weeks, one city to another. Buses. Trains. Racketing. Shaking.

She cannot sleep after a performance. Katherine Mansfield's words boom like breakers. She gets up, drinks glasses of bad water. She sits at windows and stares at the circles of street lamps. She dozes and has nightmares. She cannot rest in beds; she lies on hotel chairs and sofas and carpets and gets up with patterns on her cheek.

There is no one to talk to but strangers. She wishes Steven could be with her, but she does not ask him to come. He has to be in New York. Sometimes he joins her on weekends, but he cannot do it often.

She tells a stage manager that she cannot sleep. He gives her some pills. When Steven sees her in Pennsylvania, he is shocked.

"Jesus Christ," he keeps saying. "You look awful. Is this too much for you? Do you want me to cancel?"

"No, no," she tells him.

The show is a hit, the reviews are excellent. Caro sends her mother all the clippings.

It is August now. She is almost through with the tour. She has told more managers that she cannot sleep. She takes a whole collection of pills now.

She is in Boston. Her head hurts. She adds three white Excedrins to the rainbow of tablets. She goes to the Boston Gardens and looks at the swan boats. The movement makes her dizzy. Then she gasps; she looks again. The swans are real. The swans are breathing.

She does not tell anyone; she does not want anyone to suspect that she knows the swans are real. She is supposed to have dinner with a man from the *Globe,* but she cancels. She waits until midnight. Then she sneaks out of her hotel room, down the stairs, and out through a side door.

She hurries through the dark streets to the public gardens. Nobody is around. She goes to the pond. The swans are not in sight, but she can hear them honking. She wades into the cold water; she finds the shed where the birds are crying. She pulls at the lock, but cannot break it. She weeps in frustration.

"Ma'am? I think you'd better come out of there."

A man in a uniform is shining a spotlight on her.

The lights are up; it's her cue and she can't remember her first line.

"Come on, ma'am," he is saying. "Can you tell me your name?"

She is furious with him. That's not the cue. That's not even in the script. But of course she knows her name. Everyone knows their own name. But the odd thing is, she can't remember it. And she's standing in this cold water, but that's all right; it's part of the cure.

The man starts to come into the water to pull her out. But he isn't John Murry. That is the horror.

She starts to scream.

"It's all right, Caro."

Faces are balloons above her. There is one who looks familiar. He has dark hair, and she knows the buttons on his sweater. His eyes are kind, but so worried. She wants to tell him not to look so worried, and she would if she knew what his name was. And who was Caro?

Another head, this one red. And a white coat, so she must be back at the clinic. A long sharp needle—God, she hated those—a prick. The lights go down. Everything fades to black. She waits for the applause, but there is no applause.

There is a large, round shape. There is a square. There are spiky lines on top of the square. There is a noise, and there is something moving. Caro closes her eyes. She opens them. The shapes slowly come clear. The round is a lamp. The square is a window, the lines a Venetian blind. And the noise and the shape is a woman coming into the room.

"Well," says Zoë. She sits down on the bed. "How are you feeling?"

Caro puts a hand to her head. The room is much too bright.

"I'm in your house?" she whispers.

"Don't you remember?"

Caro shakes her head. What she remembers is someone being in a cold pond, and someone's shoes filling with mud.

"What happened?"

Zoë laughs. "Oh, my God," she says. "Honey, you had one hell of a nervous breakdown. They practically had to bring you here in a straitjacket."

"Oh," says Caro in a small voice. "I don't remember."

"No, you wouldn't," Zoë says crisply. "Apparently, you took a lot of pills."

"I'm sorry."

"It's all right," Zoë tells her. "You're fine. Doctors have been all over you. They say you just need some rest."

Caro frowns. "I can't rest. I've got the play."

"It's all right. Steven's handled everything. He canceled the rest of the tour—no one's even suing you. He's a clever guy."

"Is he very mad at me?"

"No. Just worried. Like we all were."

"I'm sorry," Caro says again.

Zoë pats her hand. "Well, rest up. Maybe next year you can give it another try."

Caro shrinks back into the bed. "I'm never going to act again."

"Pity," Zoë says. "You got a lot of press. Maybe not the best kind of publicity, but certainly intriguing." She stands up. "But that's something to discuss when you're feeling better. For now, you're going to stay here."

Six months. Maybe a year.

Caro tries to sit up. "But what about you?" she asks quickly. "You shouldn't have to take care of me."

"I've no intention of it. That idiot doctor insisted that I get a nurse. I don't need her, so she might as well earn her keep looking after you. Flavia!" she calls, and a moment later, a heavy young woman comes in. "Look who's back among the living." She points to Caro. "Flavia, this is my baby."

The nurse beams. "It's good to see you awake."

"Flavia's been keeping an eye on you."

It is strange to realize that she has been looked after by someone she has not even met.

Caro stares around the bright room in bewilderment.

"How you doing, beautiful?" Steven's voice sounds warm.

"I'm so sorry," she says.

"Oh, forget it. It gave us great publicity."

"That's what my mother said. Glad to be of help."

"So you're all right?"

"I guess. I'm not doing much of anything at the moment."

"Good. Just keep on resting. Take care of yourself."

It is the same thing Caro says to Zoë.

Caro is taking a walk. It is her first day out. She circles around the bright sidewalks of Beverly Hills. It is good to be outside in the late summer sunshine.

She comes to the Premier Market. She has not been in a grocery story for a long time. She gazes around the shelves—everything looks tempting and sweet.

She decides she will cook dinner that night. Flavia is an awful cook—it will be a nice change for Zoë. There is a special on pork; she'll make a roast.

When she leaves the store, Caro doesn't feel like going back to Zoë's just yet; she decides to walk around a little longer. As she is crossing the street at Brighton, her attention is caught by a shop halfway down the block.

It is an antique store. In the window is a Georgian dollhouse.

Caro crosses to look at it. Then finally she goes inside.

"How much is the dollhouse?" she asks the woman behind the desk.

When Caro gets back home, she finds Zoë in bed with her eyes closed.

"We've had the pain when you were out," Flavia tells her.

Zoë looks bruised with exhaustion. Caro sits gently on the bed.

"I've got two surprises," she says. "One for you, one for me."

"What's mine?"

"I'm cooking dinner tonight."

Zoë snorts and opens her eyes. "Oh, my God. That should be interesting. I still haven't gotten over your soup at the commune."

"And the surprise for me," Caro goes on, "is that I've bought myself a dollhouse."

"What on Earth for?"

"Because I wanted it."

Zoë nods thoughtfully. "You had one when you were a little girl."

"Yes. I got it with the money from the angel commercial." She looks at her mother. "But it somehow—disappeared—when we moved from Westwood."

Zoë coughs. "I got awfully tired of stepping on those damned little pieces."

There is a pause. She looks at Caro. "I'm glad you got this dollhouse if you want it, honey." Restlessly, she adjusts her pillow. "I sometimes think . . . you didn't have the most crackerjack childhood in the world."

"I had a fantastic childhood," Caro tells her.

Zoë shakes her head. "No. You didn't." She plucks at the blanket. "I wonder if maybe you would have been better off with Barton, after all."

"That's ridiculous."

"I don't know. You could have had a normal life."

"Who wants a normal life?" Caro rises and kisses Zoë on her forehead. "I don't want to hear any more of this. I'm going to get the pork started."

But when she is in the kitchen, she thinks about what Zoë has said. She wonders what it would have been like if she had grown up in New York, lived with her father. She would have gone to school like a regular kid, made friends. There would have been Meg and Adam, and picnics and family vacations. If she had grown up with her father, she wouldn't have been kidnapped when she was seven years old. There wouldn't have been Greg. And Brian in high school, and Tristan dying in a hotel bathroom. If she had lived with her father, she probably would be married to someone safe now, living somewhere beautiful. Maybe she would even have a baby. But what about the acting? There would have been no acting. And no being with Zoë.

Caro sighs, shrugs, and starts to prepare the dinner.

Beverly Hills High School looks the same. There are some small differences in buildings and landscape, but the long walk down to the gym field hasn't changed. Nor the rainbow wall in the cafeteria. And the kids look like the ones who were there in Caro's time.

Caro walks around, not sure why she is there. She goes to the Swim-Gym where she watched Brian at his basketball game. She walks by old classrooms.

Finally she goes to the auditorium. Posters for an upcoming production of *Peter Pan* are everywhere. Outside the building is a bulletin board with pictures of the cast. It looks like the same board that was put up before *Bye, Bye, Birdie.*

Caro goes up to the door, but she cannot make herself go into the auditorium.

As she is turning to leave, a heavyset man comes out, talking to some students. When he sees Caro, he stops.

"Caro?" he asks. "Caro Andrews?"

He is older, redder, but it is Mr. Stein.

The blood thuds through Caro's forehead.

"I can't believe it!" Mr. Stein turns to the watching kids. "Neil, Joan, this is Caro Andrews—one of our big successes."

You're drunk. Completely smashed, she can hear him down the years. *You're out of the play.*

She looks away.

"Congratulations on your show," he is saying. "I read the New York reviews. Any chance you'll bring it to Los Angeles?"

"I don't know," Caro says. "I don't know that I really want to. It's pretty—exhausting."

"Yes." Mr. Stein's voice is discreet. "I—heard about that." There is a pause. "Well, if you do decide to do it again, keep us in mind. We'd love to have you perform it here." He gestures toward the auditorium. "It would be an honor. And come to *Peter Pan* if you can. It's a good show."

"Thank you," she tells him.

Caro is sure that she will never be able to step into that auditorium again.

There are fewer good days now, more visits to the hospital. Zoë tells Caro she doesn't mind—she says the nurses give marvelous back rubs. On the days Zoë comes home, Caro always prepares a little celebration. She puts flowers in her mother's bedroom, and has a cake waiting.

"Carrot." Zoë is chewing a slice of the latest one. "The first time around it was chocolate; the second—what was it? Vanilla?"

"Lemon, I think."

"And then vanilla. And now carrot. What are we going to do when the bakery runs out of flavors? Then I guess it'll be time for me to die."

They play gin rummy a lot. The first month or two, Caro could not win, no matter how hard she tried. Now she wins every hand.

It is a rainy evening in January, Flavia's night off. Zoë is in bed, looking at old photograph albums. Caro is in the kitchen, making dinner.

She hears her mother calling, and rushes in.

Zoë is sitting up in bed. "I have something to show you."

"You scared me," Caro tells her, annoyed. "I thought something had happened."

"Sit down." Zoë is holding open an old green leather album, one Caro has never seen before. She sits down beside her mother and squints at the faded black-and-white exposures.

Zoë taps significantly with one long red nail. "That's him."

Caro looks at the picture. It is of a young man, fair-haired, half turned toward the camera. A slight smile is on his face, as though a voice he loved had just called his name.

"Max."

Caro remembers that name. Her mother had said it before, in New York, after Tristan died. She said she understood what Caro was going through, that she had had something like that happen herself. With a man named Max. *We were going to move to Paris. But he was killed in a car crash.*

So this was Max. Gently, Caro touches the picture. He seems trusting and sweet. He doesn't look like he should have to die.

"The love of my life."

"Yes. You told me that once."

"But I don't think I told you—we were going to have a baby."

Caro is in England, walking out of the police station. There had been the sudden pain in her stomach, and then the blood, and hers and Tristan's baby was gone.

"I'm so sorry."

Zoë is shaking her head. "No, darling. There's no need to be sorry."

"What do you mean?"

Zoë is very pale. "I had the baby, darling. You're the baby."

Caro is very still. She is conscious of an itch on her forearm. She is conscious of the yellow in her mother's bedspread. She is conscious of the wind dying down around the house.

"So." The words are soap bubbles she cannot let pop. She says them very, very gently. "You are saying . . ."

"Yes."

The bubbles smash.

"But my father." Caro flushes. These ridiculous soap-opera words. "Did he know?"

Zoë also flushes. "No," she says. "He was killed before we knew about—you."

"I didn't mean Max," Caro says the name cruelly. "I meant your husband."

"No," Zoë says after a pause. "Barton never knew."

Caro stares at her. "He never knew? He never *knew!*"

"No," Zoë says. There are pink spots on her cheeks. "I met Barton right after Max was killed—you could have been his."

"But I wasn't."

"No. You weren't."

Caro stands up. She walks agitatedly back and forth across the room.

"So this man you told me was my father all my life—he had nothing to do with me."

"That's not true," Zoë says quickly. "Barton helped raise you. He loves you."

Caro stares at Zoë. "Why didn't you tell him?"

Zoë looks at her levelly. "Because I wanted the best for you. Your life would not have gone so well otherwise."

Caro stands still. "I can't believe you would do such a thing."

She walks out of the room. She walks out of the house. She is in her shirtsleeves, and the cold air chills her. She walks and walks, harder and faster.

Finally, when it hurts too much to breathe, she slows down.

She is not Caro Andrews. The man in the New York high-rise building is not her father. The lady and the little boy are not her family at all. All her life, the trips to New York have been visits to strangers.

Caro sits down on the curb. She picks up a blown leaf and sails it through the air. She can feel Barton's hug around her, Adam tugging at her hand. No. That wasn't true. They weren't strangers. They might not be family, but they were almost family.

She stands up and starts to walk again, more slowly. The man in the photograph comes into her mind. Max with his fair hair. Hair just like hers.

She turns around and walks back to Zoë's house. Zoë is lying in bed, the photograph album turned facedown on the blanket. Caro sits on the bed. She rights the album and studies the face of the smiling blond man.

"So tell me about my father," she says.

CAROLINE

"I don't want to go!" Alexander wails.

Caroline feels like shaking him.

"We have to go," she says briskly. "Zoë loves to see you. You'll have a great time. You and Flavia can watch television."

He sighs. "All right," he says uncertainly, "but will I have to kiss her?"

Caroline stares at his anxious face. She guesses how all this must seem to a child—the nurse, the hush, the strange smells, the medicine, and the skinny woman in bed.

"No, of course you don't have to." She kneels and hugs him.

It is just past sunset when she and Alexander arrive at Zoë's. The gracious light is already gone and the house seems sullen behind its row of spiky bushes. Caroline hurries up the steps.

"How is she today?" she asks Flavia.

Flavia shakes her head. "Not the best. She had the big pain again." She looks down at Alexander. "How's the big boy? You want play cards with Flavia?"

Caroline watches them go off, hand in hand. They look like a happy team. She envies them their hour in the kitchen, their game of Old Maid.

She goes softly into Zoë's room. Zoë is lying in bed, her eyes closed. An old green leather photo album is beside her.

"Zoë?" Caroline asks gently.

Zoë frowns from a place of private pain. Her eyelids tremble and open.

"Hello, darling."

"How are you feeling?"

Zoë pats her hand. "Astonishing," she says. "I'm glad you came. I have a picture to show you."

She tries to draw the album over, but it is too heavy. Caroline picks it up and holds it out so Zoë can see. She goes slowly backward through the pages, past pictures of parties and ski trips, Christmases and cruises, right back to the beginning. There is Zoë in pedal pushers. Zoë with long hair, on a sled. Zoë at a New Year's Eve party, with a glass of champagne. Zoë younger than Caroline.

"You're so beautiful."

Zoë raises a hand. She taps significantly with one long red nail. "That's him," she says.

It is the picture of a young man, fair-haired. He is half-turned toward the camera, smiling slightly.

"Who is that?" Caroline asks politely.

"Your father."

"No," Caroline corrects her gently. "That's not Daddy." She takes the book and flips forward through it. She comes to a picture of Barton and points it out. "That's my father."

Zoë shakes her head.

Caroline is very white. She stands up, and goes into the kitchen.

Flavia and Alexander are sitting at the table, intent on their game of cards.

"Flavia," Caroline says, "There's something wrong with Zoë. Her mind—she's wandering."

Flavia jumps up; the cards scatter; Alexander wails.

"Don't you worry, Miss," she says. "She had much medicine today. I'll see to her. Don't you worry."

She rushes from the room. Caroline stares at the fallen cards, at the smiling face of the Old Maid.

When Caroline comes over the following afternoon, Zoë is sitting up in bed reading the *Inquirer.*

"Hello, my darling," she says. "You wouldn't believe what's happening to poor old Burt Reynolds."

"Are you all right?" Caroline asks her.

"Never been better."

"It's just—yesterday—you—you showed me this picture—"

"Ah, yes," Zoë says.

"You told me it was my father." Caroline swallows. "Flavia said you'd had a lot of medicine."

Zoë looks at her for a long moment. "Yes," she says finally. "Maybe I had a little too much medicine."

It is an afternoon in early February. The wind is blowing in damp, dark gusts. Caroline parks in front of Zoë's house and hurries inside.

Zoë is in bed. Caroline comes into the room and sits beside her. "I can only stay a few minutes," she says. "I've got to pick Alexander up from a play date. But I was at the library today, and I thought you might like to read this."

She pulls out a biography of Shirley Temple, and puts it within Zoë's reach.

"Thank you, my darling," Zoë murmurs. "Such manners, that little girl had. An agent's dream." Abruptly, she frowns. "I don't like the woman who bought my agency," she says. "I've never liked her. She was a sneak, even when she was a child." She looks at Caroline. "I wish you'd take over."

"Oh, no," Caroline tells her. "Zoë, you can't wish that. I'd be absolutely terrible at it. You know I would be."

Zoë smiles sadly and nods. "Well, that's a pity," she says. "I've been watching that new little girl—the one in the peanut commercial. Dye her hair red, and she'd make the most marvelous Pippi Longstocking. My friend Ned at NBC might be able to set something up. You're sure you're not interested?"

"I'm sure," Caroline says gently.

She goes into the kitchen to ask Flavia to make some tea. When she comes back, her mother's room is completely different. Something that was there is not there anymore.

Caroline goes slowly over to the bed, and kneels beside it. She picks up the white hand with its long red nails.

"Zoë?" she whispers.

* * *

Caroline walks through Beverly Hills. Up Rodeo Drive, down Beverly. Across Dayton, up Camden. She has never really liked Beverly Hills, but it was Zoë's favorite place in the world.

She passes clothes shops, gift shops, restaurants. She wonders which were the ones Zoë liked best. She cannot even begin to guess.

She stops, unable to go on. She looks at the boutique in front of her. In the window is a mannequin, wearing the bright sort of scarf that Zoë had always worn. Caroline reaches forward and touches the window. In her head, she can hear her mother laughing.

Caroline is in Zoë's house, sitting on the orange rug. She is holding Alexander in her arms. He is telling her about school that day; she is forcing herself to listen. She does not let herself think about the arrangements that must be made.

The phone rings.

Caroline slowly takes the receiver.

"Caroline? Herb Waller here."

It is Zoë's lawyer. She draws in a breath.

"How are you doing?" he asks.

"I'm okay," Caroline says. "Look, I know I've got to make the—arrangements. It's just—I haven't felt quite up to it yet. But I promise—in the morning, I'll do it all."

He sounds surprised. "Arrangements about your mother? You don't have to worry. Zoë took care of all that—she planned everything out to the last detail. In fact," he says, "I was wondering if I could come over this evening, so we could go over it all."

Caroline closes her eyes with relief.

"That will be fine."

"Also, we need to talk about the will. I'll bring the papers when I come. It won't take long," he adds. "Zoë left everything to you, you know."

"No," she says. "I didn't know."

Caroline takes Alexander to Roxbury Park. She wears a sweater, keeps her hands in her pockets, but she stays cold. She wishes Zoë hadn't left her all the money. She has never been good with money, Zoë should not have trusted her.

She has no idea how much there is. Maybe it's just a little—enough to take Alexander to Greece this summer, just like Zoë had wanted to. But what if there's more? What if there's enough to buy part ownership of Little Worlds? She would love that—but Zoë would be disappointed.

Caroline jams her hands in her sweater pocket. She knows what would make Zoë happy. She can't pretend not to know. Zoë would want her to buy out the agency, and start it up as her own.

She stands very still.

If there's enough money, she'll do it. She will stay in California and run Zoë's Babies for her mother.

Caroline puts her hands over her face.

Herb Waller comes over with the papers. They are impersonal and dry; it is a shock to see Zoë's signature, sprawling and warm, at the bottom.

Numbly, Caroline agrees to everything.

Finally they go over the will. The money Zoë has left her is enough to go to Greece. It is enough to send Alexander to a good school. It is even enough to buy into Little Worlds, though not perhaps as a co-owner. But it is not enough to rescue Zoë's agency.

Caroline is chilled with relief and with regret.

The following morning, she goes to Zoë's Babies. She sits for only a moment in the foyer, and then Lisa Rodin comes out.

"Caroline," she says with a sad pout, "I was so sorry to hear about your mother. I've been meaning to call."

"Thank you," Caroline tells her. "Well. I just wanted to say that now that she's gone, I won't be working here anymore."

"Of course." Lisa is not distressed.

"And also—you once mentioned some boxes you had stored—some things of Zoë's."

"That's right. Didn't I mail them back to her?"

"No, you never did."

"Well, I promise I will. First thing tomorrow."

"Would you mind finding them now?" Caroline asks. "I don't know how long I'll be in town."

Lisa sighs. "Ariadne!" she calls, and the young secretary hurries into the foyer. "Would you go down to the basement and help Caroline find some boxes? They should be labeled." She gives Caroline a spasm of a smile. "I have to run to a meeting. Nice to see you."

Caroline finds the boxes almost at once.

"Do you mind if I go through them here?" she asks Ariadne. "I'd just like to see what's inside."

"Go ahead," the girl tells her. "I'll head on back upstairs. Good luck with everything. I'm sorry about your mother."

Caroline sits down beside the boxes. She reaches out and gently touches the side of the largest. For a moment, she does not open it; when she finally pulls the tape and folds back the flaps, she finds a jumble inside—framed photographs of Zoë's child actors, a papier mâché parrot, a Moroccan wall hanging, a Mexican sarape, and piles and piles of yellowing scripts. The other boxes are much the same. Caroline goes through everything, then carefully repacks it all.

She sits with the boxes for a moment more, and finally she stands up. No matter where she lives, no matter where she goes in her life, she will always find a place for these things of her mother's.

Zoë's memorial service is on Saturday.

Caroline is the first one to arrive. She is greeted by a Mr. Millhouse. He is tactful, respectful. He suggests she go into the chapel and see all the tributes.

Zoë had said in her letter to the lawyer that she didn't want any flowers, but Caroline knows she would have enjoyed these mountains of blossoms. Zoë's favorite flowers were orchids; their scent hovers all over the chapel, smelling like her perfume. Caroline half turns, thinking that her mother is coming down the aisle.

She bends down and reads some of the cards; she does not recognize many of the names. Then she sees a handwriting she knows very well.

"Missing you, Zoë. Barton."

He had sent her orchids.

* * *

Other people are starting to come into the chapel now; Caroline does not want to see them. She hurries to the small enclosure reserved for the family and sits down. She is the only one there.

The room is filled now. The service starts. It is extraordinary. Zoë, who had planned it all, could have been a producer. It moves like a variety show. There is music—a blues artist Zoë had loved from a piano bar. There are video clips of some of Zoë's babies. There are speeches, a lot of laughter.

Everyone who talks about Zoë uses the same word—"original."

Caroline is proud of her mother. She knows that she herself is not original at all. She and Alexander are all that is left of Zoë, and they are neither of them original.

The service is over. Caroline waits until the room is empty, then she rises and leaves through a side door. As she is going toward the parking lot, she hears her name.

"Caroline?"

She stops and looks back. A tall, dark-haired man with glasses is coming toward her.

"Yes," she says. "I'm Caroline."

He smiles. "I knew you couldn't be anyone else. I'm not sure if you'd even remember me. I once—"

"Steven Lasky," she says.

"That's right." He is delighted.

"It's good to see you again."

He takes her hands. "I'm so sorry about Zoë. You somehow never think anything could happen to a person like her."

"No."

"I didn't even know her that well, but she was a big influence in my life. Does that sound crazy?"

Caroline shakes her head. "I think a lot of people felt that way about her."

They walk together toward the white Mercedes.

"What are you doing now?" she asks. "The last time I saw you, you were getting ready to apply to college."

"You're right. God, that was a long time ago. Well, I'm a publicist now."

"In Los Angeles?"

"No. I live in New York. I came out just for this."

Caroline smiles. "Zoë would have loved that."

"I know." They walk in silence for a moment. "She told me you were living in New York, too."

"Well, I was. I don't know what I'm going to do now."

They have reached the car.

Steven looks at her. "What would you like to be doing?"

"I think I'd like to start a museum of antique dollhouses."

"That sounds great. If you ever need any free publicity, you know who to come to."

Caroline shakes her head. "Thanks, but I'm not sure I'm really going to be doing it."

"Why not?"

"Oh, I don't know. Inertia. We'll see."

They stand in silence by the car.

"Whenever I saw Zoë, she always used to talk about you," Steven says finally. "You and your little boy. She was so proud of you both."

Caroline is silent. They were neither of them originals.

"And what about you?" she asks quickly. "Do you have any children?"

"No. No family at all. I was married once, after college, but it didn't work out."

Caroline nods. "I saw the announcement of your engagement in the newspaper. I was very put out." She feels herself blush. She cannot believe she has said that.

Steven blinks. "Were you, really?"

"Yes."

He smiles at her. "Well, listen," he says. "I'm sure you have a million things to take care of—I should let you go." He pulls out a business card from a case in his pocket. "But when things calm down, if you'd ever like to meet for coffee, give me a call. Here or in New York."

Caroline leaves the mortuary and drives up Midvale, to Zoë's old apartment building. She has not been there since Zoë made the move to Beverly Hills.

She parks the car and starts up the brick path. It is the same path that she walked up when she was seven years old, on her first visit to California. That had been quite a day. Seeing palm trees for the first time. And hibiscus. And orange blossoms. And Zoë.

She goes back to the courtyard of the complex, to the swimming pool. It is smaller than she had remembered, but just as blue. The same cracked concrete surrounds it, the same faded redwood deck chairs sit by its side.

Caroline takes off her shoe and dips a foot in the water. It is freezing on this February day. She thinks about Zoë, and what Zoë would like her to do. Then she lifts her arms and dives, fully clothed, into the water.

And, until the people come rushing out of the apartment building, it is one of the happiest moments of her life.

CARO

It is an afternoon in early February. The day is blustery and Zoë seems restless.

"You know what I'd love," she says suddenly. "A pomegranate. I've been thinking about one all day—God knows why I've gotten so Biblical."

It is good to have Zoë want something again.

"I'll get you one right away," Caro tells her. "I'll run down to the market. Will you be okay with Flavia for a few minutes?"

"Of course."

The wind is blowing in dark, damp gusts. Caro walks briskly into Beverly Hills and buys the pomegranate. She pauses, holding the dry, fleshy redness; it looks oddly evil.

On the way home, she pauses for a moment in front of a shop that sells antique jewelry. There is a large tigereye brooch in the window. Caro can see herself wearing that brooch, using it to pin up a brown-and-tan Hermes scarf, standing on shipboard, watching waves.

As she looks at the brooch, someone has come up silently behind her. Caro can see the reflection, hazy, in the glass of the window. It is a woman, smiling, wearing a large hat. It is Zoë.

Caro turns around. She is alone on the street.

She runs the blocks back to Zoë's house. She can feel the itch of perspiration sliding down her sides.

She reaches the house. By the time the front door is halfway open, she knows. Something that was there is not there anymore.

Flavia comes out of the bedroom, her face slick with tears.

"Oh, Miss Caro," she says.

Caro looks down at the brown paper sack in her hand. She drops the pomegranate.

Zoë has been taken away. The ambulance has gone discreetly down the street, and turned the corner. Zoë would have enjoyed seeing the ambulance. She would have watched it from her window, speculating on who had died. But she would have wanted things to be a little more exciting—lights flashing, sirens blaring.

Caro goes back to the house. The stillness is shocking. She goes into Zoë's bedroom. The bed has been made forever; the quilts will never be disturbed again. She goes into Zoë's big walk-in closet. She closes her eyes and takes deep breaths. The closet is a Zoë perfume. Caro breathes until she is dizzy.

She sits down on the floor. She sees a cardboard box, hidden under some hanging evening dresses, and pulls it out.

It is a box from the agency, full of old client files. Caro goes through it slowly, looking at each yellowing eight by ten photograph. There are little blond girls in short, dotted swiss dresses. Little boys in cowboy hats, holding up six-shooters. One set of twins, naked in their play pool, giving their dog a bath.

How strange to think that they were all grown up now. Did they ever even remember that, when they were little, they had wanted to be movie stars? Caro can imagine one of them saying to her own children, "When I was your age, I wanted to be an actress. And there was this woman who helped me—this woman who wore bright scarves."

It would be nice to think that Zoë was remembered that way.

She keeps going through the pile. At the very bottom, she comes upon one last picture. It is of a little blond girl, sitting on a brick walkway, and holding a daisy. Caro smiles. She remembers when that picture was taken. She remembers fighting with Zoë over what dress she should wear. She had wanted to wear her new frilly pink one; Zoë had insisted on this pinafore. And of course, Zoë had been right.

Caro stares at the photo of the little blond girl looking wistfully past the camera. How strange—that in all that pile of photos, she should be the only one who ended up an actress.

* * *

The phone rings. Caro leaves the closet and goes to answer it.

"Hello?"

"Hello, dear." It is Herb Waller, her mother's lawyer. "How are you doing?"

"All right, I guess. You know."

"Yes, I do." His voice is heavy and sad. Caro suspects that he had been in love with Zoë for years.

"I was wondering if I could drop by sometime later today. There are some—arrangements—I'd like to go over with you."

"That'll be fine." Caro has not even thought about the arrangements, but of course they needed to be made. It is a relief to find she does not have to do it herself.

"There won't be that much. Zoë left pretty clear instructions. And I'll go over the will with you, too. Again, it's not very complicated. She left everything to you, you know."

When she hangs up the phone, Caro goes into her mother's closet again and sits back down on the floor.

She left everything to you . . .

Caro does not want everything. She does not really even want anything. It seems wrong that she should take her mother's money; she cannot think of anything to do with it that would be significant enough.

Her eye falls on the box of stills again.

The memorial service is on Saturday. The Westwood Mortuary is not far from the apartment where Caro grew up. It is strange to think how many times they passed this place, she and Zoë—sitting together in the car, talking about an audition, or a dress, or a movie that had just come out.

Caro parks her mother's white Mercedes at the back of the lot and gets out of the car.

She is wearing bright red.

She comes out of the lot and looks down Glendon Avenue. There used to be a Will Wright's ice-cream store near the corner, where she and Zoë always had sodas on Saturday nights. The shop has long since gone, but the stippled brick building is still there. For a moment, Caro teases herself, pretending that she has come to Westwood for no other reason than to get a peppermint ice-cream soda with her mother.

She goes into the mortuary. A man called Mr. Millhouse greets her and leads her to the chapel. She is the first one there.

She sees flowers everywhere. There is one arrangement especially eye-catching, a big vase full of Zoë's favorite orchids. Caro goes over to see who they are from; when she reads the card, she smiles.

Caro is pleased for her mother—after being divorced from her for over twenty years, her ex-husband has sent her flowers.

Other people are starting to come into the chapel. The sight of everyone wearing black is too much for Caro. She hurries to the enclosed area, where the family is to sit.

She is the only family.

The memorial service is wonderful. It is as well organized as the Academy Awards. There are video clips, a bar pianist playing blues songs, and speeches by all the people who loved Zoë. Over and over again, the word "original" is used.

And Caro thinks: I am an original, too.

At the end of the service, Herb Waller goes to the podium and suggests to the audience that they give Zoë her favorite thing on Earth—a standing ovation.

Caro stands and cheers and imagines Zoë on that stage, taking her bow.

She waits until everyone has left the chapel, then she starts to step out through the side door.

"Caro!"

She turns.

It is Steven Lasky.

"I don't believe it," she says.

She goes over and hugs him for a long moment. When she pulls back, they are silent.

"Zoë would have liked your bow tie," she tells him. It is yellow with a design of martini glasses.

"I know she would. She gave it to me."

They walk outside. It is a bright, manic day, with cold wind-flung birds.

"Let's go to the beach," Caro says.

He pauses a moment. "All right."

"Let's take Zoë's car. We can leave yours here."

They get into the Mercedes.

"What is this?" Steven asks. He reaches up and touches the little chain and medallion looped around the rearview mirror.

"It's St. Jude. He's the patron saint of lost causes. She always said the two of them had a lot in common."

Steven smiles. "I wonder if she considered me a lost cause."

"Oh, no. But I wonder about myself, sometimes."

She starts the car, and heads west on Olympic.

"Zoë and I used to go to one of the little beaches near Venice—would that be all right?"

"That'll be great."

"We used to have a picnic there at the end of every summer. Right before school started."

"Do you want to stop at a grocery store? We could have a picnic, too."

"No. That's all right."

They drive in silence.

"So what do you think you'll do now?" Steven asks at last.

Caro shrugs.

"I don't know if you'd be interested, but we've got some news about the show," he tells her. "A guy called me up last week, asking if you'd consider doing a college tour."

Caro shakes her head. "No, thanks. I think I've done all I can for Katherine Mansfield."

"Ah, yes," Steven says, "but maybe she hasn't done all she can for you."

"I think she has." She looks over at Steven and smiles at him.

"Actually," she goes on carefully, "I may stay here for a while. I might try to start up a little agency—for child actors."

"And call it Caro's Babies?"

She laughs. "God. Am I completely nuts?"

"Maybe," Steven says.

"I've been thinking about it a lot. Being a child actor really isn't such a bad thing. It makes you feel very special. I'd like to do that for a kid."

"Wouldn't it be easier just to take over Zoë's agency?"

She shakes her head. "There isn't enough money to buy the place back. And I'd rather start my own. Maybe. None of this is certain."

"Well, if it becomes certain, you know who you can count on for free publicity."

Caro reaches over and squeezes his hand.

"Actually," she says, "There's something else I want to do before I even think about all that."

"Yes?" he prompts her after another silence. "Do I get to be told?"

"Well," she says, "it sounds a little crazy, too. I want to find out about a man called Max."

"Max?" Steven says slowly. "Who is Max?"

Caro smiles. "I'll tell you when I find out more."

"Should I be jealous?" Steven asks.

"No."

"I see." Steven clears his throat. "And in all these plans of yours, is there any possibility that one day you'll have time to be with me?"

She looks briefly over at him and smiles.

"Maybe I will," she says.

They reach the beach, and walk to the sand.

"It's freezing," Caro says, "and we've got nothing to sit on. You'll ruin your suit."

"It doesn't matter."

Steven sits in the sand and looks out at the ocean. It is high afternoon, and the sky is dark blue and screaming.

"I'll be back," Caro tells him.

She kicks her shoes off and starts to run.

She runs and runs and runs. The wind is strong against her face. The sand arches and swoops above her in a fine white spray.

She is starting to get tired. Her legs begin to ache. But she runs and she runs.

She looks back. She has gone so far she cannot even see Steven any longer. She keeps on running.

CAROLINE/CARO

It is Caroline's birthday. She is having a party that afternoon—nothing big, just the family and Trina and a few women from the board of the miniature museum. For the moment, everything is under control. Steven has gone out to Balducci's to get the cake, the sandwiches have been made, and the baby is still napping in her room.

Caroline sits down a moment on the velvet sofa that had been Zoë's.

It is Caro's birthday. She didn't want to celebrate, pointing out that it was obscene for a child actress to turn thirty. But Steven had insisted. He had flown out from New York, and was taking her to Chasen's that night.

She has an hour before she needs to get ready. She tidies the living room, and clears up all traces of the day's work. It looks like she's got a chance to sign Gretchen Oldman, but she doesn't want to think about that now.

She sits down a moment, on the velvet sofa that had been Zoë's.

The baby wakes and begins to fuss. Caroline goes into the nursery.

"Zoë, Zoë," she says. "It's a happy day. It's your mama's birthday."

She picks the baby up from the crib and walks back with her to the living room. The ottoman is covered with gifts—the antique necklace from Steven, the wooden shelf Alexander had made, the cashmere sweater set from Barton and Meg, the mini shadowbox from Trina. And so many cards—the side table is filled with cards.

The phone rings. Caro answers it and a smile spreads over her face when she hears the news. Gretchen is going to sign with the agency. Caro hangs up the phone and goes to the desk. She starts making a list of possible projects for the girl—Heidi, Dagmar in *I Remember Mama,* and why not a remake of *A Tree Grows in Brooklyn?* Gretchen would be a marvelous Flossie Gaddis, and if Caro could take time off from the agency, she just might consider auditioning for Katie Nolan. Exhilarated, she sighs.

Steven comes back with the cake.

"Let me see!" Caroline begs, but he laughs.

"Are you kidding? You have to wait till the party."

But he shows the cake to baby Zoë, and she claps her hands.

Steven comes to pick Caro up. He kisses her and gives her a small package wrapped in silver paper.

"I don't want to open it now," she tells him. "I don't want to open it till tomorrow."

"But your birthday will be over then."

"That's the point," she says. "I want there still to be one surprise left."

The sandwiches and tea are all gone. Suddenly the lights are switched off. Steven and Alexander come in, carrying the large chocolate cake.

"Happy Birthday to you . . ." everyone begins to sing.

The main course has been cleared away, and there is a pause. Suddenly the beaming waiter comes bearing a lighted cake.

"Happy Birthday to you . . ." Steven begins, and the whole restaurant joins in.

"Make a wish and blow out the candles!" Alexander says.

Caroline looks around at the room full of smiling faces.

"But I have nothing to wish for."

"Make a wish and blow out the candles!" Steven says.

Caro looks into his smiling face.
"But I have nothing to wish for."

"But you've got to make a wish!"

"All right, then." Caroline straightens up.
Caro laughs and raises her arms to the sky.
"I wish for the moon—" they cry.

"—and a pair of orange ice skates."